THE GRAY PHANTOM

To H. B., The Other Helen

Originally published in 1921.

Published by Wildside Press for release in countries where it is in the public domain.
Visit us online at wildsidepress.com.

THE GRAY PHANTOM

HERMAN LANDON

WILDSIDE PRESS

To H. B., The Other Helen

Originally published in 1921.

Published by Wildside Press for release in countries where it is in the public domain.
Visit us online at wildsidepress.com.

CHAPTER I
A TRAGIC INTERLUDE

HOURS AFTERWARD, WHEN THE tragic spell had broken and scraps and odds of the affair began to throng the memories of those present at the opening performance of "His Soul's Master," several persons remembered that a curious hush had preceded the fateful moment.

No one could tell why, but of a sudden all sounds had ceased. Subdued whispers, the creaking of seats, and the froufrou of garments had stopped as abruptly as if a silencing signal had gone through the little auditorium. The spectators had sat motionless, momentarily holding their breath, and even the voices of the actors had faltered for an appreciable second or two. The stillness had been charged with an uneasy tension, and it seemed as though a telepathic whisper of warning had been communicated to the gathering.

Vivian Tennant, as frivolous as she was delicately molded, declared the following day that the silence during those few moments had been so intense that she was positive she had heard a pin drop from the coiffure of the woman on her left. Alex Hammond, forty and cynical, would have ascribed the spell to a touch of necromancy had he been a believer in such childish things. Mrs. Hungerford Cather, a frail little widow with a melancholy disposition, said she felt just as though she were at a séance and a ghost was expected to appear any moment. The others described their impressions with varying degrees of vividness, but all of them agreed in having felt the creeping approach of a silent and invisible horror.

Only Helen Hardwick, whose fresh young charm and frank brown eyes made her seem strangely out of place in that motley gathering of rouged lips, sophisticated banter and gowns suggestive of the Parisian boulevards, was singularly uncommunicative in regard to what she had experienced during the weird interlude when the Thelma Theater became the scene of one of life's grimly realistic tragedies. And her silence was all the more remarkable because she had seen, heard and felt more than any of the others.

The Thelma, with its walls of common red brick and severely plain architecture, might have suggested anything but the setting of a dark and mysterious crime. Outwardly the building, located in a section of New York largely given over to tenements, unsoaped children and garlicky odors, presented an air of solidity and matter-of-factness that left the imagination untouched and gave no hint of the interior. The inside was as colorful and fanciful as the outside was unlovely and prosaic, and it was rumored that Vincent Starr, the eccentric owner, had spent a fortune on the decorations.

Like many another rich man, Starr had his hobby. The newspapers and the critics had scoffed and railed when he opened the Thelma and dedicated it to the uplift of dramatic art. He held the Broadway productions in lofty contempt, declaring that they catered only to the vulgar tastes of the rabble. Admission to the Thelma was by invitation only, and the auditorium seated exactly ninety-nine persons, for it was Starr's firm opinion that out of the city's five million only an infinitesimal few were able to appreciate true histrionic art. Members of the daily press were never admitted, and the only critics present at the performances were the representatives of two or three obscure journals who shared Starr's esthetic views.

The owner and director of the Thelma was prejudiced against music at theatrical performances, and where the orchestra pit should have been was an exquisite statue in marble representing Aphrodite springing out of a foaming sea. Along the walls were friezes picturing the nine muses, the work of a famous mural painter, and the domed ceiling showed colorful glimpses of Dionysian festivals. Scattered throughout the auditorium and in niches in the walls were superb vases containing flowers whose fragrance filled the air.

The effect of the whole was sumptuous rather than harmonious, and it was characteristic of Vincent Starr's freakish tastes and clashing impulses. And among the audience at the *première* of "His Soul's Master" there was not one but thought that the brilliant and fanciful setting lent a touch of incongruity to the tragic byplay enacted off stage.

The moment she stepped into the box reserved for her father and herself, Helen Hardwick felt she was in a strange and somewhat oppressive atmosphere. The faces in the audience were unfamiliar, and everybody stared at her in a way she could not understand until she suddenly remembered that among these people she was something of a celebrity. Vincent Starr, who sneered at the biggest dramatic successes of the year, had not only accepted her play for production at the Thelma, but was himself playing the principal rôle, and he was indulging in much self-flattery over having discovered a budding genius in the author of "His Soul's Master." That explained the curious glances turned in her direction.

It was both amusing and bewildering, she thought. Nothing but a whim had caused her to enter her play in the prize contest conducted by Starr to obtain suitable material for his theater, and its acceptance had been the greatest surprise of her twenty-three years. Her only other serious attempt had been a sketch produced by a dramatic society at Barnard in her junior year. "His Soul's Master" had been a slightly more ambitious effort, and it had been inspired by vague emotions which she herself could hardly understand, but for all that it was a simple, artless thing with a theme as old as the story of the Garden of Eden. It was nothing more than an allegorical fantasy depicting the forces of evil and good struggling for possession of a man's soul. How a play of that kind could have appealed to an eccentric and highly sophisticated genius like Vincent Starr was beyond her.

But the curtain had been up only a few minutes when she began to understand. In the part of *Marius*, the mortal for whose soul the spirits of light and darkness were contending, Starr had found a rôle that matched his temperament to perfection. The opening monologue, in which *Marius* revealed himself as tiring of a life of refined villainy and roguish adventures, had not proceeded far before she saw that the rôle had so gripped and stirred him that he was living the part rather than acting it. The lines throbbed and sparkled with life and passion, and Starr was completely submerging his own emotions in those of the hero.

It did not take Helen long to see that it was the character of *Marius*, rather than the flimsy fancy woven around it, that had caused Starr to accept her play. She had heard he was vain and egotistical, and no doubt he reveled in the opportunity for self-exaltation that the rôle afforded him. As the play went on from scene to scene, another impression began to take root in her mind. Here and there in the lines she noted an odd cynical twist or a bit of ambiguous phrasing that she was sure had not been in the manuscript. The tempting voices and gestures of the spirits of darkness were more appealing than she had intended, and the exhortations of the spirit of light were correspondingly feebler. She thought she understood why Starr had found excuses for not admitting her to any of the rehearsals.

She was inclined to resent the liberties he had taken with her lines, but again she was carried away by his impassioned rendition of *Marius*. The very lifeblood of the character seemed to pulse in Starr's veins. *Marius* had seemed very real to her while she was writing the play, but not so real by far as she now saw him on the stage of the Thelma Theater. She leaned forward and watched him with growing interest and wonder. It was as if a being that had existed only in her thoughts and in her heart had suddenly materialized in flesh and blood.

It was weird. Now and then there came a touch of subtlety, an odd turn of speech, or a telling gesture that she instantly recognized, although she knew it was interpolated by the actor. She had heard and seen them all in imagination, but not clearly enough to reproduce them on paper. The gestures impressed her most. She knew and recognized them all, from the slightest to the most elaborate, although she had visualized only a few of them clearly enough to be able to put them into the play. It seemed as though the actor, in expanding and vivifying his rôle, had made use of material that had existed only in the playwright's mind.

Impulsively she reached out her hand and placed it over her father's. Mr. Hardwick, curator of the Cosmopolitan Museum and an authority on Assyrian relics, started as if his mind had been roving among prehistoric scenes.

"Why, child, your hand is cold!" he whispered anxiously. "Aren't you well?"

"Yes, dad. I'm all right." Her large brown eyes avoided his searching gaze. "How do you like my play?"

She scarcely heard his answer. For a moment she had turned her eyes from the stage and let them wander over the dimly lighted auditorium, and of a sudden a face in the last row of seats held her glance. It was a striking face, though Helen would not have called it beautiful. Somehow the curve of the haughtily tilted chin repelled her. The features were perfect in a cold, unalluring way, and the faint curl of the lips and the designing look in the eyes made her think of a Velasquez portrait. The woman sat alone, the seats to right and left of her being unoccupied, and the heavily shaded electric light on the wall at her side drew a thousand flashing tints from the jewel in her hair.

It was not the face that held Helen Hardwick, but rather the fixed, shrewdly scrutinizing look with which the woman was regarding Vincent Starr. She followed his every motion and gesture with the sly persistence of a cat watching a mouse. Now and then she bent forward, and her lips twitched in a knowing way, as if she were thinking of something that pleased and amused her even while it startled her a little. Helen, studying her with a puzzled look, found herself wondering whether it was the man or the actor that interested the woman so profoundly.

With an effort—for the woman in the rear of the house had already begun to pique her imagination—she once more turned her eyes to the stage. Again she marveled and wondered. She had an odd feeling that something was going on before her eyes which her reason told her could not be quite real. Starr's perfect mastery of the rôle seemed almost supernatural. The slight, quick motions of the hands, the occasional backward toss of the head, the odd habit of gazing down at the finger tips when in deep thought, the set and swing of the shoulders, the minor but characteristic peculiarities of speech and gesture—all belonged to the *Marius* she had seen and known, and Starr's re-creation of him struck her as uncanny.

Of a sudden she felt a little dazed. She shot a quick glance over the auditorium. No one but herself and the woman in the rear seemed to have noticed anything unusual. Again her eyes went back to the stage; and then, as if a hazy idea in the back of her mind had all at once leaped into dazzling clarity, she bent abruptly toward her father.

"Dad—look!" she whispered tensely, tugging at his sleeve. "Don't you see? It's—"

She stopped, shrugged a little, and her hand dropped limply to her knee. The fall of the curtain and the flare-up of the lights seemed to have blotted out an illusion. Mr. Hardwick, gray and lean and looking rather uncomfortable in his full-dress suit, adjusted his glasses on his thin nose, and looked at her gravely.

"My goodness, child! What *is* the matter?" he murmured.

"Nothing, dad. I forgot that—that you wouldn't understand." She drew the palm of her hand across her forehead. "Isn't the air stifling?"

"Too much excitement for you, I am afraid." He smiled as if his practical sense had found a satisfactory answer. "Your mother was just like that. Whenever she got a bit wrought up, she always said things that I couldn't understand. Now—"

The hangings parted and Vincent Starr stepped inside the box. Helen gave him a swiftly appraising glance. His face was flushed and he looked tired, as if his last ounce of energy had been spent in the emotional tempest of *Marius*, but a swift look of animation brightened his face as she introduced her father. The first thing one usually noticed about Vincent Starr was his pale, placid eyes. They seemed to give the lie to his magnetic smile, his vivacious manners, and his deep and perfectly modulated voice. As once or twice before in his presence, Helen felt fascinated and repelled.

"You are doing my daughter a great honor," murmured Mr. Hardwick.

"Not at all." Starr laughed softly, but Helen thought she detected a slight discord that might have been due to either nervousness or fatigue. "Miss Hardwick has placed me under a very great obligation. Her play is splendid. The last act is particularly strong, as you will see in a few minutes. You must give me your opinion of—"

Helen heard no more. She had glanced toward the rear of the house just in time to see a mysterious smile on the face of the woman seated in the last row. In vain Helen tried to read and interpret it. Presently the woman took a pencil from her bag and began to write on a page torn from her programme. Finally she summoned an usher, handed him what she had written, and nodded in the direction where Helen was sitting. The attendant glided away, and a few moments later he stood bowing before Starr.

"A lady sent you this, sir," he announced.

Starr murmured an apology to Helen and her father and unfolded the note. His face, dark and almost effeminately smooth—the face of a dreamer rather than a man of action—showed a look of boredom hinting that he was weary of receiving notes from feminine admirers. Then, as he glanced at the writing, his expression suddenly changed. A look of fear crossed his face, but it vanished so quickly that Helen could not be sure she had read its meaning correctly. He crumpled the note in his hand and glanced at his watch.

"It's almost time for the curtain," he murmured, quite himself once more. "I hope to see both of you later."

With that he was gone. Helen stole a glance at the woman in the rear. Her face bore an expression of amusement and sly triumph, but it afforded no clew to what the note had contained. Then the lights faded out and the curtain rose upon the final act. The scene depended for its full effect on almost total darkness, and the only illumination in the house was a smoldering camp fire in one corner of the stage and the small red lights over the exits. *Marius* stood in the center, almost totally wrapped in shadows, and in the distance were heard the strains of strange, wild singing. The spirits of evil were creeping out of the darkness to make their last sorcerous appeal.

Helen felt herself tingling with suspense. She did not know why, unless it was due to the look of fear she had seen in Starr's face as he read the note. She glanced toward the rear, but the auditorium was now so dark that she could no longer see the mysterious woman, although she imagined her hair ornament was gleaming dully in the gloom.

Of a sudden she opened her eyes wide, straining her pupils against the darkness. She could not be quite sure, but she thought a shadow had emerged from one of the exits and was gliding silently toward the woman in the rear. She sat very still while little shivers ran up and down her back, and she was vaguely wondering at an odd change in Starr's voice. It drooped, grew hoarse and uncertain, and there were pauses between the words. She felt he was trying to conquer a sense of unreasoning dread. A feeling of dizziness seized her, but her imagination formed a picture of a dark shape stealing softly, silently toward where the woman sat.

Acting on an irresistible impulse, she rose and hurried from the box, deaf to her father's mild remonstrance. Without volition on her part, her feet seemed to carry her swiftly up the heavily carpeted aisle. She heard a jumble of noises in her head and felt a tightening at the throat. She rounded the last tier of seats and rushed forward, guided only by a feeble red gleam over one of the exits. A dim shape, a shade darker than the surrounding dusk, was moving a few feet ahead of her.

All at once, as if the hesitancy in Starr's voice had cast a deadening spell over the actors and the audience, an uneasy silence fell upon the house. Helen sensed it as she sped along in the wake of the creeping shadow. A few steps more, and she could make out the woman's figure, vaguely outlined against the gloom, and just behind it stood the shadowy shape whose furtive movements Helen had followed since she left the box.

The happenings of the next few moments were like a swift, horrible dream. Suddenly she felt limp and cold. Within reach of her arm a hand moved, and the motion seemed to strike a hideous note through the surrounding stillness. A cry rose and died in her throat. She staggered back against a post and stood there motionless while a dark shape brushed past her. She recoiled as a hand touched hers in passing, and she caught a fleeting but unforgettable glimpse of a face.

It was gone in a moment, but the swarthy features, framed by coarse black hair that reached to the shoulders, the flat, short nose, the thick and jutting lower lip, the great eyes with their lambent flames that seemed to send streaks of fire into the darkness, gave her a feeling that something evil and loathsome had passed.

CHAPTER II
"MR. SHEI"

FOR A MOMENT LONGER she leaned against the pillar. Then she heard laughter—laughter that was low and sibilant and edged with the insinuating twang that sometimes characterizes the laughter of a madman. It was soft and gentle, yet she thought it was the most fearful sound she had ever heard. It gripped and shook her, and she knew instinctively that it came from the woman in the rear.

Something urged her forward, but her nerves and limbs rebelled. Others beside herself must have heard that soul-shaking laughter, for the hush that had fallen over the house ended abruptly in a jumble of loud sounds. The curtain descended with a rhythmic chugging, there were exclamations of surprise and horror, and the audience sprang from their seats as the lights went on. With startled faces they looked to left and right and rear, and several of them excitedly inquired what had happened. No one seemed to know, but as if moved by a single impulse, they scrambled in the direction whence the laughter came. Then they stopped, huddled in a half circle, and stared.

What they saw seemed all the stranger by contrast with the flowery scents in the air and the rich and brilliant hues of the surroundings. All eyes were fixed on the woman whose peculiar demeanor had aroused Helen's interest. Her extravagant attire and her wild, gypsylike beauty seemed typical of the oddly assorted characters who made up Vincent Starr's circle of intimates. A filmy drapery embroidered with gold-touched flowers hung like an iridescent fog over her gown of silver tissue. Her bare arm was flung out over the top of the next seat, and her head had fallen back against the elbow.

Murmurs of awe and consternation fell from the lips of the onlookers. Before their eyes the pallor of death was creeping into the woman's face, and her cheeks and forehead were beaded with the perspiration of the death struggle. Now and then her figure writhed with a slow, snakelike motion. A film of gray was gradually dimming the luster of the eyes. Only the lips were still red.

As if to fling a taunt in the face of approaching death, the woman was laughing. It sounded wildly unreal and fantastic, and the spectators stood as if gripped by an unearthly enchantment. It seemed as though the woman's spirit was flitting away on waves of hysterical mirth.

The sounds grew husky, then ceased. The woman's glazing orbs looked out over the fringe of faces. A fluttering ray struggled with the blinding film before her eyes, and she seemed to be looking for someone who was not there. She stirred as if trying to gather her waning energies. Her lips trembled, a few faint sounds broke on the tense silence, and again her gaze strayed gropingly over the crowd.

"Mr.—Mr. Shei," she whispered.

Those closest to her recoiled as from a physical blow. The name spoken by the dying woman had contributed the final touch of weirdness to the scene. The two words went from mouth to mouth in a succession of solemn whispers. Faces turned rigid and white, and men and women looked at one another with mute fear in their eyes.

Then someone with more presence of mind than the others, suggested calling a physician. A strain of drawling laughter from the dying woman mocked the proposal. It rose to a shrill pitch, then died abruptly in a low sing-song moan that was like a chant of death. The lips were still moving, but the onlookers knew, even without the sagging of the body and the broken light in the eyes, that the woman was dead. A spell seemed to have lifted and an oppressive essence appeared to have gone out of the air.

"Awful!" wailed a woman, edging away from her place in the huddled throng. "I shall hear that laugh as long as I live. And what was that she said about Mr. Shei?"

The name and the prefix were all anyone had been able to make out, but they had been enough to send a thrill of fear and astonishment through the crowd. Of the mysterious "Mr. Shei" little was known except that he was a versatile and very elusive criminal, with a penchant for deep scheming and spectacular tactics, and that so far the police had matched their wits against him in vain. He flashed in and out like a meteor, without leaving trace or clew, and his audacity and impudence were as dumfounding as the magnitude of his exploits.

"Did she mean," inquired someone, "that Mr. Shei was here—that she saw him?"

"What else could she have meant?" The speaker cast an uncertain glance at the dead woman. The grayness and the rigidity of her features clashed bizarrely with the brilliant coloring of her gown. "Likely as not Mr. Shei murdered her."

"But there is no wound. And she made no outcry. She only laughed. And such a laugh! I can hear it still!"

"Mr. Shei is diabolically clever," observed another, "and he goes about his business in his own way. It would be quite in character for him to kill without inflicting a wound and to let his victim go to her death laughing."

The group fell silent. Helen, who had remained in the background, trying to control her sense of horror while she pondered what she had seen, touched the arm of the woman in front.

"Who is she?" she inquired.

"Don't you know?" The woman, busying herself with a vial of smelling salts, gave Helen a puzzled look. "Why, she is Virginia Darrow. Never attend her studio parties? That's strange. But I forget that you are something of a stranger among us, Miss Hardwick."

Helen smiled faintly, and the next moment her attention was attracted to her father. Mr. Hardwick had joined his daughter shortly after the lights went on, and until now he had been a silent spectator. With difficulty he elbowed his way through the crowd to the dead woman's side, and regarded her closely. Presently he raised her right arm, which had hung limply at her side. Just above the elbow was a small, faint discoloration, not unlike the puncture made by a hypodermic syringe. He nodded thoughtfully and seemed about to speak, but just then Vincent Starr, followed by several members of his company, came up the aisle and wedged a path through the huddled spectators.

He seemed to take in everything at a single comprehensive glance. He was pale, and his fingers trembled, but Helen noticed that he had taken pains to arrange his attire before coming out to ascertain the cause of the commotion. His long and glossy hair was neatly combed, his cravat was carefully adjusted, and just the proper width of cuff showed beyond the edge of his sleeve. She watched him narrowly while he questioned those about him. Somehow she sensed that it was in keeping with Vincent Starr's character to be squeamish about the minor details of his appearance even when face to face with a tragedy. Suddenly, as she heard him issue orders to right and left, she remembered the note Virginia Darrow had sent him, and she wondered, without knowing exactly why, whether he would say anything about it.

At the same time she was forced to admire his quickness of wits and the ease with which he mastered his feelings. In an incredibly short time the police had been notified of the occurrence and the doorkeepers had been given orders to allow no one to leave the building. Starr, in his habitually suave tones, asked his guests to be seated and expressed his regrets that such an unpleasant affair should have taken place under the roof of the Thelma. There would be an investigation and a great deal of questioning, he explained, but it would be only a formality. If the mysterious Mr. Shei—he smiled as he spoke the name—had invaded the Thelma, he would undoubtedly be caught.

The crowd scattered among the seats in the auditorium and lapsed into the small talk with which one sometimes masks an inward turbulence. Helen, seated beside her father on a lounge in a corner, let her glance roam aimlessly over the scene. She supposed she would be questioned along with the others, and she wondered how much or how little she would be able to tell. Now that she tried to clarify the confusion in her mind, she saw that during the evening she had received two sets of impressions. Both had been equally strong at the time, but now they seemed to clash and quarrel with each other, and one of them had all but vanished with the drop of the curtain. Yet she felt it was the more important one of the two. The other had to do with the face she had glimpsed in the shadows. With the varicolored lights glowing on all sides, her recollection of it seemed unreal and fanciful. It appeared to be a thing of darkness and dreams. Her one remaining impression of it was a sense of malignity and horror. She felt words were inadequate to describe it.

She shrugged her shoulders slightly, as if to banish harassing thoughts, and turned to her father. His face was drawn and a trifle pale, and she remembered the family physician had once said something about an incipient heart ailment and the necessity of avoiding excitement. She tilted her face close to his.

"I'm sorry I got you into this, dad," she said.

Mr. Hardwick drew himself up. His face brightened with affection and the pride of parenthood as he gazed at his daughter's figure, straight and slender and strong as the trunk of a young birch. Her simple frock of white taffeta with touches of coral at the waist possessed that subtle individual charm which fashion designers can only imitate. Her dark, loosely coiled hair, with stray wisps caressing her healthily tanned cheeks, seemed in constant mutiny against the petty tyrannies of hairdressers.

"I might have known something was to happen." Mr. Hardwick's tones were gently playful, as if he were anxious to turn his daughter's thoughts from the tragedy. "Something always happens where you are. You are a storm petrel, my dear."

"I was born under Uranus, you know. That explains everything." She smiled whimsically. There was a touch of the child in the firm oval of her face and the smooth curves of mouth and nose, but the deep-brown eyes held a surprising store of worldly wisdom. She quite baffled her father at times. The impulses of April and June seemed to be constantly clashing within her, and they filled his autumnal days with a never-ending round of surprises.

"I wonder," he said, eyeing her curiously as a new thought came to him, "whether Uranus had anything to do with your leaving the box before—before it happened."

"It's always safe to blame Uranus," she parried. "He is such a convenient scapegoat. I don't know what I would do if—"

She was grateful for the interruption that came just then. The law was already at work, and she sat back and watched the swift precision of its mechanism. Two policemen, one heavy and red-faced, the other lean and sharp-visaged, walked into the theater and stationed themselves beside the body with the air of zealots guarding the coffin of Mohammed. She gathered from the few words they exchanged with Starr that a cordon had been thrown around the building a minute and a half after the call reached the precinct station. They were followed shortly by a puffy little man who let it be known that he was a deputy from the office of the chief medical examiner. The latter had barely begun the usual inspection of the body when two other men entered the auditorium.

One of them, barrel-chested and somewhat pompous in his manners, seemed to be a representative of the district attorney's office. The other, angular and as loose-jointed as a marionette, with lazy, cinnamon-colored eyes and a complexion that seemed to indicate that he drank too much coffee and smoked too many cigars, was recognized by Helen at first glance. Uranus had brought them together once before. She remembered that his name was Lieutenant Culligore, and that he was attached to the homicide squad of the detective bureau. As his glance flitted slowly over the room, his mind seemed to register each detail without slightest effort. Helen noticed that he gazed at her a trifle longer than on the others, but his face betrayed no recognition.

Then began the questioning, conducted by the stout man from the district attorney's office, while Lieutenant Culligore made an occasional jotting in his notebook. The members of the audience were interrogated briefly and pointedly, and each one in turn was permitted to depart after leaving his or her name and address. Helen marveled at the matter-of-factness of it all. It seemed almost ruthless, this volleying of questions over a body which was scarcely cold, but she recognized the brisk efficiency with which the procedure was carried out. None of the witnesses had much to tell that was significant, and the only important points brought out were the dying woman's strange laugh and her mention of Mr. Shei.

Culligore, as was his habit when impressed, curled up his lip under the tip of his nose when these facts were stated, and the stout man raised his brows and nodded grimly.

"Looks as though Mr. Shei had been up to another of his little tricks," he muttered.

Culligore pursed his lips and chewed a dead cigar. There was a slow twinkle in his eyes which seemed to say that life wasn't quite so serious as it seemed, despite the sordid and ugly affairs with which he came in daily touch.

Helen did not know how it happened, but the house was almost empty when her turn to be questioned came. Her face showed no sign of the trepidation she felt as she stepped forward. She knew, as she turned her face toward the stout man, that three pairs of eyes were watching her with more than ordinary intentness—her father's, Lieutenant Culligore's, and Vincent Starr's.

The stout man gave her a listless look as he inquired her name and address. She fancied he was sniffing inwardly, and that after looking her over he had decided that she probably could give no information beside what had already been brought out. At any rate, his questions were few and perfunctory and gave her no opportunity to practice the evasions she had mentally rehearsed while the others were being questioned. As she turned away, she saw a mildly reproachful look in her father's face and one of amused understanding in Culligore's.

"Well, doctor?" The stout man turned on the medical examiner, whose rubicund face wore a puzzled scowl. "What do you make of it?"

The examiner wagged his head. Being a man of science, he was strongly averse to forming hasty conclusions.

"There is an abrasion on the right arm that might have been caused by a hypodermic syringe," he announced.

"And the laugh—how do you account for that?"

"I am not accounting for it, but there are certain drugs that produce exhilaration and laughter. Most of them have to be taken into the system by inhalation, however, in order to produce such an effect."

"I see." The stout man looked a bit impatient. "In plain words, then, it's a case of murder?"

"I wouldn't say that. It might prove a far-fetched guess."

"All quibbling aside, don't the scratch on her arm look as though somebody had shot a dose of poison into her with a needle?"

The examiner pondered. "It could mean that, but it doesn't necessarily follow. An autopsy will be necessary to establish the exact cause of death. Why should a murderer use a hypodermic injection when there are so many simpler and easier ways of accomplishing the same result?"

The stout man guffawed. "Mr. Shei never picks the simple and easy way. When he wants to pull off a crime, he always dresses it up in flossy trimmings. And he always plays safe. Now, my idea is that the safest thing in the world to kill a person with is a hypodermic syringe. It makes no noise, there's no smoke, no bullet, no powder marks, no anything, and it don't leave any clews behind."

The examiner smiled skeptically, as if he had his own views on the subject. "The autopsy will tell. What I fail to understand is why you seem so certain that Mr. Shei, as he calls himself, has had a hand in this affair."

"Miss Darrow saw him, didn't she?"

"She called out his name, if I understood the witnesses correctly, but she did not say she had seen him. It's possible she imagined she saw him. The same drugs that produce exhilaration and laughter also produce hallucinations. However," and he pulled a cigar from his pocket and lighted it carefully, "whether Miss Darrow did or did not see Mr. Shei is for you gentlemen to decide. Good-night."

He strode out. The stout man made a wry face and stroked his chin. Evidently the medical man had given him something to think about. Helen, too, had found food for reflection in the doctor's statement. She stood beside her father a few feet from the others. She had remained for no other reason than a feeling that Culligore, who had been watching her covertly from time to time, might try to detain her if she made a move to go. She believed the lieutenant had rightly guessed that she had not told all she knew.

Starr, who had unobtrusively slipped out of the building while the late colloquy was in progress, returned with the report that he had questioned the doorkeepers and the watchman, and that they had seen no suspicious looking characters about the place. They were positive no one had entered or left the building either before or after Miss Darrow's death. Starr ended by inquiring whether it were not possible that the murderer, granting that Miss Darrow had been murdered, was still hiding in the building.

The stout man rather scouted the suggestion, but he instructed the two uniformed officers to make a thorough search.

"If this is Mr. Shei's job, you can bet your sweet life he's made a safe get-away," he grumbled. "He probably sneaked out through one of the fire exits."

The two policemen withdrew. Starr, gliding about with the softness of a panther, found a piece of drapery and covered the body. Helen's lids contracted as she followed his movements. It struck her as odd that during the entire questioning he had made no reference to the communication Miss Darrow had sent him a few minutes before her death. She wondered whether he had forgotten it or was deliberately withholding it. In the latter case, what could be his reason?

"How about the motive?" suggested Lieutenant Culligore. It was one of the few times he had spoken since the investigation began. "Know of anybody who could have had a reason for getting Miss Darrow out of the way, Mr. Starr?"

Starr stood for a moment with head lowered, deep in thought. Then he slowly shook his finely proportioned head. "No, I don't. I knew Miss Darrow quite well. As far as I am aware, she had no enemies. I can't imagine why—"

He checked himself. Then he gaped, and his eyes widened, and he looked as though an important matter had just occurred to him. Finally, with a sheepish smile, he began to search his pockets.

"This dreadful affair has upset me completely," he murmured; and then, as if in answer to the question that had flashed through Helen's mind a few moments before, he produced a crumpled piece of paper. "If I had not been so flustered I should have shown you this at once," he added.

He smoothed out the message and handed it to the stout man. The latter's face clouded as he read it aloud:

Mr. Shei, like a fool, rushes in where angels might fear to tread.
V. D.

A pause followed the reading. Culligore's upper lip brushed the tip of his nose, a sign that he had found a problem to ponder. A blank expression came into the stout man's face. He looked bewilderedly at Starr.

"What do you suppose she meant by that?" he asked.

"That's just what I wondered when the note was brought me," explained Starr, a blend of sadness and self-reproach in his tones. "Miss Darrow was a strange woman, full of subtleties and strange whims. The note startled me at first; then I decided it was only a jest. At any rate, it was time for the curtain, and I dismissed the matter from my mind. Now, in the light of what has happened, I can see it was meant as a warning."

"Warning?" echoed the stout man.

"Undoubtedly." Starr gazed regretfully into space. "In some manner Miss Darrow must have become aware that Mr. Shei was in the house, and she chose this method of warning me of his presence. I was a fool not to see it."

He paced back and forth, running his fingers through his thick hair and muttering self-reproaches. The stout man looked as if he were trying to untangle a mental knot. Again he read the note.

"If Miss Darrow wanted to tip you off that Mr. Shei was in the house, why didn't she say so in plain words?"

"Facetiousness," said Starr grimly. "Virginia Darrow was the kind of woman you would expect to be facetious at her own funeral. Why didn't I realize that she was trying to warn me? I remember now that she behaved in a peculiar manner all evening. Whenever I happened to look in her direction, I found her gazing at me in a strange way. I didn't understand then, but I suppose now that she was trying to send me an ocular message. When that failed, she sent me the note. Oh, why didn't I—"

He made a gesture of distress and self-disgust. Helen, watching his every movement, remembered that it was Miss Darrow's odd way of staring at Starr that had first attracted her attention to the woman. The recollection started a train of new thoughts, but Culligore's voice interrupted it.

"If Miss Darrow was right and Mr. Shei was in the house," he told the fat man, "then you and I might as well hand in our badges and look for new jobs."

The other jerked up his head. "You don't think that—" he began in startled tones, then broke off and grinned complacently. "Not a chance of that. Mr. Shei couldn't have been in the audience. I gave all of them a pretty stiff quiz, and every one gave a good account of himself. Anyhow, they're the kind that get their names and pictures into the society columns of the Sunday papers. A bunch of harmless nuts—that's all."

He looked at Starr, as if realizing that the epithet had been a trifle brusque, but the manager seemed amused rather than offended.

"I think you are right," he murmured. "The audience was composed of invited guests. I am willing to vouch for every one of them. Furthermore, you have their names and addresses, and you can communicate with them whenever you wish. If Mr. Shei was really in the theater, he came here as an unbidden guest. In all likelihood he stole in while the house was dark during the first scene of the last act, and departed as soon as he had accomplished his purpose."

It sounded plausible enough, Helen thought; yet her mind was heavy with a giddying whirl of suspicions and contradictions. She slanted a reluctant glance toward the chair containing the body. With a shiver she turned away, and a look at her father's drawn and tired face warned her that he should be in bed. Then she glanced at the man from the district attorney's office, and finally at Culligore. His face was a mask, but his occasional glances in her direction troubled her. The two uniformed officers had not yet returned from their search, and she wondered what they would have to report.

Once more her eyes flitted over the little group, and then, with a suddenness that choked a cry in her throat, everything was blotted from sight. In a twinkling impenetrable darkness had descended upon the house. Somewhere a door banged. She felt her father's tightening clutch on her arm. The stout man swore. Dark shapes were darting hither and thither. She heard a fragmentary cry, followed by a crash and a succession of thuds. A thrust sent her sprawling to the floor, and her mind drifted into a state of semi-stupor during which she was conscious of nothing but the swift and silent movements of the shadowy shapes.

Voices and the return of light jolted her mind back to consciousness. She struggled to her feet and blinked her eyes at the strange scene. Her father, dazed but apparently unharmed, sat a short distance away, with his back to the wall. The stout man, seemingly unconscious, lay in a twisted heap on the floor. Culligore was staring about him groggily and muttering something about a blow on the head. A policeman, one of the pair who had been sent off to search the house, was helping Starr to his feet.

With the attention to detail that comes in moments of great bewilderment, Helen noticed that Starr made a ludicrous picture. His attire, so faultless and immaculate a few minutes ago, was now in a sorry state of disorder. A streak of crimson stained his shirt front, and he held a handkerchief to his nose. He wabbled drunkenly across the floor, but all at once his figure stiffened and a blank look came into his face. His lips formed unspoken words as he raised a finger and pointed toward a seat in the last tier.

As she followed the pointing finger, things swam in confusion before Helen's eyes. Starr, speechless and crestfallen, was indicating the chair where the body of Virginia Darrow had been. As she stared stonily toward the empty chair, Helen felt an impulse to cry out. She came a few steps closer, then stopped with a shudder and dazedly swept her hand across her forehead.

"It's—it's gone!" she cried huskily.

CHAPTER III
HELEN EQUIVOCATES

ACROSS THE BREAKFAST TABLE Mr. Hardwick looked anxiously at his daughter. The wild-rose color that usually flooded her cheeks had faded a trifle since last night, and her eyes were less bright. Most of the time the curator's mind browsed among relics of the past, but his perceptions were amazingly keen where his daughter was concerned.

"Mr. Shei gave us quite a shock last night," he remarked.

Helen kept her eyes down while she poured his coffee and added two and a half lumps of sugar and the usual portion of cream. Then she stirred it for him, knowing he would be quite apt to forget to do so himself. Despite the half dozen titles bestowed upon him by universities and learned societies, she felt he needed looking after.

"Don't forget that you have a lecture engagement this afternoon," she admonished as she passed the cup across the table.

Mr. Hardwick nodded and sipped. "It is a most extraordinary case. The murder of that poor woman—assuming that it was a case of murder—seemed wholly unprovoked. I gathered from the conversation among the officers that no motive was in evidence. It looks like a wanton, despicable crime."

Helen crumbled a piece of toast. "Professor Warburton is coming to see you at three this afternoon."

"I have a memorandum of the appointment on my desk." Mr. Hardwick smiled faintly. "Our minds seem to be pulling in opposite directions this morning. This Mr. Shei interests me. He appears to be a remarkable criminal. His audacity and the originality of his methods are unparalleled. I don't know that I ever encountered anything quite so mystifying as the circumstances surrounding the murder last night. How the murderer went in and out without being seen is beyond understanding, and the subsequent removal of the body was the most amazing part of it all. There seems to be neither method nor reason in that. One thing appears certain. Mr. Shei could not have accomplished what he did unless he had been aided by accomplices. What do you think, my dear?"

Helen's head was lowered over her coffee cup. The captive sunlight in her hair gleamed and flashed.

"Your extra pair of glasses are at the optician's," she reminded him. "Don't forget to stop for it."

Mr. Hardwick looked at her helplessly; then carefully, and from force of habit, he folded his napkin.

"I wonder whether the police will ever learn Mr. Shei's identity," he murmured musingly. "So far the scoundrel has contrived to mystify them completely, but some day his egotism and love of self-glorification are apt to cause his undoing. In the meantime, however, he is likely to do a great deal of mischief. The fellow's effrontery is colossal, and his fearlessness and brains render him most dangerous. In some respects he bears a very close resemblance to that other notorious rogue, now reported to be in retirement."

Helen drew a quick breath. She bent her head a little lower over her cup. Her right index finger traced a design on the tablecloth.

"Another cup of coffee, dad?" was her only reply.

Mr. Hardwick appeared not to have heard. "You know who I mean. The man they used to call The Gray Phantom. For several years he was regarded as one of the cleverest and most dangerous criminals the world has ever known."

Slowly Helen raised her head. Her eyes, as they met her father's, were steady and bright.

"That was because the world didn't understand him," she said with emphasis. "The Gray Phantom wasn't really a criminal. He was only a—a sort of human dynamo whose energy happened to be turned in the wrong direction."

"Isn't that a distinction without a difference? A Robin Hood is an enemy of society despite the glamour with which he surrounds himself. However," and Mr. Hardwick's face softened quickly, "I am deeply in The Gray Phantom's debt. He saved your life twice, and but for him I would now be a lonely and heartbroken old man."

Helen nodded eagerly. "And the Assyrian collection, dad. You spent most of your life gathering it, and you were almost overcome with grief when it was stolen. The Gray Phantom risked his life and liberty in order to recover it and restore it to you. He wouldn't have done that if he had been just an ordinary criminal."

"True," admitted Mr. Hardwick. "I shall be under obligations to The Gray Phantom as long as I live. The man has a number of excellent qualities, whatever may be said of his past. On the whole, it is not surprising that you have taken an interest in him."

Helen's eyes were lowered again.

There was a mingling of tenderness and worry in Mr. Hardwick's face as he looked at her. "I know just how you feel," he said softly. "A man who is trying to live down a dark past always exerts a strong romantic appeal on a woman of your impressionable age. I don't know why it is, unless it pleases her to think he is doing it for her sake. It makes me think of your play, 'The Master of His Soul.' All last night, until the interruption came, I was wondering whether your *Marius* was not The Gray Phantom."

Helen sat rigidly still for a moment. Then her lips began to twitch. She flashed her father a smile.

"Sometimes, daddy dear, you show a wonderful understanding of things that have nothing to do with Assyriology."

"I was right, then." His face sobered. "I hope you realize that, despite The Gray Phantom's admirable qualities, there is a gulf between him and you. But you are just as level-headed as was your mother, and I have no fear that the impulses of your heart will get the better of your judgment. We were discussing Mr. Shei. There seems to be a striking similarity between his methods and those of The Gray Phantom, except that the latter was never known to stoop to murder." He paused for a moment and studied her averted face. "You puzzled me last night, dear. You will admit that your conduct was—er, peculiar."

"It's getting late, dad," murmured Helen, a bit confusedly glancing at her wrist watch. "You should have been at your office half an hour ago. And this is the first time I've known you to take an interest in a murder case."

"Once during the evening you gripped my hand and tried to point out something to me," pursued Mr. Hardwick, heedless of her remark. "You spoke incoherently, and I had not the faintest idea what it was about. Then, a minute or so before the tragedy, you left the box and hurried away. Still later, while the officer was questioning you, I felt you were concealing something."

Helen, her fingers tightening about a fork handle, shook her head. "I answered every question he put to me."

"I know, dear. Yet you withheld a secret of some kind from him."

"Not exactly. I—I merely refrained from telling him something that—that I might have told."

"Something you had heard or seen?"

She hesitated for an instant. "If I had told all I had seen and heard, I wouldn't have been telling half of what I knew."

Mr. Hardwick leaned back against the chair and pondered this cryptic statement. He seemed puzzled rather than hurt by his daughter's evasive answers. Suddenly she looked up, saw the troubled expression in his face, and impulsively pushed back her chair and ran up behind him.

"Please don't ask me any more questions, dad." She put her arms around his neck and tilted her face to his. "It is true I held something back, but at the time I didn't know why. I merely felt that it wouldn't do to tell. This morning, after lying awake most of the night, I knew I had done the right thing." She gave a little laugh. "Isn't it just like a woman to act first and look into her reasons afterward?"

"I—well, I suppose so. And what were your reasons?"

"Would you be hurt if I told you I would rather not explain them just now?"

"No; I trust you. Experience has taught me that I can depend upon you in spite of your mysterious little ways and madcap pranks. There is one thing I wish you would tell me, though." He stopped, fumbling for words. "Was your reticence last night prompted by a wish to shield someone?"

"No," was her prompt reply, and her eyes gazed frankly into his. "What put such a thought into your head?"

"I scarcely know. You'll think I am an old fool, but it occurred to me that perhaps you had discovered something that led you to think that Mr. Shei and The Gray Phantom are identical."

"And you thought I was protecting The Gray Phantom? What an idea! But you were wrong, dad—absolutely wrong."

"Then I am glad." Mr. Hardwick rose and put his arm around her waist. "My goodness! Almost ten o'clock, and I have been sitting here gossiping like an old woman. You have taken a load off my mind, dear child. I was really worried."

She laughed, whisked a few crumbs from his coat, straightened his tie, and kissed him.

"And I hope," added Mr. Hardwick banteringly, "that Uranus won't lead you into any more foolhardy adventures."

Again she laughed, but her face sobered the moment he turned away and left the room. A wiser, maturer expression settled over the wide-set eyes and the vivid lips. It seemed as though her talk with her father had left a disquieting impression in her mind. She moved absently about the room, setting things in order here and there, but the far-away gleam in her eyes told that her mind was scarcely aware of what her hands were doing. Presently she stopped before the open window and looked out. A building was going up across the street, and the groaning of derricks and screaming of steam whistles jarred discordantly in the back of her mind. Near the curb a group of laborers were mixing concrete, and a powdery substance was drifting in the air.

She came out of her abstraction with a little start. Her eyes were on the window sill, and she spelled out the characters she had written in the thin layer of dust.

"G-r-a-y P-h-a-n-t-o-m," she mumbled, puzzled and somewhat annoyed with herself. The faint pencilings in the dust seemed all the stranger because she had not been thinking of The Gray Phantom. Instead, her mind had been occupied by Mr. Shei and what the morning newspapers had said about the tragedy in the Thelma Theater. The accounts she had read had been largely speculation and conjecture. The dying woman's strange laughter and her mysterious allusion to Mr. Shei had afforded material for columns of vivid and imaginative description. The medical examiner had reluctantly admitted that Miss Darrow's death might have been caused by a poison administered hypodermically, but he had added that the symptoms were strange to him, and that he knew of no drug producing just such effects. A number of toxicologists had been interviewed, but they had declared that the few facts at hand were not sufficient to enable them to form an opinion, and the disappearance of the body rendered it doubtful whether the cause of death would ever be learned definitely.

Only one thing seemed beyond dispute and that was Mr. Shei's complicity in the affair. The elusive and highly accomplished rogue already had a score of astounding crimes to his record, and the Thelma murder was hedged with all the mystery and baffling detail with which he loved to mask his exploits. Miss Darrow's dying words were scarcely needed to turn the finger of suspicion in Mr. Shei's direction. The absence of clews, the uncertainty in regard to the motive, the audacity that marked the crime itself as well as the subsequent snatching away of the body, all indicated a boldness and a finesse that left little doubt of Mr. Shei's guilt. Even if his own hand had not executed the crime, it seemed practically certain that his mind had planned and conceived it.

But who was Mr. Shei? The whole train of surmises and theories pivoted on that question. Not much was known of him save that he had a passion for tantalizing the public and keeping the nerves of the men at headquarters on edge, and that his achievements had not been equaled in scope or brilliance of execution since The Gray Phantom's retirement. He took a diabolical delight in flaunting his name before the world while keeping his person carefully out of the reach of the law's long arm, and even the name was a challenge to the police and a teaser for the public imagination. Someone versed in dead languages had discovered that the word "shei" was the ancient equivalent of the modern x, the symbol of the unknown quantity, and it was generally agreed that the name fitted the elusive individual who bore it.

Yet the name meant nothing. It was only an abstraction, for it afforded no clew to its owner's identity. The night before, while she sat beside her father in the Thelma Theater, a vagrant flash of intuition had come to Helen. She had seen the solution of the mystery in a swift, dazzling glimpse. The revelation had stunned and nearly blinded her, and thoughts had crowded upon her so thickly that she would have been quite unable to clothe them in words. The idea carried to her by that intuitive flash had seemed clear and unquestionable. It still seemed so, but her talk with her father had disturbed her a little and turned her thoughts in a new direction.

Again she looked down at the tracings in the dust. A smile, faint and wistful, reflected her softened mood, and a light of wonder and gentleness flooded her eyes. She reached out a hand to obliterate the telltale pencilings, but something restrained her. Besides, a freshly forming layer of dust was already blotting them out.

The telephone rang in the adjoining room, and she hurried away to answer.

"Miss Hardwick?" inquired a drawling voice which she instantly recognized. "Lieutenant Culligore speaking. I'm at the Thelma Theater. Wish you'd come over right away. I want to ask you a few questions."

Before she could reply, he hung up. Her face grew suddenly tense. Culligore's brusqueness piqued her, though she knew it was characteristic of the man, and she felt he had taken undue advantage of her by giving her no chance for argument. She did not wish to see him, yet she knew she could not escape him by merely ignoring his request. Anyway, she reflected as she hastily dressed for the street, it would be interesting to learn Culligore's theory of the murder.

A ride in the subway and a short walk brought her to the door of the Thelma. On the wall, at each side of the entrance, were posters stating that until further notice there would be no more performances of "His Soul's Master." Helen viewed the announcement of the withdrawal of her play without much regret. She had partly anticipated it, and last night's occurrence had given her weightier things to think of. As she passed through the foyer, a policeman nodded stolidly and in a way that told her she was expected. She passed unhindered into the auditorium.

At first she could see nothing. Every door was closed, and the vast room was full of silence and vague shadows. Presently, as her eyes grew accustomed to the dusk, she glanced toward the chair that had been occupied by Miss Darrow. She looked quickly aside, and saw that she was standing not far from the pillar that had supported her when the creature with the loathsome face brushed past her. The scene, which had seemed dim and immaterial while she was out in the sunlight a few minutes ago, now recurred to her with disagreeable vividness. Of a sudden the air about her felt heavy and oppressive.

A figure was moving up the aisle toward where she stood. The dawdling gait and the slouchy attitude told her it was Culligore, and she braced her nerves for an ordeal. In a few moments her quickly working wits had found a way of handling the situation.

"Good-morning, lieutenant," she said pleasantly as he came up beside her. "I suppose you are looking for clews. Any success?"

"Nope," he replied complainingly. "That's why I sent for you, Miss—"

"You have found no trace of the body?" she quickly cut in, anxious to maintain the rôle of questioner.

Culligore shook his head. She felt his eyes on her face, though he did not appear to be looking at her. Practicing a trick cultivated by his profession, he was studying her without seeming to do so.

"Don't you think it strange that the murderer should go to all that risk and trouble to remove the body?" she went on.

"Murderer? There must have been three or four of them, at least. There was some mighty fast work done when the lights went out, and one man didn't do it all. I've got a bump in the back of my head as big as a hen's egg. Selfkin, the man from the district attorney's office, is in bed with a fractured skull, and Starr looks as though somebody had hit him on the nose with a brick. One of the gang must have tampered with the switchboard back of the proscenium arch just before the others swooped down on us and carried away the body."

"But what was the object? Wasn't the murderer's purpose accomplished with the killing of Miss Darrow?"

"Hard telling. One thing is sure. As long as the body is missing there can be no autopsy, and I'll bet a pair of yellow socks that that's exactly what they wanted. Not that I pretend to understand it all, but it seems reasonable that they didn't care to have the exact cause of Miss Darrow's death become known."

Helen pondered this statement for a moment. "How about the motive for the murder?"

"We're pretty much in the dark there, too," admitted Culligore. "I don't suppose, though, that it was just by accident that Miss Darrow happened to die a few minutes after she had sent Starr a note warning him that Mr. Shei was in the house."

"Oh!" Helen gave a quick start. "You think she was killed because she had in some manner discovered Mr. Shei's identity?"

"Maybe." Culligore, with legs spread out and hands in trousers pockets, seemed engrossed in a study of Helen's bright-trimmed hat. "My mind isn't made up on that point. Mr. Shei's schemes go pretty deep. Maybe you can tell me—"

Again Helen interrupted him. "Have you discovered how the murderers got in and out of the building?"

"They didn't leave any tracks behind them, but there is a door in the rear of the basement that they might have used. It's supposed to be locked, but I satisfied myself a while ago that the spring lock can be picked. That the body was carried out that way is as good a guess as any. But look here, Miss Hardwick," and something that might have been a grin drifted across his face, "you're pretty good at firing questions, but it's my turn now."

She stiffened, seeing she would have to assume defensive tactics. She sent him a quick glance, but his face, always inscrutable, was even more so in the dusk.

"I asked you to come here, hoping the surroundings would refresh your memory of what happened last night," Culligore went on in his usual placid drawl. "You needn't repeat what you said then. What I'm after is the things you *didn't* say."

"I don't believe I understand."

Culligore's chuckle sounded like a snort, though she knew it was meant to be good-natured. "Oh, yes, you do. I didn't do much talking last night, but I was watching you all the time. We'd met before, you know, and I could read you like an open book. I knew you were just as long on brains as on looks. Though you answered every question, you weren't telling anything. All the while you were holding something back. Isn't that true?"

She hesitated, having an uncomfortable feeling that Culligore was seeing through her and that any attempt at evasion would be useless.

"What do you want to know?" she asked.

"That's a lot better, Miss Hardwick. You might begin by telling me where you were sitting when the disturbance began."

"Why, I—I wasn't sitting anywhere."

"Standing up, then?"

"I wasn't standing, either."

"Oh, I see. You were lying down?"

"No, not even lying down."

Culligore gave her a strange look. "If you weren't sitting, standing, or lying, you must have hung suspended in the air. Was that it?"

Helen smiled engagingly. She had found time for deliberation while quibbling, and now her mind was made up. "I was so frightened I could neither stand up nor sit down. I was leaning against that pillar over there." She pointed.

"How did you happen to leave your seat?"

Helen told him of the flitting shadow that had caused her to leave her father and run to the rear of the house.

"And what did you see while you were leaning against the pillar?" was Culligore's next question.

Helen searched her mind for words vivid enough to recount her impressions during the terrible moments just before the drop of the curtain, but she felt her description was both hazy and fragmentary. Her picture of the face that had flashed past her in the dark was blurred and unreal, like one's recollection of a dream.

When she had done her best, Culligore walked back and forth for a time. Standing in an attitude of strained tensity, she wondered what his next question would be. Suddenly he stopped squarely in front of her, and again she had an uncomfortable feeling that his deceptively lazy eyes were reading her thoughts.

"What else?" he demanded quietly. "What you have told me so far is pretty good, but you're still holding back the most important thing—the thing you didn't want to tell about last night."

"How—how do you know that?" she asked.

He gave another snortlike chuckle. "Common horse sense tells me. The reason you didn't tell about the things you saw while leaning against the post was because you were afraid they would lead you on to a subject you didn't want to discuss. You were afraid that if you got started you might get tangled up and wouldn't be able to stop."

Helen could only stare at him. He had stated the truth far more clearly than she herself could have done.

"What was it, Miss Hardwick? I think you had better tell."

She stood silent, twisting her figure this way and that, and all the while wishing that he would take his eyes from her. Jumbled thoughts thronged her mind, and she felt her power of resistance slipping from her. Finally Culligore swung round on his heels, and a sigh of relief escaped her.

"The thing about you that puzzles me more than anything else is that your hair isn't red," he told her. "The rest I can savvy easily enough. I can even tell what it was you were holding back last night. Want me to?"

His tones were soft and teasing. She squirmed, torn between anxiety and despair. His face was expressionless, but she felt he was inwardly laughing at her.

"All right, then," he said, taking her silence for assent. "You couldn't have had more than one reason for keeping mum last night, and that reason was that you wanted to shield somebody. There is only one man on earth you could have wanted to shield, and that man is The Gray Phantom."

"No!" she cried. "You're mistaken! I wasn't—"

"Easy now." All at once his tone changed. "There's such a thing as protesting too much, you know. I don't take much stock in what I read in the Sunday papers, but there's a lot of talk going the rounds about a romance between you and The Gray Phantom. Most of it is pipe dreams, I guess. Anyhow, it's nobody's business, and it makes no difference. All I'll say is that if I was The Gray Phantom and had a girl like you fighting for me, I'd be willing to go through hell-fire for her every day in the week. You're loyal clean through and—"

"But you're wrong!" she interrupted emphatically. His words filled her with a great fear, but there was a kind of rough tenderness in his voice that warmed her.

"I knew you'd say that, but you have to hear me through. I take off my hat to The Gray Phantom. He always played the game according to the code, even when he cut those fancy didos that put gray hairs in almost every head on the force. I shouldn't say it, but it goes just the same. The Phantom's been lying low now for some time. Nobody seems to know where he is. He's shown himself only twice, and each time he came out in a good cause. They say he's going it straight, and it's rumored that a certain young lady has had a lot to do with his turning over a new leaf."

He paused, and for a moment his eyes rested on her averted face.

"It's hard work for a leopard to change his spots. Some people say it can't be done. The Phantom's human, like the rest of us. Maybe he's got tired of the straight and narrow path and gone back to his old tricks under a new name. Just for the sake of argument we'll say he has. And I've got a hunch that last night you saw or heard something that made you think that Mr. Shei is The Gray Phantom."

The assertion staggered her, though she had known all the time that he was leading up to it. Using almost the same words, her father had expressed the same idea at the breakfast table, and it was the similarity of the phrasing that startled her.

"No—no!" was all she could say.

"Then will you please tell me," said Culligore, his tones both gentle and insistent, "why didn't you come out with what you knew last night?"

She fell back a step, feeling suddenly weak as she realized that his question was unanswerable. A confusion of ideas churned and simmered in her mind. Her lips moved, but no words came.

"You've answered me," declared Culligore. "You think Mr. Shei is The Phantom. Maybe you're right, and maybe you're wrong. What I wanted to know was what you thought. And let me tell you something." A foolish grin, one of Lieutenant Culligore's infrequent ones, wrinkled his face. "I hate my job less whenever I meet up with one of your kind."

Helen did not hear what he said. She felt as if the swirl of thoughts and emotions within her had suddenly turned into a leaden lump. She glanced involuntarily at the chair in which Virginia Darrow had sat, and of a sudden she fancied she heard laughter—slow, tinkling laughter that sounded like a taunt flung in the face of an approaching specter. She knew the sounds existed only in her imagination, but with a low, long drawn-out cry she turned abruptly and fled toward the door, conscious only of a fierce desire for sunlight and air.

No one detained her. She ran across the street. An idea was slowly working its way out of the turmoil in her mind. She opened her bag and counted her scant supply of bills. Then she looked about her. Half a block down the street she saw the sign of a district messenger office. In a few moments she was inside, hastily scrawling a note which she had addressed to her father. A taxicab was passing as she stepped out on the street. She hailed the driver, and he drew in at the curb.

"Erie station—West Twenty-third Street," she directed breathlessly.

As the cab started she slumped back against the cushions and gazed rigidly out the window. Despite the bright sunlight, things blurred before her eyes, and there was only one clear thought in her mind.

She was on her way to The Gray Phantom, for she alone knew where to find him.

CHAPTER IV
AZURECREST

IT WAS GROWING DARK when she reached the end of her journey, and the dusk made it easy for her to elude the little knot of idlers on the station platform. With frequent backward glances she hurried down a path that skirted the edge of a village nestling at the foot of a hill which was outlined against the horizon like a great funnel-shaped cloud. On its apex was Azurecrest, the hermitage of The Gray Phantom.

Helen found the motor driveway that circled its way upward in spiral fashion, for the hill was too steep to permit cars to reach the top by direct route. She had visited the place once before, in the course of one of the perilous adventures she and The Phantom had shared together. The residence, a sprawling structure of stone, tile and stucco, had been built by The Phantom shortly after his retirement, and she had marveled at the precautions he had taken to protect his privacy. The inhabitants of the village understood that the place was occupied by a wealthy and leisurely gentleman who was spending the remainder of his life in ease and solitude on the desolate hilltop. Though consumed with curiosity, they never ventured near Azurecrest, guessing accurately that they would not be welcomed. Occasionally they saw one of the servants, but the owner never permitted himself to be seen except by his most intimate associates.

The tang of late autumn was in the air, and Helen's head cleared as she walked briskly up the zigzagging driveway. The railway journey had been long and tedious and punctuated by innumerable stops, and she had been too distracted to think clearly. Now she began to search her mind for a plan, but she soon saw that planning was impossible. Her trip to Azurecrest had been prompted by one of those sudden impulses that usually dictated her conduct, and she had been conscious of no other motive than to put an end to her fears and doubts. She had thought that a talk with The Gray Phantom would quickly end the suspense.

Reaching the gate in the picket fence that encircled the apex of the hill, she touched an electric button. While waiting she looked about her. The Susquehanna, like a cocoon thread, wound in and out among the hills and valleys in the distance. The moon, shining through a vapory gauze, splashed a misty sheen over bowlders and trees.

She heard a dog's shrill bark, and a masculine figure came down the graveled walk toward the gate. As he drew nearer and the pale moonlight fell on him, she saw he was stocky and coarse-featured, and she guessed he was one of the sentinels that were always stationed about the place.

"What do you want?" he asked ungraciously as he reached the gate.

"I wish to see Mr. Vanardy," she announced, using the name by which the occupant of Azurecrest had been known before he became The Gray Phantom.

She thought the man repressed a start, but she reflected that his evident surprise was natural enough, since visitors seldom came to Azurecrest.

"Mr. Vanardy, eh?" He drew an instrument from his pocket and flashed an electric gleam in her face. For a long moment he studied her in silence. "You mean The Gray Phantom?"

"Yes."

He hesitated, still searching her face in the light of the electric flash. It was plain that the appearance of a feminine visitor at the gate of Azurecrest had aroused his suspicion.

"What do you want to see him about?" he demanded gruffly.

"Tell him Miss Hardwick wishes to see him. I think that will be sufficient."

She drew herself up as she spoke and regarded him steadily. As if decided by her cool and level tones, the man lowered the light and turned away, and in a few moments he had been swallowed by the shadows cast by the tall trees. Helen controlled her impatience. She understood that The Gray Phantom was obliged to exercise care every moment of his life. Despite his new mode of existence, he was still an outlaw in the eyes of the police, and a number of outstanding charges made it necessary for him to observe every precaution.

Again the man emerged out of the shadows. This time he said nothing, but peered at her furtively as he opened the gate and motioned her to step through. He closed and locked the gate carefully, then walked ahead of her up the graveled walk. A great shaggy dog slouched at his heels and wagged its tail energetically, as if disturbed by the arrival of a visitor. Helen's guide stopped under a portico and opened a door. A dim light shone on his face as he turned and told her to enter, and his expression gave her a twinge of misgiving. She tried in vain to analyze it, and the next moment the disturbing impression was gone.

"Wait," he said, indicating a chair.

Helen felt relieved as soon as the door closed behind him. The room was large and pleasant, and the oak-paneled, cream-colored walls made an attractive background for the furniture and decorations. Each little detail suggested The Gray Phantom's instinctive taste for beauty and proportion, and it suddenly occurred to her that this was the same room in which he had received her on her previous visit to Azurecrest.

Footfalls sounded in the hall, and all at once she grew confused. She wondered how she was to broach the subject that had been in her thoughts constantly since last night. She started to rise as the door opened, but in the next instant she sat back and swallowed an exclamation of surprise. She had expected to see The Gray Phantom, but the person who entered was a short, slightly humpbacked man of about fifty. He jerked his head toward her by way of a bow, and as he smiled she noticed that his mouth was crooked.

"My name is Hawkes," he announced in soft, lisping accents. "I am the secretary. I understand you wish to see Mr. Vanardy. Have you an appointment with him?"

A faint touch of uneasiness mingled with Helen's impatience. The Gray Phantom had never mentioned that he had a secretary, and she doubted whether he was in the habit of making appointments.

"I have no appointment," she said, mastering her vexation and disquietude, "but I think Mr. Vanardy will see me if you mention my name."

"Ah! Then you are a friend of his?"

"I have met him several times."

"To be sure," said the little man. He rubbed his hands, which seemed abnormally large for one of his sparse stature. "But, if you know anything at all about Mr. Vanardy, you must realize that he has to exercise caution, particularly in regard to the people he meets."

Helen rose, a faint flush of indignation in her cheeks. The next moment she sat down again, for she realized that Hawkes' argument was reasonable. The Gray Phantom's existence was precarious enough to warrant every conceivable precaution.

"I know Mr. Vanardy will see me if you tell him who I am," she declared, looking straight into the little man's eyes.

"Quite likely. But I have orders, and I dare not disregard them. Be good enough to answer one or two questions. To begin with, what is the nature of your business with Mr. Vanardy?"

Helen's patience was almost exhausted, but her sense of humor came to her rescue. Her lips began to twitch.

"Tell Mr. Vanardy," she said, "that the subject I wish to discuss with him has to do with a certain Mr. Shei."

The little man's eyes opened wide. She fancied his hand shook a trifle as he made an annotation on the pad he carried.

"Quite so," he murmured, quickly controlling himself. "You have come here on business connected with a certain Mr. Shei. Just one more question. Very few people know there is such a place as Azurecrest. How did you happen to find it?"

"Mr. Vanardy once gave me the directions. But you are exerting yourself needlessly, Hawkes. I am sure all that is necessary is to mention my name to Mr. Vanardy."

"Perhaps so." The humpback made another annotation on the pad, after which he put it in his pocket. "I'll repeat to Mr. Vanardy what you have just told me." He walked out of the room.

Helen could not tell why, but the silence that fell upon the room as the door closed impressed her uncomfortably. She did her best to muffle a faint inward whisper of warning, a premonition that something was wrong. Hawkes' questions had left a train of disturbing thoughts in her mind.

She waited a few minutes, then got up and began to pace the floor in an effort to quell a rising nervousness. She glanced at the pictures on the walls, but they did not seem to be the same as those that had hung there on her last visit, and they failed to interest her.

Presently she stepped to the window and looked out. The trees were nodding drowsily in the gentle night wind. The mist rising from the lowlands on all sides of the hill gave her a curious sense of remoteness from the world.

Then she drew back a step suddenly. Someone was passing the window, and she caught a momentary glimpse of a face. For a second or two a pair of large and oddly piercing eyes were fixed on her. Then the figure vanished, but the vision left her white and shaken. A hoarse cry rose to her lips. Unless her imagination had deceived her, the face that had just passed the window was the same swarthy, loathsome face she had seen in the Thelma Theater scarcely twenty-four hours ago.

Seized with a great fear, she ran across the floor and opened the door. The face, with its squatty features and long black hair fluttering in the breeze, had crystallized all the vague misgivings she had felt since she entered the house. For the moment she was unable to think, but an unreasoning impulse to flee drove her swiftly down the long hall. She felt she must escape from Azurecrest at once.

She had nearly reached the end of the hall when she came to a dead stop. She stood rigid, listening. Somewhere a laugh sounded. The staccato accents seemed to fill the house with volumes of hideous sound. Each vibrant note conjured up a fearful picture before her eyes. She staggered back against the wall, stopping her ears to shut out a repetition of the sound, but the echoes of it lingered in her imagination. She knew the laugh well. It was the same kind of laugh that Virginia Darrow had taken with her into eternity.

CHAPTER V
PERPLEXITIES

MINUTES PASSED, EACH DRAGGING a train of monstrous fancies before Helen's mental vision. The tips of her fingers shut out all sounds from her ears, but the laughter still dinned and echoed in her imagination. It reminded her of the haunting strains of glee that had come from Virginia Darrow's dying lips. Somehow this laughter was different, but the difference was so subtle that she could but vaguely sense it. It was loud and delirious, in contrast to the gentle, dirgelike notes that had characterized the other.

She could stand the suspense no longer. Sped on by fear, she ran in the direction where she thought the door was. She brought up against a stairway instead. A noise caused her to lift her head. Down the stairs, lurching and sliding, came a woman. Her hair was wildly tousled and her clothing in disorder, and peal after peal of harsh laughter cut through the silence as she scurried down the steps.

Then she saw Helen, and she stopped as abruptly as if she had dashed against a material barrier. Clutching the railing with one hand, she wagged drunkenly from side to side. Her face was ashen, but her skin was clear and smooth as a young girl's. The eyes, unnaturally wide and bright, stared down at Helen with fierce intensity. She had ceased laughing, but the lips were still agape, as if suddenly frozen into rigidity.

Helen forgot her fears as she saw the strange look in the woman's face. She wondered whether it meant madness, terror, or intoxication. It seemed to be neither, but rather a blending of all three. Slowly, with the outspread fingers of one hand pressing against her breast, the woman came down the remaining steps. Her great eyes were still fixed on Helen, but the mad flame in their depths was gradually yielding to a look of sanity.

"What are you doing here?" she demanded. Her voice was dry, and she spoke with little hissing sounds, as if each word were exhausting her breath.

Helen winced as the woman clutched her arm. Streaks of gray in the tumbled masses of her black hair clashed sharply with her youthfully rounded face, and Helen guessed that the contrast had been brought about by some terrifying experience.

"Do you know where you are?" the woman went on, tightening her grip on Helen's arm.

"This is Azurecrest, isn't it?" Helen's words voiced an indefinite doubt that had been stirring faintly in the back of her mind since she saw the face at the window. "I came here to see the Gray—to see Mr. Vanardy."

"Azurecrest?" The woman's mind seemed to be slowly struggling out of a daze. "Yes—that's what they call the place. But there is no Mr. Vanardy here. You have been deceived, just as I was. Those monsters! Do you know what will happen to you if you remain here?"

Helen shrugged as if to fight off a stupor that seemed to be gradually infolding body and mind.

"They'll inject the fever into your veins," the woman told her, without waiting for an answer. "The fever that always kills. Sometimes it kills quickly, but most the time very slowly, just as it is killing me. You will not feel much pain. You will laugh and sing and dream strange dreams. Those are always the symptoms. At first, before the fever reaches the last stage, you will laugh loud and hilariously—like this." She threw back her head, and then came an outburst of screaming laughter that made Helen shudder. "That's how it sounds at first. But later, when the fever has burned out your strength and destroyed your reason, the laughter will be low and soft and lilting. Then it sounds like this." She gave a series of low, tinkling sounds that were like a requiem set to laughter.

Helen shivered. Just so had Virginia Darrow gone laughing to her death. The coincidence seemed rather weird. The stark realism of the imitation gripped her, and yet she wondered whether she were dreaming or whether the woman beside her were reveling in the fancies of a maniac.

The other stiffened suddenly. She seemed to recall something which her encounter with Helen had temporarily blotted from her mind. Placing two fingers across her lips, she cast a swift glance up the stairs. For a brief space she stood tense, listening.

"The woman who watches me went to sleep and I stole away from her," she whispered. "We must try to get out before they begin looking for me. You must come, too. It won't do for you to remain a moment longer. S-sh!"

Silent as a wraith she stole down the hall. Helen, scarcely knowing what she was doing, followed dazedly. She did not know what to think, but there was an undertow of vague dread in her jumbled thoughts and emotions. What she had just heard sounded wildly fantastical, like the raving of a deranged mind. Yet she had a feeling that something was dreadfully wrong. The strange laughter and the face at the window appeared to give a background of reality to what the woman had said. They seemed to suggest, too, that there was a connecting link between Azurecrest and the tragedy in the Thelma Theater. It was this circumstance, bewildering and almost unbelievable, that clogged the functioning of Helen's mind and rendered her willing to be led along by her guide.

The door was unlocked and they passed unhindered into the open. In a dull and indifferent fashion Helen thought it strange that the woman's loud laughter had not already betrayed them, but then it occurred to her that perhaps such outbursts were common at Azurecrest. After what she had already seen and heard, nothing would have surprised her greatly. She wondered how her companion meant to overcome the obstacles of the locked gate and the high picket fence. Perhaps, in her beclouded state of mind and eagerness to escape, she was not even giving them a thought. Or perhaps—

Her guide stopped so abruptly that Helen, who had been following close behind, nearly ran into her. Out of the mist and shadows came a low, rumbling growl. A huge, black shape bounded toward them.

"The dog!" exclaimed the other. "I forgot—oh!"

The beast, rearing on hind legs, sprang at her throat and felled her. She lay prone on the ground, the dog crouching over her with jaws slavering and forefeet pawing her body. Helen stood motionless in her tracks. The dog's eyes and teeth gleamed menacingly in the moonlight, and she knew that the slightest move would precipitate an attack upon her. Her mind, clearing rapidly under the stress of danger, was seeking a way out of the predicament when hurried footsteps came down the walk.

"Cæsar!" called a gruff voice.

The dog let go its hold as a man came running toward them. He stopped and gathered the fallen woman in his arms, and Helen recognized the individual who had met her at the gate on her arrival. With scarcely a glance in her direction, he turned and walked toward the house with his burden. Helen feeling the gleaming eyes of the beast on her face, dared not move. As she stood wondering what to do, a shadow fell across the graveled walk and a second man came toward her.

"Back to your kennel, Cæsar!" he commanded, and the dog obediently slunk away. "Excellent watchdog, but a bit ferocious when he is kept on half rations. Won't you come inside, Miss—er, Hardwick? Hawkes told me about you. I am Mr. Slade. Sorry to have kept you waiting."

His manner and appearance were pleasant enough; yet Helen felt an impulse to run. The things she had seen and heard since coming to Azurecrest were highly mystifying, and they had left a number of questions and suspicions in her mind. She glanced quickly toward the picket fence, then in the direction whence Cæsar had disappeared. Something told her that a whistle would set the dog snapping and snarling at her heels if she should try to break away. She decided that her hope lay in diplomacy rather than flight.

As if he had read her thoughts, Slade touched her arm and escorted her to the house. She sensed that a trying ordeal was ahead of her, and she was already steeling her nerves for it. She had faced danger many times, and her buoyant nature always responded to the demands of a crisis with a quickening of wits and rising courage.

"I trust Miss Neville didn't annoy you" murmured Slade apologetically as he opened the door and conducted her down the hall. "A very difficult case of paranoia. She gets quite violent at times, and she is subject to all sorts of hallucinations. Tonight she broke away from her nurse and would no doubt have attempted to scale the fence if Cæsar hadn't interrupted her."

Helen walked beside him in silence. She had already wondered whether Miss Neville could be quite sane. Oddly enough, Slade's words almost convinced her that the woman was of sound mind, though perhaps she was suffering from the effects of illness and shock. Helen had conceived an immediate and instinctive distrust of Slade, despite his smooth-flowing speech and suave manners.

He ushered her into the same room she had left so hurriedly upon hearing the laughter, and placed a chair for her. A look at his face in the electric light gave edge to her misgivings, but at first she could not tell what there was about him that repelled her. According to all standards, he should have attracted her and inspired confidence in her. His personality contained that blend of strength and gentleness which she had liked in men ever since her days of inconsequential hero worship. He had the strong jaw and high forehead that often go with aggressiveness and mental keenness, and he carried his tall figure with the easy grace of a man of the world. His presence would have been quite magnetic if only— But Helen could not finish the thought. There was an unnamable something about him that eluded her mental grasp.

"Quite a sad case, that of Miss Neville," he continued. "She was once a very brilliant woman, but her genius was consumed by its own fire, so to speak. I might as well tell you that she is my half-sister. For her own good and to avoid unpleasant notoriety, I am keeping her here under the care of a physician. Her friends believe that she is traveling abroad, and so far I have succeeded in keeping the true state of affairs secret. There is a possibility, though a very remote one, that she will recover."

Helen made no comment. Though his eyes were lowered seemingly on the floor, she felt he was watching her and wondering whether she believed him. She thought it strange that he should have taken her into his confidence in regard to matters which one usually does not divulge to strangers. There were a number of questions on the tip of her tongue, but she thought it better to hold them back.

"I suppose," Slade went on in melancholy tones, "that she told you the usual story of mistreatment and persecution?"

"She seemed very excited." Helen weighed her words with care. "I don't remember all she told me, but she said something of a fever that was gradually killing her, and she seemed very anxious to get away from this place."

"Yes, the fever is one of her hallucinations. She imagines that she is suffering from a strange disease. And not only that but she thinks everybody around her afflicted with the same mysterious malady. The idea is firmly rooted in her mind that the disease has been deliberately communicated to her by enemies. No doubt she told you of a kind of laughter that is supposed to be one of the symptoms of the strange ailment."

"She not only mentioned it, but she gave me a demonstration. It sounded a bit—creepy."

"I can readily believe it. It must have been very unpleasant for you. I take it that she told the story convincingly enough to make an impression on you, or you would not have started to run away with her."

He smiled as he spoke, and all at once Helen saw the reason for her instinctive dislike of him. The smile was of the lips only. There was no responsive gleam in his eyes. And his eyes, she now perceived, were hard and dispassionate as bits of porcelain.

"She frightened me, and I didn't know what to think," she guardedly admitted. "I suppose I followed her on the impulse of the moment. I do most things on impulse, you see."

"That's the privilege of youth." He laughed, but his eyes were as glossy and expressionless as fish scales and seemed to veto his vocal merriment. "Luckily you wouldn't have got further than the gate, even if Cæsar hadn't intervened. It would be very embarrassing if Miss Neville should escape from us some night and expose her condition to the world. There is slight danger of that, though. I have taken all necessary precautions. However, your meeting Miss Neville here and noticing the state she is in, makes the situation rather awkward. I should dislike to have the matter get into the newspapers. I have been frank with you, hoping you would see the delicacy of the situation from my point of view."

"I never gossip about people's misfortunes," declared Helen with emphasis.

"Thank you. I know I can depend on you, Miss Hardwick. I hope Cæsar didn't frighten you. By the way," and suddenly he seemed to remember something, "my secretary told me you were inquiring for Mr. Vanardy."

Helen started slightly. For an hour she had been wondering why she had seen nothing of The Gray Phantom and why her request to see him had been met with evasions and cross-questioning.

Slade regarded her with polite curiosity. "I have seen your name in the newspapers, Miss Hardwick. You wrote the play that Vincent Starr produced at his theater. Only a little while ago I was reading of the peculiar tragedy that interrupted the first performance last night. I wonder whether your visit here has anything to do with that occurrence."

It was a strange question, Helen thought. "I—I would rather talk over my errand with Mr. Vanardy in person," she stammered. She was chilled and confused by his steady gaze. "Isn't he here?"

Slade's lips twitched. "You know, of course, that Mr. Vanardy is the genial rascal who used to be known as The Gray Phantom. You needn't answer; I see that you do. It strikes me as rather odd that a young lady of your evident refinement and culture should be associated with a man of that type. Pardon my impertinence. The fact of the matter is that Mr. Vanardy is not here. He left Azurecrest some time ago."

"What?" Helen half rose from the chair. With a great exertion of will power she steadied herself. "Mr. Vanardy not here? Then where is he?"

"That I don't know. I purchased Azurecrest from him through a broker. I never had any dealings with the man himself. In fact, at the time I bought the place I didn't know that it had been occupied by The Gray Phantom. You see, I had been looking for a secluded spot where Miss Neville could live quietly and without fear of unwelcome intrusions. Azurecrest seemed to answer the requirements, and so I bought it."

Helen stared at him, unable to disguise her bewilderment. Slade's statement amazed and shocked her. She had not been in correspondence with The Gray Phantom, but at their last meeting he had told her to communicate with him at Azurecrest if she should ever need him. She thought it strange that he had not sent her word of his removal.

Slade was sauntering leisurely back and forth across the floor. Now and then, as he looked at her, his eyes gave her a chill. She made a strong effort to gather her thoughts and master her feelings. Something, she did not know just what, told her that the occasion demanded a cool head and steady nerves.

A motor horn sounded in the distance. Evidently a car was winding its way up the hill. The thought gave her a vague sense of comfort. She sat up straight.

"I told the man who met me at the gate that I wished to see Mr. Vanardy," she remarked. "Later I told Hawkes the same thing. Neither one intimated that Mr. Vanardy was no longer here. I was asked a lot of useless questions and asked to wait. Then—"

"My dear Miss Hardwick," smoothly interrupted Slade, "you must understand that the circumstances under which my half-sister and myself are living here make it necessary for me to be very cautious with regard to visitors. My servants have orders to subject all callers to careful inspection and cross-examination. For instance, how do I know that you are not a newspaper reporter looking for a sensation?"

Helen smiled; the suggestion seemed so absurd. Once more the blare of a horn sounded in the distance.

"And that reminds me," Slade went on in slightly altered tones, "that you have not yet explained your presence here. I asked you a moment ago whether it had anything to do with what happened at the Thelma Theater."

"So you did." Helen's smile, though tantalizing, was the kind with which one masks an inner turbulence.

"I am waiting for your answer." Slade seemed as suave and urbane as before, but his eye was a trifle frostier and his tone carried a peremptory note. Helen glanced at the window. A glare like that of a motor car's headlight was approaching the house.

"Your question is very peculiar," she replied with a haughtiness which she did not quite feel, "and I see no reason why I should answer it."

"No?" Slade had ceased his pacing of the floor, and Helen wondered whether it was by design or accident that he had stopped with his back to the door. "Perhaps the question will seem less peculiar if I word it differently. What did you mean when you told Hawkes that the business you wished to discuss with Vanardy had to do with Mr. Shei?"

Helen felt a tingle of suspense. There was a sneer on Slade's lips and his frigid eyes filled her with a vague dread. She tried to parry the question with banter, but the words would not come. She twisted in her chair, and suddenly, as the door behind Slade's back came open, her gaze grew rigid and a look of consternation filled her eyes. She gripped the arms of her chair and very slowly raised herself to her feet, all the while staring intently at the figure whose arrival had been heralded a few minutes ago by the headlight's glare.

The newcomer seemed startled at first, then he smiled. Slade stepped aside and bowed deferentially to the man in the doorway. Then he noticed Helen's transfigured face.

"You two seem to have met before," he remarked.

Helen advanced a step. She drew a long, trembling breath. A staggering realization flashed through her mind as she gazed rigidly into the newcomer's smiling face. It was the same realization that had come to her with such unnerving force in the Thelma Theater. It had grown hazy and vague during the intervening hours, and the quick succession of events had left her wondering.

Now she knew that her first intuitive suspicion had been correct. Her mind seemed to reel and spin. She hardly knew that her lips were moving, but her voice, hoarse and scarcely audible, was uttering a name:

"Mr. Shei!"

CHAPTER VI
THE PHANTOM ORCHID

CUTHBERT VANARDY SAT IN his library at Sea Glimpse and tried hard to fix his mind on Paxton's *Botanical Dictionary*. Despite his best efforts it was a hopeless task. His thoughts would go gypsying, and every now and then the print would blur and fade or dissolve into fanciful images that had nothing to do with hybridization and cross-pollination of orchids.

A problem had been teasing Vanardy's imagination for months. He had struggled with it in idle moments, while resting from more ambitious experiments. Specimens from his gardens were shown each year at the horticultural expositions in New York and Boston, where they created much favorable comment among experts and caused endless speculation concerning the identity of the anonymous exhibitor, who had private and excellent reasons for remaining unknown. The problem he was now working on, however, was merely a diversion from his more serious work.

He wanted to create a gray orchid. It was to be a particular shade of gray—a dim, mystic gray, like the color of the sky just before dawn or the hue of the sea in a light fog. The novelty of the idea appealed to him and the task was proving difficult enough to give him gentle stimulation. Furthermore, gray always had been his favorite color. And he had almost decided that the hybrid, when once evolved, should be known as The Phantom Orchid.

It was merely a whim, of course—the vagary of a mind so active that it must be working even at play. For the matter of that, he often told himself that of late years his life had been little else than a succession of fancies and dim shades of reality. The gardens he had planted and the products that gained such flattering comment in the horticultural journals had been nothing but a tangible expression of a passionate desire to blot out the past and efface that other self whom the outside world called The Gray Phantom.

In those other days he had gone, like a rollicking Robin Hood, from one stupendous adventure to another. Without thought of sordid gain, but merely to assuage an inborn craving for excitement, he had dipped into a whirl of exploits that caused the public to gasp and hold its breath. The police, bedeviled and outwitted at every turn, had gritted their teeth and muttered anathemas even while admitting that The Gray Phantom always played the game fairly and that his victims, more often than not, were villains of a far blacker dye than he.

It had been a mad carousal, and for a time it had given The Phantom all the thrills his nature craved. Nearly always his left hand had tossed away what his right had plucked. Mysterious and untraceable contributions had poured in upon hospitals, orphan asylums, societies for the protection of animals, and other philanthropic organizations. Widows, invalids, and paupers were befriended in a way that caused them to believe in a return of the day of miracles. Dreamers starving in garrets and inventors struggling to keep body and soul together were tided over many a trying crisis.

Through it all The Gray Phantom had maintained an elusiveness that confounded the keenest man hunters among the police and wrapped his identity in a mysterious glamour. Simple-minded people wondered whether he were a being of flesh and blood, or a shade on earthly rampage. His one arrest, back in the early stages of his career, had settled their doubts once for all, but an astonishing escape a few days later caused them to wag their heads and speak in hushed tones of a rogue whose feats and juggleries bewildered them.

The Phantom laughed quietly at their perplexity. The performances that awed and puzzled them seemed simple enough to him. He was merely unleashing his imagination and giving free sway to his boundless energies of body and mind. In another age he might have been a sea-roving viking or a builder of ancient empires. At times, when one of his softer moods was upon him, he wondered why his restless spirit and the fires within him could not have found a different and more soul-satisfying outlet. Then his thoughts would go back to dimly remembered days, with their shadowy recollections of early orphanage and the peccadilloes of street urchins, and somehow he thought he understood.

But as time passed his restless moods came back with increasing frequency, and little by little he lost taste for the life he was leading and the adventures that had made his sobriquet known from coast to coast. Then there came lapses between The Gray Phantom's exploits, and finally they ceased altogether. The world, not knowing with what lavish hand he had flung away his spoils, supposed he had collected his treasures and gone into hiding, and the police grimly predicted that he would reappear as soon as he had squandered his ill-gotten gains. No one guessed that The Phantom had built a hermitage on a desolate hilltop where, surrounded by a few of his art treasures and a small group of faithful followers, he was trying to reconstruct his life in peace.

"Azurecrest" was the name he had given his secluded retreat, and there he had tried to destroy the links that still chained him to the past and to blot out the tantalizing visions of other days. For a time he had almost succeeded; then a restlessness had come upon him for which the desolate hilltop afforded no relief, and he felt that his mountain retreat, with its collection of relics and reminders of bygone times, was too closely associated with the things he wanted to forget. Finally he had disposed of the place through a broker and purchased a narrow strip of land by the sea. He could not analyze the obscure motives and hidden impulse that had impelled him to seek seclusion at Sea Glimpse, a slender tongue of wooded land surrounded on three sides by jagged coast line and in the rear by forest and farm land. But while at work clearing the ground for his garden he had felt a grateful remoteness from things he wished to forget, and a measure of peace and satisfaction had come to him while he put his unpracticed hands to strange tasks or wandered among the trees and listened to the murmurs of the sea. He often wondered whether he would be content to spend his life in this secluded nook of the world where, safely hidden and secure from intrusion, he could devote himself to his hobby and his books.

The question came back to him again as he closed his Paxton and got up to light the reading lamp. For months he had felt that the links connecting him with the past were snapping. The Gray Phantom had emerged from retirement only once, and then he had ventured forth in a good cause. In a little while, perhaps, he would be dead and almost forgotten. The gray orchid, if Vanardy should ever succeed in bringing it out, would be the living symbol of whatever had been good in his other self. The thought more than once had appealed to his imagination and the whimsical strain in his nature.

He turned toward the window, but he had taken only a few steps when he stopped and looked dreamily into space. Memories thronged his mind and a face appeared out of nowhere—a woman's face. For months it had haunted him in his idle moments, inspiring him with vague and exhilarant emotions. He saw it now, softly radiant among the shadows, an enchanting embodiment of the bloom and freshness of youth that pursued him with the persistence of a delicate scent or the strain of an all-but-forgotten song.

"Helen!" he murmured.

The vision grew a little clearer. Now he could almost see her figure, slim and straight and moving with the easy swing and grace of a young antelope. Echoes of her voice came to him, clear and unaffected and vibrant with joyous vivacity, each melodious note touching an harmonious chord within him. He remembered that her face had given him a curious impression of youthful buoyancy mingling with the soberness of maturity. Her quick intuition, coupled with a strain of subtlety in her nature and a trace of precocious sophistication that was both puzzling and enchanting, had seemed to bridge the years that lay between them. The vitalic sheen and the subtle aroma of her hair had given him a foolish desire to see what sun and wind would do to it if she were to loosen it and romp in his garden.

He sighed musingly. Months had passed since he had last seen her. For a brief, unforgettable moment he had held her hand, and the contact had given him a gentle, all-pervading thrill and filled him with strange and tender emotions. Her eyes, warm and frank, but with a touch of shyness lurking in their depths, as if she were still a little afraid of him, had inspired him with a tingling ecstasy such as The Gray Phantom in his wildest triumphs had never experienced. Twice he had written her since then, once to apprise her of his removal from Azurecrest and once to inquire concerning her well-being, but he had neither expected nor received an answer. He had not forgotten that in the eyes of the world he was still an outlaw, a hunted thing.

Again he sighed. The vision was fading, and little of it remained with him save a misty picture of loveliness. The moon was rising over the tree tops, throwing a white sheen over the landscape and the narrow wedge of water visible between the birches and hemlocks. The old house, purchased by Vanardy in a dilapidated condition and with difficulty rendered habitable, was silent but for the creeping whispers of the wind. For a time the solitary figure at the window stood lost in thoughts. His deep-gray eyes, rather too narrow for perfect symmetry, which had been known to stab and sting like rapiers, were not soft and luminous. Small wrinkles radiated from the outer corners, but the eyes themselves were animated by the slow twinkling gleam that characterizes the individual who sifts all the ups and downs of life through a sieve of whimsical imagination. The sensitive nostrils and the full arch of the lips denoted a penchant for distilling the maximum of thrills and emotions from the magic of existence. Here and there his face was lined and scarred, and even in repose there was a tension about the lean, tall figure that made one think of a cocked trigger.

A knock sounded, and he turned quickly. Through the door waddled a fat man with a woe-begone expression and a multiple chin. He groaned and puffed as if the task of carrying his elephantine body through life was not a light burden. The newcomer was Clifford Wade, once The Gray Phantom's chief lieutenant and now the major-domo of his little household.

"Wade," observed The Phantom, eyeing the fat man with disapproval, "you are getting soft. This easy and carefree existence is demoralizing you completely."

The other placed a stack of newspapers and a few letters on the table, then slumped into a chair and gazed ruefully down at the protruding curvature of his stomach.

"I know, boss. I piled on two more pounds last week. Pretty soon I won't be able to go for the mail any more. If you'd only say the word, I'd round up the old gang, and we'd turn a few more tricks like the ones we used to pull in the good old days. I'd work off this fat in no time."

The Phantom shook his head. "No, Wade. You will have to try some other form of fat reducer. I am through with the old life for good. It was exciting while it lasted, but the novelty has worn off. It was only a sort of emotional eruption, anyhow."

Wade scowled, then delivered himself of a startling exclamation: "Hang the women!"

The Phantom raised his brows in surprise. "What's your grievance against the fair sex, Wade? Hanging is pretty serious business, you know. What atrocious crime have the women perpetrated against you to deserve such cruel punishment? You don't look like a man suffering the pangs of unrequited love. Your heart is intact, I hope?"

"Oh, my heart's all right," Wade complained. "It's yours that I'm worrying about. Lately I haven't been able to dope you out at all, boss. If I didn't know you as well as I do, I'd say you've gone plumb dippy. There was a time not so long ago when you went in for big game—real he-man stuff. There were a lot of men on the police force who used to have a funny feeling around the solar plexus whenever The Gray Phantom's name was spoken. You cut some fancy didos in those days, boss. Now—now you're poking seeds into the ground and talking of reforming." Wade made a gesture of great disgust.

"Granted," said The Phantom, smiling, "but is that any reason for exterminating the feminine sex?"

"You bet it is. The trouble with you is that you've got too much girl on the brain, boss. You were all right until that pretty little skirt with the big baby eyes happened along."

"Oh, you mean Miss Hardwick?" There was an odd tension in The Phantom's tones.

"That's who I mean. She's easy on the eyes and all that, but she's sure raised the devil with you. The old kind of life was good enough for you till she bobbed up. It was then you started all this mushy talk about going straight and changing your ways. I know because I've been watching you."

The Phantom was strangely silent. Twice he crossed the floor, then paused before the window and looked out into the shadowy landscape. There was a pensive gleam in his eyes, as if Wade's speech had turned his thoughts into new channels. Suddenly he laughed, and the new expression that came into his face suggested that he had seen an all-revealing flash.

"I am much obliged to you for that bit of psychoanalysis," he told the fat man. "You're right, Wade—absolutely right. I was a fool not to see it before."

"Not to see what?"

A faint smile flickered across The Phantom's face. "That Miss Hardwick has had a great deal to do with my determination to change my ways. I hadn't realized it until you spoke just now. I had been inclined to give myself all the credit. Thanks to your somewhat crude but accurate statement of the case, I can see now that all of it belongs to her."

Wade's round little eyes, imbedded in layers of flesh, stared uncomprehendingly at The Phantom. "I don't get you at all, boss."

"Then don't try. Your heart is in the right place, Wade, but you lack imagination and there are some things that you and I can't view from the same angle. Miss Hardwick's influence in my life is one of them. Sorry to disappoint an old pal, but my determination to stay on the straight and narrow path is stronger than ever."

Wade made a wry face. "You'll suit yourself, of course, but it might interest you to know that another man is stealing your thunder while you're dancing to the piping of a skirt." He opened one of the newspapers he had placed on the table and pointed to a black-face caption. The Phantom, looking over his massive shoulders, read:

MR. SHEI'S NAME ON DYING LIPS

His eyes narrowed gradually as he read the highly colored account of the tragedy in the Thelma Theater. There was a pucker of perplexity on his forehead when he finished.

"Wonder what Mr. Shei is up to this time," he mumbled, gazing thoughtfully at the floor. "I've been following the fellow's exploits for some time. This is a bit out of the ordinary—eh, Wade?"

"You said it, boss. And you can bet your sweet life he's getting ready for something big this time. Unless I'm a poor guesser, the affair at the Thelma last night was only the beginning. Mr. Shei's schemes run deep, and he never strikes a blow unless he's got an object in view. There's something strange about the murder of that woman, boss."

The Phantom nodded. "Looks as though you were right, Wade. Mr. Shei is out after big game this time, and in all likelihood the Thelma affair is only the prelude. But I don't see how—"

"There's another thing about this Mr. Shei," interrupted the fat man. "Maybe you've noticed it. I don't know how many jobs he's pulled off, but every one of them has shown the slickest kind of workmanship. What's more," and Wade's eyes peered cunningly into the other's face, "most of them look as though you'd had a hand in them yourself. That's what I meant when I said another man is stealing your thunder."

The Phantom started; then a thin smile parted his lips. "Yes, I have noticed it, Wade. I have studied Mr. Shei's methods as carefully as has been possible from the superficial and distorted newspaper accounts, and I have observed that he has done me the questionable honor of adopting some of the methods and stratagems I used to practice in the past. In a number of instances he has copied my technique so closely that I've often wondered whether I've been walking in my sleep or whether my old self has come back in a new form. It's been almost uncanny." He laughed musingly. "What do you make of it, Wade?"

"I think you'd better take another fling at the old game before this Mr. Shei gets a monopoly on it."

"I didn't mean that. How do you account for the similarity of methods?"

The fat man pondered. "Somebody has studied your tricks and put them into practice. Somebody that's been close enough to you to watch you in action. Maybe," and the glow of a sudden idea lighted up his face, "a member of our old crowd. Say, boss, wouldn't it be a joke on you if Mr. Shei should turn out to be a graduate of your own gang?"

"Worse than a joke," said The Phantom grimly. He paced the floor with quick, short steps, his hands clenched at his back. "I have given the mysterious Mr. Shei a great deal of thought in the past few months, and I fear you are right. His tactics so closely resemble mine that I suspect he learned them from me at firsthand. In the old days I often took a sort of foolish pride in teaching my methods to the more adaptable ones among the members of my organization. It pleased me to watch their development under my training. I didn't realize then what I was doing. Now—" He shrugged as if to dismiss a futile regret. "Yes, it's quite likely that Mr. Shei is a former pupil of mine."

"Well, what are you going to do about it?"

The Phantom stopped abruptly, gazing at the fat man with a far-away gleam in his eye, as if they were miles apart.

"I thought The Gray Phantom was dead," he murmured. "It appears I have been mistaken. If Mr. Shei is a product of The Gray Phantom's brain, then my old self is still active. For every crime committed by Mr. Shei, The Gray Phantom bears responsibility." He gave a dismal laugh. "And I thought I had destroyed most of the links connecting me with the old times."

"Well," said Wade again, this time a little testily, "just what are you going to do about it?"

The Phantom did not answer immediately. He was staring absent-mindedly into space. Presently he looked at his watch; then he nodded thoughtfully.

"Wish you would pack my grip, Wade."

The fat man started from the chair. "Not going away?"

"Yes; there's a train for New York a few minutes past midnight. In the morning, bright and early, I shall start a little campaign."

"Campaign?" Wade's eyes bulged. "What kind of campaign?"

"The biggest one of my life, I think. I am going out to lay The Gray Phantom's ghost. In plain words, I propose to go on the warpath against the mysterious Mr. Shei. I fancy it will be quite an exciting little tussle, Wade."

CHAPTER VII
MR. SHEI SHOWS HIS HAND

IN THE DUSK OF the following morning a tall, gray-clad figure alighted from a train in the Grand Central terminal, glanced cautiously to right and left among the thin scattering of passengers, and with a furtive air traversed the vast concourse and gained the street by one of the side exits. With the habitual vigilance of a hunted man, he paused for a few moments under the canopy and scanned the face of each loiterer and passer-by. A dull, discordant din testified that the city was awakening, and a pale shimmer of dawn was shattering the mists hanging like a gauzy veil over Manhattan. Finally the gray-clad figure moved on, walked a block and a half to the west and, selecting an unpretentious restaurant, stepped in and ordered breakfast.

The Gray Phantom's campaign was on.

Perils lurked everywhere. Though he had changed his ways, he had not yet paid off his old scores. He still had the law to reckon with, for the outstanding charges against him were grave and numerous enough to send him to prison for the rest of his life. The capture of The Gray Phantom, once one of the most celebrated of rogues, would create a profound sensation and confer great fame on the captor. Once it became known that he had emerged from his hiding place, the entire city would be converted into a huge man-trap with claws set to catch the celebrated outlaw.

That was not all. The newspaper accounts of the police inquiry into the Thelma tragedy, which The Phantom had carefully perused on the train, had hinted rather broadly that Mr. Shei and The Gray Phantom were identical. It was pointed out that Mr. Shei's exploits were the only ones in recent years that had equaled The Phantom's as to magnitude and daring, and that there were many points of similarity in the methods of the two rogues. To be sure, The Phantom had never been known to stoop to murder, but this did not necessarily eliminate him as an object of suspicion, and it was significant that the commission of the crime had been hedged in with all the subtlety and mysteriousness that characterized The Gray Phantom's tactics. It was predicted that if The Phantom were apprehended, the mystery surrounding the identity and the movements of Mr. Shei would be cleared up automatically.

The Phantom smiled faintly as he finished his breakfast and walked out. His step was elastic, and his eye held the steely gleam which his former associates had learned to interpret as a sign that their leader was bent on some stupendous adventure. It was still early, and there was only a thin sprinkling of traffic in the streets, and the chances of his being recognized were correspondingly slight.

As yet he had no definite plan in mind. His decision to make war on Mr. Shei had been made suddenly and largely on the impulse of the moment. It was in keeping with his determination to blot out that part of himself which the world knew as The Gray Phantom. The realization had come to him in a flash that the work of his other self was being carried on vicariously by the person known as Mr. Shei. If his suspicions were correct, and if the latter was indeed a disciple of his, then Mr. Shei was a part of the past he had vowed to uproot and destroy. His regeneration would not be complete until this object had been accomplished.

He chuckled a little as he walked along. It was odd, he thought, that Wade should have guessed the motive for his determination to tear his past to shreds. Throughout his striving and reaching for something higher and better, The Phantom had vaguely and instinctively felt that the bright, brown eyes of Helen Hardwick were his lodestars, but Wade's crudely phrased remark had been needed to make the impression clear. He knew it was largely because of Helen's faith in him that he was now attacking the hardest and most perilous task of his career. Vaguely he wondered what she would think when she heard of his latest adventure, and he felt a fleeting temptation to tell her of his decision. He rejected it, however, resolving it would be time enough to make his plans known to her when they were in a more mature shape.

The sight of a knot of curious idlers outside a drug store in Times Square caused him to quicken his steps. He knew the psychology of city crowds and that the merest trifle is sufficient to attract a throng, but this gathering seemed to have been drawn together by something out of the ordinary. As unobtrusively as he could, he wedged his way through the little crowd, consisting mostly of homeward-bound night workers and belated pleasure seekers, and now he saw the object of their interest was a small square of paper pasted to the pane of the show window. A flicker of surprise crossed The Phantom's face as he read the typewritten inscription:

> For the diversion of the public and the edification of the police,
> I beg to announce that my next, and so far, greatest, coup will
> be directed against the seven wealthiest men in New York City,
> whose names I shall take a pleasure in announcing in a day or

two. By a unique and sensational method of persuasion these gentlemen will be induced to transfer half of their respective fortunes to me.

Mr. Shei.

A grin tugged at The Phantom's lips as he read the announcement a second time. Mr. Shei, in flaunting his intentions before the eyes of the public and the police, was living up to time-honored traditions of melodrama. It was of a piece with the rascal's erratic and extravagant nature, and the boastful phrasing of the announcement, as well as the incidental taunt flung at the police, was quite characteristic of him. Yet, despite the pompous claptrap with which Mr. Shei was adorning his project, the magnitude of it appealed to The Phantom's imagination. It was fully as great and daring an enterprise as The Phantom himself had ever attempted. If the scheme succeeded—and Mr. Shei's undertakings invariably did—the loot would run well into ten figures.

From remarks dropped by the bystanders he gathered that stickers bearing the same boastful announcements had been distributed during the early morning hours at various points throughout the city. Mr. Shei seemed to have spared no pains in his effort to startle the metropolis. The Phantom was edging away from the throng when a few words, spoken in low and drawling tones, caused him to look quickly aside.

"Pardon, but haven't we met before?"

The Phantom felt a faint thrill of apprehension. Recognition at this point might prove disastrous to his plans. Beside him, with tired and red-lidded eyes peering into his face, stood a tall, gaunt man whose somewhat ludicrous appearance was accentuated by full evening dress.

"I think not," he said hastily, and started to walk away. The other, refusing to be squelched, fell into step beside him.

"Now, isn't that strange?" he remarked with a wheezy chuckle. "The moment I saw you it occurred to me that your face seemed familiar. By the way, what do you think of Mr. Shei's latest?"

"Quite ambitious." The Phantom gave his uninvited companion a keen glance, and the covert scrutiny stirred several shadowy recollections in his mind. The curious individual seemed well past middle age, and his sallow complexion and furrowed face indicated decrepit health. He walked with a shuffling gait and a catarrhal affection of the nose necessitated frequent use of his handkerchief. The Phantom was trying to recall when and under what circumstances they had met before, but his face indicated nothing but annoyance at an unwelcome intrusion.

"Ambitious is the word," assented the man in evening dress. "Do you know, my dear sir, that if Mr. Shei carries out his threat and annexes fifty per cent of the seven biggest fortunes in town, his net gain will run into the billions? I can only hope that I am not one of the seven selected for shearing."

The Phantom gave him another quick glance. A gleam of humor relieved the woe-begone expression of the man's face. Again The Phantom searched his memory. The last remark had carried a strong hint to the effect that his companion was a man of great wealth.

"My name, as you probably know, although you pretend to have forgotten it, is W. Rufus Fairspeckle," continued the other, taking The Phantom's arm and turning into a side street. "I don't know how many millions I have, but I have enough to make me a shining mark for Mr. Shei's latest offensive. Ah, I see you remember me now!"

The Phantom's involuntary start had betrayed him. The mere mention of Mr. Fairspeckle's name had instantly clarified his hazy recollections. He recalled now that, some five or six years ago, he had had a brief and casual encounter with the man. It had occurred in the course of one of The Phantom's spectacular adventures, and he had almost forgotten the incident that brought them together. Now, as the memory of it flashed back into his mind, he gazed more intently at his companion.

As the man himself had intimated, W. Rufus Fairspeckle was one of the wealthiest men in New York City. Mostly through luck and partly through an inborn genius for speculation, he had amassed a huge fortune. At fifty he had retired from business, declaring that he had worked hard all his life and was entitled to a rest and a little diversion. Then he had promptly proceeded to the enjoyment of the pleasures that had been denied him in his youth, and he had gone about it with an avidity that created a great deal of jocular comment and made him known as a very eccentric individual.

"You have a long memory," observed The Phantom, glancing uneasily at Mr. Fairspeckle's formal attire. It drew many amused glances from pedestrians, and The Phantom did not care to attract unnecessary attention. "Now, if you will excuse me, I think I will wish you good morning. I have a busy day ahead of me."

"Not so fast," protested Mr. Fairspeckle, clutching The Phantom's sleeve with his long, bony fingers. "You are coming with me."

The words had a peremptory sound. The Phantom knitted his brows.

"Why, if I may ask?"

"See that cop?" Mr. Fairspeckle pointed to a blue-coated figure half a block ahead. "He's a hard-working soul and presumably he is ambitious to obtain promotion. The capture of The Gray Phantom would be quite an event in his humdrum life."

The Phantom sensed a threat. He glanced about him quickly. The streets were rapidly filling with traffic, and to break away might not prove easy. Besides, he was curious to know the reason for Mr. Fairspeckle's evident determination to detain him. Deciding to adopt the safer course, he simulated an affable smile.

"Suppose we let the hard-working cop earn his promotion some other way," he suggested. "Where to, Mr. Fairspeckle?"

"My apartment at the Whipple Hotel. We're almost there. Glad you are going to be reasonable, Mr. Vanardy. I need someone to talk to. Ever suffer from insomnia?"

"Never."

"Lucky dog! Insomnia is the bane of my existence. At times, when I can't sleep, I sit at the club and bore my friends to death. When I have no friends to talk to, I walk. Last night I walked from one end of Manhattan Island to the other and halfway back again. Oh, yes, I'm more chipper than you would think from looking at me. Well, my rambles last night explain why you see me in these togs. I was just about tired enough to fall asleep standing on my feet when I saw Mr. Shei's notice. In an instant I was wide awake again. Confound the fellow's impudence! Here we are."

The Phantom was conducted through the chastely carved portals of one of the quieter hotels in the upper Forties, and a few moments later they were facing each other across the redwood table in Mr. Fairspeckle's library. The apartment, though luxuriously appointed, was a faithful reflection of the eccentric nature of its occupant.

"You are careless, Mr. Vanardy," said Mr. Fairspeckle musingly. The partly drawn shades admitted only a vague half-dawn into the room, and the shadows lent an air of mysteriousness to his appearance. "It isn't safe for a man in your position to walk about without disguise."

"Disguises are treacherous things. I have used them now and then, but ordinarily I feel safer without them. Anyhow, no one but you is aware of my presence in New York."

Mr. Fairspeckle drew a palm across his chin. His red-lidded eyes regarded The Phantom shrewdly. "I wonder what brings you to New York at this particular time—at the very time when Mr. Shei is launching his most ambitious scheme. You will admit the coincidence is rather striking?"

"Some people might deduce from it that I am Mr. Shei," suggested The Phantom, smiling. "They would be wrong."

There was a quiver at the corners of Mr. Fairspeckle's thin lips. His eyes held a suspicious twinkle.

"Perhaps," he commented dryly. Then he fell to drumming the table with his finger tips. "What I would like to know for certain is whether I am one of the seven. You see, I wouldn't object to being murdered by this Mr. Shei. Most people think I'm leading a useless life and ought to be dead, anyhow. It won't be long until an undertaker pumps my carcass full of formaldehyde. What I object to is the idea of being swindled out of my money. No man ever got the best of me yet, and I don't intend that Mr. Shei shall make a fool of me. He can kill me, but I won't hand him a cent. I'll be hanged if I will!"

He thumped the table with his fist. There was something so ludicrous about his grim earnestness that The Phantom could scarcely repress a smile. At the same time he was conscious of a suspicion for which he could not quite account. Mr. Fairspeckle's indignation seemed not quite natural. Even the vehement thump of his fist against the table had an artificial sound. An intuition, flashing into his mind out of nowhere, held The Phantom spellbound for a moment. In the next instant he laughed inwardly at the absurdity of it, telling himself that he must hold his imagination in leash.

"It will be interesting to see how Mr. Shei intends to proceed," he casually remarked.

"It will," spluttered Mr. Fairspeckle. "You can trust him to work some devilishly clever scheme. He always does. Do you suppose," and he bent his bony frame over the table and gazed searchingly at The Phantom, "that the murder at the Thelma Theater night before last was the first episode in this latest enterprise of Mr. Shei's?"

"You mean the murder of Miss Darrow? There seems to be no doubt but that Mr. Shei had a hand in it. Everything points to—"

He paused of a sudden. All at once it occurred to him that there was something odd about Mr. Fairspeckle's question. Immediately upon reading of the Thelma murder, The Phantom had suspected that it was the prelude to another of Mr. Shei's spectacular adventures, but the suspicion had been wholly intuitive. As far as outward appearances went, there was nothing in the murder of Virginia Darrow to suggest that it was anything more than an isolated incident. It was curious, therefore, that Mr. Fairspeckle should look for a connecting link between the crime at the Thelma and Mr. Shei's threat.

"Everything points to Mr. Shei as the perpetrator of the murder," he guardedly went on, "but whether the crime has any bearing on Mr. Shei's new venture is hard to tell. It doesn't seem likely. How could he possibly further his scheme by an act of that kind? His plan is to separate seven of New York's richest men from half of their wealth. How is the death of Miss Darrow going to help him in an undertaking of that kind?"

A sly smile twitched the corners of Mr. Fairspeckle's lips. "Nevertheless," he observed, "I think that you and I agree. I am a pretty good judge of faces, and your expression a moment ago betrayed you, Mr. Vanardy. My question seemed innocent enough at first, but on second thought it startled you. Suppose we be frank. Both of us believe that the Thelma affair was the beginning of Mr. Shei's latest move. We can't see how or why just now, but we know that his schemes run deep. Isn't it so?"

The Phantom, momentarily baffled by the older man's shrewd deductions, gazed pensively at the ceiling. A jumble of thoughts and questions shot back and forth through his mind. Did Mr. Fairspeckle suspect that Mr. Shei and The Gray Phantom were identical? Or was it possible that— He did not finish the thought. The suspicion that had come to him several times during the interview seemed just as unreasonable as it was startling, and it had no firmer foundation than two or three puzzling circumstances and a tantalizing touch of mysteriousness in Mr. Fairspeckle's attitude.

"It's an interesting theory, and I've given quite a little thought to it," he finally admitted. "Strange that the same idea should have come to both of us, isn't it? Especially since there seems to be neither reason nor logic behind it. How did you happen to think of it, Mr. Fairspeckle?"

The other man stroked his lean chin with a self-satisfied air. "What's that old saw about great minds traveling in the same channel? I don't know just how the idea came to me, but I'm glad we understand each other. Now we can talk without quibbling. But first I want a cup of coffee. Hope you will join me. Haiuto!"

He fairly shouted the last word, but The Phantom doubted whether his thin and rasping voice went farther than the walls.

"Haiuto!" Again Mr. Fairspeckle's voice rose to a shrill but inadequate crescendo. "That confounded Jap's pretending he is deaf again. Excuse me, will you?"

He strode irately from the room and slammed the door. A wrinkle of deep perplexity appeared on The Phantom's brow. Mr. Fairspeckle puzzled and intrigued him. Either he was a very slippery individual, or else ingenuousness itself. When he returned and announced that Haiuto would serve their coffee in a few minutes, The Phantom searched his face in vain for a sign of guile. If anything, he was a little more affable than on leaving the room.

"That fool doctor of mine tells me I mustn't drink coffee," he confided. "Tells me it's bad for my nerves and keeps me awake. But my nerves are worn to a frazzle, anyhow, and I never can sleep except when I want to stay awake. What were we talking about? Oh, yes—Mr. Shei."

He clasped his hands across his diaphragm. A smile, at once beatific and diabolical, came over his face.

"Do you know," he went on in confidential tones, "that I don't care a rap if Mr. Shei carries out his scheme as far as the other six are concerned. Of course, I don't know for certain who they are, but it's a safe bet that they are no friends of mine. I have a hunch that every one of them belongs to the old ring that fought me tooth and nail while I was climbing up in the world. It's a long story, and I'm not going to bore you with it, but you can see why I have no love for them. I could die happy tomorrow if I could see them lick the dust today. I feel different toward you, Vanardy. We had a tilt once, but you fought fairly. The others tried to knife me in the back. They can go to blazes for all I care."

"Then you and Mr. Shei seem to have at least one aim in common," The Phantom pointed out. He smiled genially, but his eyes were studying every shifting expression in Mr. Fairspeckle's face. For once he felt certain that the older man was not dissembling. The glint of wrath lurking in the depths of his weak eyes and the vindictive sneer about his lips told that he had spoken in all sincerity.

"We have," he declared grimly. "I hope he sends the other six to the poor-house. But I have no intention of letting him pluck me, you understand. That's where our aims clash. He can go as far as he likes with the others, but I'll fight like a drunken Indian before I give him a red cent. I'll see myself in Hades before I—"

A knock and the opening of the door interrupted him. A Japanese with a face as expressionless as mahogany entered with a tray and served them coffee.

"Strange character, Haiuto," observed Mr. Fairspeckle when the servant, silent as a wraith, had retired. "I think he would cheerfully commit hara-kiri if I asked him to do such a senseless thing." He sipped his coffee with an air of keen enjoyment. "Great bracer for fagged nerves, eh? Would you believe that for days at a time I live on nothing but coffee? But let's get back to the subject. What shall we do with this pestiferous Mr. Shei?"

"What would you suggest?" cautiously inquired The Phantom, lifting the cup to his lips.

A beam insinuated itself in the creases of Mr. Fairspeckle's face. "Now we're getting down to essentials. As I said, Mr. Shei can fleece the other six to his heart's content, but he's got to keep hands off me. When I saw you standing in front of the drug store reading Mr. Shei's announcement, I was turning a little plan over in my mind. Then I didn't quite see how to work it, but I do now."

Again The Phantom brought the cup to his lips. He regarded his companion inquiringly.

"You and I are going to handle Mr. Shei together," declared Mr. Fairspeckle. His face glowed as if a pleasing prospect were warming his soul. "We will put a crimp in his scheme and show him—why, what's the matter, Vanardy?"

The Phantom had slouched down in his chair, and now his head began to wag from side to side.

"Nothing," he murmured dazedly. "I just feel a bit drowsy. Would you mind opening the window? The—the coffee—"

His eyes rolled, then the lids fluttered and closed, and he sagged limply in the chair. With a gratified chuckle Mr. Fairspeckle stepped to the other side of the table and regarded him gloatingly.

"The Gray Phantom isn't half so clever as he's supposed to be," he mumbled. Then his hand went out and touched a button. A moment later, Haiuto stood at attention in the doorway.

"Haiuto," inquired Mr. Fairspeckle, "how much chloral did you mix in Mr. Vanardy's cup of coffee?"

"Plenty," said the servant, and this time the ghost of a grin flickered across his face. "He sleep long time."

Mr. Fairspeckle nodded elatedly. "Take him to my bedroom," he instructed, "and make him comfortable."

With an ease which showed that he possessed all the agile strength of his race, Haiuto carried The Phantom into one of the adjoining rooms in the suite, placed him on the bed, and adjusted a pillow under his head. For a few moments he stood peering down into the motionless man's face. Then he silently left the room and closed the door behind him.

A minute later The Phantom raised himself to a sitting posture and blinked his eyes at the sunlight streaming in beneath the drawn window shades.

"You are fairly clever, Mr. Fairspeckle," he said half aloud, "but you ought to modernize your methods. Drugged coffee has gone out of fashion. Hope I didn't kill the potted fern at the window behind my chair."

CHAPTER VIII
THE VOICE ON THE WIRE

THE GRAY PHANTOM LAY on his back in W. Rufus Fairspeckle's ample bed and tried to grasp the meaning of what had happened. His host's attempt to drug him savored strongly of melodrama, and it seemed somewhat grotesque in view of the fact that it had occurred in an up-to-date and centrally located hotel. What puzzled him most was the motive behind the attempt. If Mr. Fairspeckle suspected that he was Mr. Shei, why had he not handed his guest over to the police? On the other hand— But his conjectures in that direction brought The Phantom face to face with a theory that made his thoughts whirl.

His eyes flitted over the room. The color combination was restful, but the decorations, and especially the pictures, bespoke rather extreme tastes. He had gathered, from what little he had seen of the surroundings, that Mr. Fairspeckle was occupying a luxurious apartment consisting of several rooms and that it had been fitted up to suit his individual requirements. Haiuto, the rat-footed Japanese servant, seemed to be his only companion.

An hour passed, and The Phantom's cogitations brought him back to the starting point. Nothing seemed certain beyond the indubitable fact that Mr. Fairspeckle was a highly mysterious individual. The rest was full of vague and hazy surmises. The Phantom waited patiently, wondering what his host's next move would be, for he had decided to play a passive rôle for the present. He explored his pockets and was thankful that his automatic had not been taken from him. Evidently his jailer was depending on the drug to keep him in a harmless condition.

His keen ears detected footsteps approaching the door, and in a twinkling he was lying prone on the bed, simulating the complete insensibility that comes with drug-induced sleep. The door came open, then furtive steps crossed the floor, and The Phantom felt a pair of sharp eyes on his face. His regular breathing seemed to satisfy the silent watcher, for after a little he turned away. As he reached the door, The Phantom flicked open an eyelid and saw Haiuto. Evidently the servant had entered the room to make sure that the effects of the drug were not wearing off.

The door closed almost noiselessly. Again The Phantom sat up. A glance at his watch told him it was a few minutes after two. He slid his feet from the bed and tiptoed cautiously to a window and raised the shade. As he looked out, an undersized figure on the opposite sidewalk instantly caught his eye. As far as appearances went, the man might have been only an idler engaged in the pastime of ogling the feminine passers-by, but The Phantom's practiced eyes saw at once that he was there for a purpose. The stealthy glances which he occasionally leveled at the windows of Mr. Fairspeckle's apartment gave an unmistakable clew to his mission.

The Phantom's brows contracted as he quickly lowered the shade. Was it possible someone had seen and recognized him on his way from the station and later trailed him to Mr. Fairspeckle's apartment. The thought was annoying, for he disliked having his movements hampered by spies. Then, as he turned away from the window, another possibility suggested itself. Perhaps Mr. Fairspeckle, and not himself, was being kept under surveillance of the fellow on the sidewalk. The theory was startling and rather improbable; yet it coincided with the suspicion that had kept flashing in and out of The Phantom's mind.

He examined the mechanism of his automatic and made sure the cartridge chamber was loaded. He sensed a hint in the air that before long he might have occasion to use the weapon. He was in the act of returning it to his hip pocket when of a sudden he pricked up his ears. From somewhere in the apartment came a series of faint, clicking sounds. At first he tried in vain to identify them, but finally it came to him that someone was using a typewriter.

"Typewriter?" he mumbled. The word seemed to hold a hidden significance, but for a while his mind was unable to grasp it. He did not believe that either Mr. Fairspeckle or Haiuto had occasion to use such an instrument, yet he was almost certain that the sounds were coming from one of the adjoining rooms. The clicks were slow and irregular, he observed, indicating that the writer was unfamiliar with the machine and was having some difficulty picking out the characters on the keyboard.

He stole to the door and opened it a crack. The sounds became louder, and the writer's awkward groping for the keys was more noticeable now. For a moment The Phantom stood listening; then his figure grew suddenly tense. A thin smile hovered about his lips as he recalled that the announcements which Mr. Shei had distributed throughout the city had been written on a typewriter.

It might mean little or nothing, but there was a keen glitter in The Phantom's eyes. In itself the clicking of the machine signified scarcely anything, but in conjunction with other circumstances it was fairly suggestive. With noiseless tread The Phantom tiptoed in the direction whence the sounds were coming. Now and then he darted a quick glance about him, as if expecting a rear attack from the Japanese servant, but Haiuto was nowhere in sight. He traversed several rooms before he came to a dead stop in a doorway.

At a table near the window, with his back to The Phantom, sat Mr. Fairspeckle. He was hunched over a typewriter, laboriously poking at the keys with the index finger of each hand. Silently The Phantom approached until he stood directly at the older man's back. Mr. Fairspeckle, all his energies centered on his difficult task, noticed nothing. Leaning slightly forward, The Phantom cast a swift, comprehensive glance at the paper in the machine. Then his twinkling eyes looked downward. On the desk, at Mr. Fairspeckle's elbow, lay a little pile of papers. The topmost one was partly covered with typewriting, and the wording was precisely the same as that on the paper in the machine.

The Phantom had seen enough. He drew his automatic from his pocket, then waited until Mr. Fairspeckle stopped writing and pulled the sheet from the machine.

"You seem to be fairly busy, Mr. Shei," he observed in soft tones.

Mr. Fairspeckle jerked up his shoulders, then sat as rigid as if suddenly turned into a statue. Finally, with slow and spasmodic motions, he turned his head and looked into the muzzle of The Phantom's automatic. A startled look leaped into his eyes and his sallow face turned a shade paler.

"You!" he exclaimed.

"I watered one of your ferns with the coffee Haiuto handed me," The Phantom explained. "A cruel way to treat an inoffensive plant, I'll admit, but there was nothing else handy. Mind if I have a look?"

Lowering the weapon a trifle, he picked up the sheet of paper Mr. Fairspeckle had just drawn from the machine. Watching the older man out of the tail of an eye, he read the typewritten lines:

> In accordance with my promise, I herewith announce the names of the seven gentlemen whom by certain means at my disposal I shall persuade to hand over half of their respective fortunes to me.

Then followed a list of seven names, each one suggestive of untold wealth and vast influence in the financial world, and The Phantom smiled as he noticed that W. Rufus Fairspeckle was one of them. By way of signature Mr. Shei's name was typed at the bottom of the announcement.

"Not bad," commented The Phantom. "By including yourself among the seven victims you make sure that no suspicion becomes attached to the fair name of W. Rufus Fairspeckle. Anyhow, since you are one of the richest men in town, it would look rather odd if your name were omitted. Congratulations, Mr. Shei."

The other looked stolidly into the muzzle of the automatic. The Phantom's sudden and unexpected appearance seemed to have paralyzed his tongue.

"You could save a lot of time by taking carbon copies," suggested The Phantom, riffling the sheets lying beside the machine. "You will need a hundred or more to plaster the town effectively. I understand now why you took that long walk this morning. There's nothing like having a pleasant pastime when one can't sleep. What I don't understand is how you meant to put your plan into effect."

A sickly smile cruised about Mr. Fairspeckle's bloodless lips.

"Oh, I don't expect you to let me in on the secret," The Phantom went on. "With your past performances in mind, I have no doubt you would have executed your threat in a manner becoming your genius. There's only one thing about your achievements that has disappointed me. I don't see why you had to copy my methods so slavishly. For a while I was almost certain that Mr. Shei was one of my former associates, and that's why—" He checked himself on the point of explaining why he had come out of hiding. "Couldn't you have shown a little more originality?"

An inarticulate mumble came from Mr. Fairspeckle's lips. His fingers fidgeted nervously over his knees.

"Well don't try to explain. I suppose the police will attend to that part. There will be quite a sensation when it becomes known that W. Rufus Fairspeckle is the mysterious Mr. Shei. I wonder what drove you to it. You were bored with the life of a gentleman of leisure, I suppose, and then you had a goose to pick with your old enemies. I take it that was your chief motive. Well, Mr. Shei—"

A dulcet tinkle interrupted him, and he glanced quickly at the telephone on Mr. Fairspeckle's desk.

"You may answer," he said after a moment's hesitation.

Mr. Fairspeckle reached out a trembling hand for the instrument. He put the receiver to his ear and spoke a feeble "Hello" into the transmitter. In the next instant his face went blank. "It's for you," he announced, gazing dazedly at The Phantom.

"For *me*?" The Phantom stared incredulously at the instrument. To the best of his knowledge, his whereabouts was known to nobody but Mr. Fairspeckle and the Japanese servant. Quickly gathering himself, he placed the automatic within easy reach and took the telephone from Mr. Fairspeckle's hand. He started as a voice came over the wire.

"Mr. Shei speaking," it announced in level tones. "If you value Miss Hardwick's life, I would advise you to abandon your present plans. That is all."

Then a click, and the connection was broken.

CHAPTER IX
THE HOUSE OF LAUGHTER

"Mr. Shei!"

Time and again through the night following her arrival at Azurecrest, Helen's lips soundlessly formed the name she had involuntarily spoken upon seeing the man in the doorway. She tossed restlessly on her bed, her mind in that curious state on the boundary line between slumber and wakefulness when the imagination forms shadowy images and one's thoughts reach for elusive realities.

Now and then, as a wild strain of laughter shattered the silence, she sat up and stared into the darkness. A cold tingle would trickle down her spine as the sounds rose to a hysterical crescendo, then fell to a gentle tinkle that made her flesh quiver, and finally died down to a haunting echo. Then, her sense of horror engulfed by overwhelming drowsiness, she would fall back against the pillow and drift into a state of soothing stupor.

Finally dawn broke. Flickering wisps of sunlight fell on the floor, lighting up the dark corners and dispersing the evil host with which her imagination had peopled the gloom. A fresh breeze caressed her hot forehead and cooled the fever in her blood. She sat up and rubbed her eyes. Outside, the sun was glimmering on treetops and long stretches of lawn. The bright, pleasant room afforded a sharp contrast to the strident discords and monstrous visions that had distressed her throughout the night.

Her recollections were still vague. Gradually a train of memories swept upon her. It all came back to her now—her arrival at Azurecrest, her failure to find The Gray Phantom, the strange laughter and the hideous face she had seen at the window, Miss Neville's amazing story and the intercepted flight, and finally the appearance of the man at the sight of whom she had cried out the name of Mr. Shei.

Again her recollections grew dim. Things had gone dark before her eyes as soon as she had spoken the name. She had heard a jumble of voices, and she believed someone had forced a drink down her throat. A sedative, perhaps, for after that she had known nothing but the intermittent outbursts of laughter and their accompaniment of strange fancies. She shuddered as she remembered them. Several voices, she felt sure, had joined in the chorus of unnatural laughter. It could mean only one thing—that more than one inmate of the house was afflicted with the mysterious fever so vividly described by Miss Neville.

Her mind was clearing rapidly now. She realized she was surrounded by dangers which she could neither gauge nor understand. Of one thing only could she be certain. Her eyes, while resting on the man in the doorway, had pierced the veil of mystery which had concealed the identity of the mysterious Mr. Shei. The discovery, confirming a suspicion that had first come to her in the Thelma Theater, had shocked and bewildered her, and on the impulse of the moment she had heedlessly called out his name.

Now, in a calmer mood, she reproached herself for her indiscretion. She wondered whether Mr. Shei would dare let her live, now that she had penetrated his secret. If he were as ruthless and unscrupulous as she supposed him to be, he would in all likelihood seal her lips forever. She might promise not to betray him, but Mr. Shei was too shrewd and cautious to rely on promises. He would be more apt to adopt the only course consistent with his safety.

She shivered a little. Physical fear she had never known, for there was a strain of recklessness and audacity in her nature that blinded her eyes to dangers, but the thought of death gave her a chill. She did not know exactly why, but never before had life seemed as enticing as now. A determination to live spurred her mind to frantic effort. She would outwit Mr. Shei by her woman's weapons. She had done some skillful fencing with them on several occasions in the past, and she could use them again. Already she was casting about for a plan. Perhaps, by a little clever acting, she could convince Mr. Shei that her calling of his name had been nothing but a hysterical outburst and without significance. If she succeeded in this, he would have no reason for taking her life.

The thought buoyed her. She turned a smiling face to the door as it opened and admitted a woman carrying a tray. She was thin and slatternly, and she sighed repeatedly while transferring the breakfast dishes to a table which she placed beside Helen's bed.

"Eat, you poor thing," she admonished, a world of melancholy in her tones.

Helen sipped the coffee. It was strong and fragrant and gave her a needed stimulus.

"Why do you call me 'poor thing'?" she inquired.

The woman heaved another sigh. "I'm not saying. I can hold my tongue when I want to. That's how I keep my job in this place. It's a shame, though—really it is."

"What is a shame?" Helen, looking into the slattern's saturnine face, with its ludicrously doleful expression, felt an impulse to laugh in spite of her misgivings.

"You're so young and pretty. That's why I call it a shame. Oh, well, we all have to go that way sooner or later."

Helen, unpleasantly impressed by the innuendo, tasted the toast. "Which way?" she asked in casual tones.

"That would be telling." A long sigh racked the woman's scrawny chest. "I hear a lot of things around this place that I never tell. Better eat hearty, dear. It might be your last— Gosh! I almost said something that time, didn't I?"

Helen, conquering her forebodings, ate in silence for a time. The slattern's funereal face and dismal insinuations were casting a spell of gloom over her which she found hard to shake off. Finally she tried a direct question.

"Do you mean that they are going to kill me?"

The woman clasped her hands across her chest and raised mournful eyes to the ceiling. "You mustn't ask questions, poor dear. You'll find out soon enough. Anyhow, there's a better world than this."

With this piece of doubtful consolation she gathered the dishes and, with another disconsolate sigh, walked out of the room. Helen tried to tell herself that the woman had merely been exercising her imagination and that her doleful hints had come out of thin air. The meal had refreshed her, and her spirits rose while she bathed her face in cold water and arranged her attire. Having finished, she viewed herself with satisfaction in the mirror. Her elastic health and strength had obliterated nearly every trace of her distressing night.

A knock sounded on the door, and Mr. Slade walked in. Helen instantly steeled herself for an ordeal. Slade, she had already guessed, was Mr. Shei's right-hand man. He was smiling affably, but something told her that her life depended on the outcome of the interview.

"I trust you had a restful night, Miss Hardwick?" he suavely inquired after seating himself.

"I slept like a top," Helen assured him with a smile that belied her real emotion. "You see, I was all fagged out when I retired. I have a faint recollection that I was a bit hysterical, too. I suppose it was on account of that affair at the Thelma Theater the other night. I received quite a shock."

"Naturally," assented Slade, regarding her with a mingling of admiration and doubt. "Yes, you seemed somewhat upset last night. You probably have no recollection of it, but you fainted completely away, and one of the maids put you to bed after the physician in attendance upon Miss Neville had administered a sedative. I don't suppose you remember any of that?"

"It's all news to me," declared Helen innocently. "I'm sorry to have been so much trouble."

Slade made a deprecatory gesture. He edged his chair a little closer to the small table at which Helen was seated. She felt his cold gaze searching her face, and to hide her confusion she began tracing figures in the dust that had accumulated on the surface of the table.

"Last night we were discussing The Gray Phantom," Slade remarked, and she started a trifle at the mention of the name. "I regret I can give you no inkling as to his whereabouts. I suppose you are very anxious to find him?"

"Rather."

"Isn't it strange that he did not give you his new address?"

"He may have written and the letter gone astray," suggested Helen. A flush had tinged the healthy tan of her cheeks the moment Slade introduced the subject of The Gray Phantom. Looking down at the table, she noticed confusedly that her hand had been influenced by the thoughts that were uppermost in her mind. In the thin layer of dust she had absently traced The Gray Phantom's initials. It was a habit of hers, cultivated since childhood, to sketch figures and designs on whatever surface was handy, and she had often told herself she must overcome it.

"Perhaps," was Slade's comment. He looked at her in a way that caused her to wonder whether he had noticed the pencilings in the dust, and she erased them with a quick sweep of her hand. "By the way," he went on, "our conversation last night was interrupted by a—a certain person. Remember?"

Helen knew that the critical moment had come. She made a pretense of searching her memory.

"I was very tired," she said, carefully choosing her words, "and I recall very little of what happened. I seem to remember, though, that a motor horn sounded while we were talking."

"Yes, and then?" Slade bent eagerly forward.

Helen's strained face indicated intense mental effort. "Then— Isn't it odd that I don't seem able to remember a thing after that?"

"It is," admitted Slade, and there was a subtle change in the quality of his voice. "Perhaps I can refresh your memory. Suddenly a man's figure appeared in the doorway. You stared at him in a way signifying that you had seen him before. Then you spoke a name."

"A name?" echoed Helen. "What name?"

"A name that has been on a great many lips of late—Mr. Shei's."

"Isn't that strange?" murmured Helen. "I wonder what on earth made me mention that name. I suppose, though," she added quickly, "that it was because Mr. Shei's name had been in my mind off and on ever since that terrible occurrence in the Thelma Theater. Yes, that must be the reason."

"The *only* reason, Miss Hardwick?"

"What other reason could there be?"

Slade smiled in a way that awoke Helen's dislike. "Well, it's conceivable that you were under the impression that the man in the doorway was Mr. Shei. That would not only have explained your excitement, but also give ample reason for uttering his name."

Helen opened her eyes wide. "But—but I don't even remember seeing the man," she protested artlessly, "so why should I suppose him to be Mr. Shei?"

"The fact remains that you spoke Mr. Shei's name just before you fainted away. Let's get at the subject from a different angle, Miss Hardwick. Do you know who Mr. Shei is?"

Helen, having a curious feeling that her life was trembling in the balance, shook her head.

"You don't know his other name—the name by which he is known to the world at large?"

Again Helen made a negative gesture, and in the same instant she became aware that Slade's frosty gaze was following the movements of her right hand. Before she realized what was happening, he had left his chair and stepped up behind her, and now he was leaning over her shoulder and looking down at the table.

"So, you lied," he muttered in tones that sent a shiver through her body, at the same time pointing to the table.

Helen looked down. She gave a violent start. While she had been fencing verbally with Slade, her hand had betrayed her. In her preoccupation she had not realized that another couplet of initials had appeared in the dust. With a sensation of defeat and despair she stared down at the telltale characters—the first letters in Mr. Shei's other name.

CHAPTER X
A SHOT

AT NOON OF THE same day a scene equally tense, but of quite a different character, was being enacted in the library of W. Rufus Fairspeckle.

Dazedly The Gray Phantom set the telephone down. In tones too low for the older man to catch, he mumblingly repeated the startling message that had just come to him over the wire: "Mr. Shei speaking. If you value Miss Hardwick's life, I would advise you to abandon your present plans."

One by one, and in the order in which they had been spoken, the words trickled into his benumbed consciousness. He had heard Mr. Shei's voice over the wire. He had been mistaken, then, and the shrunken and wizened man seated before him with eyes staring and mouth agape could not be Mr. Shei. Even the evidence of the typewritten slips lying on the desk seemed to mean nothing against the fact that the notorious rogue had just communicated with him by telephone.

"What—what's the matter?" stammered Mr. Fairspeckle, who, not having the faintest inkling as to the nature of the message received by The Phantom, was at a loss to understand the latter's demeanor. "Anything wrong?"

The Phantom scarcely heard him. The significance of the last part of Mr. Shei's message came to him in a flash. In a twinkling his mind was functioning again. His eyes were threatening, like miniature thunder clouds. A new and dynamic impulse seemed to dominate his whole being. He snatched up the telephone directory and found a number. Then he fairly hurled himself at the telephone, frantically jigged the hook up and down, shouted a number into the transmitter, and waited breathlessly till the connection was established.

A woman's voice, evidently that of a servant, answered. Miss Hardwick was not in, she explained, and when pressed for further information admitted that she had not been seen since breakfast the previous day. Mr. Hardwick, ill at ease because of his daughter's absence, was instituting inquiries for her in various directions, and the servant did not know where he could be reached.

The Phantom's eyes blazed as he set the instrument down with a slam. Mr. Fairspeckle, a flabbergasted look in his bulging eyes, seemed utterly at a loss to comprehend what was going on. For a moment The Phantom eyed him narrowly, then cast a bewildered glance at the typewritten slips, and finally turned abruptly on his heels and dashed from the room.

No one interrupted him. He suspected that Haiuto was lurking somewhere in the background, but he saw nothing of the sly-footed servant as he rushed from the apartment and, forgetting the existence of the elevator, scurried down three flights of stairs. The ferret-eyed individual whom he had seen from the window was still standing at the opposite curb, but he did not deign a single glance in The Phantom's direction. Block after block, spurred on by a medley of anguishing doubts and suspicions, The Phantom continued his heedless progress, conscious only of the one agonizing thought that something had happened to Helen Hardwick.

Presently he awoke to a realization of the futility and recklessness of his conduct. His fears for Helen Hardwick had blunted his wits and stultified his reason, making him forget his old-time caution and nimbleness of mind. To no purpose he was rushing blindly into a net of dangers. With a mutter of disgust at his childish impetuosity, he drew in his steps and turned into a convenient doorway. A glance up and down the street assured him that, thanks to luck alone, his headlong course seemed to have attracted no attention. He scanned the crowd on all sides, but there was no sign of either espionage or pursuit. He had vaguely expected to be followed by the keen-eyed watcher he had seen on the sidewalk outside the Whipple Hotel, but the man was nowhere in sight. For the present, at least, The Phantom was safe. Now he must think clearly and act coolly.

He could not rid himself of the suspicion that Helen's volatile nature and venturesome disposition had led her into some fearful predicament. He knew she had an infinite capacity for handling difficult situations, but the knowledge gave him scant comfort. He revolved the problem of her disappearance in his mind. She had been missing for more than twenty-four hours. He sensed a dim significance in the fact that she had passed out of sight the morning following the tragedy at the Thelma Theater, and of a sudden he asked himself whether there could be any possible connection between her disappearance and the death of Virginia Darrow.

Several circumstances lent plausibility to the theory. Chief among them was the mysterious warning The Phantom had received from Mr. Shei, the man who was generally believed to have been implicated in Miss Darrow's death. The Phantom's mind was working swiftly now, leaping barriers and rushing straight to conclusions. It was Helen's play, he remembered, that had been produced on the night of the tragedy, and it was very probable that she had been present at the *première* performance. Knowing her as he did, he thought it conceivable that she had come into possession of some vital facts bearing on the tragedy. Her inquisitive mind, though untainted by vulgar curiosity, was always dipping into mysteries of one sort or another, and it was possible that on this occasion her natural bent had led her into conflict with Mr. Shei.

Almost before he realized what he was doing, The Phantom was in a taxi-cab, shouting to the chauffeur to drive him to the Thelma Theater. It seemed the logical starting point in his search; at least, he did not know where else to begin, and by visiting the scene of Miss Darrow's death, he might be able to pick up some clew to Helen's movements.

The doors were open, and he thought this somewhat strange in view of the fact that a poster on the outer wall announced that the performances of "His Soul's Master" had been discontinued, but the circumstance did not linger long in his mind. The box office and lobby being empty, he passed unchallenged into the auditorium. For a few moments, while his eyes grew accustomed to the dusk, he stood just inside the door, trying to call back to mind each detail of the tragedy as it had been narrated in the newspapers, and presently there came to him a conviction that he was not alone, but that someone was watching him intently.

He could not account for the impression, for no sound reached his ears, and the interior was only a mass of gently undulating shadows in which he saw no indication of another's presence. The atmosphere was somewhat oppressive, and a multitude of faint scents lingered in the air, hinting that the theater had not been ventilated since the last performance. Glancing sharply into the gloom about him, The Phantom groped his way down the center aisle, then explored the passageways at each side of the house, and finally looked into each of the boxes. His search availed him nothing, and at length he was forced to admit that his imagination had tricked him.

Walking to the rear of the house, he stood with his back against a pillar, and gazed toward the last row of seats to the left. It was there, according to the diagram he had seen in one of the papers, that Virginia Darrow had sat when seized with the strange fit of laughter. Again he wondered what bearing the woman's death might have on Mr. Shei's latest venture. The connection, if there was one, seemed so remote that he came to the conclusion that Mr. Shei must be at work on a very intricate and deep-laid scheme. Then it occurred to him that his speculations, founded on insufficient facts, were a waste of time. They were not helping him to solve the mystery of Helen Hardwick's disappearance.

As was his habit when he wished to concentrate his mind on a problem, he took a cigarette from his case, then struck a match against the sole of his shoe. Absently he held the fluttering light to the tip of the cigarette, and inhaled.

Suddenly he sprang aside, for a sound, all but too faint for his ears to detect, had warned him of danger, and in the same instant a sharp crack and a flash of fire leaped out of the darkness. Then an object whizzed past his head and with a thudding sound imbedded itself in the pillar against which he had been leaning.

In a moment he had extinguished his cigarette. He could see now that its glowing point, together with the match, had made him a target for the person who had fired the shot. The bullet had passed so close to his head that, but for his quick and agile backward spring, it would undoubtedly have killed him. His narrow escape had an exhilarating effect, and he dashed toward the point where he had seen the flash of fire, determined to capture the would-be murderer. It was his impression that the shot had been fired only a dozen feet away, and he did not think the man could have escaped.

In the gloom he could not distinguish objects clearly, and he dashed head-long against a post. The contact sent a stinging sensation through his head, and in the same moment a figure glided silently past him and was swallowed by the shadows at the other side of the house. Again The Phantom rushed forward. A swiftly moving object, a shade darker than the surrounding dusk, was discernible down the aisle leading to the boxes at the right. The Phantom darted after it, but when he reached the point his quarry had disappeared. For an instant he stopped, uncertain which way to turn, and in the midst of his perplexity the varicolored lights along the walls were flashed on.

The Phantom whirled round. Near one of the exits in the rear of the house stood a tall, slenderly proportioned man. His long, glossy hair was rumpled, and even at a distance The Phantom could see that his features, so regularly molded as to give an impression of effeminacy, were intensely pale. He approached swiftly. The two men eyed each other intently before either spoke.

"You are Mr. Starr, I believe?" began The Phantom, recognizing the other from photographs he had seen in the newspapers.

Starr nodded. His right hand was clutching a revolver. Coming closer, The Phantom noticed that his nose was discolored and swollen, probably the result of the attack that had preceded the disappearance of Virginia Darrow's body.

"I owe you an apology for intruding like this," he went on, "but the formalities can wait. There was a shot fired here a few moments ago, and I believe it was meant for me."

"I was at work in my office upstairs when I heard something that sounded like a revolver shot," explained Starr. "I armed myself and came down to investigate." His voice, at other times perfectly modulated, was a little husky, and he seemed unduly conscious of his disfigured nose. He maintained a tight grip on his pistol while regarding The Phantom with a look of suspicion.

"We ought to search the house at once," suggested The Phantom. "The scoundrel can't have gone far."

Starr readily acquiesced, but from time to time while they went on with the search The Phantom felt the other's stealthy gaze searching his face, and each time he saw a look of dawning recognition in Starr's eyes. He thought nothing of it, for the capture of the man who had fired the shot seemed of far greater importance. Deep in his mind was a faint and remote hope that the fellow, if caught, might be persuaded to tell something of what had happened to Helen Hardwick.

They searched every conceivable space in the auditorium, back of the stage, and finally in the storerooms and dressing rooms down below, but without avail. As they abandoned their quest The Phantom thought he saw signs of increasing nervousness on Starr's part.

"Strange how the scoundrel disappeared," he remarked when once more they stood in the back of the auditorium.

"No stranger than what happened here night before last." Starr spoke with a touch of petulance in his voice and manner. "Mr. Shei and his henchmen seem to have a knack of walking through solid walls. What I object to most is his evident determination to make my theater the scene of his diabolical activities. By the way," and he fixed The Phantom with a look of mingled perplexity and suspicion, "haven't you and I met before?"

"Not in person, unless I am mistaken." The Phantom, alert against the slightest threatening move on the other's part, smiled faintly. "The newspapers have been kind enough to give me some publicity from time to time, and you may have seen my photograph. Suppose we let it go at that."

"As you wish, of course," murmured Starr, his lips twitching, "but we shall be able to talk to better advantage if we first complete the introductions. I was almost certain I recognized you at first glance. You are The Gray Phantom. But don't get startled," he quickly added as The Phantom suddenly stiffened. "My interest in life is purely esthetic. I am trying, in my small and humble way, to uplift the drama from the sordid depths into which it has fallen through the stupidity and avarice of managers. The capture and punishment of criminals interest me not at all. To be perfectly frank with you, as between the police and a fascinating rogue like yourself, my sympathies are with the latter."

He made an expressive gesture, and The Phantom watched with interest the slight, quick and marvelously impressive motions of his hands. Though this was his first meeting with the man himself, the gestures, as well as the characteristic backward toss of the head, seemed oddly familiar.

"I think you are mistaken about one thing," Starr went on, his nervousness returning. "Is there any reason why anyone should wish to put you out of the way?"

"None that I know of," replied The Phantom thoughtfully. "I suppose I have enemies, but it didn't occur to me that anyone was after my life until that shot was fired."

"And weren't you a bit precipitate in jumping at the conclusion that the bullet was intended for you? Suppose you give me the details."

The Phantom told him the meager facts of the firing of the shot.

"There you are!" exclaimed Starr when he had finished. "The fellow couldn't see your face. All he saw was the match, and he used that as a target, knowing you were holding it directly in front of your face while lighting the cigarette." He took a few quick, nervous steps back and forth. He clenched and unclenched his hands as if trying to quell a rising trepidation. Suddenly he paused directly in front of The Phantom. "That bullet was not intended for you, but for me," he declared emphatically.

"Are you sure?"

"Not sure, but I have the best of reasons for supposing that such is the fact. I have had several intimations of danger in the past few weeks, but it isn't necessary to go into details. Since night before last I have wondered what prompted Miss Darrow to send me the facetiously worded note hinting that Mr. Shei was in the house. If she were alive I am sure she could tell us several interesting things about— But what's the good of supposing? Miss Darrow will never be able to tell what was in her mind when she wrote me that note. Only one thing is certain. She was killed because she had, in some unexplained manner, learned Mr. Shei's identity."

The Phantom regarded him narrowly. "Some people seem to be of the opinion that I am Mr. Shei."

"Rot! The similarity between your tactics and those of Mr. Shei is only superficial. The essential difference ought to be plain even to a stupid head-quarters detective. Besides, you never took life or— But the idea is too absurd to waste breath on. Let us be practical. You have not yet explained why you are honoring the Thelma Theater with this visit."

The Phantom was about to reply when one of the doors in front was pushed open and the shadow of a masculine figure fell across the floor. After a glance into the face of the newcomer, The Phantom sensed danger and tried to retreat into a corner where the dim light held out a faint hope of brief security. But it was too late.

"Stay right where you are," commanded the man who had just entered. "Didn't know The Gray Phantom was back in town. Step out here where I can look at you."

Starr had known him. One of the men whom he had just entered didn't know the only Phantom's share. In fact, see one anywhere, can look around.

CHAPTER XI
AN EAVESDROPPER

THE PHANTOM SHRUGGED HIS shoulders and stepped forward, concealing his misgivings behind a smiling and carefree exterior. He knew Lieutenant Culligore from past encounters with the man, and he had learned to respect him for his shrewdness as well as his sense of fairness. Now he looked straight into the muddy and deceptively lazy eyes of the man from headquarters. Once The Phantom had assisted him in solving a singularly perplexing mystery, but he knew that Culligore was not the kind of man to let sentiment interfere with duty.

There were times when it was difficult for The Gray Phantom to realize that he was still an outlaw and that several prison sentences were hanging over his head. The poignant fact came back to him now as he gazed into the eyes of one of the keenest man hunters of the detective bureau.

"You sure have nerve," observed Culligore, a trace of reluctant admiration in his tones. "Don't you know there's a warrant out for your arrest?"

"Several of them, I believe," calmly replied The Phantom.

Lieutenant Culligore took a cigar from his vest pocket and lighted it with elaborate care. Then he turned to Starr.

"Mr. Shei's gang certainly handed you an awful wallop the other night," he observed, gazing frowningly at the disfigured organ. "That's a peach of a nose you've got."

Starr flushed angrily, but controlled himself.

"I've got a few words to say to this gentleman privately," Culligore went on, inclining his head toward The Phantom. Starr, accepting his dismissal as gracefully as his indignation permitted, walked out. Culligore's small eyes, twinkling humorously through a cloud of tobacco smoke, followed his progress till the door closed behind him, then he slowly turned toward The Phantom.

"Starr is my idea of a perfect gentleman," he musingly observed. "He can get mad clean through and still keep his coat on. Was the shot fired at you or at him?"

"Shot?" For a moment The Phantom stared bewilderedly. "How did you know?"

"My sense of smell is fairly good," said Culligore, sniffing. "I noticed there was powder smoke in the air the moment I walked in. What became of the bullet?"

The Phantom explained. With a listless air the lieutenant examined the point where the leaden slug had entered the pillar. "I'll bet a pair of pink socks that the rascal who fired the shot is a safe distance from here by this time. What I'd like to know is whether he was aiming at you or at Starr."

"Starr thinks the bullet was meant for him," said The Phantom thoughtfully. "He may be right, but I have my doubts. He is the imaginative type that believes he is being pursued by secret enemies and all that sort of thing. On the other hand, I can't see why anybody should waste a chunk of good lead on me, unless—" He stopped short as an idea suddenly occurred to him.

"Unless Mr. Shei should have a goose to pick with you," Culligore filled in, and The Phantom marveled at the way the detective had read his unspoken thought. "It's always safe to look for a shower of bullets whenever The Gray Phantom bobs up. By the way," and Culligore frowned disapprovingly, "what's the idea? Don't you know the climate in this town is mighty unhealthy for a man like you?"

"I am aware of it." The Phantom's lips tightened into a grim line. "But I had to risk it, Culligore. I couldn't sit idle while— But first let me ask you one question. Some people seem to think that I am Mr. Shei. Do you agree with them?"

Culligore pulled thoughtfully at his cigar. His eyes seemed to be searching every remote corner of The Phantom's mind. "No," he said finally, "I don't. And I don't see it makes any difference. You're The Gray Phantom, and that's reason enough for me to pinch you. There are times when I hate my job, but duty is duty. I wish you hadn't shown up just at this time. Some of the higher-ups are dead sure you are Mr. Shei, and the whole town is on tenter hooks on account of the notices posted last night. Everybody expects Mr. Shei to strike, but nobody knows where the blow is going to fall. You can see how things are. Why the devil didn't you stay where you belong?"

"I couldn't," replied The Phantom. Then he regarded the lieutenant with a slow, carefully measuring glance. Culligore was one of the few men he had met whom he could instinctively trust. There had been clashes between them in the past, but the lieutenant had always fought fairly. Choosing his words with great deliberation, The Phantom explained why he had come out of hiding to cross swords with Mr. Shei.

"That's just like The Gray Phantom," was Culligore's comment when he had finished. "You stick your head in the noose just because somebody else is copying your tricks. Well, anyhow, I admire your nerve. Too bad you and I belong to opposite camps. We could have a lot of fun tracking Mr. Shei together." He shook his head as if to banish a pleasing but impossible hope. "No use wishing things were different, though. I don't exactly like the idea, but I've got to take you along to headquarters."

"You will have to take me in an ambulance, then." There was a note of challenge in The Phantom's tones and his figure tensed perceptibly. "You'll never take me alive, Culligore. It simply can't be done. And you will have the scrap of your life before you take me dead. I am going to see this thing through if I have to fight the whole police department of New York City. The fact that Mr. Shei is stealing my tactics isn't the only reason. I learned something this morning that is of vastly more importance. By the way," and The Phantom fairly jabbed the question at the lieutenant, "have you seen anything of Miss Helen Hardwick?"

Culligore's lazy eyes opened a little wider. "Not since yesterday morning. She and I had quite an argument about Mr. Shei. We were standing almost exactly where you and I are standing now. She knows how to fence with words. I haven't made up my mind yet whether she or I got the best of the argument."

The Phantom smiled despite his impatience. "What did she think of Mr. Shei?"

"How can anybody tell what a woman thinks? You can make a guess, of course, but the chances are either that you are wrong or that you are making just exactly the kind of guess she wants you to make. Miss Hardwick left me pretty much up in the air, but I have a feeling all the time that she had discovered something that led her to think that you were Mr. Shei."

"Oh," mumbled the Phantom; then he stood silent for a few moments. "Where did Miss Hardwick go from here?"

Culligore shrugged. "Ask me something easy. She walked out of that door, and that's all I'm sure of. There was another question or two I wanted to ask her, and that's why I dropped around here today, thinking she might show up again. She seemed very much wrought up over Mr. Shei."

With an impetuous gesture The Phantom placed his hand on the lieutenant's arm.

"Miss Hardwick has disappeared," he announced quickly, "and I fear she has blundered into the clutches of Mr. Shei."

"Eh?" The mask of listlessness dropped in a twinkling from Culligore's face. He was instantly tense and alert. "What's that?"

"I called up her home this morning. Nobody seems to know what has become of her. A little later I received a telephone message warning me that— But I see I shall have to tell you the whole story in order to make things clear." Briefly The Phantom related his encounter with Mr. Fairspeckle, the events that had occurred at the apartment of the retired financier, and finally the warning message that had come over the wire. "Now you can understand," he concluded, "why I don't intend to submit to arrest until Miss Hardwick has been found."

Culligore's cigar had gone out while The Phantom was speaking. Now he lighted it again, sent a few clouds of smoke curling toward the ceiling, then peered intently into The Phantom's face. Finally he jerked his head up and down as if he had seen a light.

"The thing to do," he declared, "is to take the shortest route and go direct to Mr. Shei and ask him what he has done with Miss Hardwick."

The Phantom laughed bitterly. "Beautifully simple! The only difficulty is that we haven't the slightest idea who Mr. Shei is or where to find him. Otherwise your suggestion is capital."

An odd smile curled Culligore's lips. "Sometimes The Gray Phantom isn't playing in very good form. But then every man gets a bit foolish when he has a girl on the brain. Your thinking cap isn't on straight today, or you wouldn't have let Fairspeckle pull the wool over your eyes the way he did."

"Fairspeckle? You don't think—"

"He acted oddly all morning, didn't he?"

"Yes, but—"

"And didn't he try to put you to sleep by drugging your coffee?"

"True, but he—"

"And didn't you see him typing the notices with Mr. Shei's name at the bottom?"

"But the telephone message?"

"Yes, I know," said Culligore patiently. "That's where he duped you to a brown finish. You would have seen the trick at once if your thinking machinery had been in good condition. I don't know Fairspeckle, but from what you have told me he must be a sharp one. My experience has taught me never to trust a man who can't sleep nights. It's a bad conscience that keeps him awake in the first place, and a man suffering from loss of sleep is likely to go in for any kind of deviltry. Maybe that's what happened to Fairspeckle. Anyhow, the way he pulled the wool over your eyes proves he is a slick one."

"Then you think Fairspeckle is Mr. Shei?"

"If he isn't, why should he be typing those notices? Just look at it this way. Fairspeckle saw that you suspected him. He didn't like that a bit. To throw you off your guard, he pretended to suspect *you*. You caught him with the goods when you saw him typing the notices. Right away you started in denouncing him as Mr. Shei. Then, right in the midst of a dramatic moment, the telephone rings. The voice at the other end asks for you. You're told that Mr. Shei is speaking and that Miss Hardwick will suffer unless you keep hands off. That gives you a jolt, of course, and all you can think of is the girl. You don't stop to question whether the man at the other end is really Mr. Shei. For all you know he might be Tom Brown or Bill Jones, but you're too excited to think of that. I don't blame you. I'd been just as easy if I had been in your place."

A blank look crossed The Phantom's face while Culligore was speaking. It was quickly followed by an expression of mingling comprehension and self-disgust.

"I see it now. I've been as gullible as a ten-year-old. The message purporting to come from Mr. Shei was meant to divert my suspicions from Fairspeckle. He might have been prepared for some such emergency, or else he signaled Haiuto while I wasn't looking. The Japanese could easily have gotten in touch with one of the members of Fairspeckle's gang and instructed him to call me up and give me the prearranged message. But just how it was done doesn't matter. The important point is that I was taken in. I am wondering now whether the threat in regard to Miss Hardwick was pure bluff, or whether she is really in danger."

"I wouldn't take chances," cautioned Culligore. "If I were you I would call on Mr. Fairspeckle tonight and have a confidential chat with him. He may not want to talk, but maybe you can persuade him. Of course, as an officer of the law, I must warn you there mustn't be any rough stuff." Culligore's twinkling eyes gazed toward the ceiling.

"Then you have abandoned your intention of dragging me over to headquarters?"

Culligore did not answer directly, but the faint grin on his lips was eloquent. "I would advise you to watch your step," he said softly. "The moment it becomes known that The Gray Phantom is in town, there will be the niftiest little man hunt you ever saw. I wish you luck. In the meantime, I'm going to tackle the case from another angle. I'd give a pair of pink socks to know just when, where, and how Mr. Shei is going to strike."

He tilted his chin against his hand and lapsed into deep thought. When he looked up, several minutes later, The Phantom was gone. Very softly, with a twinkle in his eyes, he stepped to a recess in the wall toward which he had cast an occasional furtive glance during his talk with The Phantom. On a marble shelf extended across the niche were a number of potted ferns, and behind them was a small window, artistically decorated to render it opaque.

Culligore, noticing that it stood open a crack, pricked up his ears and listened. From the other side came a faint, scraping sound, as if someone were hiding there.

Culligore nodded elatedly as he tiptoed away. He seemed immensely gratified at having verified his suspicion that his interview with The Gray Phantom had been overheard.

CHAPTER XII
MR. SHEI STRIKES

A FINE DRIZZLE WAS in the air and the street lights emitted a blurred and languid sheen. For an hour The Gray Phantom had been pacing the sidewalk across the street from the Whipple Hotel, impatiently waiting for the lights in Mr. Fairspeckle's suite to go out. His coat collar was turned up and the brim of his soft hat was pulled low over his forehead. Taking Culligore's warning to heart, he had resolved not to endanger his project by running unnecessary risks.

The passing pedestrians gave him scarcely a glance, and he told himself that the inclement weather was a point in his favor. Evidently neither Culligore nor Starr had mentioned his presence in the city, for he could see no signs of accelerated activity on the part of the police, as there would have been if the news had leaked out that The Gray Phantom had come out of hiding. The solitary watcher whom he had seen from the window of Mr. Fairspeckle's bedroom earlier in the day had evidently quitted his task, for he was nowhere in sight.

Throughout the late afternoon and early evening, The Phantom had been harassed by fears for Helen's safety. At times he had scarcely been able to control his impatience, but his eagerness had been cooled by the knowledge that a headlong rush into danger would only render the situation worse. His interview with Culligore had not only helped to clarify his mind, but it had left him with a renewed conviction that the emaciated and dour-looking ex-financier was Mr. Shei.

Again he cast a speculative glance at the windows of Mr. Fairspeckle's apartment. All the lights but one had been extinguished since he last looked in that direction, and he guessed that the occupant had retired to his bedroom. His imagination pictured the old man sleeplessly pacing the floor, chuckling softly to himself while his mind evolved nefarious schemes. It was The Phantom's plan to take him completely by surprise and if possible wring a confession from him. But above all else he was determined to ascertain whether Fairspeckle knew anything about Helen's whereabouts.

He waited fifteen minutes longer, then adjusted his hat and collar and walked briskly across the street. With the air of one belonging on the premises he entered the hotel and, not thinking it safe to use the elevator, walked toward the stairway in the rear. A few drowsy loungers sat in chairs in the lobby, and the clerk was engaged with a late arrival, so no one noticed him. The long, heavily carpeted hallways were silent and deserted, for the Whipple was catering chiefly to the staid and respectable element that retires early and sleeps soundly.

The Phantom ascended three flights of stairs, then turned down the corridor toward Mr. Fairspeckle's apartment. Reaching the door, he stopped and listened, but no sound came from the interior. After a cautious glance behind him, he took from his pocket a compact case which he always carried when engaged in enterprises like the present, and from its silk-lined grooves extracted a small metallic tool. In a few moments the lock had yielded to his deft manipulation, and he stepped inside.

Again he stopped and listened. The hallway in which he stood was lighted only by a tiny electric bulb in the ceiling, and its glow was so faint that the surrounding objects were scarcely distinguishable. At first he could not hear the slightest sound, and he was about to proceed when a curious impression caused him to draw in his steps. Perhaps his imagination was deceiving him, but he thought someone was sobbing, and he had a distinct impression that the sounds were coming from the door at his left.

In an instant he had pressed his ear against the keyhole. Now he could heard the sounds quite clearly, but the soblike effect was gone, and instead they made him think of someone gasping and spluttering. Mystified, he tried the lock and pushed the door open. The room was dark, and he ran his hand along the wall until he found the electric switch. As the light flashed on, a mutter of amazement fell from his lips.

On a bed at the farther end of the room, with hands and feet bound and a gag firmly adjusted to his mouth, lay Haiuto. The servant, a look of mute pleading in his bulging eyes, was tugging impotently at the ropes around his ankles and wrists.

"What's happened?" sharply inquired The Phantom, but renewed splutterings called his attention to the fact that the gag prevented Haiuto from speaking. He removed the cloth while repeating the question. Haiuto, breathing hard, licked the bruised portion of his mouth.

"Don't know," he finally managed to say. "I sleep. Then noise at door. Before I can get up, somebody walk in. All is dark, like tomb of Iyeyasu. I get awful crack on head. Then sleep again. Don't know anything else."

With a moan Haiuto sank back against the pillow. A startling suspicion flashed through The Phantom's mind. Without troubling to release the servant's limbs, he ran from the room and opened a door at the farther end of the hall. He had thought it led into Fairspeckle's bedroom, but his sense of direction had become somewhat confused, and he found himself in the library instead. Faintly through the darkness he glimpsed the bright nickel trimmings of the typewriter at which the ex-financier had been at work earlier in the day. He groped his way across the floor, turning in the direction where he thought Fairspeckle's bedroom was. A soft tinkle brought him to a dead stop.

The telephone was ringing! Acting on impulse, he fumbled about in the dark till he found the instrument, then lifted the receiver to his ear and spoke a low response into the transmitter. The answering voice sent a quiver through his being. He recognized it at once, for he had heard it before.

"Mr. Shei speaking," it was saying, and the cold, precise tones were edged with a taunt. "I perceive you have chosen to disregard the warning I gave you a few hours ago. Unless you abandon your plans at once, Miss Hardwick will die. That is absolutely final."

A faint click signified that the connection was broken. For a few moments The Phantom stood rigid, scarcely able to comprehend the import of the message. It had been spoken in tones so emphatic and sinister that he was left in no doubt regarding the speaker's sincerity. But how had the man at the other end of the wire learned that The Phantom was in Fairspeckle's apartment? The telephone call, coming a few minutes after The Phantom's arrival, had been so accurately timed as to indicate that he had been followed to the Whipple. Yet that did not seem quite possible, for he had been particularly alert against that very thing.

Finally he put the telephone down. He tried to stifle the new and poignant misgivings with which the voice had inspired him. He remembered the other message he had received from the person purporting to be Mr. Shei. He had been deceived then, unless his own and Culligore's deductions were all wrong, and he would not be so easily imposed upon again. Doubtless the second message, like the first, was only a clever hoax on Fairspeckle's part. Well, in a few moments he would probably know the truth.

His fears and doubts were only partly quieted when he stepped softly from the room. Time and again there flashed through his mind a suspicion that something was wrong with the theory Culligore had implanted in his mind, but his thoughts in this direction were hazy. The binding and gagging of Haiuto was a disquieting and perplexing circumstance that did not seem to fit into the woof of the lieutenant's ideas in regard to Fairspeckle.

The Phantom passed through another door, then stopped short and stared in astonishment at the scene that met his eyes.

He was in Mr. Fairspeckle's bedroom. A single electric light, the one he had seen while standing on the sidewalk opposite the hotel, glowed softly in a wall fixture. In a morris chair in the middle of the room, with the folds of a dressing gown hanging loosely over his bony frame, sat W. Rufus Fairspeckle. He sat so still that, if his eyes had been closed, The Phantom would have suspected that he was either asleep or dead. He was bound and gagged in the same manner as Haiuto had been, but it struck The Phantom as vaguely significant that his right arm was bared to the elbow.

As he stepped closer, he became oddly impressed by the strange expression in the old man's eyes. They looked straight ahead in a fixed, unseeing way, and there was a gleam of merriment in their dim depths that clashed sharply with the pallor on the shrunken cheeks. It seemed as though Fairspeckle's soul was indulging in fancies of which his physical self was unaware, and the whole effect impressed The Phantom as uncanny.

He leaned forward and examined the exposed arm. Just below the muscles of the elbow, and directly over one of the smaller veins, was a puncture and a congealed drop of blood. The puncture was so small that it might have been inflicted with a needle prick. In a roundabout way The Phantom's mind went back to the scene in the Thelma Theater as it had been pictured in the newspapers, and with an inward start he remembered that just such a puncture had been found on the right arm of Virginia Darrow.

Though as yet he could not grasp the meaning of it, the coincidence acted as an electric shock on his nerves. He tore away the gag from the old man's lips and vigorously shook his arm.

"What's the matter?" he inquired.

The red eyelids quivered a little. The look of hilarity flickering in the depths of the orbs grew a trifle more pronounced. It was almost grewsome, but The Phantom's sense of perplexity was stronger than his repugnance.

"Can't you speak?" he asked sharply. "What is the meaning of this?"

Fairspeckle's chest heaved feebly. The motion was accompanied by a plucking movement of the fingers. The hands and feet strained impotently against the fettering cords. Then the lips fluttered, exposing a row of uneven teeth, and in the next instant a shiver ran down The Phantom's spine.

Through the fluttering lips came a laugh such as he had never before heard. It sounded hollow and cracked and as unreal as if produced by a mechanical contrivance. The Phantom had an uncanny sensation that the dead, if they were capable of producing sounds, might laugh just like that. Then he remembered the vivid descriptions he had read of the mocking laughter that had come from Virginia Darrow's dying lips, and a hazy suspicion entered his mind. He took a jack-knife from his pocket and swiftly slashed the cords around Fairspeckle's arms and legs.

Although released from his bonds, the man in the chair scarcely moved. The feet scraped gently against the floor, and the arms fell limply to his sides. Weird snatches of laughter were still trickling through his lips, but the expression of insane merriment in his eyes was slowly yielding to a look of returning reason.

The Phantom looked helplessly about him, and suddenly his eyes fell on a sheet of paper lying at the old man's feet. Mechanically he picked it up and glanced at the typewritten lines. From the smudged and indistinct type he was vaguely aware that he was gazing at a carbon copy. A word here and there attracted his attention, and presently he was reading the communication from the beginning. It read:

> Dear Friend: The poison which has been injected into your veins tonight has been accurately adjusted to produce death within seven days. You will have lucid intervals, but you will be gradu-ally growing weaker and weaker. Consult as many high-priced specialists as you wish, and if they can help you, you are to be congratulated. There is only one antidote, and that is the secret of a confederate of mine. It will be supplied you for a consideration. The exact terms will be communicated to you in a few days. By that time you will probably have been convinced
>
> that your life is absolutely in my hands.
>
> If misery loves company, I trust you will find consolation in the fact that six others are in precisely the same predicament as yourself.
>
> Mr. Shei.

The sheet dropped from The Phantom's fingers. If what he had just read seemed grotesque and absurd, a glance at the man in the chair conferred a semblance of hideous reality upon it. Mr. Shei had struck the threatened blow, and he had struck sooner than expected.

Fairspeckle's laughter had ceased and a look of reason was coming into his waxen features. The expression of ribald mockery had left his eyes, and now they were fixed on The Phantom's face in a dull, suspicious stare. With a start The Phantom awoke to a realization of his predicament. If he were caught in Fairspeckle's apartment, the police and the public would be firmly convinced of what they already suspected—that Mr. Shei and The Phantom were one. Not even Culligore's keen mind and generous impulses would suffice to save him from arrest and imprisonment. And there was Helen—the thought gave him a spinal chill. Perhaps at this very moment she was confronted by some terrifying peril. And if he were arrested, then his last chance of helping her would be gone.

His mind made up, The Phantom ran to the telephone in the adjoining room. He called a number, and presently he was answered by an operator at police headquarters. His inquiry for Culligore elicited the information that the lieutenant was out and would probably not return until morning. The Phantom hesitated for a moment, then spoke hurriedly into the transmitter:

"This is important. Send a doctor and a couple of detectives at once to the Whipple Hotel, suite 36. You will find something very interesting. That's all."

With that he hung up, and a few moments later he had left the apartment and was briskly walking down the stairs.

CHAPTER XIII
A MESSAGE FROM MR. SHEI

THE CITY, CONSUMING THE news of Mr. Shei's amazing coup along with its coffee and toast the following morning, reacted to the sensation much as a child might react to the sight of a fabled monster. The whole affair seemed monstrous, unbelievable—and yet the facts could not be reasoned away. Seven of the city's wealthiest men had been inoculated with a malady of such a mysterious nature that the most celebrated physicians in New York City had admitted they were unable to diagnose it.

An air of bafflement and suspense hung over the city. Mr. Shei's name was on every tongue, and the blow he had struck was discussed by groups that gathered on street corners, in cafés, and in public squares. Among the seven victims were several of the most important capitalists in the country, so the effect of Mr. Shei's astounding maneuver was an assault on the financial nerve center of the nation.

The name that, next to Mr. Shei's, was most often spoken in the street corner discussions, was that of The Gray Phantom. The spectacular nature of the coup, as well as the daring and resourcefulness exhibited by its perpetrator, seemed ample proof that The Gray Phantom had returned to his old ways under the *nom de guerre* of Mr. Shei. No one else, it was argued, could have engineered an achievement of such magnitude without bungling and falling into the clutches of the police. Already wagers were being placed on The Phantom's ability to evade capture until he should have consummated his plans.

At ten o'clock, just as newsboys were raucously crying the latest extras, a taxicab stopped before a dingy establishment in a squalid and disreputable section of the lower East Side. The Gray Phantom alighted, hurriedly tossed the driver a bill, then disappeared in a basement entrance. The door was opened by a surly-looking man wearing a soiled apron, and The Phantom took a seat at one of the tables in the rear. He looked nervously at his watch. Lieutenant Culligore, whom he had reached by telephone at police headquarters, had promised to meet him at ten sharp, and he had suggested Lefty Joe's place as a reasonably safe rendezvous.

The Phantom cast a slanting glance at the rough-looking customers scattered about the place, and just then the door opened and Culligore walked in and took a seat beside him.

"Any luck?" inquired the lieutenant, though the question seemed superfluous in view of The Phantom's dejected appearance.

"None. That's why I wanted a talk with you. How is Fairspeckle?"

The lieutenant, a little bleary-eyed and with a trace of diffidence in his manners, looked questioningly at the questioner. "Why single out Fairspeckle? He's in the same boat with the six others. Neither better nor worse, though the doctors say his age and poor health will weigh against him."

"You still think that Fairspeckle is Mr. Shei?"

Culligore hesitated. A thin, inscrutable smile hovered above his lips.

"If he is, he gave himself a dose of his own medicine," was his final comment.

"And that's precisely what I think he did." The Phantom, speaking in low tones, gave the table a resounding thwack. "Being one of the city's richest men, he knew suspicion was apt to turn in his direction, unless he was inoculated along with the others. He is easily one of the seven wealthiest men in town, and it would have looked odd if he had been omitted. And so, to ward off suspicion, he had a dose of the poison injected into his own veins, though I suppose the amount was carefully adjusted so it would produce the characteristic symptoms without causing death."

Culligore appeared to ponder. "Not bad reasoning," he remarked. "That would be on a par with the trick he played on you yesterday. Fairspeckle seems to be a shrewd old fox, the kind that isn't overlooking any bets. Maybe you're right. In that case, of course, the binding and gagging of the Jap was a blind."

The Phantom nodded.

"Well, whoever Mr. Shei is, he certainly put one over last night," was Culligore's rueful comment. "He seems to have a gang of highly trained followers who do exactly as he tells them without batting an eyelid. Last night, between ten o'clock and two in the morning, he sent one or more of his men to the homes of each of the seven victims. In two or three instances the servants were bribed, I understand. Anyhow, Mr. Shei's men got in by some hook or crook. Four of the seven were caught in bed and trussed up before they could say Jack Robinson. Two of the others were tapped on the back of the head when they returned home from the theater, and one got his in a taxicab. Mr. Shei made a clean sweep."

"What do the doctors say?"

"Most of them are doing some fancy stalling to cover up what they don't know. The high muckamucks of the profession are holding a consultation this morning to decide what's to be done. One of them let slip the information that the symptoms look something like a combination of rabies and delirium tremens, but he believes the disease is produced by one of the ancient poisons that were known to the Asiatics. The fact that the doctors are keeping mum is a bad sign. It will be interesting to see how many of the patients will cough up Mr. Shei's price for the antidote. If all of them come across, Mr. Shei will rake in a good many millions."

"Billions, rather, I should say." The Phantom smiled wearily. "If successful, the experiment will be unique in that it will demonstrate just how much a billionaire considers his life to be worth. But that isn't what I wanted to talk with you about. Culligore, I still think that Fairspeckle knows where Miss Hardwick can be found."

"Well?" Culligore gazed noncommittally into space.

"I wonder if some sort of pressure couldn't be brought to bear on him to make him divulge what he knows. Last night he was in no condition to be questioned, and today, I can hardly make a move without running the risk of being arrested."

"I should say you can't!" declared Culligore explosively. "It's as much as my job is worth to be seen here talking with you. The Gray Phantom is a marked man, if ever there was one. Fairspeckle and the Jap swear you were in the apartment late last night, and Fairspeckle believes—or pretends to believe, which amounts to the same thing—that it was you who squirted the poison into his veins. Of course, he doesn't pretend to know just how it happened, but he remembers seeing you just as he was recovering his senses. You'd better take my advice and lie low for a while. I'll see what I can do with Fairspeckle, though I haven't any high hopes. I'll have him watched, and it's just possible that we can squeeze some information out of him. But look here. Aren't you starting this thing from the wrong end?"

The Phantom gave him a puzzled glance.

"When Miss Hardwick left the Thelma Theater day before yesterday," pursued Culligore, "I could have sworn she was on her way to see you. She didn't say anything about her plans, but that was the idea I got from her actions."

The Phantom shook his head. "If she started for my place, she never got there. I called up on the long distance this morning, and was told that nothing has been seen of her. Of course, something may have happened to her on the way."

"Well, I wouldn't worry just yet. The young lady has a lot of spunk, and I'll bet a pair of pink socks she knows how to take care of herself. It mightn't be a bad idea to get in touch with her father. He may have had some news from her since yesterday. I must be on my way. Mr. Shei is putting gray hairs on my head."

Culligore rose, and the two men shook hands. They parted after the lieutenant had once more admonished The Phantom against exposing himself to arrest. For a moment or two after the detective had left the place, The Phantom looked dubiously at the door through which he had departed.

"There's something strange about Culligore," he mumbled. "I wonder if he—"

He did not finish the thought, but with a shrug of the shoulders he stepped out and looked warily up and down the sidewalk. Culligore's warning had not been needed to impress upon him that caution was necessary. He sniffed danger in the very air he breathed as he slunk across the street, walked a block to the east, then ducked into a deserted doorway. A taxicab appeared, and he signaled the driver. For a moment he hesitated as to his next move, then Culligore's parting advice occurred to him and, after consulting the small notebook he carried, he gave the chauffeur the address of the Hardwick residence.

The cab started. The Phantom glanced sharply through the windows. A familiar and yet intangible sensation had been with him constantly for the past hour. Now and then, at long intervals, he had had a fleeting impression that he was being watched. Now, as the cab chugged its way down the avenue, a sixth sense told him he was being followed, yet he could detect no sign of pursuit in the welter of traffic. He tried to dismiss the impression, knowing that in his present state of high mental tension his senses were not to be trusted.

He alighted in front of a modest brownstone house, its rigid exterior relieved by sprawling vines and flowers in the window boxes. The female servant who opened the door announced that Mr. Hardwick was at home, and The Phantom gently pushed past her. In the room he entered, a thin, stoop-shouldered man was pacing back and forth with hands clasped at his back. He stopped abruptly at sight of The Phantom and peered blankly into the visitor's face.

"You know me?" inquired The Phantom.

"It's—it can't be—The Gray Phantom?" A startled look appeared in Mr. Hardwick's deeply furrowed face. He came a few steps nearer. "But you *are* The Gray Phantom, I see. I recognize you from your photographs. Where is my daughter?"

The Phantom was a trifle taken aback by the sharply spoken question. "Then you have received no word from her? I telephoned your house shortly after my arrival in the city and was told she had been missing for twenty-four hours. I was in hopes you might have heard from her this morning. That's why I called."

"I have not seen my daughter since breakfast day before yesterday," explained Mr. Hardwick in quavering tones. "In the afternoon I received a brief message from her announcing she did not expect to be home for dinner and telling me not to worry. She is an impetuous child, and it isn't the first time she has caused me anxiety. Her message made me very uneasy, for she had been acting strangely ever since—since—"

"Since the affair at the Thelma Theater," guessed The Phantom. "Listen, Mr. Hardwick. I am as deeply concerned in what has happened to her as you can possibly be. I intend to find her, no matter where she may be. Can you trust me?"

Mr. Hardwick's dim eyes searched The Phantom's face for a long time. At first there was a look of doubt and suspicion in the old man's countenance, but it faded gradually away.

"I believe I can," he declared. "I know what your past has been, and I confess I have disapproved strongly of the friendship between you and my daughter. She is still impressionable and there are romantic notions in her head, and you will forgive me if I say that you did not seem quite the proper person for her to associate with."

"I can understand that," murmured The Phantom. "Your attitude was quite natural in view of the circumstances."

"And so," continued Mr. Hardwick, "when your letters came I did not feel justified in giving them to her. I was not unappreciative of what you had done for her and me, but I feared she might form an unsuitable attachment. In short, I destroyed the letters after a glance at the handwriting on the envelope."

The Phantom smiled faintly. "I know you acted for what you thought your daughter's best interests. It is not for me to criticise your conduct in the matter. I can readily see— But wait." The Phantom's brow suddenly clouded. "How many letters did you intercept?"

"I think there were two. One came in the spring; the other late in the summer. Yes, I am quite sure there were only two."

The Phantom's narrowing gaze swept the older man's face. His lips tightened into a grim line. "The letter I mailed in the spring was the one in which I told your daughter of my removal from Azurecrest to Sea Glimpse," he explained in tense tones. "I had promised to keep her informed of my movements so that she could communicate with me if she should ever need me." He paused for a moment. "Have you any idea where your daughter might have gone? Didn't she say anything that suggested what her plans were?"

"She talked rather incoherently at breakfast, but said nothing about intending to go away. When I received her message later in the day, it occurred to me that she might have gone in search of you. You had been mentioned several times in our talks together, and I thought that—"

"If her intention was to find me, she probably went to the wrong place," gravely interrupted The Phantom. "Not knowing of my removal to Sea Glimpse, she naturally would look for me at Azurecrest. I sold the place through a broker and never even learned the name of the present owner. But her going to Azurecrest doesn't explain her absence for the past twenty-four hours. She would naturally return at once upon learning that I was not there. The trip by train takes only two or three hours. I fear something must have happened to her on the way. Well, we shall soon learn—"

He dashed across the room, snatched up the telephone from its stand in a corner, and, after being connected with the long-distance operator, gave his old number at Azurecrest. A wait followed. The Phantom stood tense and rigid, while Mr. Hardwick dazedly drew his palm across his forehead. He gazed expectantly at The Phantom while the latter spoke briefly into the transmitter. Finally, with a puzzled look in his face, The Phantom hung up.

"The present owner of Azurecrest is a Mr. Slade," he announced. "I just had him on the wire. He tells me nothing has been seen of Miss Hardwick, or of any person resembling her."

Mr. Hardwick looked as if he did not quite know whether to feel relieved or discouraged. The Phantom grasped his hand.

"Don't worry," he said in a tone of hopefulness which he was far from feeling. "We will find your daughter. I shall communicate with you as soon as I learn something."

He squeezed the older man's hand and walked out. Though he could not understand why, his interview with Hardwick and his brief talk with Slade had intensified his fears and misgivings. It seemed as though the mystery of Helen's disappearance had become darker and deeper. Suddenly, as he stood irresolute on the doorstep, he heard someone call his name. A limousine had silently drawn up at the curb, its sides of burnt sienna flashing brilliantly in the sunlight, and at the window, beckoning him with a smile and a nod, he saw a woman's face. He stepped forward, and the woman leaned slightly from the window.

"If you will step in," she whispered, "you may learn something of interest concerning the young person you are looking for."

The door opened invitingly. The words had exerted a magical effect on The Phantom, and without a moment's hesitation he entered. As the car glided away, he noticed that the woman had a young, dark face, a figure almost serpentine in its slenderness, and that there was an air of gay insouciance about her smartly embroidered frock and rakish picture hat that seemed to clash with the subtlety and craftiness expressed by her pale-green eyes.

"You are very reckless, my dear Phantom," she murmured. "Please don't ask to what happy circumstance you owe the invitation to ride with me. I abhor ceremonious speeches. I am Fay Dale, though that probably don't interest you, and I have a message for you from Mr. Shei."

The bluntness of the statement made The Phantom catch his breath. He wondered whether it was the vivacious eyes of Fay Dale that had been following him all morning and giving him the haunting impression of being watched.

"As I said, you are very reckless," Miss Dale went on. "Twice within the last two days you have been warned to abandon the course you are pursuing, and you have paid no heed whatever. There's such a thing as carrying audacity to a fault, you know. Doesn't the safety of a certain young lady mean anything to you at all?"

"Everything!" exclaimed The Phantom impulsively. "You said you had something to tell me about her."

"I have, but you mustn't be impatient. I have something very important to tell you. You have seen fit to meddle in an affair that doesn't concern you in the least. You have been warned that your conduct is endangering the life of the young lady, but evidently you have not taken the warnings seriously. I can assure you that Mr. Shei never makes idle threats. It is his wish that you leave New York at once."

A taunting laugh was on The Phantom's lips, but he held it back. "Why?" he demanded.

"Because Mr. Shei doesn't care to have you interfere with him. He is now engaged in the most important enterprise of his life, and he would rather not be opposed by such a formidable enemy as yourself. I shall be perfectly frank with you, even at the risk of inflating your vanity. You are the only man of whom Mr. Shei stands in fear. He has a profound respect for your genius. He laughs at the police and snaps his fingers at public opinion, but he knows The Gray Phantom is a dangerous adversary. At this particular time he can brook no opposition. That's why he requests you to leave New York immediately."

"I am flattered," murmured The Phantom, gazing reflectively out of the car window. "What I cannot understand is how Mr. Shei learned of my plans."

Miss Dale gave an amused laugh. "One of Mr. Shei's agents saw you in Times Square the morning you arrived. You have been watched ever since. Mr. Shei has sources of information that would amaze you if I were to tell you about them. And he is just as resourceful in other ways. Don't you think you had better swallow your pride and comply with his wishes?"

"Suppose I were to refuse?" The Phantom temporized, trying hard to restrain his impatience.

Miss Dale looked straight into his eyes. There was a hint of cruelty in her tightly compressed lips.

"There are ways of breaking even such a stubborn will as yours," she coldly declared. "The young lady is absolutely in Mr. Shei's power. That gives him a means of persuasion that ought to impress even you. Nothing in the world can save her if you disobey his wishes."

Her tones carried an emphasis that caused The Phantom to give her a sharp glance. There was a curl to her lips and a gleam in her eyes that impressed him even more strongly than her words. His mind worked quickly.

"If Mr. Shei will return Miss Hardwick safely to her home, I will leave New York on the next train," he promised.

She laughed frigidly. "You must think Mr. Shei is a fool. He would lose his hold over you the moment he released Miss Hardwick, and what guarantee would he have that you would carry out your promise?"

"My word of honor."

"It would be enough under ordinary circumstances, but not in this case. Evidently you do not realize the gravity of Miss Hardwick's position, or you would not quarrel with Mr. Shei's terms." She shrugged her slight shoulders. "Well, you shall soon be convinced that Mr. Shei is not to be trifled with. From Miss Hardwick's own lips you shall learn what a desperate predicament she is in. After that, my dear Phantom, I think you will be more amenable to reason."

There was a question on The Phantom's tongue, but just then the car drew up in front of an apartment house facing Central Park, and Miss Dale conducted him through an ornate entrance, then up three flights in the elevator, and a little gasp of admiration escaped The Phantom as they passed into an exquisitely furnished apartment. Save for the prevalence of the feminine touch, exemplified in gorgeous but meaningless trifles and gewgaws, it met the emphatic approval of The Phantom's discriminating eye.

Miss Dale excused herself and entered an adjoining room, and he was left alone for a few minutes. He strained his ears and listened. From faint sounds coming through the closed door he imagined she was at the telephone. The cold gleam in her eyes as he had helped her from the car was still haunting him, and he wondered what she had meant when she promised that from Helen's own lips should he learn the nature of her predicament.

The frigid, insinuating smile was still on her lips when she returned to the room in which she had left him.

"Your curiosity shall be gratified in a few moments," she announced, seating herself and regarding him with a cold, impersonal gaze. There was an air of quiet self-reliance and efficiency about her that enabled him to understand how she could be a valuable assistant to Mr. Shei. Neither spoke, and presently the silence was interrupted by the ringing of the telephone in the other room.

"Answer, please," she said lightly, the faintest trace of malignant satisfaction in her tones. "I think Miss Hardwick is on the wire."

Puzzled and tormented by vague suspicions, The Phantom passed to the telephone. The woman followed a short distance behind.

"Hello," he said tensely.

He started violently as he recognized the answering voice. He would have known it among a million voices despite the hysterical catch and the staccato accents that tended to disguise it. It spoke a few jumbled and disconnected phrases, then broke into a stream of loud and wild laughing in which he detected the same note of maniacal glee that had characterized the ghastly laughter of W. Rufus Fairspeckle.

CHAPTER XIV
THE ELUSIVE MR. SHEI

SPASMODICALLY THE GRAY PHANTOM pressed the receiver closer to his ear. The laughter at the other end of the wire rose to a shrill crescendo, then ended abruptly in a harsh and discordant twang.

"Helen!" shouted The Phantom.

No answer came; nothing but a muffled thud that sounded as if the person at the other end had suddenly dropped the receiver. His face white, The Phantom turned to Miss Dale.

"Are you convinced now?" she murmured, a silken smile hovering about her lips. "And don't you think you had better obey Mr. Shei's wishes and leave the city immediately?"

The Phantom mopped the clammy perspiration from his forehead. A moment ago his face had been distorted from horror; now a look of rage glittered menacingly in his eyes. "Mr. Shei will pay for this," he muttered thickly. "When I have finished with him, he will wish he had never been born."

"And just what do you propose to do?" Miss Dale airily waved her slim, white hand. "As a measure of self-protection, knowing that he could not control you by any other means, Mr. Shei has caused Miss Hardwick to be inoculated with the same malady that killed Miss Darrow, and which will kill seven of the city's wealthiest men unless they comply with his wishes. There is only one thing which can save her, and that is the antidote. It is in the possession of a Malayan scientist, one of Mr. Shei's most devoted followers, and it will be administered only when you have carried out the terms I have explained to you."

The Phantom stood silent while trying to fight down the surge of emotions that threatened to swamp his reason. Suddenly his roving gaze was fixed on the numbered tag above the mouthpiece of the telephone instrument. His lids contracted a little.

"Brilliant idea, my dear Phantom," drawled Miss Dale. "For once you are quite transparent. It is your intention, as soon as you leave my apartment, to call up the telephone exchange and trace the call, thus learning Miss Hardwick's whereabouts. It would be simple, for it was a long-distance connection, and such calls are always recorded. I will save you the trouble, however. Miss Hardwick is at Azurecrest."

"Azurecrest?" echoed The Phantom, momentarily a trifle dazed.

Miss Dale seemed to find his perplexity highly amusing. "When Mr. Shei learned the place was for sale, he bought it anonymously through an agent. It seemed an ideal spot for certain experiments he had in mind. Hoping to find you there, Miss Hardwick went to Azurecrest the day after Miss Darrow's death, and for divers reasons it was thought best to detain her."

The Phantom muttered an exclamation. Slade had lied to him, then, when The Phantom had called up Azurecrest earlier in the day and inquired for Miss Hardwick. Slade, he now suspected, was one of Mr. Shei's agents, and under the circumstances it was not surprising that he had disclaimed all knowledge of Helen. The Phantom might not have accepted his denial so readily if he had had the faintest inkling that Mr. Shei was the present owner of his former retreat.

Suddenly he whirled round on his heels and started abruptly from the room.

"Wait a moment," commanded Miss Dale as he reached the door, and a subtle quality in her tone caused him to stop. "How impulsive you are, my dear Phantom. I suppose you mean to rush madly off to Azurecrest and rescue the fair damsel. Stop and think for a moment. Surely you don't imagine I would have told you Miss Hardwick's whereabouts unless I had been absolutely certain that you were powerless to act."

The Phantom saw the weight of the argument at once. He moved away from the door.

"Glad you are willing to listen to reason," murmured Miss Dale. "You see, you could accomplish nothing at all by going to Azurecrest alone. The place is very carefully guarded by a little army of picked men, not to mention a few savage dogs. Of course, you might ask the police for assistance, supposing that you were on good terms with them, but what would be the result? If Mr. Shei and his followers are put in jail, Miss Hardwick will die, and so will the seven others. In fact, if anything at all happens to Mr. Shei and the members of his organization, the antidote will be irrevocably lost. I believe you grasp the idea, don't you?"

The Phantom's expression showed that he did. There was a baffled look in his eye that testified to his thorough appreciation of Mr. Shei's ingenious precautions.

"In other words," Miss Dale went on, her tones now soft and purring, "you have the best reasons in the world for not wishing the police to annoy Mr. Shei. In a way, Mr. Shei has compelled you to become an ally of his as a result of having Miss Hardwick in his power. It is really an excellent arrangement. And the police, when they understand the situation, will not be inclined to risk the lives of the seven wealthy men by forcing Mr. Shei to take extreme measures. Ah, you are beginning to understand at last that Mr. Shei is practically invulnerable."

"So it would seem," mumbled The Phantom, at last finding his voice.

"And don't you think you had better be reasonable and accept Mr. Shei's conditions? If you decide to be sensible, the antidote will be administered to Miss Hardwick as soon as Mr. Shei's plans are consummated, and she will not be one whit the worse off for her experience. On the other hand, if you choose to be disagreeable—" Miss Dale paused significantly.

The Phantom's tense face bespoke a great mental effort. One by one he reviewed the details of Mr. Shei's brilliant precautions. He could not see a loop-hole anywhere. As far as his imagination could stretch, the only result of obstinacy would be certain death for Helen. Yet the cup of defeat was a bitter draft. Never before had The Gray Phantom surrendered to any man; but now the life of one dear to him was in danger. He made his decision promptly.

"Mr. Shei wins," he announced with a bow. Then he walked out, oblivious of the triumphant smile that curled Miss Dale's lips. His brow was clouded as he descended in the elevator and walked out on the sidewalk. He was aware that the dragnet was thrown out and that he was endangering his liberty by going about so boldly, but arrest and imprisonment seemed a minor matter now. For the first time in his life he was a defeated man. Worse still, he could not rid himself of fears concerning Helen's safety.

Presently he paused as a new and even more disturbing thought flashed through his mind. He had accepted Mr. Shei's terms in the hope that by doing so he would insure Helen's safety. He wondered if he had been too gullible, and he dodged into a doorway while considering the question. He had been under a terrific tension the past few days, and his mind had not been working with its customary agility. Now it occurred to him that he had nothing but Miss Dale's word for it that Helen's life would be spared if he yielded to Mr. Shei's terms. He had relied on her promise, not because of blind faith in her, but rather because Mr. Shei would gain nothing by killing Helen. He was merely using her as a means of suasion whereby to hold The Phantom in leash and prevent interference with his plans, and once she had served his purpose there was no reason why he should do her harm.

But The Phantom was far from satisfied. At Azurecrest, Helen must have heard and seen things that if divulged would constitute a great danger to Mr. Shei and his organization. Her keen perceptions and inquisitive nature were always delving into whatever was strange and mysterious. Would Mr. Shei dare let her live after her usefulness to him was past? Again, as he repeatedly asked himself the question, a cold perspiration broke out on The Phantom's brow.

Once more he made a quick decision, completely reversing the one he had made in Miss Dale's presence. He glanced quickly at his watch. If he remembered correctly, there would be a train for Azurecrest inside twenty minutes. Single-handed, relying only on his quick wits and agile strength, he would beard the lion in his den.

But first he was anxious to learn whether Culligore had made any progress toward clearing up the other phases of the mystery, particularly in regard to Mr. Fairspeckle. He entered a convenient telephone booth and called up the police department. Luck was with him, for after a brief delay he heard Culligore's voice over the wire.

"Oh, Fairspeckle! Why, he's vamoosed. Slipped away right from under the eyes of a doctor and a nurse. Can you beat it?"

The Phantom's veins tingled as he hung up. Fairspeckle's disappearance was final proof that he had correctly guessed the identity of Mr. Shei.

CHAPTER XV
DR. TAGALA

HELEN'S LITTLE WRIST WATCH showed a quarter past four.

Getting up from the chair, she roamed aimlessly about the room. Presently she stopped at the table and gazed down. The initials she had heedlessly scrawled in the dust were still there. The faint tracings that had betrayed her knowledge of Mr. Shei's identity seemed fraught with fate now. With a few idle strokes of the hand she had signed her own death warrant.

She could not have mistaken the sinister gleam she had seen in Slade's eyes as he looked down at the letters in the dust. His eyes had spelled her doom just as surely as the tracings on the table spelled the name by which Mr. Shei was known to the world at large. And the slam with which he had closed the door told even more eloquently than words that her life was forfeit.

Suddenly she felt a little hysterical. The fatal secret she had learned, the spectacular intrigues of Mr. Shei, even the scrawl in the dust seemed so trivial now that she felt an impulse to laugh. It was grotesque, she thought, that such a little thing as a couple of initials traced on the surface of a table should mean the blotting out of her life.

The house was very silent. No one had entered the room since Slade's departure, and she had spent the intervening hours in a state of musing detachment. Her thoughts and fancies flitted about in circles, and she had a curious impression that only her mind was functioning and that her emotions were numb. The slanting rays of the sun glimmered pleasantly on the furniture and she wondered abstractedly whether she should ever see the sunlight of another day. She glanced down at her dress, trimmed with delicate touches of red, and the thought struck her that perhaps she was wearing it for the last time. It was odd, she mused, that the prospect held no terror for her, and that her only feeling was a sense of dull, aching void.

Voices in the hall outside started her out of her reverie. The Gray Phantom's name, spoken in excited tones, sent an emotional quiver through her being and awoke her from her lethargy. Sensations, gentle and stimulating ones, stirred in the depths of her consciousness.

"The Gray Phantom," she whispered, looking pensively at the door. He had inspired her with emotions that she had never been quite able to understand. At times they had terrified her by their strangeness and power, for she had felt as if they were rousing new impulses within her and sweeping her along toward an unknown destiny. His career, bright and swift as the flash of a meteor, had intrigued her imagination even while she felt awed and a little frightened at the stories she heard about him. Of late he had tried to throw off the shackles of the past and start a new life, and she had watched his efforts with a strange and bewildering sense of sponsorship.

The voices in the hall had ceased now, but the name that had been spoken was still echoing in her ears and vibrating against hidden cords in her consciousness. Of a sudden the prospect of death, which a few minutes before she had contemplated without fear, filled her with dread and poignant regrets. The mere mention of a name had inspired in her a vehement desire to live.

She tiptoed to the door. It did not surprise her that Slade had left it unlocked. The picket fence, the ferocious Cæsar, and the attendants made such a precaution unnecessary. She stepped out in the hall, then looked hesitantly about her, but she could see nothing of the men whose voices she had heard a few moments ago. At the end of the hall a door stood open, and she moved silently in that direction. Entering, she ran her eyes over long white benches on which were bottles, jars, and odd-looking apparatus. There was a reek of chemicals in the air, and she guessed it was a laboratory of some sort. It all seemed a little strange to her, but in the next moment her attention was engaged by voices coming through a partly open door at one side of the large room.

"Oh, it's serious enough," one of them was saying, and she instantly knew that the speaker was Slade. "The Gray Phantom is the only man alive who can stop Mr. Shei's game."

The words were spoken in a tone of reluctant respect that gave Helen a thrill. Coming from an enemy, it was a striking tribute to The Phantom's genius and power.

"Ah, The Gray Phantom! I have heard the name. One of your fascinating master criminals, is he not?" The second man spoke with the exaggerated precision that characterizes the educated foreigner. "But why does The Gray Phantom interfere in the affairs of Mr. Shei?"

Slade chuckled grimly. "That's hard to tell, Doctor Tagala. Perhaps for a number of reasons. Maybe he dislikes to see another man excel him at his own game. There's such a thing as professional jealousy even among crooks, you know. All we know for certain is that he arrived in New York the day Mr. Shei's notices were posted. One of our men saw him, and he was watched almost from the moment of his arrival. His actions indicated plainly that he had gone on the warpath against Mr. Shei. Confound the infernal meddler!"

"But Mr. Shei is a resourceful man," observed Doctor Tagala. "He surely can devise some means whereby this impudent fellow may be restrained."

"He has already done so. As you know, he motored back to New York early this morning, but I had a long-distance telephone conversation with him a few minutes ago. He made a very good suggestion, but the execution of it will have to be left to you."

"To me?"

"You remember hearing me speak of the young lady who came here looking for The Gray Phantom. Her name is Helen Hardwick, and she is much too astute for her own good. She's learned a number of things that won't bear repeating, and among them is the identity of Mr. Shei. Of course, as soon as I found out how much she knew, I saw that she would have to be put out of the way, and I told Mr Shei so over the telephone. He over-ruled my plan; or, rather, he suggested an improvement."

"What was it?"

"To let the young lady remain on earth five or six days longer; in other words, until Mr. Shei had cashed in his chips. You see, doctor, The Gray Phantom has quite a crush on the young lady, and he would rather go through hell fire than have a single hair on her head hurt."

Helen felt the blood rushing to her head.

"I am beginning to comprehend," remarked Doctor Tagala. "It is Mr. Shei's plan to keep The Gray Phantom in check by threatening to inflict harm on the young lady. An excellent idea, but a trifle vague."

"Oh, there's nothing vague about it, and it involves something far more substantial than mere threats. Can't you guess, doctor?"

There came an interval of silence. Evidently Doctor Tagala was exercising his imagination. Helen crept a little closer, then peered through the narrow crack between the door and the jamb. Only two or three feet from her, with his lips curled into a leer, sat Slade. Her eyes traveled a little farther until she saw Doctor Tagala, and suddenly she caught her breath. It required all her self-control to keep from betraying her presence. She had seen the face twice before, first in the Thelma Theater and later at the window of the room in which Slade had interviewed her shortly after her arrival at Azurecrest, and on each occasion the sight had given her a chill. The coarse and brutal features, framed by black hair that reached almost to the shoulders, stood out in sharp contrast to the man's cultured speech and polished manners. Again, as she saw the brutish lips and the flaming eyes, she received an impression of something evil and loathsome. She leaned weakly against the wall, and then she heard again Doctor Tagala's voice.

"I am very poor at making conjectures. You will have to enlighten me."

"Well, then, Mr. Shei's orders are that you are to inoculate the young lady with the laughing fever. You will calculate the dose just as you did in the cases of the seven millionaires. The Phantom will be told that the antidotes will be administered on the one condition that he goes back to his bailiwick and keeps his hands out of Mr. Shei's affairs. That will keep him on his good behavior for a week, and by that time Mr. Shei will have cleaned up."

"And the young lady?"

Slade laughed unpleasantly. "She knows too much, as I have already told you. A little knowledge is a dangerous thing. Much knowledge is apt to prove fatal. You will merely forget to administer the antidote when the time comes."

Doctor Tagala gave a rumbling laugh. Helen felt a sudden chill. She leaned weakly against the wall. Inoculation with what Slade had called the laughing fever seemed far more dreadful than death itself.

"By the way, doctor," Slade went on, "I hope the antidote is safely hidden?"

"You may rest assured on that point," Tagala declared. "I have hidden it so securely that not even Mr. Shei knows where to find it."

"Good. That being the case, our seven millionaire friends would be in a bad fix if a sudden misfortune should befall you."

"Nothing on earth could save them," said Tagala emphatically. "The secret is in my exclusive possession. No other man could diagnose the malady, much less prescribe a remedy. The lives of the seven gentlemen are absolutely in my hand."

"Then there isn't the slightest chance of Mr. Shei's plans falling through?"

"Not the slightest. The seven gentlemen will pay Mr. Shei's price, and within a week we shall all be rich beyond the dreams of avarice." The gloating tones hinted that Doctor Tagala's imagination was luxuriating in enchanting visions. "By the way, when do we inoculate the young lady?"

"Better wait till evening," suggested Slade. "There will be less danger of interruption then."

Helen turned away. She feared an involuntary cry of horror would betray her if she remained longer. Steadying herself with great difficulty, she stole out of the laboratory and slipped back into her room. Her watch showed half past five, and the inoculation would probably not take place for an hour or two. In the meantime she wanted to think and if possible find a way of escape, but the fierce pounding of the blood against her temples seemed to preclude clear thinking.

Her only distinct thought was that she must flee from Azurecrest no matter what dangers and difficulties she might encounter. She felt that The Gray Phantom would gladly fling his life away in order to protect her, but in this instance his hands were tied. He could not make a single move without rendering her predicament worse, and that fact would restrain him, much as he might rebel against his enforced inaction. Mr. Shei's men would point out to him that her safety depended on an unresisting attitude on his part. He could not know what she had just learned from the conversation between Slade and Tagala, that it was their intention to take her life, anyway.

Somehow, she told herself, she must manage to escape from the horrors awaiting her at Azurecrest. Even being clawed and torn by the savage dog seemed preferable to the slightest touch of Doctor Tagala's hand. She shuddered whenever her imagination conjured up a vision of his repelling features, and a hoarse cry rose in her throat at thought of being inoculated with the fearful malady. Miss Neville's maniacal outbursts were still ringing in her ears, and she remembered the hideous strains that had poured from the lips of the dying woman in the Thelma Theater.

The recollections filled her with sickening terror. With ghastly visions floating before her eyes, she rushed blindly from the room. The hall was deserted, and she scurried down the stairs as if pursued by a monster. She reached the outer door without hindrance, and a flickering hope began to stir within her as she scanned the wide stretch of lawn surrounding the house. The long shadows cast by the trees gave her an additional sense of safety. Swiftly, without a backward glance, she started to run. Her hopes rose higher and higher as she plunged into the thick shadows among the trees. In a few moments now, if her flight remained unnoticed, she would have reached the fence. Somehow she would manage to scale it, or maybe she could find an opening somewhere.

She quickened her pace, but of a sudden a low, rumbling growl sent a chill through her veins. She stopped, stood crouching behind the scraggy trunk of a hemlock, and glanced wildly in all directions. With great leaps and skips, a huge, black form was rushing toward her, its teeth gleaming ominously between slavering jaws. In a few moments it would be at her throat, and then— Once more a vision of Doctor Tagala's repulsive features filled her with dread. Again she looked about her, then raced swiftly in the direction where the shadows were thickest. Behind her the underbrush crackled beneath the paws of the savage beast. In a moment or two he would be snapping at her heels.

Again hope rose within her. A squatty shed loomed within a narrow clearing. With the strength of frenzy she sped toward it. If she could reach it before the dog could overtake her, she would be temporarily safe. A great terror urged her on with the speed of the wind. Now the dog was snatching at the hem of her fluttering skirt, but she was already at the door. With a final exertion of strength she pushed it open and rushed in, then slammed it shut behind her. With a deep breath of relief she lurched against the wall. Suddenly she recoiled as from a blow.

"What are you doin' here?" queried a gruff voice.

She stared into the dusk around her. A few wisps of waning sunlight straggled in through a small window in the rear. Gradually, as her eyes grew accustomed to the dusk, she descried a stocky figure leaning over a shovel. It was the sour-faced individual who had opened the gate for her on her arrival at Azurecrest. Little by little, as her pupils responded to the dim light, she took in each detail of the scene. An amazed gasp slipped from her lips.

An oblong space had been torn up in the center of the flooring and on each side of it were little mounds of dirt. Instinctively she stepped closer and looked down into a rectangular hollow. She had a weird sensation that she was looking into a grave, and with a shudder she glanced up into the man's face.

"What—what's that?" she asked hoarsely, indicating the hollow.

The man guffawed. "Better not ask questions, miss. This is a nasty job, and you'd better clear out."

He looked aside just then, and she followed his glance. In a corner of the shed she saw a heap vaguely resembling a human form. Her feet seemed to drag her forward in spite of her horror, and she lifted the blanket that covered the figure. Then she stood rigid, her tightly drawn lips stifling the cry that rose in her throat. At once she recognized the features of Miss Neville, the woman whose maniacal laughter had startled her the night she arrived at Azurecrest. The face was white and rigid now, but the wraith of a ghastly smile lingered on her lips. A long, shuddering moan escaped her, and then she sank limply to the floor.

She had a weird sensation, during the hours that followed, that she was treading on the brink of oblivion. A merciful mist seemed to obscure everything. She was dimly aware of being carried from the shed and placed on a long, white table. Through the haze that engulfed her she glimpsed the repulsive features of Doctor Tagala. She felt a sting in the arm, and then a sickening substance raced through her veins. For a time she felt as though unseen hands were wafting her body through a limitless void. Somewhere—far away, she thought—there was laughter, and she had a curious impression that it was coming from her own lips.

Dawn came, and a flood of sunlight brightened the void through which she was roaming. The strange and wild fancies that had flitted around her throughout the night seemed to melt away, and now she saw things more clearly. She was standing at a telephone, and over the wire came a voice that sounded strangely familiar. Words poured from her lips, but they seemed futile and meaningless, and then an involuntary contraction of laryngeal muscles filled the room with wild strains of laughter. It frightened her, and just then a hand jerked her away.

"That'll do," said a voice, and she thought it was Slade's. "The Gray Phantom has heard enough."

CHAPTER XVI
CHECKMATED

A MASS OF JAGGED, elongated clouds hovered like scowling specters over Azurecrest. A raw wind sighed moodily among the birches and hemlocks as The Gray Phantom reached the apex of the hill. Stopping within fifty yards of the high picket fence, he glanced toward the house that once had served him as a retreat and shelter against the activities of the police. The white trimmings of doors and windows gleamed faintly in the dusk and here and there a light twinkled through the trees.

The Phantom turned away and walked a few paces toward the fence. On the trip from the city he had tried to exclude Helen from his mind, for each thought of her was maddening, and he needed a cool brain and a steady nerve if he were to accomplish his purpose. By sheer force of will he had tried to forget the hysterical laughter he had heard over the wire and which had told him with grim eloquence what had happened to her. To keep disturbing thoughts from his mind, he had outlined several plans of procedure and prepared himself for the difficult and perilous task that awaited him.

After a brief search over the rugged ground, he stopped at the side of a huge bowlder and cleared away an accumulation of dry twigs, dead branches, and rotting weeds. After the obstruction had been removed, an opening barely large enough to permit him to crawl through appeared at the base of the rock. It slanted gently into the ground, then widened into a tunnel in which he was able to walk upright. During his sojourn at Azurecrest it had often occurred to him that an emergency exit might some day prove desirable, and he had built the tunnel in consequence. He had not happened to mention the existence of the passage when he sold the place, and he did not think it likely that the new owner had discovered it. Though he had never had occasion to use it during his occupancy, it now gave him a distinct advantage in that it enabled him to enter the house secretly and by an easy route.

Reaching the farther end of the tunnel, he fumbled along the wall until he found a spring deftly hidden in a crevice. Evidently the mechanism was still in good working order, for a door swung squeakily on unoiled hinges. He passed inside, touched another spring, and the door swung shut. In another moment he had switched on an electric light.

The room was narrow and almost square, and there were neither windows nor visible doors. It was supplied with air through ingeniously hidden ventilators and The Phantom had fitted it up for brief occupancy. Occasionally it had suited his mood to retire to the hidden chamber and read one of his favorite books.

Throwing off the light overcoat he had been wearing, he then examined his automatic and the little pocket case in which he carried a number of carefully selected tools that had stood him in good stead in numerous emergencies. Despite the advantages afforded him by the tunnel and the secret room, he would be surrounded by dangers at every step. He had no doubt Mr. Shei's henchmen would kill him on sight, and he could not afford to toss his life away recklessly while Helen was in danger.

He glanced at his watch. It was only a little after ten, and sounds reaching him through the ventilator shaft warned him that the occupants of the house were still about. As soon as the house had quieted down a little, he would try the first plan on his programme. If that failed, he was holding two or three others in reserve.

For half an hour he waited, then a sliding panel opened at his touch on a spring, and he ascended a narrow spiral stairway that terminated in what appeared to be a blank wall. His hand touched a lever, and The Phantom passed through an aperture that instantly closed behind him. He was standing in a dark room in a seldom frequented part of the house. He advanced a few steps, then stood still, listening. Someone was laughing, and in the darkness the sounds impressed him even more forcibly than they had in the light of day. He walked on, trying desperately to exclude the agonizing accents from his ears. Hurriedly he opened a door, then as quickly drew it to again. Someone was passing in the hall outside.

He waited till the footsteps moved away, then looked warily out. A tall figure, walking with a brisk, swinging gait, was turning into one of the rooms farther down the corridor. As soon as the door had closed behind him, The Phantom followed on tiptoe. Noticing that the hall was deserted, he bent his ear to the keyhole. Two voices, one of them speaking with a distinct foreign accent, were talking in tones signifying that they had reason to be well pleased with themselves. They were discussing the progress of Mr. Shei's adventure and congratulating themselves on the prospect of becoming immensely rich within a few days.

The Phantom, listening intently, was learning several facts of interest. The two speakers were addressing each other as Doctor Tagala and Mr. Slade, and he gathered from divers remarks that the latter was in charge of affairs at Azurecrest while Mr. Shei was watching developments in New York. Doctor Tagala seemed to be the scientist who had discovered the poison that was the chief factor in Mr. Shei's scheme.

Having absorbed a great deal of useful information, The Phantom raised his head from the keyhole. Then, he flexed his muscles and drew the automatic from his pocket. Here was his opportunity for putting his first plan to the test. It was cruder than the alternative ones, but it might also prove vastly more effective. His hand closed around the knob. With automatic in one hand he softly pushed the door open, entering so silently that for several moments neither of the two men in the room was aware of the intrusion.

He gazed for an instant at the singularly repulsive face of the man addressed as Doctor Tagala, then gave his companion a fleeting glance of inspection, noticing that Slade had the strong jaw and aggressiveness of manners that usually go with a domineering personality. Only the eyes, shifty and unmagnetic, gave him a suspicion that there was a weak strain in the man's moral fiber. Smiling affably, with every nerve in his body atingle, he advanced to the table.

"Good-evening, gentlemen," he said softly.

With a hoarse cry Slade sprang from his chair, but Doctor Tagala gave the intruder only a cold, impersonal glance.

"Sit down, Slade," ordered The Phantom, "and both of you keep your hands on the table." He made a significant gesture with the automatic.

Slade stared and looked as if not quite certain that his eyes were to be trusted.

"How the devil did you get in?" he exclaimed explosively. He tried hard to get a grip on himself, but the twitching of the lines around his mouth showed that he was ill at ease. "But then," he added, steadying his voice with an effort, "I suppose anything is possible for The Gray Phantom."

"Ah, so you are The Gray Phantom." Doctor Tagala seemed mildly impressed. "I have heard a great deal of you, and I have felt some curiosity in regard to you. I must confess to a great disappointment, however. I did not think a man of your genius would descend to such crude methods. Of you I had expected subtlety and finesse. Bah!"

Slade was rapidly regaining his self-control, but he kept his hands obediently on the table. From time to time he cast an uneasy glance into the muzzle of The Phantom's pistol.

"I can't imagine how you got in," he admitted. "How you got past the picket fence, the dogs, and the watchmen is too much for me. But, now that you are here, what do you intend to do? I suppose it has something to do with Miss Hardwick?"

"Precisely, Slade."

The other sneered. "Don't you realize that there's nothing you can do? What you heard over the telephone wire should have warned you to keep hands off. Miss Hardwick's life is absolutely in our power."

"For the present, yes; but I think the situation will soon be reversed."

"How?"

The Phantom's lids contracted and his eyes held a steely glitter as he looked down at the man in the chair. Then he cast a quick glance over his shoulder. At any moment someone was apt to enter and deprive him of his advantage.

"I intend to fight the devil with fire," he announced. "In other words, I am going to fight your Mr. Shei with his own weapons. Mr. Shei works through fear. He hopes to induce his seven victims to surrender half of their fortunes to him by putting the fear of death into them. Now, it's a poor rule that doesn't work both ways."

"Suppose you come to the point," suggested Slade sneeringly.

"Very well. I understand that you, Slade, are in charge here during Mr. Shei's absence. I want you to do two things at once. One of them is to release Miss Hardwick immediately; the other, to have the antidote administered to her."

Slade's eyes left the automatic and gave The Phantom an insolent glance. "A bit dictatorial, aren't you? Has it occurred to you that I might refuse?"

"Certainly." The Phantom smiled, but his eyes were hard as steel. "Mr. Shei has probably considered the possibility that his seven victims may refuse to accept his terms, but he feels fairly sure that in the end they will submit. His whole scheme is based on the idea that a man will do almost anything to escape death. So will you, Slade; especially when I convince you that you will never leave this room alive unless you do as I say."

Slade shifted uneasily in his chair. A tinge of gray was slowly creeping into his face.

"Make no mistake, Slade," The Phantom went on. "It's true there are no bloodstains on my hands, but this time I am gambling for higher stakes than ever before in my life. I could kill you without the slightest scruple."

His eyes, as he looked down at the other man, were keen as rapiers. He spoke each word with an emphasis that spelled terrible earnestness. Slade winced and writhed beneath his lowering gaze.

"What—what do you want me to do?" he stammered.

The Phantom felt a thrill as he saw that the other was yielding. He had judged him correctly at first glance. Slade, despite his swaggers and blustering, was at heart a coward.

"In the first place, you are to instruct Doctor Tagala to administer the antidote to Miss Hardwick immediately. I will give you exactly sixty seconds. If you have not obeyed by that time, you will be a dead man."

To emphasize the threat, The Phantom took out his watch. Slade turned a quavering glance on the scientist. He opened his lips to speak, but Doctor Tagala anticipated him.

"I dislike to interrupt such a dramatic scene," he declared in drawling tones edged with a faint trace of sarcasm, "but it has proceeded far enough. You see, my dear Gray Phantom, that even if Mr. Slade should give me such absurd instructions as you request, I would refuse to comply with them. Furthermore, in order to save you needless waste of energy, let me inform you that the antidote is concealed in a place where I alone know where to find it. We are protected against every conceivable emergency."

The Phantom felt a presentiment of defeat, but his face, tense and threatening, showed not the slightest sign of it. With a quick movement he turned the pistol from Slade and pointed the muzzle straight at Doctor Tagala's head.

"All right, doctor," he said crisply, "in that case let me warn you that I could kill you with just as little scruple as I could Slade."

But the scientist only folded his arms and smiled. A look of patient amusement crossed his swarthy and evil face.

"That is an excellent example of what you Americans call bluff," he drawled. "You can't frighten me, for I know you have not the slightest intention to kill me. If you take my life, the antidote will never be found, and then the charming young lady will die. Mr. Shei anticipated just such a situation as this when he made me the sole custodian of the antidote."

A trace of disappointment passed over The Phantom's face; a sense of bafflement took hold of him as he realized that, thanks to Mr. Shei's ingenious precautions, his first plan had failed disastrously. Still pointing the pistol, he backed slowly toward the door.

"Mr. Shei wins this time," he frankly acknowledged, "but he will lose in the end. The Gray Phantom was never beaten yet. I wish you good-night, gentlemen."

With that he was out of the door and running swiftly down the hall. With a cry of rage Slade sprang from the chair and started in pursuit, blowing a pocket whistle as he ran. Men appeared from every direction, and Slade shouted orders that the house and grounds be thoroughly searched at once. The men scattered, and in a few moments the search was on.

But The Gray Phantom, safe in his hidden chamber, was already at work on the details of his next move.

CHAPTER XVII
DOCTOR TAGALA'S DISCOVERY

A GLANCE AT HIS watch as he entered the secret room showed The Phantom that daybreak was not far away. In a little while it would be highly unsafe for him to walk about the house; besides, the execution of his next move depended for its success on darkness and quiet. To jeopardize his project by a reckless move would be the height of folly and might result in disastrous consequences. Much as his fears and anxiety urged him to immediate action, The Phantom decided to wait till the following night.

He lay down on the cot and slept by snatches. Now and then, as a faint but terrifying sound came down the ventilator shaft, he awoke with a start. Peals of unnatural laughter, sounding remotely in the darkness of the hidden chamber, started a cold sweat on his forehead. By sheer physical force he would shut out the sounds, knowing that for the present he could do nothing, but the mutterings that fell from his lips and the convulsive clenching of his hands boded no good for Mr. Shei and his followers.

Morning came, and he tried to fix his mind on his forthcoming move. A grim look came into his face as he contemplated the step he was about to take. Ordinarily he would have shrunk from it in disgust, for it was an expedient he had never employed in the past. Now, however, with the life of Helen Hardwick in danger, he must employ whatever means might prove effective. It was no time for niceties or scruples. Besides, there was no reason why he should be restrained by ethical considerations when dealing with blackguards like Mr. Shei and his retainers.

The hours dragged. A troubled look on his face, The Phantom paced the floor of the narrow chamber. His plans for the night were complete except for one detail. Cudgel his brain as he might, there was one small but important matter that continued to puzzle him. Evening came, and the solution of the difficulty still eluded him. He was a little faint from hunger, for he had not eaten for twenty-four hours, and he wondered if his brain would not work better after a visit to the pantry. In a little while the house would quiet down for the night, and then he could safely leave his hiding place.

At last he was ready for action. He gave his automatic a careful inspection. Into his pocket he put a coil of thin but strong rope which he had unearthed from an old chest. Then he turned off the light and ascended the spiral stairway. After listening in vain for sounds, he tiptoed out in the hallway, then down the main stairway. The entire house seemed immersed in sleep, and even the strained laughter had stopped for a time. Evidently the occupants of the house, never guessing that he was hiding in their very midst, supposed that The Gray Phantom had left Azurecrest.

He felt more alert after gratifying his hunger in the well-stocked pantry. By the back stairway he returned to the second floor. Silent as a shadow he walked down the hall, pausing briefly before every door and listening. It was important that he should locate Doctor Tagala's room, for his whole plan revolved around the scientist. Also, he was anxious to take the doctor completely by surprise.

At one of the doors he stopped longer than before the others. A faint reek of chemicals filtered through the keyhole, and in a vague sense the odor suggested Doctor Tagala's nearness. Neither light nor sound came through the tiny opening, so evidently there was no one in the room. The door was locked, but a simple operation with one of the tools in his case opened it readily, and he stepped inside.

He peered sharply into the darkness before he thought it safe to snap on his electric flash light. As the small point of light played over floor and walls, he knew at once that the room was a chemical laboratory. Chemistry had always held a strong fascination for him, and his knowledge of the science was far more comprehensive than the average layman's. Something prompted him to glance twice at the long rows of bottles stacked on shelves around the room. Stepping closer, he read some of the labels, and suddenly he gave a faint chuckle of elation. The problem that had puzzled him all day was at last solved. From its place on the shelf he took a small bottle containing a colorless fluid, and slipped it into his pocket. The chemical was a very ordinary one, but he expected it to serve a highly useful purpose.

Again he darted the electric gleam over the room. At one side was a door, and as he bent his ear to the keyhole he heard sounds of deep and regular breathing. Something told him that the sleeper was Doctor Tagala, for it seemed only logical that the scientist should occupy the room adjoining the laboratory. Quickly extinguishing his flash light, he turned the knob and noiselessly pushed the door open, then stepped softly in the direction whence the sounds of breathing came. Once more he brought his flash light into play, but only to assure himself by a swift glance that the sleeper was Tagala.

A faint, triumphant grin curled his lips, and then the flash disappeared in his pocket. For a moment, standing in utter darkness, he tensed his muscles for action. In an instant he pressed his knee firmly against the sleeper's chest and wound his fingers tightly around Tagala's throat. A harsh rumble sounded in the doctor's windpipe, but the firm clutch over his Adam's apple prevented an outcry. He writhed, squirmed, doubled up his knees, and attempted to fight with his arms, but The Phantom gradually increased the pressure on his throat, and his struggle grew feebler and feebler. Finally, when he was nearly exhausted, The Phantom took out a cloth with which he had provided himself before leaving the secret room, and applied it as a gag. The doctor made only a feeble show of resistance while his arms and legs were bound, and finally The Phantom took the limp form on his back and started from the room.

Every inch of the way was beset with perils. A board creaking under the double weight of captor and captive might bring on a sudden attack, or one of the occupants of the house might be encountered in the hall. But luck was with The Phantom, and in a short time he had placed his burden on the cot in the hidden chamber. Panting from the strenuous exercise, he removed the gag from his prisoner's mouth, then switched on the light.

The doctor, breathing stertorously, his face almost black from the recent choking, wriggled his arms and legs in a futile effort to free himself. Seeing it was hopeless, he subsided and looked dazedly about him. His eyes opened wide as he saw The Phantom.

"You—again!" he exclaimed.

The Phantom smiled at sight of his stupefaction.

"You didn't suppose I would give up so easily; did you, doctor? You don't seem particularly pleased to see me. No doubt you thought I left Azurecrest after the fizzle last night. I suppose you are wondering where you are. It is enough for you to know that you will never leave this room until we have had an understanding, and that for the present you may regard yourself as my prisoner. Your confederates will never find you, and you may as well reconcile yourself to the fact that they are unable to help you."

Tagala, gradually recovering breath and wits, looked balefully at The Phantom.

"You—you will suffer for this!" he muttered thickly. Again he strained at the cords around his ankles and wrists, but he soon saw that it was useless. "We know how to deal with meddlers."

The Phantom smiled complacently. As yet it had not occurred to his prisoner to cry for help, and The Phantom had no fear of the result if he should do so. Though Slade and the others were not far away, they were as harmless as if they did not exist. Save for the ventilating shaft, the room was practically soundproof, and the exits were so completely hidden that they would never be able to locate the chamber.

"We shall see," was his calm response. "Mr. Shei appears to be a very shrewd man, but even he has his limitations. The infirmities of age are beginning to show a marked effect on his strategy. He is too old for this sort of thing."

"So," said the scientist, "you think you know him?"

The Phantom nodded. "I had an encounter with him some years ago, and he proved to me then that he had extraordinary astuteness. As a matter of fact, he was a little too much for me. The other day I ran into him by accident, and we had quite a pleasant little chat."

Tagala lay motionless on the cot while his eyes, slowly recovering their customary brilliance, searched The Phantom's face.

"The police are laboring under the delusion that *you* are Mr. Shei," he dryly observed.

"Oh, well, the police are not particularly bright at times." The Phantom shrugged. "Now, doctor, you and I are going to have a very serious talk. I was outmaneuvered last night, but this is my round. I shall convince you by a very simple method that it will be wise for you to place the antidote in my hands."

Despite his humiliation and physical discomfort, the doctor gave a contemptuous laugh.

"Fool!" he snorted. "Every move you make is fore-doomed to failure. We have provided against every possible emergency. Our plan is already a certain success. Only this afternoon Mr. Shei telephones me from New York that everything is going well. A group of the most celebrated physicians in America have held several consultations without practical results. They are utterly at a loss to diagnose the disease or to prescribe even a palliative. Poor idiots! It took me years to perfect the toxin, and they have only a few days in which to combat its effects. On the seventh day after the inoculation, the seven subjects will be doomed unless the antidote is administered in the meantime. After the seventh day it will be too late. Mr. Shei told me that two of the subjects are already in a mood to discuss terms. Perhaps by tomorrow they will place half of their fortunes at Mr. Shei's feet."

"You seem very confident of success," observed The Phantom.

"Our success is already assured. In a few days I shall be wealthier than I ever before dreamed of being. Some people scoff at money, but it is an excellent thing for all that. All my life, while pursuing my scientific investigations, I have had my eye on what you Americans call the main chance. I never dreamed that I should realize my hopes through an accidental discovery. Ever hear of the datura plant?"

The Phantom shook his head.

"It grows in great profusion in my native soil, the Malay States, but it can be transplanted or produced almost anywhere. It is an odd plant, from four to six feet high, with wide-spreading branches and black flowers that are shaped like trumpets. Children have been known to die after eating the seeds, which are very poisonous. A few years ago, after an extensive tour in Europe, I returned to my native land and was called upon to treat a child who had eaten a great quantity of the seeds. It was then I made the discovery that shall make me a wealthy man in a few days. It was a mere accident, but isn't our whole life a series of accidents?"

He smiled philosophically, for he had quite recovered from the effects of his recent humiliation.

"If you will permit me to explain a little further," he went on, "I think you will understand how invincible we are and how foolish it is for you to oppose us. The poisonous property of the datura plant is known as daturin. It is a very curious drug. Its active principle is a mixture of a kind of atropine and hyoscyamine, but the true nature of the component alkaloids has never been fully determined. It is one of the mysteries of nature. Among the symptoms of datura poisoning are hoarseness, dryness of the mouth, dilation of the pupils, disturbed heart action, bad memory, and a curious vocal affection that produces involuntary laughter. No chemical antidote had been either known or suggested until I made my accidental discovery. It has suited my purpose to keep that discovery to myself."

There was an elated smirk on his face, and The Phantom turned away in disgust.

"I came to America," continued the doctor in oily tones, "and by mere chance made the acquaintance of our remarkable Mr. Shei. I shall not weary you by reciting all the details. I happened to mention my discovery to Mr. Shei, and his brilliant mind immediately conceived the idea of putting it to a highly profitable use. Like all great things, his plan was simplicity itself. His theory was based on the fact, so aptly stated by yourself last night, that the average run of mortals can be most effectively controlled through the factor of fear. He suggested that if a deadly malady were communicated to a number of wealthy men, they could easily be persuaded to pay almost any price for a sure antidote, especially if the antidote were the exclusive property of an individual or an organization.

"That was the beginning of the idea. It required quite a little elaboration. The chief factors in the plan were the poison and the antidote. The antidote was in readiness, but the poison had to be so adjusted that it would produce death within a specified time unless the antidote were administered meanwhile. If the plan was to succeed, we must be in a position to tell the subjects that they would die within a certain number of days unless they paid our price for the antidote. You probably know, since you appear to be an educated man, that the ancient Chinese knew how to adjust poisons so as to produce death within a certain time. All my life I have been making special studies along that line, and my discoveries proved very valuable in connection with Mr. Shei's project. Yet, for a long time, I was unable to adjust the poison with sufficient accuracy. With Mr. Shei's assistance I fitted up a laboratory here and began making additional researches. It was necessary to have human subjects for the experiments, and Mr. Shei furnished me several. Two or three, who were inoculated in the early stages of the work, failed to react properly to the antidote, and one or two of them were unfortunate enough to die."

"You murdered them, in plain words," suggested The Phantom curtly.

"Harsh word, my dear Gray Phantom. As a whole, the experiments were highly successful. I discovered how to adjust the poison so as to produce death within a specified time. We were now ready to go ahead with the plan. Mr. Shei selected the victims, and I showed a number of his most trusted men how the poison was to be injected. Each of these, with an assistant, was assigned to one of the seven victims chosen by Mr. Shei, and the whole number of inoculations were successfully accomplished the other night. In a few days—"

"What about Miss Darrow?" inquired The Phantom brusquely. "What did you gain by murdering her?"

"Really, I wish you would drop that unpleasant word from your vocabulary. Miss Darrow had been unfortunate enough to learn certain facts which were detrimental to Mr. Shei. She had been watched constantly, and she was followed to the Thelma that night. Her actions were peculiar, and Mr. Shei's agents suspected she was on the point of making embarrassing revelations. I was in New York at the time and happened to be within reach, so the agents communicated with me. I arrived just in time to prevent unpleasant consequences. In another moment she might have made some very damaging disclosures. In fact, she had already sent a peculiarly worded note to that remarkable person whose name eludes me."

"Vincent Starr?" suggested The Phantom.

"Precisely. Mr. Starr is one of your highly temperamental geniuses. Just how much Miss Darrow had learned will never be known, but I thought it advisable to act promptly. The amount of poison I injected into her veins was carefully calculated to produce death within a few minutes."

The Phantom mastered his sense of loathing. What he was learning might prove highly useful later on.

"Wouldn't a knife thrust have been quicker and safer?" he suggested. "Even in the few minutes between the inoculation of the poison and Miss Darrow's death she might have blurted out all she knew."

"There was slight danger of that. The poison always blunts one's mental faculties, especially when given in such a large dose. It was very unlikely that Miss Darrow would speak coherently in the brief interval while the poison acted. A quick thrust with a knife would perhaps have been safer, but we needed the moral effect."

"The—*what*?"

The satisfied gleam in the doctor's eyes testified that he was quite at ease once more, despite the cords that incapacitated him for action.

"Yes, the moral effect was valuable. You see, the seven victims selected by Mr. Shei had to be impressed with the deadliness of the poison. Unless they were thoroughly convinced that the poison would kill, they might not have been amenable to reason. Miss Darrow's death, coming just a day or two before the seven were inoculated, was a valuable object lesson."

An oily smile creased the scientist's swarthy features. Once more, despite his uncomfortable position, he seemed hugely content.

"No doubt," admitted The Phantom ironically. "Mr. Shei doesn't seem to have overlooked anything. What I can't understand is why you, a man of scientific attainments, should consent to do the bidding of such a blackguard."

"Wealth is a very excellent thing," said Tagala musingly. "It is even more desirable than fame. Mr. Shei has put me in the way of acquiring a great fortune, so why should I not serve him?"

"And what are you going to do with the money after you have acquired it by such vile methods, granting that your scheme succeeds?"

"Enjoy life, my friend." The doctor's repulsive features were wreathed in smiles. "I have a great capacity for appreciating the beautiful things in life. Nature works by contrasts. She treated me very shabbily as far as physical characteristics are concerned, but by way of compensation she gave me a taste for the only things that really matter. I intend to surround myself with luxuries that an Indian maharajah might envy. I intend to feast my eyes on the costliest and the best the world can produce. Now perhaps you understand?"

The Phantom nodded. Inwardly he tingled and glowed, but his face showed nothing but boredom and disgust. The insight he had just obtained into Tagala's character would have an important bearing on his plan.

"And now that we understand each other," the doctor continued, "let us terminate this rather dreary farce. This little room is pleasant enough, but I never sleep well in strange places, and these cords are not inducive to repose."

"You will be free to go wherever you please as soon as we have settled the little matter I mentioned a moment ago."

"Ah! Then you persist in your foolish determination. Your experience last night should have convinced you of the futility of your efforts, but I see you are as stubborn as ever."

"More so," The Phantom assured him. "I have discovered a new weapon since last night. Before you leave this room, you will have told me where the antidote is hidden."

Tagala grinned insolently. He tilted his head back against the pillow and complacently regarded The Phantom.

"You are very amusing," he murmured. "I thought that—"

He stopped and looked toward a corner of the ceiling. The Phantom followed his glance, and his figure tensed perceptibly. From somewhere above their heads came strains of soft, lilting laughter, edged now and then with a hysterical vibration. A pallor began to spread over The Phantom's face.

"There, my dear Gray Phantom," said the doctor elatedly, "is your answer."

The Phantom clenched his fingers spasmodically. His face was hard and his eyes held a strange gleam.

"You are mistaken, doctor." He clipped off the words with sinister precision. "Until a moment ago I had silly scruples about employing my latest weapon. After hearing that," and he inclined his head toward the corner of the ceiling, "I have concluded that any methods are fair when dealing with scoundrels of your type."

"That is obviously true," assented Tagala cheerfully. "The only difficulty is that any methods you employ are certain to prove ineffective. Please don't make any more threats against my life. I should laugh, and that would be impolite."

The Phantom came a step nearer the cot. "No," he said grimly, "I have no intention of doing anything so futile. I have the best reason in the world for not wanting you to die just yet. Also, I have discovered a much more effective way of dealing with you."

An odd emphasis in his tones seemed to impress the doctor. A flicker of uneasiness crossed his face, but it was gone in a moment.

"Ah!" he murmured derisively. "I might have foreseen it. You mean to force me to surrender the antidote by torturing me. It is an improvement on your previous method, but it will prove just as useless. Torture is unpleasant but I can endure any amount of it."

"Mistaken again, doctor. Torture is a little too crude, and I am not sure you are the type of man that could be influenced by it. The plan I have in mind is subtler and surer. You told me a moment ago that your highest aim in life is the enjoyment of beautiful things and the pursuit of pleasure."

"I told you the truth." This time there was a trace of bewilderment in Tagala's tones.

From his pocket The Phantom drew the bottle he had taken from the laboratory. He studied the label with a preoccupied air, then held it so the man on the cot could read the inscription. Tagala's eye narrowed in perplexity.

"I have been told," said The Phantom casually, "that a single drop of this fluid, when injected into the eye, is sufficient to cause blindness."

The doctor's hands and feet strained spasmodically against the cords. A quick muscular contraction told that The Phantom had found his sensitive spot.

"Blind men are not particularly appreciative of the luxuries and pleasures you so vividly described a while ago," The Phantom went on. His voice was soft, but there was a faint throb to his tones. "What good will it do a man to accumulate costly and beautiful things if he can't see them?"

A grayish tinge crept into Tagala's face. His eyes, with a look of horror lurking in their depths, were fixed rigidly on The Phantom's face.

The Phantom held the bottle to the light. A faint but ominous smile was playing about his lips.

"Just a drop of colorless liquid!" he murmured. "But what a different complexion it would put on your prospects, Tagala! All the money you hope to get through Mr. Shei would be only so much rubbish. All the wealth in the world couldn't relieve your misery. Don't you think you had better reconsider?"

The scientist's lips fluttered, but no words came. A look of abhorrence accentuated the repulsiveness of his face.

With a quick movement The Phantom stepped toward the cot. The doctor wiggled and squirmed, but was unable to move.

"Perhaps, just to convince you that I am in earnest, I had better begin by blinding the left eye now," The Phantom went on, bending slightly over the trembling man. With two fingers of one hand he pressed back the lids of the doctor's left eye while holding the bottle in the other. The scientist rolled from side to side, but the firm pressure of The Phantom's knee against his chest checked his efforts. Finally, as The Phantom was tilting the little bottle against the exposed eye, a great sigh of horror broke from the doctor's lips.

"Stop!" he cried, almost overcome by terror. "You have won. I will do anything you demand. Only don't blind me!"

CHAPTER XVIII
THE FIGURE ON THE STAIRS

THE PHANTOM COULD SCARCELY hold back a cry of exultation as he saw the abject fear written in Doctor Tagala's face. Knowing how ingeniously Mr. Shei had laid his plans and guarded against every imaginable emergency, he had not been altogether certain that his artful contrivance would succeed. But the scientist's acute distress was ample proof that Mr. Shei had been outmaneuvered and that The Gray Phantom was master of the situation.

"It appears Mr. Shei has overlooked something, after all," observed The Phantom in tones that expressed his elation. "Now, doctor, let me warn you that evasions and trickery will only aggravate your position. Where is the antidote?"

Tagala seemed to be making an effort to gather his scattered thoughts. "If I tell you, will you release me at once?" he asked shakily.

"All I promise is to spare your eyesight," declared The Phantom, still holding the little bottle in dangerous proximity to the scientist's terror-filled eyes. "You will have to be content with that, and I am really letting you off very easily. Now answer my question."

The doctor glanced at the bottle, gave an involuntary shudder, and seemed to be trying hard to think clearly.

"The antidote," he finally managed to say, "is hidden in the wall of my bedroom, exactly one foot from the window and directly above the head of the bed. The wall is apparently solid, but if you will carefully run your hand over the space I have indicated, you will find a slight protuberance. A light pressure on it will release a hidden panel, and inside you will find a number of small bottles, each one containing a full course of treatment. You will find complete directions on the label."

The Phantom searched his face, but found no signs of guile. "I hope, for your sake, that you have told the truth," he said sharply. "I shall be back as soon as I have verified your statement."

He examined the cords around the doctor's feet and hands and saw that they were securely tied. Then he stepped out of the little chamber, carefully closing the sliding door before he ran up the stairs. Even now he could scarcely realize that his stratagem had succeeded. There were still dangers and obstacles in the way, but somehow he would win out. He would take as many bottles as his pockets could hold, then he would find Helen, and they could easily make their escape through the tunnel. His imagination pictured Mr. Shei's discomfiture when he should learn that this stupendous scheme had failed.

The Phantom drew his revolver before stepping out in the hall. The slightest slip or a chance encounter might easily reverse the situation and turn the tables against him. His feet glided soundlessly over the floor till he came to the laboratory. A quick glance up and down the corridor assured him that so far he was safe. He opened the door and entered the bedroom at the side of the laboratory. Now he took out his electric flash, placed his automatic within easy reach on the bed, then gingerly ran his fingers over the area specified by Doctor Tagala.

In a short time he had found the slight protuberance mentioned by the doctor, but he hesitated for several moments before pressing it. First he carefully examined the surrounding space, looking everywhere for hidden wires. Even when controlled by terror, the wily scientist was not to be trusted, and The Phantom had no intention of walking blindly into a trap. His search satisfied him, however, and finally he placed a finger on the tiny projection and pressed inward. Almost instantly a narrow portion of the wall opened. Within, arranged in an orderly row on a shelf, stood a number of small bottles.

He drew a long breath of intense relief. Before him was visible proof that he had frightened the truth out of the scientist. His head swam a little as he contemplated his success. Each one of the bottles would have netted Mr. Shei a fortune if the audacious plan had succeeded. What seemed more wonderful still, one of them would save the life of Helen Hardwick. The Phantom's hand trembled excitedly as he reached out and clutched one of the bottles.

In the next instant his hand darted back. Something was wrong, for the bottle was immovable, as if clamped down with rivets, and a hideous suspicion flashed through The Phantom's mind. Simultaneously there came a loud clanging which reverberated throughout the house, confirming his agonizing suspicion that a gong had been released the moment his hand touched the bottle. He had blundered into a trap, after all. For an instant he marveled dazedly at the almost uncanny scope of Mr. Shei's precautions.

Then suddenly alert and tense once more, he put the electric flash light back into his pocket and snatched up his automatic. The clangor of the gong, resounding throughout the entire house, was almost deafening. Overhead doors were slamming and voices shouting excitedly. From the direction of the stairs came a tumultuous clatter, and above the hubbub he caught the

insistent tones of Slade's commands. He cast a glance at the window, its out-
lines delineated by a gray dusk against the darker background. But flight was
out of the question, for he could not leave Helen behind him. The Phantom
steeled himself for battle. Often in the past he had fought against overwhelming odds, and this time something far greater than his life depended on the
outcome.

Every vein tingling, he left the bedroom and crossed the floor of the laboratory. Maintaining a steady grip on his automatic, he pushed the door open
and stepped out into the hall. A chorus of shouts greeted his appearance. Men
in various stages of attire were running excitedly up and down the corridor,
but all stopped at sight of the tall, tense figure standing with his back against
the laboratory door. His eyes, hard as steel and swift as speeding arrows,
surveyed them narrowly with a long, comprehensive sweep. The barrel of his
automatic, held in readiness for instant action, glimmered ominously in the
dim light shed by a single bulb in the ceiling.

"The Gray Phantom!" was the hushed whisper that went back and forth in
the huddled crowd. A spell seemed to fall over them as they stared at the man
of whose amazing exploits they had heard and read, but whom few of them
had seen until now. But their inaction lasted only a few moments. Some of
the bolder ones were already crowding forward.

"Stop!" cried The Phantom. The gong had ceased ringing, and his voice
rang sharp and clear down the hall. "The first man that moves will get a
bullet."

Momentarily awed by the metallic tones, the crowd fell back. The Phantom's glittering eyes seemed to encompass them all in their sweep, and there
was an air of desperate determination about his tense, slightly crouching
figure that impressed them strongly.

The situation was the most critical The Phantom had ever faced, yet he felt
a tingle of triumph as he surveyed the huddled throng. Any one of them could
have crippled or killed him with a well-aimed shot, but not a hand moved. For
the moment, at least, he was holding them in subjection through the sheer
strength of his domineering personality and his attitude of utter fearlessness.

Someone laughed, and The Phantom's eyes turned to Slade, standing on
the outer fringe of the crowd. He held a pistol in his hand, but the muzzle was
pointed downward.

"You must be crazy," he said contemptuously. "Can't you see that you are
outnumbered eleven to one?"

"I hadn't taken time to count," said The Phantom calmly. In the same
instant a crack and a flash of fire came from his automatic. One of the crowd,

more intrepid than the others, had ventured forward as he spoke, and now a yell of pain signified that The Phantom had aimed straight.

Slade scowled. On his face was a look of mingled wonder and rage.

"Mr. Shei's orders are not to kill you unless necessary," he explained, "and I have been hoping you wouldn't make it necessary. Mr. Shei has the highest admiration for you."

"Thanks," said The Phantom dryly, and for a mere instant his thoughts went back to the ludicrous figure of Fairspeckle. "It's too bad I can't say that the sentiment is mutual."

Slade's scowl deepened. He seemed inclined to instruct his men to advance, but something evidently restrained him.

"You ought to know by this time that Mr. Shei is invincible," he declared impressively. "You are a wonder in some ways, but a fool in others. How you keep slipping in and out of this house is beyond me. Not that it matters, for you have sung your last tune. What have you done to Doctor Tagala?"

A thin smile hovered about The Phantom's compressed lips.

"I suppose you have kidnaped him," Slade went on, "but we will find him before long. You see, Mr. Shei foresaw even such a possibility as that, and prepared for it. He anticipated that pressure of some sort might be used on Tagala to make him reveal where the antidote is hidden, and so he prepared the trap you walked into a moment ago. The bottles, as you may have guessed by this time, contain only water. The real antidote is elsewhere, and Tagala is the only man who can put his hand on it."

"So I understand." There was a momentary flicker in The Phantom's eyes which indicated that Slade's words had suggested something of importance to him. "Mr. Shei is amazingly clever—but there is such a thing as being *too* clever."

Slade looked as if he sensed a hidden meaning which his mind could not quite grasp. Presently he shrugged and fixed his frosty gaze on The Phantom.

"I'll give you just one more chance to surrender," he warned. "Throw down your pistol and tell us where Tagala is, and I promise you will not be harmed."

"Very anxious to learn Tagala's whereabouts—aren't you, Slade? Without Tagala you can't find the antidote, and without the antidote your beautiful scheme goes to pieces. It would be very awkward for you if you shouldn't be able to deliver the goods when your seven victims have come around to the point where they are willing to pay your price."

Slade mumbled something under his breath. Again The Phantom's eyes darted over the fringe of sullen faces in the background. He was gambling for Helen's life and his own, and he still held one card in reserve.

"Tagala seems to be the key to the whole situation," he went on. "I have hidden him in a place where you will never find him, even if you search from now till doomsday. Men sometimes die of hunger in three days, especially if they do a lot of fretting in the meantime. Slade, why don't you order your men to shoot me?"

The last sentence was spoken in taunting tones, and Slade's face showed that the gibe had gone home. Inwardly fuming, he glared savagely at The Phantom.

"Is it because you realize that, if I am killed, Tagala will die with me?" The Phantom's smile told that he once more felt he was master of the situation. "Is that the reason, Slade?"

Slade grumbled inarticulately. He glanced gloomily at the men lined up behind him. Then he looked again at The Phantom, and his face took on a baffled look. He seemed unable to account for the fact that one man, single-handed, was holding nine at bay. Suddenly, as his glance flitted up and down The Phantom's tense figure, his face brightened a trifle. He whispered something in the ear of the man at his side, and the latter immediately hurried away.

The Phantom felt a twinge of misgiving. It was evident from the gratified smirk on Slade's lips that an inspiration had just occurred to him and that he was planning a surprise of some sort. The Phantom wondered whether the resourceful Mr. Shei had provided against this latest emergency as he had against the others. He waited in a state of tremulous tension, and presently a slight sound drew his attention to the stairs at the end of the hall.

He glanced aside out of the tail of an eye, and then sudden despair took hold of him. Halfway up the stairs, gazing blankly down upon the scene in the hall, stood Helen Hardwick. There was a look in her face that caused a groan to break from The Phantom's lips.

Suddenly he stiffened. In an instant he saw the meaning of the elated smile on Slade's face. Directly behind Helen he discerned a crouching figure, evidently the man who had left the hall a few minutes before.

"Splendid!" ejaculated Slade. "I see you have already glimpsed the idea. At this very moment the muzzle of a pistol is pressing against Miss Hardwick's back. The slightest pressure on the trigger will send a bullet through her heart. You cannot fire at him, much as you would like to do so, for Miss Hardwick's figure makes an excellent bulwark. Will you admit you are beaten?"

Torn between rage and despair, The Phantom gazed rigidly at Helen. The stolid expression on her face showed plainly that she had not the faintest inkling of what was going on. Now and then her lips twitched as if she were on the point of laughing. Of the figure crouching behind her only an elbow and a narrow strip of shoulder were visible. An anguished cry rose in The Phantom's throat as he saw the full infamy of Slade's ruse.

"I shall begin to count," said Slade in triumphant tones. "If, by the time I come to ten, you have not signified by throwing down your pistol that you are willing to surrender, Miss Hardwick will die instantly."

A hush, charged with an electric tension, followed the ultimatum. Then, slowly and evenly, Slade began to count:

"One—two—three—four—five—"

CHAPTER XIX
A FUTILE SEARCH

WALKING WITH HIS USUAL listless and shuffling gait, Lieutenant Culligore mounted the steps in front of police headquarters and entered the office of Inspector Stapleton of the detective bureau. It was late in the afternoon, and Culligore might have quickened his steps and carried himself with more animation if he could have known that at this very moment The Gray Phantom, seated in the secret chamber at Azurecrest, was planning his second move against the redoubtable Mr. Shei.

Stapleton, a huge, thick-necked man with a reddish face and a tendency toward irascibility, looked up with a scowl as the lieutenant walked in.

"Well, what's new?" he demanded.

"Nothing," said Culligore patiently and flopped into a chair beside the inspector's desk, "except that our friend Mr. Shei seems to be getting away with it."

Stapleton glared at a pile of newspapers he had been reading. His temper was on edge from his perusal of several editorials that chided the bureau for its failure to circumvent Mr. Shei.

"Two of the seven moneybags are already showing the white feather," Culligore continued, "and two or three of the others are getting wabbly. By the end of the week I guess most of 'em will be ready to pay Mr. Shei's price. I don't know how he means to manage the transaction, but I'll bet a pair of pink socks he'll figure out a safe way."

"What are the doctors doing? Still loafing on the job, I suppose?"

"They're up a tree—every mother's son of them. They can't dope out the disease at all. If they had seven months instead of seven days, they might be able to do something, but as it is, they're at the end of their tether. Their only hope is that one of the seven will be obliging enough to die before the others, so they can perform an autopsy."

Stapleton jerked his head savagely to one side. "This is the twentieth century and we're living in a civilized country," he muttered. "A man can't put over a thing like that in these times."

"Just what I've been telling myself for the last three days," admitted Culligore. "I've been saying it can't be done—but Mr. Shei is going right ahead and doing it."

"And he's pulling the trick right under our noses," supplemented the inspector. "That's what gets my goat. It's plain as day that Mr. Shei is The Gray Phantom. Nobody but The Gray Phantom ever got away with a thing like this, and this job has all the ear-marks of his work. Well," and his huge fist descended on the desk with a slam, "we'll get him yet, and when we do I'll see to it that he's put away for keeps."

Culligore drew the palm of his hand across his mouth as if to stifle one of his infrequent grins.

"Keeping something up your sleeve again?" demanded the inspector, who had noticed the gesture. "If you've got something on your mind, why don't you spring it?"

The lieutenant shifted his lanky figure in the chair. "I've been trying all day to get a line on Fairspeckle," he said slowly, without directly answering the inspector's question. "Strange how that old duffer vamoosed. I tried to question the Jap valet, but all he knows is that there are two bumps on his head where there was only one before. The doctor and the nurse got rough treatment, too. Of a sudden the lights went out, and old Fairspeckle seemed to go out with them. Anyhow, he was gone when the doctor came to." Culligore paused to light one of his vicious-looking cigars. "Something odd about that old goat's disappearance—eh, inspector?"

Stapleton stared hard at his subordinate, as if trying to read the thoughts stirring behind his stolid countenance. "Of course there is," he said irritably. "There's something odd about every disappearance. Just what are you driving at? You don't doubt that Fairspeckle was kidnaped by Mr. Shei's agents?"

"I doubt everything, inspector. Know of any reason why Mr. Shei should go out of his way to abduct the old geezer?"

"No, I don't," admitted Stapleton after some thought. "The kidnaping of Fairspeckle doesn't seem to fit into the pattern of Mr. Shei's scheme. What's your idea, Culligore? You don't suppose Fairspeckle kidnaped himself?"

"Stranger things have happened, inspector. By the way," and the lieutenant reached into his pocket and took out several typewritten slips, "I meant to hand you these yesterday, but was too busy with other things. I found them beside the typewriter on Fairspeckle's desk. What do you make of them?"

Stapleton picked up the slips and glanced at them. His eyes widened into a stare as he read the typewritten lines. He read them twice, and then he transferred his gaze to Culligore.

"Holy mackerel!" he muttered. Then he sat silent for a time, wriggling his ample frame to and fro in the chair. "Why, these things make it look as though Fairspeckle was Mr. Shei."

"They show that the mystery isn't quite so simple as you thought, inspector. They sort of knock the pins from under your theory that The Gray Phantom is Mr. Shei."

For a few moments longer Stapleton's bewildered eyes rested on the slips. Then he read aloud the list of names beneath the introductory paragraph, and the pucker on his forehead deepened. Finally he looked quizzically at the lieutenant.

"Yes, I noticed it, too," said Culligore. "There's something wrong about that list. Looks as though Mr. Shei, whoever he is, hadn't followed his original programme. Seven men were inoculated, but only five of them are named in Fairspeckle's list. The other two names don't jibe."

Stapleton pondered for a while. He seemed to have great difficulty readjusting his thoughts to a new fact.

"And here's another interesting thing," Culligore pointed out. "Every one of the seven men mentioned in Fairspeckle's list was a member of a ring that fought him tooth and nail some years ago."

"And this is Fairspeckle's way of getting even with them," ventured the inspector.

"Maybe," said Culligore guardedly. "Anyhow, a fairly strong motive could be made out of it."

"But how do you account for the fact that Fairspeckle didn't carry out his original programme?"

"I'm not trying to account for it just now. There might have been a slip of some kind. *If* Fairspeckle is Mr. Shei, the fact that he revised his list doesn't really cut any ice. Any man has a right to change his mind."

Inspector Stapleton sat up straight. He looked at Culligore in a determined way. "What I can't understand is why you didn't show me these slips yesterday. You say you were too busy with other things. I'd like to know what other things could be more important. Never mind that, though. The thing to do now is to find Fairspeckle."

Again Culligore drew his palm across his mouth. "And when you have found him, inspector, what are you going to do with him?"

"Eh?" Stapleton seemed to think the question a strange one. "Do with him? Why, we'll see to it that he gets the stiffest sentence the law provides. If we once get our hands on him we'll put him in a place where he won't be able to trouble us for some time."

"Aren't you overlooking something, inspector?"

Stapleton stared perplexedly at his subordinate.

"What about the seven capitalists?" the lieutenant went on. "They'll die like rats unless the antidote is administered in time. You can't make Mr. Shei fork over the antidote by putting him in jail. He's wise enough to know that as long as the antidote is in his possession he has a hold on us, and he won't be likely to give it up. He knows we are not going to let seven of the biggest men in the country die just for the sake of sending him to jail. The fact is, inspector, that Mr. Shei has us sewed up in a sack."

Stapleton seemed about to make an indignant reply, but it died on his tongue. Evidently Culligore's argument had made a strong impression. He dropped back against the chair and peered diffidently into space.

"I'm hanged if I'm going to sit with arms folded and let Mr. Shei put this thing over," he muttered at last. "He's a slick crook, but there ought to be a way of dealing with him."

"I think there is, inspector," agreed Culligore, leisurely rising from his chair. "I can't see it just yet, but maybe my mind will work better after a little walk. So long, inspector."

He shuffled from the room, followed by Inspector Stapleton's puzzled gaze. After leaving the headquarters building, he walked to a near-by restaurant and ordered a substantial meal. He seemed in no hurry, for he ate slowly and lingered for a considerable time over his coffee and cigar. An observer, noticing his languid air and phlegmatic expression, might have thought that Mr. Shei was farthest from his mind. It was dark when he left the restaurant, and it was a little after eight o'clock when, after a leisurely stroll in a zigzagging direction, he reached the Thelma Theater.

His decision to visit the Thelma once more might have been due to the fact that it had been the scene of several mysterious incidents which were more or less directly traceable to the activities of Mr. Shei. The death of Virginia Darrow had occurred there, and the bullet that had missed The Gray Phantom by such a narrow margin was still imbedded in one of the pillars. But Culligore's expression gave no indication of his purpose as he stood on the sidewalk across the street from the theater and glanced up at the windows of Vincent Starr's private office on the second floor.

The windows were dark, so evidently Starr was not there, and the entire structure presented a gloomy and lifeless appearance. Culligore hummed a little tune as he walked to the nearest street intersection, then cut diagonally across the thoroughfare, continued half a block to the west, and finally ducked into a dark basement entrance. The ease with which he made his way suggested that he had traveled the same route before. After walking down a dirty and foul-smelling passage, he emerged into a vacant space bordered at one side by the rear wall of the theater.

He crossed the inclosure, then ran down a short stairway, and brought up against a door. Now he took a number of keys from his pocket and tried several in the lock before he found one that fitted. At last the door came open, and the lieutenant, locking it carefully behind him, stood in the basement under the Thelma Theater.

On all sides was total darkness. For a time he stood still, listening for sounds, but nothing but dull and distant noises from the outside reached his ears. Having satisfied himself that he was apparently alone in the basement, he took out his flash light and began a thorough and comprehensive search. With the electric flash peering into every nook and corner, he explored the dressing rooms, peeped behind piles of discarded scenery, examined odds and ends of stage property, looked into the barrels and boxes in the dusty storerooms, and even tapped the walls here and there to assure himself that there were no hollow spaces.

At last he gave up. His search had taken almost an hour and it had been complete and painstaking in every respect, yet Lieutenant Culligore seemed not quite satisfied. On his face was a look of hesitancy that seemed to suggest a lingering suspicion that something might have eluded him. Standing in the center of the basement, he extinguished the flash light, for it had been his experience that his other senses were more acute when his eyes received no impressions.

For a little while, standing in impenetrable darkness, he scarcely breathed. He had a curious sensation that a faint sound was passing him and dissolving in the dank air. It was so slight and elusive that his ears could scarcely detect it, yet it appealed to his imagination with peculiar insistence. It might have been either a moan or a sigh, or perhaps a cry coming from a great distance. Somehow, though he could not analyze the sensation, he fancied it expressed a great, overwhelming anguish. Whether it came from above, below, or the sides he could not determine, but it inspired him with a haunting feeling that he was not alone.

Again he took up the flash, and instantly the impression vanished, as if it had been a wraith fleeing from the light. Once more, step by step, he went over every square foot of the basement, covering the ground he had already searched so patiently, but he found nothing that gave the slightest clew to the peculiar sound. Finally, half inclined to believe that his imagination had deceived him, he ascended the stairway and continued his search on the ground floor. With dogged determination he explored the space in the wings and back of the stage, then went up and down the aisles in the auditorium.

His inspection of the boxes was fruitless, and he found nothing of significance in the little niche where, on his previous visit to the Thelma, he had strongly suspected that an eavesdropper was hiding. Finally he went through the offices on the street front, occupied, as was indicated by the brass plates on the doors, by the treasurer, business manager, and stage director. Here also his quest was unavailing, and nothing now remained but Vincent Starr's private office on the upper floor.

The moment he entered, Culligore felt as though he were invading the den of a sybarite. His flash light, flitting slowly over the room, revealed soft color harmonies and exquisite decorations. Faint and delicate perfumes mingled with the fresh and alluring scents of flowers. Culligore's feet sank deep into costly rugs as he moved about the office, peeping behind chairs, desks, and cabinets, and occasionally sounding the walls for hollow spaces. After an hour of intense and patient effort, he was forced to admit that he had exerted himself needlessly and that his impressions while standing in the basement could have been nothing but figments of his fancy.

Finally he sat down in the luxuriously upholstered chair beside Starr's desk. His watch showed a quarter past eleven, and he tried to reconcile himself to the thought that the only thing he could do was to go home and sleep. He was disappointed, for he had hoped that his search would yield some tangible results. He scowled a little as his gaze roamed idly over the orderly piles of papers on the desk. The ink stand, the paper cutter, and the pens were all of ornamental design. The only plain and undecorative objects in the room were the two telephones standing at one side of the desk. It struck him as a little odd that there should be two of them, but then he noticed that one was an automatic instrument without outside connections and communicating only with the various departments in the building.

Presently he yawned ostentatiously. He could not quite understand his reason for remaining after his fruitless task was done, nor could he comprehend the feeling, vague but uncannily persistent, that the next few minutes would bring some startling developments.

A gentle buzzing caused him to sit up straight in the chair. The telephone was ringing, and instinctively he reached out his hand for one of the instruments. He spoke a soft "hello" in the transmitter. There was no response, but the ringing continued. A little dazedly he hung up the receiver and peered fixedly at the other telephone. He jerked it to him, thrust the transmitter to his ear, and instantly the buzzing ceased.

A gasp of amazement fell from his lips. Someone was calling on the automatic telephone, the one that had no outside connections. The person calling must be inside the building, then, despite the fact that his patient search had convinced him that there was no other human being within the four walls of the structure.

THELMA THEATER

Located still. There was no other sound but the wind in the trees
throughout.

CHAPTER XX
TRAPPED

"Hello—hello!" shouted Culligore into the mouthpiece. From head to foot
he was tingling with suspense. It was one of the rare occasions within recent
years when he felt the thrill of excitement.

A hoarse and rasping voice responded, but at first he could make out no
words. The person at the other end seemed to speak with great difficulty and
was evidently on the verge of hysterics.

"Speak a little louder, can't you?" urged the lieutenant. "Who are you?"

A jumble of split words and syllables sounded distantly in his ear. Now and
then, between efforts to speak clearly, came a titter and a giggle that awoke a
startling suspicion in Culligore's mind.

"Tell me who you are," he said in loud tones.

A short, cracked laugh came over the wire. It was followed by a groan, as if
the speaker were despairing over his inability to make himself understood.
Then he tried again. "Fair—Fairspeckle."

"Oh!" Culligore's teeth clicked out the exclamation. He nodded at the instrument, as if the name just spoken had confirmed a suspicion in his mind.
"Where are you, Mr. Fairspeckle?"

"I can't—can't tell you," came gropingly over the wire.

"Haven't you any idea?"

"None. I'm locked in a—a room, and I am—dying! For God's sake get me
out!"

"Listen, Mr. Fairspeckle," said Culligore tensely. "You're somewhere in the
Thelma Theater, and I am going to find you. It may take some little time, but
don't worry. It won't be very long."

A groan of relief mingled with pent-up suspense sounded in Culligore's ear,
and then he slammed the receiver back on the hook. His eyes were twinkling
and there was a new eagerness in his face. He jumped up from the chair and
took a step toward the door. Then he drew back, and in the next moment his
face had resumed its habitual sluggish expression and there was nothing in
his manner to indicate that anything out of the ordinary had happened.

The door opened and in walked Vincent Starr. The theatrical manager, faultlessly attired in evening dress, topcoat, and silk hat, shrank back at sight of the man standing beside the desk. Then, recognizing the lieutenant, he instantly gathered himself.

"You startled me, Culligore," he explained with an apologetic laugh. "So many strange things have happened in this place that I am naturally a little nervous. I often come here late at night to read or write, according to my mood, but of late I approach the place in fear and trembling." He eyed the detective inquiringly. "I wonder what brings you to my private office at such an hour."

"Hope you don't mind my snooping," said Culligore genially. "I have been looking around a bit. There were a couple of things I wanted to get straightened out in my mind. As you say yourself, there have been a lot of strange doings in this place, and I've got a sneaking suspicion that Mr. Shei is back of them all."

Starr doffed his hat and ran his fingers through his long, glossy hair. The discoloration of his nose had diminished greatly, but his face was still pale and drawn.

"That's precisely my idea," he said nervously. "I shall never feel safe until that scoundrel is behind iron bars. Unless he has a private grievance against me, I am at a loss to understand why he can't keep away from my theater. By the way, did you obtain any light on the things that were puzzling you?"

"Not much," said Culligore disgustedly, with a furtive glance at the telephone. "I searched every square inch of the place without finding what I was after."

"Yes?" Starr seemed politely curious. "I infer, then, that you had a definite object in view, that you were not just searching at random."

"Oh, no." Culligore looked about him as if not quite at ease. "I suppose we're alone?"

"Not another soul in the building. You can speak as freely as you like."

"Then I'll tell you exactly what I think. The way Mr. Shei's men have been sneaking in and out of this place is mighty suggestive. Just why they should be turning your place into a rendezvous is something I don't understand, but that's exactly what they seem to be doing. They were right on the job the night you opened your new play. They gave Virginia Darrow a shot of poison just at the psychological moment, before she could spill what she knew. Then they sneaked the body away right under our eyes, and we have not yet discovered how they managed it. Only the other day, somebody took a shot at either you or The Gray Phantom. All this looks mighty odd."

"It does," assented Starr. He took out a jewel-studded case and lighted a cigarette. His pale, uneasy eyes did not leave the detective's face for a moment. "What is your theory?"

Culligore looked musingly into space. "Mr. Shei is very clever, but he is of flesh and blood, like the rest of us. There must be a simple and natural explanation for all these strange doings. I'll bet my hat that he has found a secret entrance to your place."

"Impossible," said Starr promptly. "This theater was built according to my own directions and my own architects supervised every detail of the construction."

"That may be, but I still stick to the idea of a secret entrance. Don't you see, Mr. Starr, even if you didn't have such an entrance made when you constructed your theater, Mr. Shei's men may have drilled a hole through the wall or the floor somewhere? Nothing else explains how they have been slipping in and out of the place."

"But why?" demanded Starr, and his fingers trembled as he took the cigarette from his lips. "Why should they do such a thing?"

Culligore smiled faintly while his muddy little eyes scanned the other's face.

"I think you can make a pretty fair guess," he said dryly.

Starr's face turned a shade paler. For an instant there was a look of positive dread in his eyes, but it vanished quickly. A sad smile came to his lips.

"I see I must be frank with you," he murmured, "much as I dislike to discuss matters pertaining to my private life. Don't ask me to go into details, for there are excellent reasons why I should not do so. In plain words, I do not care to incriminate myself. I have not always been what I am today. There was a time, quite a number of years ago, when I led a very violent life and when the law and I were not on the best of terms. I made enemies—a number of them—and it is possible that they are pursuing me today. In fact I—"

He paused, and his narrowing gaze slanted to the floor. Culligore repressed a start. In the intense silence of the moment he heard a faint buzzing. Somewhere, in one of the offices on the ground floor, a telephone was ringing, and he guessed that Fairspeckle had grown impatient and was calling one of the other departments of the intercommunicating system.

"In fact," Starr went on after a moment's pause, quickly controlling his astonishment, "if I were to come face to face with Mr. Shei today, I strongly suspect that I would recognize in him one of my old enemies. Don't ask me to explain any further, Culligore. You will appreciate the delicacy of the matter."

"I do, and you've said enough to explain the funny doings that have been going on here. I want you to answer one question frankly. Have you any idea who Mr. Shei is?"

"Have you?" was Starr's prompt rejoinder.

Culligore chuckled. "Maybe I have and maybe I haven't. I'm pretty sure of one thing. Some people think The Gray Phantom is Mr. Shei, but they're dead wrong."

Starr's lips twitched into a knowing smile. "I agree with you, there, Culligore. Shall we go a step farther? With The Gray Phantom eliminated, the range of available suspects narrows down to one man. Am I right?"

"I think you are on the right track, Mr. Starr."

The theatrical manager, once more quite composed, seemed to find a great deal of amusement in the speculative drift of the conversation.

"It is diverting to try to read other people's minds," he observed. "I wonder how close I can come to an accurate reading of yours. A detective's thoughts travel a devious route, but I will try to look at the situation from your point of view, taking all the circumstances into account. If you were to mention the name of the one remaining suspect, I fancy it would be W. Rufus Fairspeckle."

Culligore stared as if dumfounded at the other's astuteness, but his lips curled into the faintest grin as soon as Starr averted his gaze.

"You might as well admit that I was right," said the manager with a smile of elation. "For once a mere layman has read your mind like an open book. The next question is what has become of Fairspeckle. Do you suppose—"

He broke off short. His glance darted involuntarily to the automatic telephone on the desk. Its summons sounded clear and distinct in the tense silence. Once more a tinge of gray crept into his face. With a tightening of the lips he looked furtively at Culligore.

"Strange!" muttered the lieutenant, fingering the green cord attached to the instrument and tracing it to the sound box. "Someone is calling on the private wire. And you just told me that you and I were alone in the building."

The buzzing continued. Starr stared helplessly at the instrument, but out of the tail of an eye he was watching the expression on the detective's face. Finally, with a jerk of the shoulders, he emerged from his daze.

"I don't understand it," he murmured, "but we shall soon see what it means."

He sat down and drew the instrument to him. His face took on a look of determination, but there was also a baffling and inscrutable expression that might have puzzled the detective. But Culligore's thoughts seemed to be elsewhere. He looked as though he foresaw a critical moment and realized that quick thinking and prompt action were necessary. While Starr was speaking into the telephone, he looked quickly about the room. From his vest pocket he took a small box and removed the lid, exposing a reddish substance that looked like salve. Rubbing a little of it onto his finger tips, he softly crossed the room and quickly smeared a thin coating of the reddish material on the doorknob.

Starr hung up the receiver just as the little box disappeared into Culligore's vest pocket.

"I don't understand it," said the manager frettingly. "Someone was speaking. It was a man's voice, but I couldn't make out what he was trying to say. It is very mysterious." He smiled faintly. "It's beginning to look as though I was mistaken and there was someone else in the building besides you and me."

"It certainly looks odd," admitted Culligore. "I searched everywhere, but we might as well go over the ground again."

Starr acquiesced readily, and Culligore saw to it that the manager preceded him out of the room. He noticed with gratification that the other's fingers closed firmly around the knob as he opened the door, and he knew that Starr was too preoccupied to take heed of the faint smear left on his hand from contact with the greased metal. He chuckled inwardly as he followed the manager down the stairs and through the offices in front of the building. After a brief and somewhat perfunctory search, they entered the auditorium.

"Shall I switch on the lights?" whispered Starr, walking beside the detective.

"I wouldn't. If there's a prowler around the place, we don't want to warn him. My electric flash will do."

For a time they conducted the search in silence, the detective cautiously darting the electric gleam over floor and walls and into dark corners. Finally he paused before a niche in the wall and pointed to an aperture behind the marble shelf that spanned the opening.

"Do you know," he whispered, "that the other day, while I was talking with The Gray Phantom, I had a funny feeling someone was hiding back there and listening to our conversation? Who do you suppose it could have been?"

There was no response. Culligore had been peering into the recess behind the marble ledge. Now he looked up quickly, but Starr was gone—and the twitching of the detective's lips signified that the manager's sudden disappearance did not surprise him greatly. In an instant he was amazingly alert. Jerking his electric flash hither and thither, he moved quickly back and forth within the narrow space where he had last seen the manager, sweeping the surrounding objects with his electric gleam and examining the surfaces of chairs, pillars, walls, and decorative articles.

Presently he brought up in front of one of the larger pillars supporting the balcony. He had previously noticed its huge dimensions, and now he gauged them again with a quickly calculating eye. It was there The Gray Phantom had stood when the mysterious shot was fired the other day, and Helen Hardwick had been leaning against the same pillar when the curious individual with the repulsive features glided past her.

The electric gleam moved swiftly over the white surface of the post with its ornate trimmings of dull gold. Again, as once or twice before, he wondered whether there was any hidden significance in the fact that The Gray Phantom had stood in this identical spot at the moment the shot was fired. Was it possible that the skulking assailant had feared that The Phantom was about to make an important discovery, and was that why he had fired the shot? Culligore pondered the question while scanning every square inch of the pillar.

Suddenly the electric gleam stopped at a point near the floor, and Culligore could scarcely repress an exclamation of elation. His ruse had succeeded, for on the white surface of the post was a faint discoloration which signified that Starr's hand had recently touched that particular point. There were no other marks, and this one was only a few inches from the floor. Culligore's fingers ran quickly over the surrounding space, and occasionally he pressed his thumb firmly against the wood, but without discovering anything. His hand slid downward to where the rich Persian carpet was neatly tucked around the base of the post, and suddenly his exploring fingers touched a slight knoblike projection. He pressed firmly, and he felt an exultant tingle as there came a soft, whirring response. A panel in the post, ingeniously hidden in the gold-lined grooves, was sliding back, forming an aperture.

The electric gleam showed a look of keen elation on Culligore's face. His discovery had taken only a minute or two of valuable time, for he had moved fast since he noticed that Starr was gone. Yet, but for a happy inspiration and the resultant reddish stain on the post, he might have searched for days without finding the opening.

Now he squeezed his figure through the narrow aperture, at the same time pocketing his electric flash and drawing his automatic. His feet encountered the upper rungs of a ladder that pointed straight down. He descended rapidly, making no sound. At the bottom was a narrow passage extending in the direction of the street, and at its farther end he saw a faint glow. He approached quickly, warned by a sixth sense that he had no time to waste.

He came to a door. It stood open a crack, and through the narrow opening he saw a strange scene. An elderly man, with a thin and haggard face and sunken eyes that stared about him in an agonized way, was lying on a cot.

Starr, bending over the recumbent man, was winding pieces of rope around his feet and hands and drawing them into tight knots.

"There, Mr. Fairspeckle," he tauntingly declared when he had fastened a gag around the other man's mouth, "I don't think you will work loose a second time. Even if you should, you will find that the telephone is out of order."

He laughed, turned away from the cot, and uttered a gasp as he looked into the muzzle of Culligore's pistol. Every trace of color faded from his face, but he gathered himself quickly.

"You are a most astounding person, Culligore," he remarked coolly. "I wonder how you found your way down here. Not that it matters," he added with a shrug, "but I am naturally curious. I won't press you for the information, however. Any way I can be of service?"

"Yes, Mr. Shei," said Culligore, emphasizing each word and looking straight into the other's eyes, "you can hold out your hands and not make any fuss while I put the handcuffs on you."

Starr laughed derisively. "Sorry not to be able to oblige you, but I have a distinct aversion to handcuffs. Won't you sit down and be comfortable? An underground room like this has many advantages. In the chests you see against the walls I occasionally store things that the police and private detectives would give a great deal to be able to lay their hands on. It is an excellent hiding place, and it serves several other purposes besides."

"So I see," muttered Culligore with a glance at the man on the cot. Fairspeckle's face bore a dazed look and he seemed to understand nothing of what was being said, but his staring eyes held an expression of terror.

"I would like to know," murmured Starr, fixing his pale eyes on the lieutenant's inscrutable face, "how and when you learned that I was Mr. Shei. I was under the impression that you suspected Fairspeckle."

"I meant you should be," said Culligore with a dry chuckle. "I knew somebody was listening behind the marble ledge the day I had that talk with The Gray Phantom upstairs, and I guessed it was either you or one of your men. I pretended to believe that Fairspeckle was Mr. Shei, and I encouraged The Phantom in thinking the same thing, but all the while I was talking for the benefit of the fellow behind the marble slab. I had a pretty good suspicion as to who Mr. Shei was, and I wanted to throw him off his guard. Once a man gets careless it isn't hard to catch him."

Starr grinned appreciatively. "I'll admit that you are far shrewder than you look, Culligore, but I am not so sure that I have been guilty of carelessness. That remains to be seen. What I am curious to know is when you first began to suspect that I was Mr. Shei. You see, I have nothing to fear from you, so I frankly admit the fact. But I would like to know by what sort of reasoning you were led to suspect me."

"There wasn't any course of reasoning," said Culligore, maintaining a steady grip on his pistol. "It was only a flash here and there. The first flash came when I saw the note Virginia Darrow sent you the night she died. I guessed then that she had learned in some way that you were Mr. Shei, and she wanted to tease you with it. A little later, when you were handed that bump on the nose, I didn't know exactly what to think. Then it came to me that, if you really were Mr. Shei, you would have yourself assaulted along with the others to turn suspicion away from you. It was a clever move, Mr. Starr, but it didn't fool me for long. Well, a number of other things happened that strengthened my suspicion, but I wasn't really sure until I walked into this room tonight."

Starr scowled a little. "You are a bit disappointing, Culligore. I had hoped you would give me an example of fine-spun deductive reasoning of the kind that always drips from the lips of story-book detectives. Just one more thing before we close this pleasant interview. How do you account for Mr. Fair-speckle?"

"Oh, that part was fairly easy. Fairspeckle is a strange sort, but he never did any real harm. He's been troubled with insomnia, and when a man can't sleep, he's likely to do any foolish thing, from writing poetry on a park bench to murdering his mother-in-law. The deeper the mystery, the simpler the explanation. That has been my experience, and it has held true in Fairspeckle's case. I'm not dead sure of my facts, but I can make a pretty close guess. The night Mr. Shei's notices were posted, Fairspeckle had been roaming the town as he always did when he couldn't sleep. He saw one of the notices in Times Square and, being one of the seven richest men in town, he didn't like the idea a bit. Then The Gray Phantom came strolling along, and Fairspeckle recognized him. Like many others, he jumped at the conclusion that The Phantom was Mr. Shei, and right away he began to study out a way of beating Mr. Shei's game.

"By some hook or crook he got The Phantom into his apartment, and there he tried to drug him. He had two objects in view. One of them was to keep The Phantom under cover for a time so he wouldn't be able to go on with his scheme, and the other was to get even with certain enemies of his by throwing an almighty scare into them. While the real Mr. Shei, as he supposed, was a prisoner in his apartment, he meant to carry the scheme just a step or two farther—just far enough to put fear into his old enemies. It just so happened that five of those enemies were among the seven richest men in town. Well, Fairspeckle got a typewriter and went to work and typed a new set of notices, supplementing the ones that had already been posted. I hope he had a good laugh while he was typing the seven names, for that's all the good his scheme did him. A few hours later he was kidnaped. That was another fairly clever move, Starr."

Starr seemed to enjoy the compliment. "Thanks, Culligore," he murmured. "I knew you would appreciate that little touch. After overhearing the conversation between you and The Phantom, in which I thought you made it plain that both of you suspected Fairspeckle, I saw a still more effective way to divert suspicion from myself. Since you already suspected Fairspeckle, as I thought at the time, it occurred to me to let the suspicion take firmer root by having Fairspeckle disappear. A man who vanishes mysteriously is always an object of suspicion."

Culligore nodded absently. Only half his mind had been on Starr's speech. Now, still holding the automatic firmly leveled, he came a step closer to the other man.

"I don't like to muss you up," he said softly, "so please put out your hands and make no trouble."

Starr chuckled amusedly. "You are really surprisingly simple, Culligore. Your pistol doesn't frighten me, for I know you won't use it. And arresting me won't do you any good. If you put me in jail, the antidote will never be found, and then seven of the biggest men in the country will die. Don't you see, Culligore, that there isn't a thing you can do?"

His tones were soft and teasing, and his words expressed the same idea that Culligore himself had voiced in Inspector Stapleton's presence. Slowly the lieutenant ran his eyes over the walls. The underground chamber, and especially the steel chests stacked along the side, would serve excellently as a hiding place. What more natural than the antidote should be concealed in one of the chests? It seemed—

He got no farther in his reasoning. Too swiftly for Culligore to interfere, Starr's hand moved to the wall at his side. A faint click sounded, and then blackness fell. Culligore sprang forward, but already a loud slam signified that the door had closed. He hurled himself against it, but he might as well have been pitting his strength against a brick wall.

"Trapped!" he muttered.

CHAPTER XXI
MR. SHEI'S STRATAGEM

A SWARM OF JUMBLED thoughts and emotions crowded each fraction of a second as The Gray Phantom, standing with his back against the door, heard Slade's slow and precise voice pronounce the numerals. At each distinctly spoken word he started as if a rapier had prodded his flesh. His gaze was fixed on Helen, who from her position in the stairway stared down on the scene with eyes that appeared to see nothing, and the blank look in her face told him that she was mercifully oblivious of the meaning of it all.

With the speed of lightning, stray thoughts and impressions flashed through The Phantom's mind. Slade had warned him that Helen would die when he had counted ten, unless The Phantom surrendered in the meantime. At Helen's back, shielded by her body against a possible bullet from The Phantom's revolver, stood the executioner, ready to press the trigger.

Things swam in confusion before The Phantom's eyes. He would gladly have given his life if thereby he could save Helen from her predicament. But Slade dared not kill him just yet, not until he had learned where Doctor Tagala was hidden, and so he hoped to force The Phantom into submission by threatening Helen. The plan was subtle and fiendishly clever, and more than once, as the seconds dragged by, The Phantom had been on the point of yielding. The only thing that had restrained him was the belief that his surrender would only make the situation worse. It would deprive him of his precarious advantage, and then Helen's position would be doubly desperate.

Once he glanced at the automatic in his hand, wishing that he could fire a bullet into the figure crouching behind Helen. It was a forlorn hope, for the coward knew better than to expose himself. Again Slade's voice, pronouncing each syllable with excessive precision, broke in upon his thoughts:

"—five—six—seven—"

The Phantom jerked up his head as an inspiration flashed through his mind. He still had an advantage, though his aching mind had not been able to grasp it until this very minute. Again his eyes sought the pistol drooping from his nerveless right hand.

"—eight—nine—" A note of hesitancy crept into Slade's accents, and he looked expectantly at The Phantom. Evidently he was reluctant to pronounce the final word, the word that would mean Helen's death. He vastly preferred that The Phantom should accept his terms, but his face showed no sign of yielding from his purpose.

His lips opened, and in another moment the fatal word would have been spoken. But in that brief interval The Phantom acted, and the word never left Slade's lips. Instead he uttered a long-drawn-out exclamation of amazement.

The Phantom's maneuver had been both swift and surprising. The blue steel of his automatic had flashed for an instant in the dim light, and then he had pressed its muzzle firmly against his heart. For a few moments the crowd stared in dumfounded amazement; then a startled look in Slade's face showed that he understood. He bit his lip and suppressed a cry of rage.

"If Miss Hardwick dies, I die, too," declared The Phantom in gritty accents; and the metallic gleam of his eye and the note of grim earnestness in his voice left no doubt of his sincerity. "And you can't afford to let me die, Slade. With me dead, you would never find Tagala, and then the bottom would drop out of Mr. Shei's scheme."

Slade fumed and gnashed his teeth in impotent rage. A glance at The Phantom's face, smiling and yet grimly determined, seemed to increase his fury. But The Phantom's airy confidence was all on the surface. He knew that his dramatic gesture had only postponed the crisis, and already his mind was planning another move.

At last Slade's rage cooled and his reason reasserted itself. Pointing to the stairway, he bawled an order to the man behind Helen to take her back to her room. The Phantom drew a long breath of relief as she was half led, half carried up the remaining steps; but the comfort the sight gave him was of brief duration.

Now Slade's finger was pointing at himself. "Take his gun away," he ordered the men lined up behind him. "Make a rush for him, all at once, but don't shoot. Go!"

The men bounded forward, but in the same instant The Phantom's pistol spoke twice. Two yells of pain followed the sharp cracks of the weapon, and the leaders of the rush sank to the floor. The others stopped, stared diffidently at the steadily pointing pistol, then wavered and fell back. Once more The Phantom had triumphed. He cast a quick glance at the two who had fallen. He had aimed to cripple, not to kill, and he could see that their wounds were not serious.

Slade shook his fist at the cowering men.

"Are you all white-livered kittens?" he shouted. "Are you going to let one man bluff you? Rush at him again, all together!"

The Phantom tensed himself for the attack. He quavered inwardly as he recalled that only two slugs remained in his cartridge chamber. He crouched behind the pistol, fixing each man in turn with a piercing gaze. The line advanced with a rush. Someone, more intrepid than the others, seized one of his legs and tried to pull him to the floor, but The Phantom disposed of him with a vigorous kick. The next was dispatched with a well-aimed bullet, and the third went reeling to the floor from a blow with the butt of his pistol. He took careful aim before he fired his one remaining shot, and a scream of agony told that the bullet had found its mark. Again the line wavered and broke. On the floor lay five who had been maimed by The Phantom's bullets and one who was still unconscious from the blow with the pistol. Of the original eleven combatants only five remained, but also The Phantom's ammunition was spent, and at any moment one or more of the wounded might revive and get back into the fray.

Slade's face was white with helpless rage. He could not know that The Phantom's cartridge chamber was empty. He stamped his foot and again shook his fist at the men. Taking advantage of his temporary distraction, The Phantom glided forward and, stooping quickly, snatched a pistol from the cramped fingers of one of the wounded. Then he threw down his own weapon and hurried back to his position at the door.

Slade noticed his sudden move out of the tail of an eye, but not soon enough to prevent it. He turned again to the remnant of his little army. His face was dark and bore an ominous scowl.

"We will get him yet," he declared, snarling. "Form a line and take aim, but don't shoot to kill. Aim for the arms and legs only. Don't shoot until I give the word."

The men spread out in a half circle, and The Phantom saw five pistols pointing at him. There was a malevolent grin on Slade's lips as he watched the preparations. Then he stepped to one side of the half circle.

"Fire!" he commanded.

The Phantom ducked just as a chorus of shots rang out. A stinging sensation in the shoulder told him he had been hit, but he choked back the cry of pain that rose in his throat. A dense film of powder hung in the air, and for a few moments the firing line was only a row of shadowy forms. The Phantom thought of flight, but someone opened a window and the smoke quickly scattered. In the next instant the blare of a motor horn was heard in the distance.

The men exchanged quick glances, and The Phantom fancied he saw a look of relief on Slade's face. In the muttered conversation that followed he made out the name of Mr. Shei, and new misgivings caused him to forget the stinging pain in his shoulder. Slade's handling of the situation had exposed him as a bungler, but for Mr. Shei's ingenuity and resourcefulness The Phantom had a high respect. If Mr. Shei had arrived, as the blare of the horn and the conversation among the men seemed to signify, then a new and more critical situation awaited him.

He glanced toward the end of the hall. A faint glimmer of dawn showed against the window back of the stairway railing. The night had been crowded with exciting events, and the time had passed more quickly than he realized. Again Mr. Shei's name was mentioned among the men, and then a hush fell over the group. A door opened at one side of the hall, and in the next instant The Phantom's eyes widened into a bewildered stare.

The tall man who entered and was received with such marked deference by Slade and the others was none other than Vincent Starr!

A film floated before The Phantom's eyes. It seemed almost unbelievable at first, but a succession of minor incidents and circumstances that had vaguely puzzled him at times suddenly came back to him in the light of a new significance. He had been blind, he told himself; yet it was no wonder that he had been deceived. His concern for Helen had been uppermost in his mind, and he was forced to admit that Starr had played his game very shrewdly.

The newcomer cast a swift, comprehensive glance up and down the hall, then turned to Slade, and the two engaged in a low-voiced conversation. Now and then Starr mentioned Culligore's name, and The Phantom gathered from isolated words and phrases that something of an unpleasant nature had happened to the lieutenant. He learned, too, that there had been developments that necessitated quick action on Mr. Shei's part and that the latter had made a quick motor trip from New York to Azurecrest. The Phantom absorbed these bits of news with interest, but all the time he was studying the characteristic gestures with which Starr emphasized his statements. Once before, while standing in the Thelma Theater, it struck him that there was something familiar about them, and the same impression came to him now. He was searching his memory for half-forgotten facts when Starr suddenly turned round and faced him.

"Surprised?" he inquired, and his smile exposed two rows of flashingly white teeth.

"A little, at first, but I think I understand it all now," was The Phantom's nonchalant reply. Then, of a sudden, his figure stiffened. Starr had delivered another of his oddly expressive gestures, and it had started another train of recollections in The Phantom's mind. "Starr," he added impulsively, "you were once a member of my organization."

"Only a very humble one," admitted Starr, "and it was years back, so it's no wonder you didn't recognize me at first. In those days you scarcely noticed me, but I was watching and studying you all the time. There were a lot of melodramatic notions in my head, and The Gray Phantom was my hero. I dreamed of some day eclipsing his achievements, and I think I have succeeded. You see, the Thelma Theater, for all the fun I got out of the experiment, was only a cover for my other and more fascinating activities."

"My first impression was correct, then," murmured The Phantom, addressing himself rather than Starr. "I suspected Mr. Shei was a former follower of mine and had learned his methods from me, and that's why I decided to defeat his purpose and break up his organization. Now I'm doubly glad that I took up the cudgels against you, Starr."

"Glad?" A puzzled frown crossed Starr's face. "You are a beaten man, defeated by a once insignificant pupil of yours. Why should you be glad?"

"Defeated?" The Phantom threw back his head and smiled. "Not just yet, Starr. The Gray Phantom doesn't even know the meaning of the word. Before I drop out of this game you and your crowd will be in jail."

A cloud gathered on Starr's forehead. "You are a curious character. I have beaten you at every turn. I have you so completely cornered that you can't even raise your pistol against me without endangering the life of a certain person whom you are deeply interested in. By the way, Slade has bungled this situation. He tells me that you have kidnaped Doctor Tagala and refuse to tell where he is hidden."

"He has told you the exact facts. You will never see Tagala again until I release him, and that I won't do until Miss Hardwick has been freed and the antidote turned over to me."

Starr's lip curled scornfully. "As I said, Slade has bungled the situation. He doesn't seem to understand what kind of persuasion to exert on a man like you. I think I can suggest an improvement. Miss Hardwick, as I think you know, received a dose of datura poison calculated to produce death within seven days. What is the matter?" he added quickly as The Phantom winced and touched his left shoulder. "Ah! You have been wounded!"

"Only a scratch," said The Phantom coolly, despite the sharp twinges that now and then shot through the injured shoulder. "What about Miss Hardwick?"

"As I said, the injection she received was calculated to kill within seven days. As you know, if you read the accounts of Virginia Darrow's death, the dose can be so adjusted as to produce death in a much shorter time—say fifteen minutes or half an hour. Doctor Tagala, who is a very fascinating gentleman, explained the method to me very carefully."

"I don't quite see—" began The Phantom, an uneasy flicker in his eyes; but Starr had already turned to his lieutenant.

"Slade," he crisply commanded, "in one of the drawers of the desk in the laboratory you will find several bottles of datura poison. Bring me one of those marked 'Series A.' Fetch a hypodermic syringe, too, and be quick about it."

Slade withdrew. A horrifying suspicion was entering The Phantom's mind. Starr's methods were subtler and far more frightful than his subordinate's.

"You look faint," observed Starr with a glance at The Phantom's face. A trace of sarcasm edged his words. "I'm afraid the wound is very painful. Too bad Doctor Tagala isn't here to treat it."

The Phantom was about to reply, but just then Slade returned and handed his superior a syringe and a small bottle containing a dark liquid. Starr studied the label for a moment.

"Correct," he murmured. "It's fortunate Doctor Tagala taught me how to use a syringe. In a few moments Miss Hardwick will have received a second dose of datura poison—one that will kill her inside half an hour unless Doctor Tagala should administer the restorative in the meantime."

A cry broke from The Phantom's lips. The severe pain in the shoulder, together with the terrifying realization that had just flashed through his mind, made him suddenly dizzy. He leaned weakly against the wall. In the same instant Starr, quick to seize the opportunity, wrenched the pistol from his hand.

"This is ever so much better," he murmured elatedly. "I think you will be willing to produce Doctor Tagala as soon as I have injected the second dose of poison into Miss Hardwick's veins. Hold him, Slade, till I come back."

He instructed one of the other men to follow him and hurried away, but his words kept dinning in The Phantom's consciousness. He made a strong effort to fight down the treacherous weakness that was stealing over him. He wondered why his eyes saw nothing but whirling specks and why his knees shook so. The loss of blood, he reflected, must have weakened him more than he had realized. Suddenly everything went black, and with a despairing moan he sank to the floor.

He heard Slade's derisive laugh, but it had an unreal and far-away sound.

"Dead to the world," muttered Slade, and The Phantom was dimly conscious that someone was bending over him. "Well, I hope for the girl's sake that he comes to before the half hour is up."

CHAPTER XXII
THE PHANTOM'S RUSE

THE WORDS HAD AN electrifying effect on The Phantom's nerves. Not more than a minute could have passed since Starr's departure, and his imagination pictured the scene that soon would be enacted in Helen's room. He strove valiantly to shake off the numbness that had been brought on him by horror and loss of blood.

Out of his half-closed eyes he saw Slade standing in a listless attitude a few feet from where he lay. Evidently he was depending on The Phantom's unconsciousness to last a while longer, for he was idly toying with his pistol and seemed rather bored. Two of the other men were removing their wounded comrades, and for the moment no one was observing The Phantom. A sharp realization that he must act at once quickened his thoughts and stirred his energies. His mental picture of Helen and her desperate peril stimulated his reserve forces of mental and physical vigor.

Warily he glanced about him, then crawled swiftly and silently toward the point where Slade stood. Suddenly he rose to his knees and jerked the pistol from Slade's hand. In another moment he was on his feet, stifling Slade's loud cry for help by a blow with the weapon. Without a glance behind, he ran as fast as he could in the direction taken by Starr. His mind was already at work on a plan. A new force, more powerful than mere bodily strength, seemed to speed him on. Despite physical weariness and the sharp twinges in his shoulder, he felt as if nothing could resist him. If only there was yet time—

Reaching the top of the stairs, he turned at random in the hall. A low, drawling chuckle, uttered in a voice he recognized as Starr's, drew his attention to one of the doors near the end of the corridor. He approached cautiously and looked in.

What he saw assured him that he had arrived in time. He took in the scene with a single glance. A powerful man, one of those he had fought in the hall below, was seated on the edge of the cot, holding Helen's weakly resisting hand in his huge paws. In the center of the room, with a smile of gratification on his lips, stood Vincent Starr, and The Phantom saw that he was transferring the contents of the bottle to the syringe. Evidently it was a slow and tedious task.

The Phantom waited until Starr had finished. He flexed his muscles, then lunged forward. Before either of the two men could move, the handle of his pistol crashed down on the head of the individual seated on the cot. With a fragmentary little squeal, he slid from his seat and lay prone on the floor. In an instant The Phantom had whirled on Starr, who seemed completely taken back by the sudden interruption, and jerked the syringe and the empty bottle from his hands. Then, with all the strength he could muster, he crashed his fist into Starr's jaw and sent him spinning to the floor. Thrusting the empty bottle into his pocket and gingerly handling the syringe, he fled from the room.

Despite his pain and weakness, he smiled as he sped on. Once more The Gray Phantom's quick mind and elastic energies were about to reverse a seemingly hopeless situation. But the danger was not yet past, and the hardest task was still to come. Starr, only partly stunned, would soon recover his wits, and then, with a hue and a cry, the pursuit would start. The thought made The Phantom quicken his pace as he ran toward the entrance of the hidden chamber.

A din and clamor sounded in the distance as he reached the point where a sliding panel in the wall afforded egress to the spiral stairway. Quickly closing the opening behind him, he ran down the steps. The pursuers, he knew, would never be able to locate the entrance, and for the present he was safe. He stepped inside the room and switched on the light, then placed his automatic, the syringe, and the empty bottle on the table.

Doctor Tagala was lying on the bed, just as The Phantom had left him. As the light went on, he gave a hoarse gasp of amazement and tried desperately to rise.

"Didn't expect to see me so soon again—eh, doctor?" The Phantom removed his coat and proceeded to clean and bandage his wound as well as he could. "You tricked me very neatly, I'll admit, but the ruse didn't quite succeed. Even if it had, don't you realize that you would have been left here to starve to death?"

The doctor continued to stare at The Phantom, who rather enjoyed his stupefaction. He glanced at the bed from time to time while he took several articles from a cupboard and dressed his wound. When he had finished, Tagala began to strain uneasily at the cords fettering his hands and feet.

"Useless exertion, doctor," advised The Phantom. He walked to the bed and regarded the physician with a frown. Then he quickly took the syringe from the table and placed a knee on Tagala's chest. Tagala squirmed and heaved, but to no avail. With his left hand The Phantom took one of the scientist's arms and pressed it firmly downward.

"Steady now, doctor. This is only a dose of your own medicine, you know. You seemed quite proud of it when you told me how you discovered it." The Phantom took the syringe in his right hand, between thumb and third finger, and pricked the doctor's flesh with the needlelike point. "I'm a rank amateur at this, but I'll try to manage. I believe the proper way is to inject the stuff into a vein, but that's a ticklish job, and I won't attempt it. This method is a little slower, but just as effective."

The scientist, at last perceiving The Phantom's aim, struggled frantically to free himself, but the ropes and the pressure against his chest rendered him helpless. Slowly and firmly The Phantom pressed against the piston with his index finger, gradually discharging the contents of the syringe into the physician's tissue. Tagala soon ceased struggling, and the look of mute agony in his face told that he had an acute realization of his extremity.

Finally The Phantom tossed the empty syringe aside and removed his knee from the doctor's chest. Then he picked up the empty bottle and held it so Tagala could read the label.

"Series A!" gasped the doctor, and a grayish pallor overspread his hideous features.

"You seem to know what it means," observed The Phantom. "Starr took pains to assure me that the contents of this particular bottle would produce death in thirty minutes. Now, doctor, don't you think you had better tell me where the antidote is hidden—truthfully this time?"

Every trace of color had fled from the scientist's face. He glared at The Phantom with a mingling of dread and rage in his eyes.

"Yes!" he groaned at length. "I will tell you. You have me where I can do nothing else. But, if I tell you, you will bring me a bottle of the antidote?"

"Assuredly. I am not a murderer. It isn't for me to punish you for your crimes. I am resorting to this method only because it seems the only way to influence you and save eight lives.'

"You give me your word of honor?"

"My word of honor."

Tagala heaved a vast sigh. "Very well, then. The other time I gave you an accurate description of the bottles, although I deliberately deceived you in regard to where they were." He spoke fast and raspingly, as if realizing that every moment was precious. "Listen carefully," he went on; and then he gave The Phantom clear and detailed directions which the latter memorized. He knew that this time Tagala, actuated by mortal fear, was telling the truth.

His pulses throbbed exultantly as he left the room and hurried up the steps. Shouts and scurrying feet told that Starr's men had not yet given up their search for him. The hardest and most dangerous part of the task was still ahead of him. The slightest accident or misstep might yet cheat him out of the hard-earned success that now seemed so near. He groped forward cautiously, tightly clutching his pistol, infinitely alert against the slightest sign or sound of danger. The searchers were evidently in another part of the house, for he reached the laboratory without encountering anyone.

He throbbed and tingled with suspense and excitement as he entered. Doubts and fears came back to him. Had Doctor Tagala lied to him, after all? Did the wily Mr. Shei have still another ruse in reserve? Was he once more walking into a trap? Would Helen and himself be able to escape from Azurecrest with the precious antidote in their possession? He was torn between maddening misgivings and serene hopes as he crossed the floor of the laboratory. Tagala had mentioned a closet in a corner of the room where, in an ingeniously concealed hiding place, he would find the bottles. His heart raced fast and hard as he stepped inside. His hands trembled and there was an insistent throbbing at his temples as he began to follow out the scientist's directions.

Ten minutes later, with pockets bulging and a great joy in his heart, he emerged from the closet. He had found ten small bottles in all, and each one, according to the directions on the label, contained a full course of treatment. The antidote in his possession was more than sufficient to save the lives of all of Mr. Shei's victims. But he had promised to deliver one bottle to the doctor; and with The Phantom a promise was a promise, even when made to a blackguard of Tagala's type. It would mean delay and additional risks, but he would not go back on his word. Holding the automatic in readiness for instant action, he began to make his way back to the secret chamber.

He had covered about half the distance when suddenly he heard a shout at his back. It was followed by a sharp command to halt. Other voices took up the cry until the house resounded with a chorus of harsh and excited exclamations. Clear and loud, issuing commands to right and left, the voice of Vincent Starr was heard above all the others. The Phantom paid no heed. He ran swiftly along, feeling that everything in life depended upon his ability to elude the pursuing throng. A pistol cracked spitefully; then a bullet, aimed low, whistled past his knees. The Phantom ran faster and faster, summoning all his remaining strength.

Now he was only a few feet from the wall, but a swift backward glance told him that the nearest of his pursuers was almost at his heels. He found the deftly hidden knob that controlled the sliding door, and pressed it. The wall parted, and in an instant he had passed through the opening, but someone was already tearing at his coat, and he could not close the aperture behind him. Carried on by their momentum, several men pressed and shoved against his back, pushing him precipitately down the spiral stairs. One by one his pursuers rushed through the opening at the top, shouting wildly as they slid and tumbled down the perpendicular stairway.

"Get him!" shouted Starr, one of the last to pass through the opening. "Don't let him get away this time!"

A sense of bafflement took hold of The Phantom as he saw his pursuers pouring into the little chamber, but of a sudden the glow of an inspiration came over his face. The accident that had prevented him from closing the opening had been a thing in his favor.

He had left the light on upon leaving the room the other time, and now a touch of his finger plunged the chamber into darkness. He knew it would be some time before the others found the switch. Groping in the dark, he slowly made his way to the cot and thrust a bottle of the antidote into the hook of Tagala's arm. The others would have to cut his ropes later. Elbowing his way among men running wildly hither and thither in the darkness, he came to the foot of the stairs once more. Quickly he tiptoed to the top and closed the sliding panel, well knowing that Starr's men would be unable to master the mechanism that controlled it. He chuckled softly as he descended again and once more mixed with the scampering throng below.

"Where is The Phantom?" shouted a voice which he recognized as Starr's. "Get him, men—get him! We may lose millions if he slips away from us. Can't someone make a light?"

The Phantom was crouching in a corner. "Better give Tagala a hand," he called out. "He is badly in need of help. And don't worry about your millions. They will be the least of your troubles after this."

He darted across the floor before the others had recovered from their amazement. Pushing and wriggling, he reached the opposite wall. He fumbled along its surface until he found a hidden lever. At his touch a narrow door slid noiselessly open. Beyond it was the tunnel by which he had entered the house upon his arrival. For an instant, before closing the door behind him, he paused in the opening.

"Starr," he called, an ecstatic throb in his tones, "The Gray Phantom always wins in the end."

The door closed, and The Phantom started toward the other end of the tunnel. Starr and his men would remain prisoners in the chamber until the police could reach Azurecrest and take them into custody.

With a brisk step, wholly unconscious of the pain in his shoulder, The Gray Phantom hurried toward the light of day—and Helen.

CHAPTER XXIII
THE END OF THE GRAY PHANTOM

A THIN AND STOOP-SHOULDERED old man, with a kindly gleam in his sunken eyes, gave The Phantom a warm handclasp when, three days later, he walked into the drawing room of the Hardwick's residence.

"How is Miss Hardwick?" was his first question.

"As well as ever, sir," declared her father. "The antidote seems to have worked like a charm. I needn't tell you that I am deeply grateful to you, and—" He paused and looked uncertainly at The Phantom. "I wonder if you can ever forgive me for intercepting those letters. I was a meddlesome old fool."

"You did what you thought best, Mr. Hardwick. Anyway, all's well that ends well. Please don't think about the matter."

"Thank you for saying that. I'll call my daughter immediately."

He withdrew, and The Phantom sat down. His eyes were keen and bright and there was a new vim and confidence in his manner. He had several reasons for feeling highly elated. Starr and his men, trapped in the secret chamber, had been lodged in jail. The seven capitalists were recovering rapidly following the administration of the antidote. Starr, after a thorough sweating by the police, had grudgingly revealed the whereabouts of Culligore and Fairspeckle, and they had been rescued from their uncomfortable position under the Thelma Theater. Incidentally, the room had been found to contain a great amount of loot stored up by Starr's organization. The full story of The Gray Phantom's achievements had been published in the newspapers, and strong efforts were being made to have all outstanding indictments against him quashed. His adventure had been successful in every respect.

He sprang up as Helen, with a wild-rose flush in her rather pale cheeks, ran into the room.

"Gray Phantom!" she whispered.

His smile was a trifle sad. "The Gray Phantom is dead," he murmured. Then his face brightened. A whimsical light came into his eyes. "But in my gardens at Sea Glimpse I am trying to bring out a little gray orchid that is to be planted on his grave, symbolizing whatever was good in him. I am thinking of calling it The Phantom Orchid."

"How poetic!" she exclaimed. "But I don't quite like to think of The Gray Phantom as dead. He was so splendid in many ways, just like the hero of my poor little play. All he needed was to have the good in him brought to the surface. And that reminds me—the hero of my play was *you*!"

The Phantom nodded. "I was conceited enough to suspect it as soon as I saw the reviews in the papers."

Helen looked as if her thoughts were wandering away from the present. "The weirdest experience of my life was when I saw Starr enact the rôle of the hero in my play. He actually *lived* the part. And it was then I first suspected he was Mr. Shei."

The Phantom seemed puzzled.

"I am not sure I can explain. The idea that Starr was Mr. Shei came to me like a flash, yet there was quite a little feminine logic behind it. My hero was modeled after you, but Starr enhanced the resemblance. He introduced things that were not in my play, but which made the similarity between my hero and you all the more striking. His gestures and mannerisms were all yours. As I sat there marveling at it, the name of Mr. Shei suddenly leaped into my mind. I think Virginia Darrow must have felt the same thing. From time to time she looked at Starr in the strangest way, as if she had suddenly made a startling discovery."

"Hm," mumbled The Phantom. "Perhaps that was why she sent Starr that facetious note."

"Afterward my impressions grew somewhat confused," Helen continued. "The whole thing—Starr's acting and Miss Darrow's strange conduct—seemed sort of unreal. It was as if an illusion had been shattered the moment Starr disappeared from the stage and the curtain went down. The officers argued that Mr. Shei could be nobody but The Gray Phantom. Their arguments made me very uneasy, and after my talk with Culligore the next day I felt I must see you. On the impulse of the moment I got on a train." She shuddered a little, as if some horrifying recollection had come back to her. "It all seems like an ugly dream—and I am not sure even now that I am quite awake."

For a time they sat silent, gazing dreamily into the soft sunlight.

"Helen," said The Phantom at length, "I feel as if a great black cloud had lifted from my life."

"I feel that way too."

He found her hand and held it. For a moment his thoughts went back to the day when his fingers had first touched hers.

"Helen," he murmured, "you and I have schemed together and dreamed together and shared all sorts of dangers together. I wonder if we couldn't—"

Her misty-bright eyes met his. A smile, warm, radiant, and tender, came to her lips.

"Yes," she whispered, "why couldn't we?"

EVERYTHING
SHE NEEDS

LAURA P. JONES

LAURA P. JONES

Publish by Engaging Escape Publishing
Chesapeake, VA., USA

This is a work of fiction. Names, characters, places, and incidents are a product of the author's imagination and are used fictitiously. Any resemblance to actual persons, living or dead, events, or locales is entirely coincidental.

ISBN-13: 978-1-7332720-1-8
Biblical quotations are from the King James Version (KJV) in the public domain.

EVERYTHING SHE NEEDS

Also by Laura P. Jones

CROSSROADS TO AVALON
WHISPERS OF HOPE
DANCING IN THE RAIN: A BOOK OF POEMS
THE ATTRACTIVENESS OF CHRISTIANITY

Read more of Laura's books[1]
Follow her on Twitter[2]
Follow her on Facebook[3]

---

1. https://www.engagingescape.com

2. https://twitter.com/authorlpjones

3. https://www.facebook.com/authorLPJones/

Prologue

An only child, Alana was the daughter of the most prominent family in the small town called Beautiful. Many wouldn't call it a town though, for it was more like a village spread out atop of a mountain and secluded by miles of undeveloped land. Legend has it that this was a safe place where people of different shades of color went to escape the critical eyes that judged them. Hundreds of families lived up there. It looked like a rainbow on that mountain top. Beautiful.

A railroad track ran along the grassy side of the town's Main Street, which stretched through the middle of the town. There were communities of small ranch houses and a few churches on one side, and an industrial park with vibrant family-owned businesses on the other. Some apartment buildings lined the streets near the industrial park. The younger generation, upon coming of age and wanting their independence, lived in them. When their parents grew feeble, they move back across the railroad track into the homes to take care of them until they pass on, leaving them the homes to raise families of their own. This was the cycle that sustained life in the small town of Beautiful.

Alana's father, a tall brown freckled face man, pastored the largest congregation there. Albeit, just a few more than the average one hundred members the other churches had. He was charming, and he often joked with pride that Alana inherited all his physical features, except his freckled face that is. She was tall, too, and slender with a pointy nose just like his.

It was with her mother that Alana spent most of her time, while her father tended to the business of the church. An elegant petite woman of unblemished character, she taught Alana music, art, and proper social etiquette. At sunset, she sat with Alana on the front porch, and combing her thick curly black hair, shared stories of their ancestors that were passed down to her through previous generations.

Alana especially loved the stories of her great-grandparents. Their stories, filled with romance, told of a chance meeting between two brilliant minds at a university in London, and their journey across the Atlantic to the small town of Beautiful fascinated her. She asked many questions about them, and her mother was always eager to answer, taking care to impress upon her the expectation of carrying on the tradition of being proper and well learned.

By the time Alana reached the age for formal schooling, everyone in Beautiful knew her. But she was set apart. Her parents allowed her only one friend, Lola. Alana and Lola were friends until their junior year in high school when Lola disappeared. No one in Beautiful spoke of her again then, and Alana's parents forbade her from even mentioning her name.

That changed the afternoon of Alana's seventeenth birthday. Dressed in the pair of new blue jeans and white tie-back halter top blouse her parents gifted her, she drove, alone, across the railroad track to watch an early movie in the town's one-room movie theatre on Main Street.

It was dark and empty in there. She walked down the center aisle to the front row, unaware one of her teachers, who they called Mr. Vic, followed her. He sat in the chair next to her, and after she recovered from the fright of the unexpected company, he apologized and right away told her she reminded him of her friend, Lola. A dreadful fear came over her, and she told him her parents didn't want her to discuss her friend.

Her teacher reminded her it was only the two of them in there. "If you have questions, you can ask me. Nobody has to know we discussed her." His voice was deep and soothing, and the warmth that eclipsed his hairy face made him seem harmless. Still, Alana didn't speak freely right away. Never having the opportunity to talk about it, she couldn't decide what to ask about the disappearance of her best friend.

"Don't you want to know what happened to her?" he nudged.

She nodded.

"She might have gotten herself pregnant," he said and went on to shed light on the town's unforgiving nature, which he said was what drove unwed teenage mothers out of town. After he explained it, he asked her to tell him what she missed about their friendship.

5

Alana didn't know where to start, or what anyone would care to know about them for that matter. He prompted her some more, inquiring how they met.

"We had the role of angels in a Christmas play at my dad's church."

"Angels?" He laughed. "Tell me more about your friendship with her."

She stuttered at the start, but he was engaged, offering her the words she couldn't conceive to express her deeper emotions. It freed her to share memories she never told to anyone. Memories like the good times they had dreaming of their wedding day and imagining themselves raising the children they hoped to have one day. When she laughed, he laughed too. When she grew sad, his countenance fell in concern for her.

Leaning closer to her, he twirled a few strands of her hair around his finger and glided it down the side of her face. It was the first touch of a man in that way, and, although it made her uneasy, she couldn't resist wanting to feel that touch against her skin again.

That evening, she left the theatre agreeing to meet him there the next week. She did, and they met there, again, the week after that. He exposed his desire to spend more time together, sharing his knowledge with her, but warned, being married, their frequent meetings in Beautiful would raise suspicions.

"You have to keep it a secret," he cautioned, before suggesting they meet, instead, in Langston, a city more than an hour away from Beautiful. With his soft kiss gracing her lips, Alana gave in to him.

In the following months, she deceived her parents by crafting stories to justify the time she was spending away from home. First, it was needing tutoring and more tutoring. Then, it was researching school projects at the public library. Soon, she rebelled for having to offer an excuse. Her defiance caused discord in her family, but to her, it was worth the time she had alone with her teacher in Langston.

She yearned for their drive down Beautiful's mountainside, listening to music as they traveled the long barren stretch of two-lane highway that ran alongside a wide rippling river, with fierce white waves bouncing off the top of sturdy rocks for nearly a mile. She hungered for their intimate moments at a quiet spot deep into a park, where they spread a blanket on soft green grass and lay under short stocky trees, with thick widespread branches hovering just low enough to offer the privacy they sought. Surrounded by blossoming flowers, it was perfect for their frequent getaways.

Alana loved being with him, listening and learning, accepting his kisses, his stroke of her hair, and his hands caressing her thighs. Never wanting to resist, she readily surrendered her body to him to enjoy in every way he desired, and he did. The passion they shared made it unbearable to pretend he was nothing more than her teacher when they crossed paths on the school grounds. He assured her it was to protect her, for if anyone suspected she gave her body to him, her reputation would be ruined, like Lola's. So, she agreed to settle for those private moments she was able to have with him, only in the park in Langston.

With a few weeks from graduation, Alana discovered she, too, was pregnant. She was anxious to tell him, and as soon as they were alone again in his car, she shared the news with elation.

"Who's the father?" His voice was low and cold, and it left the question dangling in her ears. She was sure she misunderstood him.

"What?" The one-syllable word came out weak and dragged in the air for a while. She searched his eyes for an explanation, but instead, found a scathing glare that left her feeling dirty. Her spirit crumbled. Alana shrunk back into her seat, wishing to disappear.

He didn't reach for her as she hoped he would. He just sat and watched in silence as the bolt of shame exploded in her heart. Her tears streamed, and Alana pressed the heels of her palms hard against her eyes to stop the flood from her first heartbreak. It seemed the pain would last a lifetime, and she vowed she'd never fall in love again.

As graduation neared and other graduating students made plans to move into their apartments across the railroad track, Alana begged her parent's permission to travel the countries of her ancestors. It wasn't an unusual request, and, in fact, it was quite fitting for her. For she had often wondered with curiosity and enthusiasm, of what those places must be like. Still, it was the only way she knew to spare them the shame of what she had done.

Her parents knew nothing of her pregnancy when Alana left home that summer, and she crafted a romantic story of love at first sight when she returned a year later, with a young daughter, she named Victoria.

Chapter One

The wide-brim straw hat hid more than just the scorching sun from her pale brown face. She thought it was best to put it on during the long bus ride from the affluent Crystal Falls to where she concluded was the middle of nowhere.

Nestled between acres of barren land to its north and a deep wooded valley to its south, the small town boasted a one-room post office and some abandoned buildings on a strip on the north side of the town. There were a few churches, too, planted among small ranch-style homes in old neighborhoods across a railroad track. The town hadn't changed much in decades. The busy Main Street that ran parallel to the railroad track was its heartbeat, but it was the churches that held families together there, and the main reason some who left came back.

It took more than a day to get there. During the long bus ride, she sat circling a diamond ring around and around her finger and fondling the delicate strands of gold necklaces, lending a subtle hint of glamour to her beige sleeveless dress. Now and then, she'd catch herself tangling and untangling the gold bracelets around her tiny wrists and wiping imaginary smudges from the tips of her red painted fingernails. A grey-bearded man sitting next to her watched from the corners of his eyes the whole ride. But that was all she could do to occupy her time. It got tiring after a while-pretending to not notice the eccentric man watching her during the long boring ride. So, she put on her hat and closed her eyes.

Hours passed before the bus turned off the well-paved two-lane highway, where the towering limbs of old oak trees shaded her window from the mid-day sun. It crossed over a river and began a strenuous crawl up a long steep mountainside. She pulled back the brim of her hat to see a thick forest of tall green pine trees gliding by her window like a mudslide. Reaching the top, the bus traveled a narrow road paralleling a gorge for miles and then breezed a lonely two-lane highway parting through a wide-open land of nothingness, before coming to a stop in front of an old post office near a railroad track.

A muffled announcement brought her to her feet.

"Beautiful."

A downpour of rain had preceded her. She peered through the window at a narrow one-story red brick building with businesses attached side by side. Some had chained steel gates. Some had boarded windows and doors. A few were open and had catchy names scribbled on canopies over their entrance.

This can't be it.

The words swirled around in her head like an album on an old record player. And somewhere lodged in the monotonous cycle was the image of her huge Victorian-style mansion in the bend of a cul-de-sac on the sprawling estate she left behind. She picked up her purse, held down her hat, and shuffled passed the grey-bearded man to get off the bus. No one else got off, but it took a while to unload her ten-piece luggage set before the bus continued out of town.

"Mrs. Davenport."

The sound of her name brought her attention to a tall well-built middle-aged man, by quick estimation, a little older than her age of forty-five. He hopped out of a pick-up truck parked across the street and half-jogged half-walked his way to her.

Years in the sun were evident upon him as he neared. His dark oval-shaped face was unshaved, and a well-toned physique peeked from beneath his blue plaid shirt with the long sleeves rolled up to his elbows. The ends of the shirt hung loosely over his blue jeans.

"You must be Mrs. Davenport." He stretched out a muscular hand to greet her. She met it with a weak handshake, unnerved by the conflicting emotions awakening inside of her.

"Pastor said the bus would get here right about this time," he said tapping his watch. "He's at a church convention and couldn't meet you as he agreed, so he asked me to come instead. How was your trip from Crystal Falls?"

Suspicion kindled within her, hearing the strange man deliver the change of plans. She quickly scanned the surrounding. Seeing the shoppers going in and out of the few open businesses greeting him with friendly waves eased her into trusting him. Besides, she rationalized, he wouldn't know her name or where she came from if the pastor hadn't told him. Observing him keenly and realizing, too, she had either to trust him or be stranded in the strange land, a gentle intuitive push to abandon the suspicion took down her guard.

"The trip was long and tiring." She spoke with a voice void of the emotions she was enduring.

He looked away from her to her bags. "Well, let me get these off this wet sidewalk. It's been raining just about every day for a week now." Fixing his eyes up to the clouds, he rambled with delight, "We don't mind though. It gets hot up here this time of year, so we welcome the rain to cool us down."

He stuck one of the smaller bags under his arm, grabbed two of the bigger ones, and carried them across the street, where he loaded them onto the back of his pick-up truck. She waited as he made the trip two more times. Finally, with the last bag under his arm, she walked across the street with him and stood by the door on the passenger side. He pushed the bag into a small space he carved out and hurried to open her door. She climbed into the seat and shuffled a bit. When he was sure she was comfortable, he closed her door and hopped in on the driver's side.

"You look like a fine lady, Mrs. Davenport. I hope you'll be staying in Beautiful for a while."

She took off her hat and smoothed down the short strands of light brown hair ruffled out of place. "And you are?" Her voice was calm, but she was still uneasy. She didn't even turn to look at him when she asked.

"I'm sorry I didn't introduce myself. They call me Slone."

"I'm Victoria. Davenport." She added her last name as if it was an afterthought. "Thank you for meeting me, Slone. I don't believe Pastor Avery would have sent you if he didn't trust you to do what I asked of him."

"No, ma'am. He wouldn't," Slone agreed before a thoughtful pause. "He said I should take you to a house on Grover Street?"

It was meant to be a statement, but it came out as a question buried in disbelief. No one had lived in the old house for more than a decade. She nodded, suppressing the anxiety she detected rising above the other emotions tightening her stomach in a knot.

"As you wish."

He started the engine, shifted into gear, and pulled onto the road. He drove a few blocks and turned onto a wider street with four lanes. Two and three-story buildings lined both sides of that street.

"This is Main Street. Here, you'll find restaurants and places to shop." He offered the information as if it was a tour.

It was vibrant with more people strolling the sidewalks. Young men hanging out of their cars with loud music stopped in the middle of the street to chat. He slowed, tooted his horn, and passed around them in the open lane. The doors of more businesses along that street were opened. Some had old men sitting on wooden benches at their entranceway. They waved as Slone passed them.

"There's our movie theater," he pointed to a building. "The movies are not current, but they keep us entertained."

She looked at the theater but strained for a better view of the higher floors, where bright colorful curtains swayed in windows.

"Those are apartments. I wouldn't live in them though. With the crowd and loud music all hours of the night, I don't see how anyone gets a good night's sleep up there."

Victoria only listened.

Further along, a smooth paved driveway curved off the street. Slone shook a finger in its direction. "Now, over there is where I would live if I didn't already own a home."

The approval sent her extending her neck toward it with curiosity, and she glimpsed a three-story building behind thick flowery shrubs and trees. Children ran around on a small playground there. She took in the quick view and then centered herself, again, in the seat, silently combing the street for a familiar sight. Nothing triggered a memory. It was like she had never been there before.

They came to the town's only traffic light at an intersection. It changed to red, and he stopped. "We have a night club too. White Roses." He motioned with a jut of his chin to a building a short distance ahead. White lights illuminated the name in big elegant letters, and a single white rose flashed on and off below it. He cut his eyes over to her. "If you're into that sort of thing."

She detected it was an inquiry but didn't respond. The light changed to green, and he turned off the street, crossing over the railroad track onto a narrow road touched with overgrown shrubs. He followed it into an old neighborhood where small ranch style homes, some painted pink, light blue, and green, sat behind chain-linked fences on both sides of the road. He carefully navigated around children playing in water-filled potholes and waved back at neighbors sitting on their front porches as he made way to the house.

"Our people are very friendly. You will love being here."

Victoria glanced over at him, forcing away from her mind's eyes images of extravagant mansions hidden behind tall neatly trimmed hedges and high walls in the quiet gated community of Crystal Falls. She reeled back her thoughts to the day she decided to come and searched within herself for confirmation she had not acted foolishly, for everything she saw suggested it would take time getting used to being there.

"How much farther before we get to the house?"

"It's on the other side of that playground," Slone pointed, assuring her they didn't have far to go. From the corners of his eyes, he saw relief warming her face.

A long train roared down the tracks, a few yards from the playground where more children played. They ran toward it with pebbles in hand, amused at the mischief that was about to ensue. Amidst the mayhem, a little girl fell, and a boy ran to her, offering a hand. She took it, and he helped her from the ground. As she dusted dirt from her knees, the boy stared. She looked away from him, brushing her hair behind her ears. It drew Victoria's attention, and she looked back over her shoulder, mesmerized.

Slone noticed. "Her name is Rayne. She lives in the house across from where you'll be staying."

"Rayne," Victoria echoed with a light voice. "She looks to be the age I was the last time I was here."

Slone lived in Beautiful his whole life and knew the people who lived there. Victoria didn't look like anyone he ever saw there before. He would remember. He was sure. "You've been here before? In Beautiful?" The shock was apparent.

She nodded. "My mother lived here. She brought me to visit once or maybe twice."

"Who's your mother?"

She was silent again.

"Is she the reason you came back?" Slone pried.

"No."

"Why did you come?"

Victoria stared out the window with hopes he would sense she didn't want to engage him further.

Discerning she didn't, he voiced, nonetheless, "I understand if you don't want to tell, but know that whatever it is that brought you back, I hope it'll keep you here for a while."

Reaching Grover Street, Slone pulled into a driveway, and stopped. Staring at the house, he added with suspicion, "It seems someone made it here before us."

The old house, in the middle of the freshly manicured yard, sported a fresh coat of olive-green paint and stood out like it was new. Tall columns at each corner of the wooden-railed front porch, spanning the full width of the house, were trimmed in beige. A matching love seat near a round table occupied the far end of the porch. There was an elegant gold lantern-shaped sconce mounted on the side of a new oval glass door. Under each window on both sides of the door, were a pair of white fan-back wicker chairs with green floral print cushion seats. Curtains swaying lightly in the open windows, suggested there was life beyond the front porch.

"Pastor Avery hired someone to prepare the house for me." She spoke with a quiet voice, as she scrutinized the work.

Slone squinted, seeing the nose of a black jaguar poking out from the carport at the back of the house.

"Is Mr. Davenport joining you?"

She shook her head. "No."

"There's a car-"

"I had it delivered ahead of me."

He unlatched his seatbelt, but she didn't move. Water dripping from an unsightly gutter hanging loosely at the side of the house caught her attention. She closed her eyes and escaped to a vivid image of her intimate guest house amidst a lush garden of lilacs and daffodils. A breath of despair ascended from deep within her, and she opened her eyes. When she spoke again, her words revealed both a longing and a sentiment.

"My mother was born here, you know. She left right after high school. She said she wanted more than what this little old town had to offer her. Such an adventurous woman my mother is. Born way before her time if you ask me."

Slone listened, both perplexed and intrigued. She was so guarded during the ride that he didn't expect more than a thank you when they arrived. But the sudden revelation begged him for conversation, and possibly even more.

"If you need anything while you're here, anything," he stressed, "You have only to ask me."

"Right now, I only need you to open my door, and if you will, take my bags inside." She was finally composed.

Slone obliged, offering his hand to help her out of the truck. She took it, noting the roughness and dirt under his fingernails. She wondered how she missed it in the earlier handshake. Steadying her feet on the ground, she straightened her dress and made her way up the five bricked-layer steps to the front porch.

"Mrs. Davenport. You finally made it," a zealous voice greeted her. She stopped to acknowledge the plump woman with a colorful head wrap, coming out of the house. She had a spirit of youthfulness and beauty that age had not stolen from her face. Her deep brown smiling eyes danced with nervous exhilaration as she stuffed a dishrag into the pocket of her apron and extended a moist hand to her.

"I'm Dorothy."

"Dorothy," Victoria repeated, accepting her hand with raised eyebrows. An awkward moment passed before Dorothy brought herself to speak again.

"I took the liberty to make some cold lemonade. I wasn't sure what you'd like, but it's been so hot these days, I reckon I couldn't go wrong with lemonade."

"Lemonade is fine." Victoria moved passed her into the house.

The beige walls in the living room were empty. Under the window to her left, sat a brown leather sofa on a shiny cherry wood floor. A matching love seat was angled near it in the corner. Centered on a colorful square rug was a glass table with a bouquet of live daffodils that brought life to the décor. To her right, a matching recliner and ottoman faced a brick fireplace that teased her memory, but she couldn't recall it.

A short narrow passageway leading from the living room opened into the family room. She went through it, passing the entrance to a kitchen on her left. A step down brought her into the family room. The two-piece floral sofa in front of a wooden center table faced a huge window. Victoria shifted the curtain and assessed the backyard.

Dorothy joined her with the glass of lemonade on a bamboo tray. She took the glass, sipped once, and gave it back to her.

"Show me to my room."

Dorothy set the tray on the center table and lead her to another narrow hallway where doors opened to three small bedrooms. She took her into one at the end. "I prepared this room for you. It's bigger than the other two. I imagined you'd prefer it. The bed is bigger, and it has a private bathroom," she gushed, pointing to it.

Victoria placed her purse and hat on the bed, brushed a hand delicately over the white cotton sheet, and looked around the room. The wood-framed bed, a small table on one side, and a six-drawer oak dresser and mirror on the other side furnished it. By the window, where a white curtain hovered about an inch from the floor, a wooden rocking chair added to the room's décor. Her private thoughts begged for something familiar.

"If you prefer, I can prepare one of the other rooms for you," Dorothy offered, noting the distant look in her eyes.

Victoria took off her shoes and sat cross-legged at the edge of the bed. "Bring me my bags."

Dorothy didn't move, so she repeated with a gentle command, "Slone is getting my bags. Help him bring them in to me. Please."

"Yes. Yes, Ma'am," Dorothy stuttered. "'So much for a warm welcome,'" she mumbled, hurrying out the room.

When she was gone, Victoria went down the hallway to view the room at the other end of it, thinking it must be in there where she and her mother slept when they visited. She was trying to remember. Or, was it the next room- the middle one? She second-guessed and peeked into that one, too. Both rooms had a white Formica dresser and a full-size bed with white metal headboard. A soft off-white rug covered the floor. She went further into the room.

Memories of her mother's arms around her, a comb going through her hair, and a goodnight kiss upon her forehead surfaced. But it could have been anywhere, a thought cautioned her. London. Milan. Dakar. Those places she was sure.

It was nearly forty years since she was in that house, and her mother never reminisced about the visit. Now, the memories she wanted to come alive were pushed back so far, she couldn't reach them. Victoria went back to her room, or what she imagined was her grandparent's room, and curled up on the bed.

I t was close to midnight when she awoke. She sat up in the dimmed room, with its only source of light coming through the bathroom door, opened about an inch. A nightgown draped over the footboard came into focus. She reached for it. At her bedside was a pair of slippers. Stepping into them, she didn't think who put them there. She was accustomed to having that type of service most of her adult life.

In the bathroom, she was jolted into a new reality. A plush red three-piece set bathmat spread out on the white ceramic flooring added a touch of class to the modest master bathroom. She retrieved a folded towel from a shelf near a single sink cherry vanity stuck to the wall and just stood. Her eyes scanned the room on their own, noting in detail, the absence of everything she left behind.

The staggered air jet design massage spa tub caught her attention. It was the one thing she was specific in her instructions to the pastor about having. Her full appraisal of it came with subdued approval, for she was not tempted to indulge in it yet. After all, it was near midnight. She settled, instead, for a warm shower to refresh from the long bus ride and crawled back into the bed.

The night passed in what she reasoned was only a few minutes. She had just fallen asleep, she felt, when a loud bang woke her.

"Edward, did you hear that?"

The words came without thought, and she sat up with her heart pounding to face the empty side of the bed. Daylight flowing through the window to the extra pillow next to her. Victoria took it and held it to her bosom tightly. It was a year since her husband died in a tragic accident, and she was not used to taking care of things on her own. She thought about their only son, Noah, and for the first time, wished she had taken his advice to not come. Another bang came louder, commanding her to see about it. She put the pillow down and got off the bed doubting her readiness for the role.

"Dear God, Edward should be here to handle this," she whined, draping a long white silk robe over the white knee-length nightgown, and hurried out to the front porch.

Dark clouds hid the sun, but the sounds of nature still greeted the hazy morning light. A bird chirped and flew from a tree with branches stretched so wide she could touch them from the wooden rail at the edge of the porch. Dogs barked in the distance, fueling her concern about what she might encounter out there. Unsure, she waited for another bang to detect the location of its source. The seconds passed in silence like hours, and after she'd had all she could stand of it, she decided to go back to her room. It was then she heard a truck coming from the back of the house. Slone brought it to a stop when he saw her and got out, pulling off his gloves.

"Good morning, Victoria." He came up the steps to greet her.

"What are you doing here?" She asked in a joyless voice.

"I came to fix your gutter before heading to church this morning. We're sure to get more rain today." He forced out the explanation amidst the disapproval in her eyes.

"You can't come onto my property at your whim. You scared me half to death," she panted with a hand up to her chest.

He narrowed in on the huge diamond ring on her finger, and her thin delicate hand resting against her brown skin. Tiny moles scattered about her chest and shoulders were exposed in the white laced V-neck nightgown Dorothy unpacked, and he draped over the footboard the night before. The robe, loosely tied around her slender waistline, left room to explore more of her. And, he did, drifting down to the white furry three-inch heel slippers he left at her bedside, too. She was not like any woman in Beautiful, he admitted, as a desire for her crept into him. His eyes met hers again, and she pulled the robe in closer, covering her shoulders.

"Wait here." Victoria disappeared into the house and returned quickly with cash in her hand. "Here. Take this. It should be enough for your troubles."

Slone didn't reach for it. "It was no trouble at all."

"Take it, nonetheless. I always pay my helpers before I ask them to leave."

"I'm not one of your helpers. It's what we do for each other in these small towns. But considering where you come from, you probably wouldn't know anything about that." He looked at her with pity and she didn't know what to do about it. No one ever looked at her that way. She thought to walk away, but her feet didn't move. Slone held her attention with a desperate hope she would say something to redeem herself, but she didn't.

"Don't you know who I am?"

The question came with a hint of royalty, which would have otherwise intrigued him, but he wasn't. He leaned back against the rail, studying her.

"Didn't Pastor Avery tell you who I am?"

"I didn't ask," he shrugged.

"You should have. I'm a very wealthy woman." She managed a twinkle between batting eyes.

Slone scoffed. "That's too bad. For when I thought of you this morning, you amounted to more than dollars and cents."

She took the words as a jab at her self-worth, and the sting was vivid. She squared her shoulders and tightened the robe around her to contain it.

Seeing the effect, Slone decided to surrender. He eased away from the rail. "I'm sorry, Victoria. You must forgive me. The women in Beautiful are usually out of bed before sunrise. I thought you would be as well. I didn't think I'd be disturbing you. I'll be more mindful the next time."

Looking at the dark clouds, certain he had done right to come, he tipped his hat to her and left, jogging down the steps. From his truck, he watched her twirl back into the house with the train of the long white robe disappearing as she closed the door behind her.

Chapter Two

Lightning lit the dark sky as Slone drove away from the house. Within mere minutes, fat raindrops splattered the roof of his truck at an increasing pace. They soon turned into sweeping sheets of torrential rain, blanketing the road ahead of him. A wind grew out of nowhere and strengthened with no warning. The trees, along the wayside, swayed and bowed to the force. In the vicious downpour, the countless potholes were soon swallowed up underwater. He navigated around them in a lineless street to make it home.

Slone came to a stop under his carport and dashed into the house. The vicious rain left him conflicted about attending the church service that morning. However, history taught him not even that unpredictable storm would deter the few faithful members from assembling. It was his responsibility to prepare the sanctuary for worship, and if the doors were locked when they arrive, they would never forgive him.

He wisely dismissed the thought of skipping church, and as he readied himself for the service, the image of Victoria standing before him in the soft white nightgown crept into his mind again. She was all he thought of the whole way home, and from shaving to feeling the warm water run down his back in the shower, the image seemed stuck on replay.

Even struggling to decide which suit to wear, a competing battle to figure out who she was, occupied a space in his head. When he settled on one, he went before the mirror and held up two ties- one black and the other striped. He tested them against the suit, over and over. After much deliberation, he stood still, as if could he listen more keenly, he would hear her voice help him decide.

Raindrops tapping against the windowpane in a slow rhythm broke the trance. He went over to it, parted two slats of the Venetian blinds, and peered through them. The storm had lost its force, almost as quickly as it developed and took the perils from the rain with it. He dressed and hurried back to his truck.

At church, he moved through his normal routine, although somewhat disengaged. From placing the Bibles and hymnals in the pew racks to filling the pitcher with water for the pastor, he labored to get past the unpleasant, yet intriguing, early morning encounter.

During the praise and worship service, he was unfocused, and he tried in vain to stay tuned in to the usual upbeat sermon. With only a few faithful members spread about the pews, it wasn't hard for the pastor to notice his disconnection, and it bothered him so much that as soon as he said the benediction, he summoned Slone to his office.

Slone went in uttering congratulatory words for yet another powerful sermon. It drew no reaction from the pastor, who, at a little over six feet tall, was a clear misfit for the brown vinyl chair behind the old wooden desk where he sat.

"Slone, I haven't had the opportunity yet to thank you for receiving Mrs. Davenport yesterday." He flipped through a folder on his desk as he spoke. "She was counting on me being there to meet her. Thank you for stepping in for me."

"You know I'm here for you," Slone interjected.

He closed the folder and, pushing it to the center of the desk, his lips formed a mysterious smirk. "You know who she is. Don't you?" His light complexion robbed him of the ability to hide evidence of the faintest emotional arousal. His face was reddened with excitement when he asked.

"Should I?"

"Slone, it's me, Myles, your best friend. You don't have to be coy with me." He leaned across the desk, and in a whisper, confessed, "I almost didn't make it through my sermon today with you sitting there looking like you saw a ghost. I was sure, you-"

The interesting flow of words came to an abrupt halt as the door swung open, and a familiar visitor, along with the church secretary, Nena, met them.

"Pastor Avery, I told her you were in a meeting, but she insisted on barging in anyway." Nena threw up her hands.

A young woman in her mid-twenties, Nena was a new member of the church and the role of church secretary, but she had already grown frustrated with the out of control visitor.

Slone eased up from the chair, but Myles cautioned him with a half-raised hand. "It's okay. I'll handle it."

Reclining in his, Myles' eyes turned cold, and he eyed the woman from head to toe as if she didn't belong there.

Her hair was cut short, dyed light brown, and shaved to the nape of her neck. It was quite different from the long braids she wore the last time she came to the church and cried at the altar. Now, her piercing brown eyes were enhanced with light purple eye shadow, and her breasts bulged from a tight-fitting colorful dress, hugging every inch of her curvy petite body. It stopped way above her knees, revealing a light-colored birthmark halfway up her right thigh. Myles was fixed on it, and she pouted from the attention, stretching the end of the dress to no avail.

"I wouldn't have come, but I need a place to stay tonight."

She regained his attention. "You don't have to justify coming here. There's no better place to seek refuge than in the house of the Lord." He turned to Nena. "Call the homeless shelter and have them to secure a bed for her tonight."

The woman's hands swept up onto her hips with anger. "The shelter?"

Slone pushed back his chair and approached her without hesitation this time. "Ronnie, wait in the sanctuary. We'll consider another option for you."

She exchanged a fierce look with the pastor, and Slone took her hand, deciding to escort her in there instead.

When he returned to the office, Myles grunted in frustration, "This is the problem with living in a small town. Every time you turn around, you bump into your past."

"Do you want me to throw her out?" Slone teased.

Myles gave the question serious thought but decided against it. "No. She's right. I should have handled her better." He picked up the folder on his desk and flipped through it without giving attention to any particular page. Then he closed it and dropped it into the desk drawer. "Dorothy is in the kitchen preparing dinner for Mrs. Davenport. Tell her to spare some for Ronnie and ask Nena to reserve a room at a motel for her."

"That's definitely better," Slone laughed, heading to the door.

"Wait." Myles stopped him and repositioned himself in the chair. "We've been best friends since first grade. I can tell if you're troubled, and I noticed you were from the pulpit today. I assumed it had to do with Mrs. Davenport, but if you don't know who she is, then it must be something else. I hope you know whatever it is, you can count on me to be there for you, for I know you would be there for me."

Slone leaned against the door observing his friend. He couldn't remember a time when Myles was not there for him. Growing up across from each other with adjacent backyards, they played like brothers, and only separated once, when Myles joined the army and he chose college instead. They returned to Beautiful, having never lost touch or the strength of their friendship. It was that friendship that helped them through the death of their parents, breakups, and heartbreaks. If there was one thing Slone knew with certainty, it was that he could count on Myles being there for him.

"You seem to think I should know Mrs. Davenport."

Myles thought back to the third grade when Slone raved for weeks on end about a girl he met in the churchyard. He held a straight face. "She said she's been here before. I thought you might recognize her."

"Do you know her?"

Myles shook his head. "No."

"Then why do you think I would?"

"I only thought you might," Myles shrugged.

"If you don't know her, how'd you know she was coming?"

"She called me inquiring about the town. Well, she called the pastor of the church, which turned out to be me."

Wanting to believe his friend, Slone asked, "Is that it?"

Myles half-nodded. "That's how it happened."

Slone watched his friend mustered up sincerity, and deciding to table further inquiry, he left the office.

Myles went to the window an shifted the verticals to assess the weather. The rain was pouring down again, and a clash of thunder forced him to pivot, plastering his back against the wall in a panic.

In that instant, Ronnie came to the door. She folded her arms and laughed.

"Still afraid of thunder, Myles?"

Summoning patience, he went to her. "What do you want from me, Ronnie?"

"Do you need a reminder?"

The quick exchange was all time allowed before Nena walked in again.

"The motels around here are booked, Pastor."

Without taking his eyes off Ronnie, he instructed Nena, "Find a hotel in Langston," and he went back to his desk.

Nena followed him, whispering, "Those hotels are expensive. We don't have it in the budget."

He reached into his pocket for his wallet. "It's on me."

"Pastor, not again. One of the Mothers might take her in for the night if you ask."

He pulled out a credit card from the wallet and handed it to her. "Make the reservation and ask Deacon Slone to take her there."

Ronnie cleared her throat to remind them she was still in the room. It prompted Nena to take the card, and she left the office without looking at her.

"Langston?" Ronnie asked, sauntering to his desk. "You don't have to work so hard to be rid of me, Myles. I would have left without you knowing if the front door-"

"You weren't going anywhere Ronnie," Myles snapped and shoved the wallet back into his pocket. "Why are you here?"

She sat in the chair across from his, and he sat too. Studying his cold hazel eyes, she tugged at the end of her dress to cover the birthmark he'd been unable to ignore.

"Today, you preached about leaving the past behind and walking, fearlessly, I believe you said, into the future."

Myles simpered. You heard the message. I don't recall seeing you in there."

"I was late, so I listened from the foyer."

His face hardened. "Then I trust you got the message. Leave the past behind."

She leaned across the desk to him. "If I didn't know you so well, I would be convinced you believe every word you said from that pulpit."

23

He pulled his chair closer to the desk. "And if I didn't know you so well, I would be convinced the only thing you want is a safe place to sleep tonight."

Ronnie stood. "How long will it be before Slone can get me out of here?"

Internally, Myles reprimanded himself. After all, as a pastor now, he should know better than to engage in such a fruitless exchange. He picked up the phone and dialed Nena's extension.

As she answered, Slone walked in and perched at the edge of her desk. Nena held a hand up to him and spoke into the phone.

"Yes, Pastor. Yes, sir. He's right here. I'll tell him right away."

She hung up the phone, and Slone dismissed the message before she relayed it. "We'll discuss Ronnie later. Right now, let's talk about you." He glided a finger down the side of her neck, shifting the excess material from her turtleneck blouse to expose the bruises it was covering. "There's only so much a turtleneck in the middle of summer can hide. I noticed this today during praise and worship. What is it this time Nena? Did you fall again?"

His voice was low, and he looked sternly at her. "Be truthful with me. Which is it? Did you fall? Or, did he hurt you again?" With each question, his voice was more commanding.

Nena got up from her chair, but he pressed in a powerfully hushed voice, "Tell me. What reason did he have to put his hand around your neck and hurt you this way?"

She felt cornered but not compelled to answer. When she spoke, her words came with a firm undertone but had nothing to do with the bruises on her neck. "Pastor Avery wants you to take Ronnie to this hotel in Langston." She handed him an index card from her desk. "Here's the reservation."

Slone accepted it without disengaging her. He was certain she was abused, but she always found a way around discussing it.

"It's still raining, but Pastor is ready for her to go," Nena stressed.

He looked away from her and examined the card. By the name alone, he knew the church would not have approved the expense. Tapping the card against his thumb, he mumbled, "He paid for this again. Didn't he?"

"He did," Nena confirmed, and they both fought a hopeless internal inquiry of what to do next.

Slone tried to decide which issue to prioritize. The evidence of a young church member being abused, or the compromising position in which his best friend and pastor had found himself. Nena, knowing Slone will do as the Pastor requested, wondered how he should proceed.

"You should ask one of the Mothers to go with you," Nena suggested. "You don't want to be seen taking Ronnie to a hotel alone." She managed a burst of laughter, as one with no concern of her own, and it nudged him to prioritize the issue concerning his best friend.

"I'll ask Dorothy. Her car is making a funny noise, and she wants me to see what's causing it. I could figure it out if she allows me drive it to Langston when we leave Mrs. Davenport's house."

"Who's Mrs. Davenport?"

Slone was dumbstruck, partly because he didn't have an answer, but mostly because her ability to detach from her ordeal with such ease baffled him.

"She's only the richest woman anyone in Beautiful will ever meet," Dorothy declared, walking in with a small covered basket on her arm. Her daughter, Rayne, followed. "And as the head of the hospitality ministry, I have the responsibility of making her feel welcomed while she's in town." She frowned. "After last night, I'm not sure if that's a blessing or a curse."

"What's a rich woman doing in Beautiful?"

"I don't know yet. She's staying at that old house across from me on Grover Street. Pastor hired a crew last week to work on it. They were quite discreet. I didn't even know they were there until they were putting on the finishing touch outside the house. Pastor gave me the job of assisting her just before she arrived yesterday."

Slone listened.

"Tell me, what did you think of her?" Dorothy asked, making her way to him. "I didn't want to ask last night while we were unpacking her suitcases. I was afraid she'd wake up and hear us talking about her. So, tell me. You met her at the bus stop and drove her to the house. She must have said something along the way. What'd you think?"

"She's interesting." He pushed out the words as if he hadn't thought about her at all, and it was his best effort at a forced assessment.

"That's all you have to say?" Dorothy's eyes pierced him in disappointment.

"You know it's a short ride from the bus stop. There wasn't time for anything beyond pleasantries. Now, if you're done gossiping, I want to ask you to go with me to Langston."

"Langston? Why?"

"Pastor wants me to take Ronnie to a hotel there."

Dorothy flashed him a blank stare that told him she needed more convincing.

"I figured if I drive your car, I can assess what's causing that noise you keep hearing."

Her expression was unchanged, and she looked back at Nena.

"He's our deacon. It wouldn't be proper that he alone take Ronnie to a hotel," Nena voiced.

Seeing it from that perspective, Dorothy agreed. She held up her arm with the basket on it. "I have to take this to Mrs. Davenport first."

"Where is Ronnie's?"

"In the kitchen."

"Put it in the basket, too. I'll let her know we're ready now."

Dorothy gave him her keys, voicing Ronnie's presence will only make for an awkward ride.

She couldn't have been righter. For most of the drive to Grover Street, Slone was quiet. Even Rayne, seated in the back next to Ronnie, was quiet, preoccupied with coloring the pictures in her coloring book and showing them to her. Ronnie responded with "oohs" and "aahs." Then it was quiet again. The silence was too much for Dorothy. She turned on the radio and for the rest of the way, sang along with the songs that were playing.

Slone stopped in Victoria's driveway, and deciding against his rationale to wait in the car, he took the basket of food from Dorothy, went up the steps ahead of her, and rang the doorbell.

Victoria opened the door and was startled at seeing him, standing there in a black three-piece suit, white shirt, and the black tie. She didn't expect it, and she struggled for words to welcome Dorothy in his presence.

"Pastor Avery told me you were coming, Dorothy. He didn't mention you were bringing company."

Dorothy whimpered an apologetic, "I thought it'd be okay since he brought you home last evening."

"Oh, don't worry about it. Come inside." She stepped away from the doorway.

Dorothy took the basket from Slone and motioned to Rayne, with her chin, to hurry in ahead of her. Slone didn't move.

"You may come in, too." Her tone was mellowed. She closed the door when he did and led the way into the family room.

"Myles didn't know I was coming with Dorothy," Slone confessed, taking her attention from the stacks of paper she had spread out on the floor.

"Myles?"

"Pastor Avery," he corrected himself.

"Still, you said you would call first," she whispered.

"I don't have your phone number," Slone whispered back.

"You didn't ask for it, but that's not the point. I don't like to be caught off guard." She fought to suppress the agitation in her voice, and they both looked toward the kitchen being mindful they weren't alone. "Besides, look at me. I'm a mess," she frowned with a delicate thrust of one shoulder and pulled up a sleeve slipping down her arm.

"You look just fine," Slone thought but decided against voicing it, taking in full view of the oversized white t-shirt and black tights she was wearing. Turning toward the kitchen with a half-raised finger, he said, instead, "That's the girl you saw at the park yesterday. She's Dorothy's daughter."

The attempt to shift the mood worked.

"She is?"

Slone nodded.

"She has the body of a ballerina. Now that I see her up close."

"Like you." The words fell from his lips.

"I am." She spoke as if it was common knowledge.

"You are?"

"I was. In my younger days." She sat on the floor and threw a pile of paper into an empty box in front of her. "And you? What's your profession?"

Slone seated himself at the edge of the sofa near her. "A mechanic."

"Was that by choice?"

He grinned. "Yes, it was. I own the business."

She looked at the box in front of her as if speaking to it. "It was my mother's dream for me, you know. To become a ballerina that is. She wanted me to be rich and famous." The last three words were tainted with sarcasm.

She paused and spoke again. "It's not that I didn't enjoy dancing, but I did it for her more than I did it for me. I do wonder what I might have been if I'd had the freedom to choose."

Slone nodded, noting she was most transparent when he least expect it.

Her attention fell back upon the box. "None of that matters now anyway. In time, life will pull you to where you're meant to be and make you into who you are to become."

"Are you... there... now? Where you're meant to be?"

The punctuated pauses exposed a depth in thought he wanted her to reach, but she was not ready to delve deeper. Not with him. She kept her attention on the box and drew silence between them.

"You are here. I take it you believe it's where you're supposed to be." It was an attempt to break the silence, and if nothing more, elicit confirmation of how long she planned to stay in Beautiful.

Victoria did not respond to that either, and it threw him in a quandary. He was smitten. That he'd admit. But he needed to know more. Who was she? Why was she there? How long will she stay? Should he explore his interest in her if she stayed? And, why did Myles kept her visit a secret? They never kept secrets between each other.

"Did you come here because of Pastor Avery?"

She looked at him. "No."

"How well do you know him anyway?"

"Well enough." That was all she was willing to divulge.

"Is it romantic?" Slone pried.

"What business of yours is that?" She fixed her eyes on him, and curiosity settled on her face.

He didn't let up. "You contacted him. Why him?"

"You are out of line," Victoria whispered through clenched teeth, and they both looked toward the kitchen again. When she looked back at him, his calm but steady eyes battled her, and she knew he wasn't about to give up.

"What's it to you that I called him?"

"I don't want to cross any lines. So, tell me why him?"

A response felt pointless, but she decided to answer anyway. If nothing more, it might stop his interrogation, she hoped. "I knew of the church, and that he is the pastor. It was a safe choice to help with my accommodations.

Are you satisfied?"

She watched Slone take it in and detected relief in his eyes. He loosened his tie. "You must forgive me for wanting to know."

The questions left her uneasy, and she warned him, "Don't come back to my home, unannounced. Are we clear?"

It was his turn to answer, but he didn't. She called it home, and it was enough to ease the quandary. It didn't seem she planned to leave any time soon.

Satisfied she made her point, Victoria excused herself and went to her bedroom. She returned with a picture of her in a slightly oversized silver sequin tank tutu, standing poised in fifth position. She went straight into the kitchen and knelt by Rayne.

"From the moment I saw you, I knew I wanted you to have this. I was a little younger than you are now when my mother had me photographed, and I've traveled all over the world since then, dancing."

Rayne accepted the picture, bright-eyed. "Will you teach me to dance, so I can travel the world like you?"

"Mrs. Davenport is here on business. She doesn't have time for that. Say thank you and put that away in my bag," Dorothy scolded her. Stripping from the apron, she apologized to Victoria. "I'm sorry. She doesn't understand what she's asking of you."

Victoria deflected the anxiety settling on Dorothy's face with an imposing tug at Rayne's cheeks that made her giggled.

Dorothy hung the apron on the door of the pantry. "It's all done," she pointed to the plate on the small table in the corner of the kitchen. "Do you need anything else before we go?"

"No. That will be all."

She gathered the basket and handed it to Slone, who had joined them in the kitchen. "We'll be out of your way, and I'll see you tomorrow."

Mrs. Davenport held Rayne's hand and led them to the door. It was well-timed, for Ronnie was losing patience. Alone in the car, she reflected on the harrowing night she had when she went home with an old acquaintance who threw her out of his apartment for refusing his sexual advances. He had promised her his sofa for the night. She thought about the friend who saw her walking in the rain and drove her to a shelter. There, she fought off a

29

man who tried to slip into her bed. The memories left her worn, and tears ran down her face.

Seeing them come out of the house, she wiped her tears with the back of her hand and shift her mind to a more pleasant thought. Myles. It was easier to relive every second of her time in his presence that day. The sound of his voice from the pulpit, the scent of his cologne when he came near her, and the love he hid in his eyes were all she needed to put her heart at ease.

Rayne ran to the car to show her the picture Victoria gave her, but Dorothy moved swiftly and snatched it. "I told you to put that in my bag."

When they were settled in the car, Slone handed Ronnie the basket with her portion of food left in it. She uncovered it and sniffed the content. Steak, mashed potatoes, and gravy. Her favorite. She couldn't wait to get to the hotel to relax and enjoy it.

During the ride, Dorothy wondered aloud about the many places Victoria traveled, the wealth she accumulated, and the reasons she came to Beautiful. With amusement, she speculated from looking for love to escaping a hitman, rambling off a list of possibilities that left Slone in stitches. He listened with his focus shifting between her outrageous speculations, and his own curious thoughts of Victoria. It was a pleasant escape from the long drive to Langston, and it kept his mind off the ticking sound from the car which he suspected was caused from the valvetrain.

Chapter Three

The morning opened to a kind blue sky with patches of fluffy white cloud scattered about it. Slone observed it from Dorothy's driveway. The welcomed break from days of persistent rain was his first opportunity to finish the work on her car and return it. If the heavens should grant him his wish, he planned to accomplish more that day.

He unhitched the car from his wrecker and rolled a pink bicycle, Rayne left in the driveway, up onto the front porch with him. Knocking the door, he called out for Dorothy, but she didn't answer. Slone went back down the steps and lingered in the driveway, willing himself the courage to cross the street to see if she was at Victoria's house. The decision came with nervousness. For a grown man, the presence of that emotion was getting the best of him, he admitted, slowing his steps as he jogged up Victoria's front porch.

He knocked on the door, but no one answered there either. He went to the backyard and noticed her car was gone. He saw, too, the grass was tall again, and weeds had sprung up in a flowerbed. Twigs, fallen from the trees in the persistent rain, were scattered about the yard. Deciding to abandon the plans for everything he hoped to do that day, he went home for his lawnmower and garden tools to take care of her yard. On a whim, on his way back, he stopped at the flower shop and bought a dozen red roses.

Victoria was still not home when he returned, and there was no sign of her either when he was done cleaning up the yard. Slone placed the roses at her doorstep, scribbled a note on the card, and left.

The sun was setting when she returned, rejuvenated. The rainy days had left her cooped up in the house. When she awoke to the beautiful sunshine that morning, she thought it a waste to not enjoy it. So, she set out to explore the neighboring towns.

Like Beautiful, they were quaint and surrounded by rolling mountainous backdrops. Charming locally owned boutiques, antique shops, and restaurants all adjoined, lined the narrow walkable downtown streets. A medieval clock tower, the tallest structure in any of the towns, marked the square. Polite unhurried shoppers sauntered around with shopping bags on their arms or sat on benches in parks near the sidewalk eating sandwiches. She ate bread at a bakery, browsed an antique store, visited a spa after lunch, and bought postcards she dropped in a mail collection box to send back to Crystal Falls.

Seeing the neatly cut grass when she entered the driveway sent her further into a state of appreciation of small towns. She decided to ask Myles to hire the gardener, she supposed, to take care of the yard. At her doorstep, she picked up the roses and read the unsigned note: *Welcome to Beautiful.*

She expected the warm welcome would come from Myles and was thankful she was not home to receive it personally. Such a gesture makes it easy to fall in love. But she came to Beautiful for a purpose, and the last thing she needed was to be distracted in an encounter with a kind heart. Ultimately, she accepted it was good she was not there and counted the delightful welcome note a perfect ending to a well-needed escapade, for, already, her time there was proving fruitless.

Day after day, since she arrived, she climbed up a pull-down ladder in her closet, entered the attic, and threw down old taped boxes packed with keepsakes her mother told her were up there. On hands and knees, she pushed them into the family room where the lighting was better, sat on the floor, and searched through them.

With each box, images of a time she only heard stories of came alive before her. Old knitted blankets, newspapers, birthday and anniversary cards, old Bibles, letters, and pictures were packed neatly in the boxes. She spread them on the floor and examined each, piece by piece.

On one of those occasions, she found a black and white picture of her grandparents on their wedding day. They were standing about a foot apart holding hands. She revered the image of such innocence but was miffed that it stood out more than their love. Shifting through more pictures, another brought her to a pause. It was of her grandfather, older than he was in the wedding picture, standing behind a wooden pulpit delivering a sermon, she assumed. Victoria glided a finger across the picture, kissed it, and pulled it to her bosom. In that church was where she last saw his face. Overcame by memories of that sad day, she broke from the task and went to her room to gather her emotions.

It was the next week before she continued searching the box. She found a picture of her grandmother sitting in a rocking chair holding a baby, Alana. More pictures of her grandmother with other women sitting in the same room where she now sat and pictures of her grandfather with other men at the church were in the box. She struggled to make sense of the images. For the most part, they all were stoned-faced. It was as if having their pictures taken was a serious act. Too few smiles for such pleasant memories, she concluded. And their fashion- so modest were the women sitting with hands crossed on their laps, wearing colorful dresses layered with heavy materials reaching the floor. The men, dressed in fat bow ties and suspenders, were stiff as a board. Sheepishly holding in laughter, she imagined herself in their time and dressed in their style.

Victoria read the old newspapers and cards and skimmed over letters she thought were too private to scrutinize fully. In one of the boxes, she found an old Bible with a list of names and the birthdays of relatives she wished she could have met. She scrolled down the list until she saw Alana's name, and she stopped. It was the last name on the list. She wondered why, in all the years, her mother didn't add her name to it. An intense sense of belonging came over her. Victoria brought the Bible into her room, wrote her and her son's name and birthdays in it, and dropped it into the dresser drawer.

She returned to the living room. And, as she did after searching the boxes, she put back the contents, taped it, and took it up the ladder to the attic, a step at a time.

It was yet another one of those days. Victoria was pushing another box across the floor in the family room when Myles visited. It was the first meeting, face to face.

"Let me get that for you," he hurried to her after Dorothy led him into the family room.

"She won't accept the help, Pastor," Dorothy warned over her shoulder, heading back into the kitchen.

Victoria opened her arms and welcomed him like old friends seeing each other after a long while. "Myles! You made it!" Her eyes sparkled. "I'm so glad to see you. I've been looking at old pictures all day," she sighed in exhaustion, "It's good to finally see a smiling face."

"I would have come sooner had I known you were hauling boxes around here by yourself." He picked up the box and swung it onto his shoulder. "Where do you want this?"

"There's a ladder in my closet. It leads to the attic." She led the way to it. Myles followed and went up the steps at an effortless pace. "You make it look easy," she remarked when he came down.

He dusted his hands together with his eyes lingering on her. "You're exactly how I imagined you. I'm so sorry I couldn't come before now to meet you."

Victoria thought about the roses left at her front door. If he hadn't been there before, then who left them? Her suspicion immediately registered, Slone.

She shrugged. "Your job is demanding. People need you. I understand." She backed away and observe him fully. "Your picture did you no justice."

"In what way?"

"You have a warm inner spirit that transcends you, physically. A camera could never capture it."

"Compliments like that assure me I'm going to enjoy having you here," Myles blushed. "For as long as you'll stay."

Frustration crept into her eyes. He stretched his arms out for her and pulled her into another embrace.

"Thank you. I needed that," she whispered when he let her go.

"I thought you might. Did you find any information on your father?"

"Not yet, but I'm sure I will. As you saw, there're more boxes up there. I intend to search all of them if that's what it takes."

And it seems that's what it would take. Over the next few weeks, she continued the search. Then a day passed before she climbed up that ladder again, weary from the arduous task that continued to be in vain. Nothing in those boxes produced a link to the father she came hoping to find.

Victoria sank into the rocking chair in her room and covered her legs with a colorful blanket she took from one of the boxes. In deep contemplation, she rocked back and forth, looking out the window.

Her memory took her far across the Atlantic Ocean and to the upper deck of a bus coming to a stop in London's Trafalgar Square. Vivid in her mind, was a man carrying a little girl off the bus. She assumed he was the girl's father but wasn't sure on what she based that assumption. Maybe it was the way he buttoned her coat around her tiny body before they left the seat. Or, it was the way he tucked her under his coat to shield her from the rain when they exited the bus. Whatever it was, it made her take notice.

"Mom, where's my father?" Victoria asked, holding tightly to Alana's hand after they got off the bus.

"You don't need one. You have me." It was her earliest memory of being curious about her father, and, at the time, her mother's response sufficed.

A time came when the response was no longer enough. Her best friend, Olivia, had invited her for a sleepover. When her parents tucked them in and Olivia's father kissed her goodnight, Victoria puckered for a goodnight kiss, too. It didn't come, and it pierced her heart and left a void she lived with since.

The phone rang, but Victoria didn't hear it. She was immersed in the memory of her mother discouraging her from ever asking about her father again. She had only asked for his name.

"Am I not enough? Don't I take care of you?"

Indeed, Alana worked continuously, taking various modeling jobs to provide a decent living for them. But she must have known it wasn't about her, Victoria reasoned.

Too young, at that time, to articulate the void she felt in not knowing her father, she decided the burden of making her mother feel inadequate was too great a price to pay.

"Mrs. Davenport," Dorothy whispered, poking her head into the room.

Victoria's focus did not shift from the window.

"Mrs. Davenport," Dorothy called again. When she still didn't answer, she came into the room and handed her the phone. "Your son is waiting to talk to you."

Distress faded from her face. "Oh my! I didn't hear the ring."

She pulled the blanket from across her legs and rose from the chair. Taking the phone, she cupped her hand over the receiver.

Dorothy didn't move.

With closed lips, stretching across her face, Victoria nudged her toward the door with her head. She finally took that hint and left.

Victoria sat in the chair and covered her legs with the blanket again. "Noah! I didn't mean to keep you waiting."

"Mother, are you alright?"

"I'm fine, son. Have you visited your grandmother yet?" Victoria spoke in one breath.

"I have. The helpers are taking care of her, but she misses you. She wants you to come home."

Her son's words stirred emotions of guilt her mother stroked as a child, and, although she always gave in to her wishes, to not cause her agony, Victoria fought the urge to do so this time. As an adult, trying to please her often came with a stifling internal conflict, so in weighing between what her mother wanted and what she needed, her needs won narrowly.

"It's lovely here, although not in the same way as Crystal Falls, of course. The people here lack such sophistication. The simplicity, though, is rather endearing. You must visit when you can pull away from your studies, son." She wanted to change the direction of the conversation, and she hoped he picked up the hint she was not interested in talking about her mother's desire for her.

"I will," Noah agreed. "I don't like that you're gone so long to such a strange place. I should be familiar with your whereabouts."

"You worry just like your father did," she laughed. "But you shouldn't. I can take care of myself. Besides, I have to do this."

"I know. Did you find any information?"

"No," Victoria sighed. "I searched through most of the boxes mother left in the attic, and I didn't even come up with a name."

"You should visit the library. It's a small town. There might be newspaper articles in the archive with pictures of grandma and her friends. you might learn something in examining them."

A loud thump outside took her attention. Then seeing a shadowy figure passed under her window, Victoria gasped.

"Are you okay?" There was tension in Noah's voice.

"It's just children playing in the yard. They caught me off guard again," Victoria said in a light voice to ease the worry, and, hopefully, delude him into believing she was indeed okay. She wasn't. There were no children in the yard, and the shadow was of a grown man. "I should go and see about them," she said.

"Okay. I'll call again soon."

His concern appeared to have lessen, and Victoria was thankful her quick thinking worked. The possibilities of why a grown man would be prowling near her window, though, left her heart racing.

With frightening images unfolding in her head, she draped a shawl across her bare shoulders and hurried out to the front porch. It brought her great relief to see Slone coming from the back of the house. He had cut down a branch that was hanging over onto the porch and dragged it to the backyard. With it gone, the porch was brightened, and she wondered why she didn't notice the tree was overgrown.

"Hello, Victoria."

She held in place the flare ends of her dress caught in a breeze and waited until he was in earshot. "You don't take orders well I see."

"It's my weakness." He stopped and looked up at the space where he had cut the branch as if studying it. "I noticed it the other day. I figured if it didn't rain today, I'd come and trim it back." Squinting from the sunlight brushing his eyes, he refocused on her. "It didn't rain today."

"You're trespassing."

"I know." The response was swift. He took off his gloves, and, wiping his hands on the pair of old blue jeans he fashioned with an untucked clingy white shirt that had sleeves reaching above his bulging biceps, he leaned against the tree with eyes on her.

"Wait there," she pointed to where he was and headed back inside the house.

"Are you thinking to offer me cash again?"

The sarcasm was bold, and it brought her to a halt. She took the three steps back to the edge of the porch and leaned over the rail. "I'm not accustomed to owing anyone. You did the work, and I must pay you."

"How about a *thank you* instead?"

It was a dare and she knew it. But being uncomfortable on the receiving end of favors, allowing the two words to pass her lips wreaked havoc within her. Slone recognized it.

"It's just a branch. A thank you would suffice," he coaxed.

Victoria straightened. "What will it cost to be rid of you?"

"You don't want that loss," he chuckled.

She pulled back with her mouth agape. Her raised eyebrows questioned his arrogance. Slone leaned up from against the tree and spoke again. This time he mustered sincerity. "You don't, Victoria."

He was not an arrogant man standing before her, she amended her perception. He was laying aside his pride and compelling her to take a second look at him. Deeper.

"Thank you for cutting down that branch," Dorothy said, bursting unto the porch with a tray in her hand. The interruption could not have been more imperfectly timed. He needed more time to woo her, and she needed more time to escape the spell.

Dorothy placed the tray on the table at the far end of the porch. On it, she had a carafe with fruit juice and three flat-bottom glasses, each with pictures of blueberries, strawberry, and slices of seeded watermelon etched in it. Untying the apron from around her waist, she voiced Victoria's earlier observation. "It sure looks brighter out here."

Dorothy poured juice over ice in one of the glasses and handed it to Victoria. Pouring another glass, she beckoned to Slone, "Come join us and have some."

He accepted and made his way onto the porch. In passing Victoria, she met his gaze and held it, but even in her best effort to appear hardened, he sensed she was rattled.

Dorothy handed the glass of juice to him when he sat. Holding up the carafe, she turned to Victoria, "This is the last of it. I'll need more fruits from the grocery store to make more for you."

"I'm going to the library shortly. I can make a stop at the grocery store after I leave there."

Dorothy looked at Victoria as if she had spoken in a strange language and stuttered a dreaded, "You'll buy them at the grocery store? Are you sure?"

Her mouth stayed open long after the questions, and nothing else on her face moved.

"Of course, I'm sure."

"You'll need to know how to pick out the good ones." Dorothy rambled off a list of different fruit and the ways to check them. "Not everything in that store is worth buying," she warned.

"Our church secretary, Nena, runs the store. She'll help you choose the good ones if you're unsure," Slone chimed in with a tone that undermined the challenges Dorothy implied. Though she tried to ignore it, Victoria noticed he didn't shift his attention from her the whole time Dorothy spoke. Now that he had hers, he faced her fully and made his words count for more.

"A good one is easy to spot if you know what to look for."

She brushed away strands of hair cast across her forehead in another breeze, and Slone finally turned away and sipped from his glass. "This is delicious. You should own a restaurant. And you know we could use another good one in Beautiful."

Dorothy threw her head back in a burst of laughter and slapped her thigh. "Lord knows we do need some good ones." When she calmed, she exposed her desire to own one but outlined a list of reasons it might not work. Slone listened and countered with ways that it could.

Victoria sipped from her glass and listened. But she observed more than she listened. She soon felt her presence fade into the beautiful sunny day, with the sound of birds chirping and cool breeze blowing, creating a compelling scene of two friends sharing their dreams. It was the feeling she yearned for. Being among the audience instead of on center stage, where her every move had to be in perfection for those observing her.

She was more certain it was what she longed for when she walked into the library, drawing only a few stares. When she joined the line at the post office, no one requested her autograph. At the grocery store, two women chatting at the door scanned her, but she was sure it was only because she was unfamiliar to them. Shifting her sunglasses up onto her head, she acknowledged the attention with a half-smile and entered the store.

The tall shelves against the walls were scanty. Wooden tables, about waist high and spaced a few feet apart, formed narrow aisles. She walked down one of them, spotting the fruits. Victoria picked up a melon and looked it over. She thumped and squeezed without a clue on what she was to glean. "Dorothy was right. I'll need help to select the best ones," she admitted.

"Mrs. Davenport."

She watched a young woman approached her with an outstretched hand, seemingly confident of who she was. Victoria extended her hand, too, with a thought the anonymity she was enjoying was over.

"I'm Nena. Dorothy called and told me to expect you. Her description was precise." Nena handed her a paper bag. "I selected a few of them already."

"Thank you." The breathless response was mostly to God that her celebrity status was still unknown.

"It was nothing," Nena fanned away the gratitude with her hand. "Feel free to look around. There's not much left on the shelves, but you might find something you can use."

A tall well-dressed young man entered the store and drew Nena's attention. With his hands behind him, his eyes brightened as he crept up to her. He was jovial, but Victoria saw excitement drain from Nena's eyes. She stiffened to abort a kiss he planted on her lips.

"Aiden, I have a customer."

Ignoring the point, he presented the bouquet of white roses he hid behind him. "I bought these for you, babe."

Victoria was amused, and the two women at the door were impressed. One of them joked aloud that she would be grateful to have a man bring her flowers.

"You should come with me to church next week, Connie. You will learn about a man who will give you more than that. His name is Jesus," Nena told her.

"I have to clean up my life first," she responded in jest.

"I keep telling you that's not how it works." Nena shook her head and faced Aiden, again. "Will you put that in my office and wait for me in there?"

Victoria watched Aiden walk away in confident strides. "He's charming. Is he your husband?"

"No." She spoke quickly and with a denunciation of the possibility.

The complexity of young love, Victoria thought and took a quick survey of the store to see if anything else piqued her interest. Finding nothing, she held up the paper bag. "This will be all." They made way to the cash register where Nena tallied the contents. After Victoria paid and left, she joined Aiden in her office and closed the door.

"You have customers. Looks like business is improving." He handed her the bouquet.

Nena took it. "It was only one customer. Mrs. Davenport. She's new in town. Those two at the door are just fueling today's gossip. There's nothing in there they want to buy." She sighed. "I don't know how much longer this store can stay open."

"If it closes, you can always work for me at the club."

She put the flowers on her desk. "I know what goes on at your club."

"Nena. You're still upset."

"I don't have the energy to be upset anymore, Aiden." She folded her arms and cut her eyes at him. "What do you want in coming here? And don't tell me it's to give me the flowers. You could have waited until I'm home this evening."

"I didn't want to wait to explain what you saw last night."

"I know what I saw."

"It's not what it looked like."

"It was pretty clear to me."

"Let me explain."

"You don't have to. Just tell me, when will this end?" Her voice was weak.

"If by this, you mean what you saw last night, it's already ended, babe." He pinned her against her desk. "It meant nothing."

She pushed away from him. "By this, I mean what we have. Us. Whatever it is that we have become. When will it end?"

He pointed from her to him and shook a finger. "We will never end. I love you, Nena." He drew her back to him and playfully brushed his lips against hers. She shifted to prevent the kiss. Aiden clutched her face. "Babe, don't. I'm trying to show you I'm sorry." She steadied, and he loosened his grip. "That girl you saw me with means nothing to me. I own the club, and girls come on to me when I'm in there. I entertain the attention because they're patrons. It's business, Nena. They mean nothing to me." He went in for the kiss again, and sensing no resistance, made it long and passionate. "You're the only woman I want," he moaned upon release.

"You're talking to the wrong woman then."

Aiden frowned. "Why do you say that?"

"From the way you were kissing and groping that girl last night, it's clear she's the woman you want."

"I had too much to drink, and things got out of control. If I knew you'd be in there, I wouldn't have let her close to me."

"I'm sure you didn't explain it that way at her apartment last night."

He laughed. "I'm trying to let you live that holy church girl life, but I have needs, Nena. You know I have needs."

She tried to walk away, but he grabbed her arm. "And you know, too, it doesn't matter who I'm with, you're my priority."

"I'm your constant, Aiden. Last night, she was your priority. There's a difference. So, if that's your explanation, you wasted your time coming." She peeled his fingers from her arm and bolted for the door.

He didn't go after her. "There's another reason why I came." His grimness accompanying the words was enough for her to halt. She faced him with exhaustion.

"The store next door to the club was robbed this morning. With you here alone, taking in cash, I need to protect you. You never know who's coming in for reasons other than to shop." He took a handgun from his waist and held it out to her. "I taught you how to use it. Don't be afraid if you have to."

Nena took it. "Why didn't you tell me that already?"

"I didn't want you to worry. I know this job means a lot."

"Was anyone hurt in the robbery?"

"No. And I don't want you to be either if they target this store."

She stood by the door, feeling their hearts fighting for each other. He, hoping she will never have to use that gun, and she, wrestling with the reality of what they have become.

As kids, they grew up playing together in their adjoining backyards, and, as teenagers, flirted with each other at the park as friends. In high school, he made her his girlfriend. When a botched home invasion ended his mother's life, she promised she would never leave him. And, she, motherless at birth, when her father succumbed to a lengthy illness, held tightly to his promise to always protect her.

The years that followed stretched their will to survive in life and love. Now, as they stood across from each other in the realization of something weightier than the overtly sexually explicit encounter she witnessed only because she needed him to change a flat tire, Nena bent her mind to accept, as he had, what they have become will never end.

Chapter Four

The narrow red brick church stood in the center of the two-acre lot. A generous portion of green grass surrounding it touched the empty rows of parking spots. Slone parked his truck and eyed the tall weeds springing up around the church in patches. It was days now since it rained.

As if everyone in Beautiful knew the sunshine wouldn't last, they took to clearing their gardens and mowing their lawns. Neighbors crossed the streets into each other's yard to share what else they hope to accomplish before it rained again.

As expected, the break was short. The low rumbling of thunder returned, and grey clouds hid the light from the rising sun. For Slone, the overcast sky made it a perfect morning for mowing the huge churchyard, for he didn't have to endure the heat from the sun. He had to hurry, though, before the rain comes.

Myles saw him from his office window, and he hastened out to help. Since the member who was responsible for the church grounds left the church, only Slone stepped up to take over the duty. With the dark clouds settling in the sky, they worked swiftly and finished just before a drizzle.

"We better get inside," Myles urged, and they rushed to lock the lawnmowers in a shed.

"You go ahead," Slone told him. "I'm going back to my shop."

"I'll see you tonight."

Slone stopped. It was their usual night for playing cards, but between the church conferences and accepting an increasing amount of speaking engagements, there was no time for that. "I look forward to it. We have unfinished business."

"Unfinished business?"

"Mrs. Davenport. You haven't told me about her yet."

Myles laughed. "The usual time then?"

"The usual time," Slone agreed, looking at the clouds and hurrying back to his truck.

Myles went up the red-bricked steps and opened the door to the foyer.

"There you are." The soft voice, marred with impatience, startled him. "Ronnie."

She stood with a frown, smoothing her hands lightly across her white crop-top sleeveless blouse before pulling it down over her navel. It barely touched the top of her tight blue jeans.

"Your secretary made me wait in here although I told her I'd rather wait in your office. Why is she even here today? Doesn't she work at the grocery store?" She shook her head annoyed.

Myles looked at the stray grass clippings on his boots. Gently tapping his feet against the door, he spoke over his shoulder. "Not many customers shop at the grocery store these days. It's opened only every other day now." He examined his boots and tapped it again. "She comes here to help out when it's closed." Myles examined his boots more carefully. A final tap left him satisfied. He came into the foyer, closed the door, and cleared his throat. "What can we do for you?"

The formality pierced her. Any other time she would readily counter it with a provocative comment but finding the words was too far-reaching. Her heart sank as they fixed their eyes on each other. His were cold and detached, ignoring the yearning in hers as he waited for her response. It came with tears settling in the corner of her eyes.

"Daddy is in the hospital, and my sisters won't let me see him. I thought I'd come here for help, but I see it was a mistake." She dabbed a finger against her moist eyes and went for the door.

Myles took her hand gently as she passed him. "It's gearing up to rain again. You shouldn't go out there."

The implied concern would have consoled her if there wasn't callousness in his eyes as she saw when she looked up at him. She turned away to escape it.

"What kind of help are you looking for anyway?" He was still holding onto her hand when he asked.

"Advice, I guess."

He let go of her. "You need a lawyer for that."

She choked back tears. "You know I can't afford one."

The desperate woman standing in front of him bore a resemblance to the innocent schoolgirl, who rested her head on his shoulders in the bleachers overlooking their high school football field, over thirty years ago. His ears were the pages of her diary where she left details of pain and rejection. Holding back tears then, too, she shared a haunting secret of her mother leaving her on her father's doorstep when she was a baby. She spoke of a tumultuous life growing up with sisters who blamed her for their father's infidelity that brought her into their lives. It tore that family apart and drove her teen-aged mother, at the time, out of town. Myles listened then, caressing the back of her neck and shoulders. That was all he could offer her. But it was different now. He had access to resources, and it was high time he gave that teenaged girl, who he loved so deeply, the help she was due.

"Come with me."

He walked briskly ahead of her into his office. At his desk, he searched through scattered papers in the drawer until he found a business card. He passed it to her. "Give him a call. Tell him I referred you."

Ronnie took the glossy brown business card with fancy gold lettering of the well-known high-priced lawyer's name printed on it. "How am I supposed to pay him?"

"The consultation is free."

"And after that?"

Myles pushed the desk drawer closed. "He owes me. Don't worry about it."

She slid the card into her front pocket and planted her hands at her waistline, taking her blouse above her navel again.

"And you. How do I thank you?"

He quipped with a wry smile, "Don't worry about that either."

Ronnie's lips curved into a disappointing frown, and he took much satisfaction from it. "You may wait in the foyer until the rain passes. I have some business to attend to privately in here."

Nena poked her head into the office. "Pastor Avery."

"Come in, Nena."

Nena stood next to Ronnie but didn't look at her. "The mothers have secured a donation of canned goods for the pantry. They asked me to collect them." She pointed to the window. "It's best I do it now since the rain has held off."

Myles looked out the window. "I was expecting more than a drizzle."

"Do you need me to do anything before I go, Pastor?"

"Yes." He pointed to Ronnie. "Find someone to give her a ride?"

"To where?" Nena asked.

"Wherever she came from."

Ronnie's tight lips parted into clenched teeth. "I came here from the hospital, but I'm going to my father's house."

Myles flinched. "Why are you going there?" The mental image of him pulling her from the grip of her stepmother on the eve of their graduation surfaced. He took her away that evening, and she found comfort in his bed that night. The day before he left to join the military, she called him amidst another argument. He helped her pack, and she left that house for the last time.

Her stepmother passed on since, but the rift with her siblings didn't end. It worsened, and Myles knew nothing pleasant could come from her being at that house.

He stepped away from his desk. "Why put yourself through that again?" There was an unsettledness in his voice. The muscles in his cheeks tightened as he grappled with her decision. It was a glimpse of the emotion she had been waiting for years to see come alive, and he hoped, too, she didn't miss it. "You promised you wouldn't."

"That wasn't the only promise made that day, Myles. I've kept mine long enough."

Never forgetting the day he left, he promised to come back and marry her, he absorbed the blow, but with little expression. "I can arrange for you to go somewhere else?"

Ronnie took the business card from her pocket and flipped it between her fingers. "You don't have to this time."

"Then at least wait until you meet with the lawyer."

"Take me to him now."

"I can't, Ronnie."

"Why can't you?"

He scratched his head. "I-"

"I'll take her," Nena budged. Expecting Ronnie's objection, she pressed, "We must leave now. The rain might not hold off long."

"Thank you, Nena," Myles spoke to urge her acceptance.

"You're not taking me anywhere but to my father's house."

"Fine. Wherever you wish," Nena said and walked out of the office to her car.

"Reconsider your decision, Ronnie."

"That's what I've done all day, and it's time I stand up to them." She stuck the card into her pocket. "You might have to rescue me again, but I'm going there." She left with no hurry to catch up with Nena.

Once inside the car, Ronnie wasted no time taking a jab at her. "No Christian should have such hate bottled up in their hearts."

Nena started the engine.

"Doesn't the Bible say you must love and not hate?"

The question was simple, but the delivery was combative. Their interaction was always that way, so Nena was prepared.

"It does."

"Why do you hate me then?"

Nena gripped the steering wheel. "I don't hate you, Ronnie." She whispered a prayer in her head for patience and guidance.

Ronnie scoffed. "I feel nothing but hate every time I see you at that church."

Nena backed out of the parking lot, and it began to drizzle again. She switched on the wiper. "It's not you who I hate. It's the disrespect you show to Pastor that bothers me."

Ronnie hissed. "It's not disrespect, little girl. We have a history. You're too young to know that."

"This is a small town. Everybody knows your history."

Ronnie cast her eyes at her. "They think they know, but they don't. Not like we know anyway."

Nena swerved around a pothole and slowed to a stop at an intersection. "People will gossip whether or not they know. But when you come onto the church property two and three times a week, demanding his attention and dress like that, you give them more to gossip about."

"It's a church. Anybody is free to come looking however they wish."

They crossed into the intersection and turned onto another street. Nena held her head steady. "You're not just anybody. As you say, people know your history with him. And it's not just about you. It's about Pastor Avery, too." She glanced at Ronnie. "The church board thinks you're a distraction. They want him to be rid of you, or they'll be rid of him. I'm telling you only because I think you should know the challenge that he's up against."

"Myles will endure. He doesn't want to be rid of me."

"The members of the church board agrees with you. They think you satisfy him. The church has lost members because they think so, too."

Ronnie rubbed her hand across her bare belly. "As I said, they only think they know what goes on between me and him, but they don't."

"Like them, I thought I knew, but watching the two of you in his office, I learned a lot more about you and him."

Ronnie studied her, astonished she read beyond the exchange of words, but said nothing.

"What I saw doesn't matter though. You're a problem for him, and you need to know."

They were silent until Nena turned into a driveway and stopped. Ronnie looked ahead at her father's house and asked, "Tell me, from what you saw, what do you believe now? You booked the hotels. You know he pays for whatever I need. Do you believe we're sleeping together?"

"It doesn't matter what I believe."

"You're right. It doesn't. But, entertain me."

Nena shifted to park. "I think he's a good pastor, who as a man, is conflicted in dealing with the emotions he has for you."

Ronnie laughed out and faced her. "You picked up all that back there?" She laughed, softer. "Damn girl. I respect that. Those judgmental folks at the church could learn from you, youngons."

"In fairness, Ronnie, you reinforce people's perception of you, and it's hurting the church and our Pastor."

"Is this why you offered me the ride? To preach to me about your pastor?" The words were riddled with cynicism.

"Yes. That was my plan," Nena confessed easily. "I couldn't ignore what I saw. I wanted to appeal to you. If you care for him as he does for you, I pray you'll consider changing the way you interact with him."

"Little girl, stop wasting your prayer. You can't change my history with Myles."

"That's too bad, Ronnie. Pastor Avery is well respected in this town, but if you keep dragging your past into his present, you will be the cause of his downfall."

Ronnie leveled chilly eyes on her and clapped. "Well done good and faithful servant. Your name is recorded in the Book of Life." She hopped out of the car and closed the door. Offering a flirty wave over her shoulder, she pranced up the stairs to the front porch.

At the door, Ronnie turned the knob, but it didn't open. She knocked on the door and waited, but nobody came. She pounded on it louder, but that effort, too, was in vain.

Nena stuck her head out of the window. "Do you want me to take you somewhere else?"

"Nope," Ronnie yelled and propped down into a chair in the corner of the porch. "I'll just sit right here and wait."

Nena drew her head back in and backed out of the driveway.

It was an hour before she returned to the church. Myles helped her unload the boxes of canned goods, expressing gratitude for the organization that donated them and thanking God for their generosity. He skirted around mentioning Ronnie, inquiring only if her trip was without incident.

"Yes, Pastor. It was."

He was hoping for the details. "I assume there were no issues at the house either," Myles dug deeper, as they carried another box into the kitchen.

"No, sir. None at all."

"Everything went well then."

"Yes, sir." She didn't want to share the conversation they had.

Myles brought the last box into the kitchen and placed it on the counter. He rested a hand on it and chuckled. "You know, I forgot you were in there."

Opening one of the boxes, Nena paused. "In where?"

"My office. With Ronnie."

"Oh."

"I wouldn't have been any less vulnerable if I remembered you were there."

"I didn't think you were vulnerable, sir."

He leaned against the counter and crossed his feet at the ankles. "You do know it's okay to be vulnerable sometimes?"

Nena reached into the box and took a few cans to the cupboard, without answering.

"We're human, fully equipped with emotions. It does no good to keep them bundled inside. The untangling of it reveals more about us than we hoped to hide," Myles continued.

Nena reached into the box for more cans, but he took them from her hands. "You don't have to keep it all inside."

She looked away from him.

"If you ever want to talk, Nena, I'm listening."

"Me? Talk about what? I'm fine."

"I've watched your eyes tell a different story for quite some time. Which should I believe? Your lips or your eyes?"

"I don't know what you mean." She let out a light laughter.

"Laughter is something I haven't heard come from you in a long while. How did that make you feel inside?"

She half-shrugged a shoulder.

He straightened. "Real laughter fills you up inside. It ascends from your belly." He placed his fingers over his. "And overflows through your eyes." His glistened.

He leaned back onto the counter and crossed his ankles again. "I didn't see that in your eyes."

She reached back into the box. "I don't know why you didn't, Pastor, but I'm fine."

"I'll accept that you want me to believe you are. But know I'm here, and I'm watching."

By evening, Nena had restocked the pantry, scheduled more speaking engagements for Myles, and lost count of the many calls she transferred to the prayer line. Happy to volunteer at the church, but worried about the paid hours she was losing at the grocery store, she transferred one last caller, Mrs. Davenport, to Myles, and peeked into his office with a quick wave goodbye. He dipped his chin to acknowledge it and spoke into the phone.

"Victoria."

"Myles. Thank God you're there. I have a flat." In her voice, she detected a touch of despair she was not used to being there. She tried to wish it away.

"Where are you?"

"I'm on Main Street." It was still there.

"Where exactly?"

She looked around for a sign to be more precise. There was none, but it was only a few minutes since she left the library, where she read numerous articles in old newspapers again.

"A couple of minutes from the library," she added.

"Do you have a spare?"

She hadn't thought of that, but remembering Edward peeling back the mat in the trunk of the car and unbolting the spare once when they were stuck on a highway, she uttered, "I'll check."

Unlocking the trunk, she saw a boy across the street watching. She thought to solicit his help, but he disappeared before she decided. Victoria shifted the mat and desperation crept into her. She pushed out a somber, "No, I don't have one."

"Don't worry," Myles calmed her. Stay in your car and lock the doors. I'll take care of it."

He ended the call and dialed Slone's number.

"Hello."

"Good. You're still at the shop. I need a favor."

"Sure. What is it?"

"It's Mrs. Davenport."

"Is she okay?" Entangled in the question was concern and panic. It took Myles aback, and he lost his train of thought.

"Um. Yes. She- she is."

Slone sighed relief.

"She called and said she has a flat tire, but she doesn't have a spare. Can you help her?"

"Sure." He dragged out the word uncommittedly. "I can, but she called you though."

"I know." Myles massaged his forehead. "But I have to see about Ronnie."

"Ronnie? What's happened to her?"

"Nothing. Her father is in the hospital. She visited him, but her sisters wouldn't allow her into his room. She's waiting at the house to confront them. You remember the fights they had there?"

Slone remembered well. He groaned a dismal, "I remember."

"A nurse has been keeping me abreast. She informed me the sisters are leaving the hospital now. I have to talk some sense into Ronnie before they see her at the house."

"Good luck. I mean that."

"We have to cancel our plans to play cards this evening again," Myles said.

"I understand. Don't worry about Mrs. Davenport. I'll take care of her." He glanced up at the round white clock on the wall. It was past five 'o clock. "Where is she?"

"Near the library on Main Street." He cleared his throat. "Thank you for stepping in for me again."

"I'm always here for you. Let me know how things work out with Ronnie. I'm praying for you, my friend."

"I'll need it."

Slone left the mechanic shop in his wrecker and reached Victoria within minutes. He stopped behind her car on the grassy part of the sidewalk. She didn't expect him but was relieved when she saw him hopped down from the truck. She shifted her sunglasses onto the top of her head and stepped out of her car.

"Slone," she said as he approached.

He took a pair of gloves from his back pocket and pushed his hands into them. "Pastor Avery said you have a flat tire."

She pointed to it. Slone walked around the car, examining the four tires before stooping to check the one that was flat.

"What happened?"

"I drove into a pothole." She crossed one arm over the other, clutching it above the elbow. "I ought to be more careful."

He came up, dusting his gloved hands. "Don't be so hard on yourself. It happens to everyone. We need better roads up here." He patted the top of her car. "Let me drive you home. I have to tow this to my shop."

"It's just a flat. Why can't you fix it here?"

"Pastor Avery said you don't have a spare, and I see you need a new set of tires." He looked at the car. "Besides, I want to check it out more closely to be sure you're safe driving around in it."

The tension within her diminished and her heart rate steadied. She turned away from him.

"Is that a problem?"

She tilted her head to him in a delicate struggle. "No."

"You seem apprehensive. I've worked on foreign cars before. You can trust me with it."

"That's not it."

"What is it then?"

Her face softened. "I've been in Beautiful for a short time, but already I see instead of making you my enemy, I should be making you a friend."

Slone pulled the gloves off his hands and smirked. "You want us to be friends now?"

"I didn't say that."

"What are you saying?"

"I'm saying I should have handled it differently."

"It?"

"Your kindness. I showed you the worst side of me, and each time you were only trying to help."

He leaned against her car. "You noticed."

She nodded.

"Why didn't you handle it differently?"

"I didn't want you to be in the way."

"Of what?"

Her brown eyes grew moist and conflicted. They were warm but burdened. Her lips quivered and parted, but no words came. He moved closer to her. "Am I in the way, Victoria?"

Her aura welcomed him into her space, and she admitted, "You're getting in the way, Slone."

"Tell me how."

"You're always showing up. Fixing things. Leaving flowers at my doorstep. Attending to me."

"What's wrong with that?"

"You're distracting me."

"From what?"

"From what I need." A single raindrop fell on her bare shoulder. She wiped it away.

"What is it you need?"

"I need you to understand that I came here for a reason and that it matters. What I want matters."

"I understand that. Why would you think otherwise?"

"I gave you some ground rules, and you didn't honor them."

"You said it yourself. I was trying to help."

"You are, but you want more."

"You're a sophisticated woman, Victoria. You shouldn't find it unreasonable for a single man of my age to want more."

"My late husband was a businessman who thought the same as you. He wanted more, too. That he could capitalize on my ability to leap through the air made me perfect for where he was in his life, but he had little regard for what I wanted," Victoria said, humorlessly. "My mother, who craved the limelight, orchestrated our marriage. As it turned out, only what they wanted mattered to them." She clutched her elbow again. "You need to know what I want matters, too."

"Why do you do that?"

"Do what?"

"Pretend you want to keep me at a distant, but when you have my attention, you open up in ways I don't expect of you."

Another raindrop fell. It landed on her arm. She wiped it and looked at the sky. "Will you take me home?"

"That's another thing you do."

"What thing?"

"Shut down after you open up to me."

A raindrop landed on Slone's shoulder. Another came quickly. He looked up at the cloud, paralyzed by her attempt to escape him, and nature giving her the way out. She wiped more drops from her shoulders, and he gave in to nature's way.

Slone hitched her car onto the wrecker and helped her up into the front seat. He made his way around it and climbed into the driver's side just as a gush of rain came down. He turned on the wiper and asked, "Have I done that to you?"

"Done what?"

"Made you feel my interest is self-serving."

"At times."

He nodded in appreciation of her honesty.

"Other times," she continued, "I believe you recognize what I need, and you attend to it. That's not so bad, I suppose."

Slone started the engine and shifted into gear. "You'll have to open up again, then, and tell me what I'm missing."

The truck rocked as he steered it off the grassy sidewalk unto the street. He glanced at her with seriousness. She took heed and spoke again.

"You're missing that I need some boundaries, so I can figure out some things on my own. Living my life boxed into what my mother wanted for me and doing what my husband wanted of me left no room for me to decide for myself."

"Is that why you came to Beautiful?"

"That's part of it."

"And the other part is-?"

"I had to breathe."

Their eyes met, and the hunger in his told her the explanation was not enough.

"To everyone, I was a performer, and that extended beyond the stage. From entertaining friends to simple conversations with Mother, I practiced a smile that came only through emotional labor. It was stifling," she confessed. "I came here so I could breathe."

"Of all the places you've been to, why here?"

She was silent. "Why Beautiful?" Slone asked again.

She fiddled with the embroidery in her white skirt, straightening it over her knees. "It's here I remember feeling most free. I was a young girl then, but when I left, I left a part of me."

He maneuvered around a corner, and straightening out of the bend, Slone cleared his throat. "It's natural to leave pieces of ourselves behind when we transition into adulthood. You're a woman now. Why couldn't you be restored somewhere else?"

She remembered a casket in a church and running down the church steps with tears streaming down her face. There were a boy and a wooden bench. She closed her eyes to preserve it. Then she opened her eyes again, remembering her mother taking her away in a hurry and putting her into a car that drove them far away. What if her mother had not taken me away? Victoria wondered silently.

"Don't shut me out," he begged.

"I don't mean to, Slone, but I don't think you're ready for the answer."

"Let me determine that."

"Fair enough," she agreed. "I left my heart here in Beautiful, and I lived my whole life wondering what might have been. There's nowhere else to find that answer. I had to come back again." She sighed heavily. "I need space and time to figure out some things, Slone, and I won't compromise that by feeling what you want me to feel. I hope that matters, and we can find a way to just be friends."

Her words clipped his heart, and he focused on the wipers, swinging back and forth, as a distraction from the pain it brought. He didn't speak again until they reached her house.

Slone drove to the back of the house at a snail's pace. He parked under the carport, hopped down, and rounded the truck to open her door.

Taking a hand he held up to her, Victoria descended into his arms. He received her fully and held her for a while. He was careful yet contending. Tender but taunting, all in one act before letting her slide to the ground. Her heart and mind collided, and she was sure the earth shifted when he put her down.

Grasping at a prayer, she silently begged "Dear God, let him hold me a little longer." In a window of consciousness, she felt his hand lingering still, at the center of her lower back, and she steadied her feet on the ground.

Assured she was balanced, Slone took his business card from his wallet and scribbled his personal phone number on the back. "If you're in need again, call me directly."

Victoria couldn't bring herself to look at him. She slipped the sunglasses back onto her face and took the card.

The sound of the rain on the carport metal roof amplified. "It might rain all night. Are you okay being here alone?" His deep voice flowed sweetly to her ears, tempting her to beg him to stay.

"Yes, I'm fine alone," she managed, convincingly. Her feet finally moved to mount the stoop.

When she entered the house, Slone called out, "Victoria, don't forget to lock the doors."

Chapter Five

Rain poured from the late evening sky like water through an open floodgate of a reservoir. Myles parked in the driveway and hurried from his car. Pulling the hood of his sweatshirt over his head, he ran to the house, skipping every other step up to the front porch. He could hear the commotion, so when his first knock went unanswered, he pushed the door open and rushed inside.

"Ronnie! No!" he shouted, dodging a large rustic candlestick holder she hurled across the living room. It narrowly missed her eldest sister, Julia, who leaned out the way just in time.

The middle sister, just two months older than Ronnie, ducked but found a chair she threw across the room and yelled, "Get out of our mother's house."

Myles grabbed Ronnie, and they both fell, landing near an overturned love seat on the floor.

Signs he had waited too long to come were all around him. Broken glasses, lamps, and picture frames were scattered on the floor. A picture of the family- the mother, father, and the three sisters that is- was trapped behind shattered glass in a frame. He swept away a piece of the broken glass near her head with his hand. In Ronnie's eyes, anger burned. She tried to push up from the floor, but he took her down by her hand.

"Don't," he warned her. The commotion waned into a single voice. "Are you okay?"

It was the youngest sister's voice. Myles lifted his head and scanned the room. The two sisters had come to aid Julia, who was leaning over a table, clutching the edge of it.

"Julia are you okay?" he echoed, scrambling back to his feet.

Ronnie followed, but Myles held her off with a stiffened hand.

"Are you okay Julia?" He asked again

She shook her head wearily. "No."

He eyed her with suspicion. With patches of gray springing along her hairline, Julia, though the eldest, was also the most dramatic. Her younger sisters readily gave her the extra attention she commanded, but Ronnie didn't in all the years she lived in that house. It made every fight, them against her.

"When will this fighting end?" Myles asked.

Julia released her tight grip of the table and looked at Myles, confused that he even asked. With a weak voice, barely above a whisper, she said, "It'll end when she leaves our mother's house. She doesn't belong here, Pastor Avery. Everybody in Beautiful knows it."

Ronnie made a desperate attempt to lunge across the room at her, but Myles barred her again and kept her back.

"This has to stop." His head went swiftly from Ronnie and back to Julia.

"We don't want her in this house," Julia pressed.

"She knows you don't, but, regardless, she's here. So, let's figure out a better way to deal with the reality." Myles managed the statement calmly and only after a firm look at Ronnie settled her.

Julia leaned over the table again, panting.

"Take as much time as you need because I'm not leaving this family tonight without a plan of resolution."

Julia pulled out a chair from under the table to sit, but the sisters convinced her to lay down instead. Holding her at the armpits, they led her to the only sofa still upright in the room, all the while warning Ronnie she will regret coming back into their mother's house. When they had Julia secured on the sofa, they took seats at opposite ends.

Myles picked up the chair thrown at Ronnie, amazed it was still intact. He dragged it across the room, observing the elegant eight-seat solid hardwood table he first saw when he rushed into the house decades ago. It was in the same spot. He replaced the chair under it and looked to where the sisters sat. The same brown sofa and center table were positioned the way he saw them, too. Surveying the room, he discovered everything was the way he remembered when he first rescued Ronnie that afternoon. Amidst their exchange of another bout of angry words, he walked back across the room, lifted the overturned loveseat, and guided it into its old position.

Pointing to it, he flashed Ronnie a stern look to quiet her. She sat in it, and he sat next to her, massaging his temples in a circular motion. "You've been fighting with each other for decades now, and nothing has changed. In every fight, you say the same thing to each other." He looked from Ronnie to Julia. "Is there anything different you have to say?"

They didn't answer him but pierced each other with fiery eyes.

"Have you ever considered the words you haven't said?"

They were silent still. The sound of rain cascading from the rooftop rose above the silence. It was pouring down harder.

"You're drowning in your noise and clinging to the weakest part of this longstanding feud, unaware your survival depends on those words that go unsaid. There is strength in accepting you have old wounds and that you resent the actions of those who caused them. Clearly, they hurt as badly today as when you were kids, but it's time you face them. You're not children anymore. You can't keep fighting the same old way evading them."

He looked around the room at each of them. Their faces were bridled with tension. "Each of you sat in my father's Bible Study class for years, and in mine, since I became the Pastor. Where did we fail in our teaching on forgiveness?"

Julia struggled up into a sitting position with the help of her two sisters. "We haven't done anything that warrants forgiveness, Pastor." Her voice was still weak.

Myles stooped near Julia. "You hold yourself blameless for your father's actions, as you and your sisters rightfully should. Nevertheless, those actions caused this family, including Ronnie, grief and a lot of pain, and he needs forgiveness."

He picked up the family portrait in the broken frame. Reflecting on what he knew about them as he examined it, he mumbled, "Your father cared for this family. If the circumstance that brought Ronnie into your lives didn't occur, you would have nothing to be angry about." He handed the picture to Julia. "But she's here, and you wanting it not to be so hasn't changed that reality in all these years."

Julia took the picture, straightened some of the broken pieces of glass left in the frame, and sobbed, "She broke it."

Myles took a seat next to Ronnie, again, and sighed. "I know. And just like the broken glass in that frame, this family has experienced brokenness, and it must be put back together. But it starts with forgiveness, and each of you has to get to that place where God can forgive you." He cast his eyes at each of them. "Matthew 6 verse 14 and 15 clearly states: For, if ye forgive men their trespasses, your heavenly Father will also forgive you. But if ye forgive not men their trespasses, neither will your Father forgive your trespasses. You see, divine forgiveness is not bestowed upon us automatically. It's conditional, and forgiving others is one of the conditions we must meet to obtain it. You say none of your actions require forgiveness. That might be so, but if others have wronged you, you'll have to forgive them first, in case you ever commit an act and want God's forgiveness."

Julia looked at her two sisters next to her. "They haven't done anything wrong for me to forgive."

Myles shuffled in his seat. "What about your father?"

"Daddy did nothing wrong either." She pointed at Ronnie. "She should be asking for forgiveness." Her voice was calm and steady. "If she hadn't come to the hospital to visit our sick father, as if she has a right to be there, none of this would be happening."

Ronnie sprang from her seat. Her blouse slid up just beneath her breasts as she leaned toward Julia, patting her chest, "He's my father, too."

Julia shook her head. "You don't know that. Your loose teenage mother left you at our doorstep, and he brought you into our home. That doesn't make him your father."

"I have a lawyer who will prove otherwise."

Julia rolled her eyes and simpered. "No decent lawyer would offer you their service. Everyone in Beautiful would know what you offered in return."

Ronnie frowned at Myles for not disputing the scathing remark. Like her, he wanted them to know he arranged for her to see the lawyer, but, questioning within himself if he had acted too hastily or unwisely in doing so, he commanded instead, "Sit down, Ronnie."

She did but snapped, "Aren't you going to tell them?"

He was sure if he didn't, she would, and at the risk of appearing disingenuous, Myles gave in to her. "I referred her to the attorney today when she came to my office and told me about the ordeal at the hospital."

The shock on the sisters' faces was expected, and he waited for their next move. Julia shook her head in disgust, and her nostrils flared as if an intolerable odor entered it.

"I should expect the two of you were working together. She's been feeding you lies since high school. But how dare you come into our home, Pastor Avery, quoting scriptures about forgiveness and pretending you want to help us when all along you're plotting against us." She placed her hand on her chest again, and the sisters reached for her.

"It's not pretense. I told you earlier you can't fight the way you used to as children. You're adults now, with legal issues. Ronnie saw it from that perspective, and she came to me for advice on the matter. Frankly, I believed the whole situation was out of my league, so I referred her to the best lawyer I knew to work on her behalf." He went to the center of the room with the sisters eyeing him. "After being here this evening, I will admit I was mistaken in my thinking. Your battle is not simply a legal one. It's spiritual, and that makes it very much within my expertise. I won't ask you to trust me to guide you through it. You know other pastors in this town. I will only ask, however, for you to trust one of us to help you heal. The decision as to who, from this point on is yours."

He asked them to close their eyes, and in respect unto God, they did. He stretched out his hands and prayed, asking God to create in them a forgiving heart. When he opened his eyes, he said to Ronnie, "The weather report has it raining like this throughout the night. I can still find someone to take you in tonight."

His voice was void of the usual annoyance, and, for that she wished he had offered to take her home and wrap her safely in his arms instead. The reality of her wish not materializing forced her to face another fact. If she wanted to be safe, and she did that night, there was only one place left. She faced her sisters. "I'm staying right here tonight- in my father's house."

Julia gasped, but Ronnie paid little attention to her. She went down the hallway and went into the room she shared with the youngest sister when she lived there.

Envisioning the rest of the night, Myles warned them, "If anyone starts another fight tonight, one of you better call me." He pulled the hood back over his head and left the house.

Sitting in his car, the depth of the pain and anger he left in there shattered his heart. In all the years he knew them, the magnitude of their problems was never clearer, and it left him feeling powerless to make a difference. Disgusted, he struck the steering wheel with great force, mulling if he was ineffective as a pastor.

The rain pelted the top of his car fiercely. Deciding to wait for the worst of it to pass, he closed his eyes and listened to his thoughts.

It was the wee hours of the morning when he leaned up from the headrest. It was quiet. The rain had calmed. He rubbed his weary eyes, and the house in front of him came into view. He was still in their driveway. The light on the front porch was on, but from the windows, the rooms were dark. He rolled down his window and listened. Even the crickets were silent. With relief, he started the car and reversed out of the driveway.

The normal ten-minute drive to his house doubled. When he finally made it, he took a warm shower and fell asleep again on a sofa in his study.

His phone ringing woke him late in the morning. Myles answered.

"You sound terrible. The evening must not have gone well with Ronnie."

He pulled up into a sitting position. "Has it ever?"

"Not that I recall," Slone chuckled. "Is there anything I can do?"

"Not yet." He scoured over his face with his dry hand. "I couldn't convince her to leave the house last night. I'll have to see what comes of that decision." He breathed and then asked, "How was it with Mrs. Davenport?"

The encounter came back to Slone in no specific order, and he couldn't decide where to start. He settled on, "She needs a new set of tires."

Myles rolled back over onto the sofa with his face toward the blank ceiling. "Can you take care of it?"

"A couple of my mechanics are working on it right now. I want to have it back to her today."

"Good. Thank you for stepping up again for me and for checking on me, as well," Myles added.

"That's what friends do. You should rest. You sound awful."

Later that evening, when he towed the car back to Victoria, she met him on the front porch and asked immediately, "How much do I owe you?"

Slone handed her the bill. "Wait here."

"Victoria."

She looked back over her shoulder at him.

"You shouldn't keep this much cash in the house. In fact, I'd rather you don't keep any at all."

She brushed her hair behind her ears. "I was getting my credit card. Do you accept that?"

"You'll have to pay at the shop."

She checked her watch. "Is it open?"

"No."

"Then how do I pay?"

"It'll be open tomorrow. You can pay then."

"I'll be there first thing in the morning."

"You'll need these first." He held up her keys.

She hung her head to hide her embarrassment and took them. "Thank you."

"That wasn't so hard. Was it?"

"What was?"

"Those two little words that slipped from your lips."

She reflected on her words, and remembering his attempts at making her say them, she held up her head, smiled, and said proudly, "It was quite easy if you must know."

They laughed, and after they settled down, she asked, "Would you like something to drink?" Hearing the offer stunned even her. She noticed Dorothy asked it whenever someone visited, but she wasn't aware she had adapted to the custom somehow.

Amused, Slone accepted, and she went into the kitchen and returned, carrying a tray with a goblet and two glasses on it. When she placed the tray on the table, Slone picked up the goblet and poured the fruit juice over ice in each glass for them. She sat, leaving plenty of space for him to sit beside her. Handing one of the glasses to her, he took the seat and asked, "Are you adjusting to life in Beautiful?"

"It's different from what I'm used to."

"How so?"

"People here are relaxed. Content."

"I imagined the same of the people in Crystal Falls- with the luxury and all."

"The more you have is the more you want. There's no room for contentment in that way of living."

"Do you miss being there?"

"I miss some aspects of it. Family, mostly. I haven't thought much beyond them."

Slone sipped while she talked.

"Here, people treat each other like family. They cross the street and go into each other's homes often as if they have a share in it. It takes some getting used to, but it's what communities should be like, I suppose."

"You don't visit your neighbors in Crystal Falls?"

"No. The homes are secured behind high gates, tall hedges, and walls. Many have cameras all around them. Besides, except for invitations to holiday parties, we have little time to visit our neighbors' homes." She looked off at the houses on the street. "Of course, people in Crystal Falls are more private and probably have possessions that are of greater value in their homes."

"You haven't visited your neighbors here either, I see."

"How do you know?"

"You said probably. I assure you, nobody in Beautiful has material possessions of greater value in their homes. At least not the likes of which you're accustomed, anyway." He pointed to a house. "Have you met that family?"

"I've seen them from time to time mowing the lawn and getting in and out of cars."

"Our parents attended the same school and had some of the same teachers. Then we went to the same school. Now, their children and grandchildren are students there. They never left Beautiful. I believe, from one generation to the next, they will be here all their lives." Of the house next to it, he pointed and uttered, "Uh. The family who lives at that house was trouble. Their parents almost took up residency in the principal's office. The eldest eventually became a pastor, and he ministered to the rest of them. Now, they're all pastors, deacons, and ministers." He pointed from one house to the next, telling her stories about her neighbors.

"Do you know everyone in Beautiful?" Victoria asked.

"Almost everyone. You can pick any street and point to a house, I know stories about the family who lives there."

"What about this house? What stories do you know about the family who lived here?"

"Many families lived here. They are of the younger generation, mostly. They move in, stay for a while, and move out. It's one of the few houses in Beautiful available for rental and has families moving in and out. It's been years now since anyone moved in though, until you." He paused. "When I brought you here you said your grandfather built this house."

"My great-grandfather built it. My grandfather remodeled it, my mother said."

"Is your grandfather, Mr. Grover?"

She nodded.

"He was a prominent man in Beautiful. They renamed this street after him."

"Did you know him?"

Slone shook his head. "I was young when he died."

"Did you know my grandmother?"

Slone thought and shook his head again. "They were before my time. Except for stories I heard about them, I can't say I knew either of them."

"What about their daughter?" Victoria was hoping he would disclose information that might lead her to her father.

"I never met her." He laughed, playfully. "You're inquiring about a lot. Are you investigating your family?"

She shrugged. "It would be interesting to hear their stories from the perspective of someone who lives here and knew them."

"For what it's worth, theirs is a legacy of honor and respect- the essence of which lives on silently in Beautiful."

She smiled, folded her arms, and crossed her legs at the knee. Swinging one leg back and forth, she met his eyes. "What about you? What is your story?"

Slone told her about his life. His father, quite a disciplinarian he recalled, owned a retail store on Main Street. His mother was a teacher at his elementary school. "She had difficulty conceiving," he divulged. "I was their only child."

"That covers your childhood. What about your adult life?"

"There's not much to tell. I left for college, came back, and built my business."

"I hope you won't consider it intrusive if I ask about a wife."

"I never married."

"Why not?"

"For years, I believed I was too young. When I opened up to the idea, I realized I was unprepared to take care of a wife. I positioned myself for the responsibility, but I didn't find a woman I was ready to call my wife."

"You had no children in the process?"

"No. I didn't want to burden anyone with that responsibility if I couldn't make her my wife."

She looked out into the yard. "I don't blame you. No one should settle when it comes to marriage and other matters of the heart."

"You know that all too well. Tell me the rest of your story."

She talked fondly of the places she lived and shared the disheartening decision to end her career as a ballerina. They talked way into the evening. The sun disappeared, and they hardly noticed. When the stars appeared, she pointed to the sky with a hand clutching his knee. "There's a view you won't find in Crystal Falls. Stars that shine brightly."

The moon drift near the middle of the sky, and finally, Slone checked his watch. "It's way past your bedtime. I didn't intend to stay so late."

"I shouldn't have kept you," she said, apologetically.

They walked to the top of the steps where he took her hand and held it. "We could have talked all night, and it would've been effortless."

She smiled.

"Being in your presence tonight felt right. I can't see how we can be just friends without settling when it comes to matters of the heart. Are you prepared to do that again?"

She lowered her head.

"Look at me, Victoria," Slone begged, and she did. "I won't hide my feelings for you, but I need to know what's in your heart, and the truth of why you're fighting it."

He waited for her to speak, but she didn't. He brought her hand to his lips and kissed it. "Have a good night."

"Goodnight, Slone," she finally said.

He waited in his truck until she was in the house. When she turned off the light, he left. At his home, Slone weighed between revealing to Myles his love for Victoria and waiting until he was sure she felt the same for him. It was the first time he grappled with sharing his feelings about a woman with Myles, for talking it out with him always gave him clarity. He brewed a pot of coffee and decided against the phone call. After all, from the little information Myles disclosed about their relationship, he couldn't be sure he didn't feel the same for her.

It was good that he didn't call that night. Between worrying about Ronnie and her sisters and combing over the numbers on the church financial report, Myles was drained.

The church finance was in jeopardy. Each month, the tithing was less than the month before, and the offering collected that week was the lowest since he became the pastor. He barely met the church expense that month. Unsuccessful in constructing a sound plan to keep the church doors open under such financial condition, he pulled the sheet over his head, and fell asleep, again, on the sofa in his study.

That night led to more nights sleeping in the study. There was an energy in the space that empowered him. He found wisdom in many of the books he kept on shelves he built against an entire wall. He experienced relief at the altar he made against one of the adjoining walls, and he drew inspiration from quotes he heard or read and wrote on colorful index cards he used to decorate it. Every night, he knelt at the altar with his face to the wall.

In that space, he was most vulnerable and free to connect with God, the source that always replenished him. It strengthened him to eulogize a classmate that week, preserve through a guest speaking engagement at another church the following week, and deliver another powerful sermon at his church when he returned.

From the pulpit, Myles scanned the congregation to see if Ronnie was there. She wasn't, and she didn't come the next week either. It wasn't unusual for her to pull a disappearing act, but it was too many weeks now, and Myles grew weary with concern.

Preparing for another night's sleep in his study, he called the attorney he recommended to her.

"I see her often," he said with a throaty chuckle. "Between me and you, I knew I was in trouble the moment she strutted into my office, swaying her hips in those tight-fitting jeans. We've been spending a lot of time together. I will owe you again if my wife finds out about this one, too."

Chapter Six

Myles stood by the window in his office, looking out into the churchyard through the raised blind. The day was the fairest in weeks now. The sun shone brightly from a cloudless blue sky, and a small patch of yellow black-eyed-susan swayed gently in a light breeze. On a whim, he let down the blinds, picked up his briefcase, and peeped into Nena's office.

"I'm leaving for lunch. Would you like me to bring anything back for you?"

Nena shifted the phone from her ear and covered the receiver. "No, thank you," she whispered and shifted her attention back to the caller.

He leaned against the doorframe and waited for her to finish the call. "Are you sure? It's on me."

She picked up a paper plate and pushed the covering aside, revealing the half-eaten steamed fish with brown rice and a colorful array of sautéed vegetables. "Dorothy brought in lunch for me."

"That looks delicious."

"It is." She scooped up a spoonful of rice.

With his next sermon prepared, and confident in his ministers to carry on a meeting he had scheduled for that evening with them, he tucked his briefcase under his arm. "I see no reason to come back then. Enjoy your lunch and call me if you need me."

She nodded with the spoon in her mouth.

Myles left, eager to indulge in the gratification he envisioned standing at the window. First on his agenda was lunch at White Roses, mainly a nightclub, but a chic restaurant by day. With a posh red-carpeted stairway leading to the bar and spacious room for dancing on the second floor, and an elegant room for dining on the first, it was a symbol of Aiden's ingenuity to attract both the saints and sinners in Beautiful.

He was careful in appealing to the two groups. A door closed off the entrance to the stairways during the day, so saints coming in to dine wouldn't risk having their intentions scrutinized. At nights, he opened it, transforming the establishment into the closest thing to an upscale night club anyone in Beautiful ever experienced.

The ambiance was enticing. Soft Jazz music, audible from the entrance, set the mood for patrons as they arrive. Well-trained greeters, who slip into sexy black and red lacy attires at nights, wore knee-length black skirts and white shirts to welcome the day crowd. They escort the patrons across the red carpet in the dimly lit dining hall and seat them at round tables covered with a white tablecloth. The warm glowing candlelight flickering inside round bamboo-woven lantern centerpiece stimulated an inner calm and made unwinding easy. Myles wasn't a regular customer. He reserved the experience for when he wanted to de-stress and treat himself to a fancy lunch or dinner. And that was all he desired when he arrived.

Only a few patrons were dining, much to his delight. The lunch crowd had dwindled, and it was at least three hours before more diners to start trickling in for dinner. He had timed it perfectly. Eating out, uninterrupted, was becoming impossible. Someone always approaches him and asks for prayer, or prayer for a family member or friend, or for money to pay a bill, or to deliver news about someone dying or nearing death. With the almost empty dining hall to himself, Myles requested a table in a corner at the back of the room and ordered his favorite potato soup for appetizer.

He wasn't expecting her but was elated to see a greeter escort Victoria into the dining room. He waved them over to his table, and she welcomed the invitation with a warm one-hand hug around his shoulder.

"You can't be tired of Dorothy's cooking," he joked, as she accepted the chair that he pulled out across from him.

"I'm not, but she's at your church cooking for the homeless." She placed her purse on the chair next to her and crossed her legs under the long red-floral flare skirt.

"If I know Dorothy, I'm sure she left plenty for you to eat at home."

"You know Dorothy well," she agreed.

"So, what brought you here?" Myles scooped a spoonful of soup into his mouth.

"The blue sky mostly. And you?"

He swallowed. "The same. I couldn't stand being cooped up in my office any longer. I had to escape and enjoy this beautiful sunshine."

"It seems a day like this is a rarity in Beautiful. I'm learning I must seize the opportunity to enjoy it when it comes."

"You're a fast learner. Our rainy season is especially long."

The young woman, waiting their table, placed a menu and a glass of water in front of her. Victoria picked up the menu and handed it back without looking at it. "I'll have what he's having."

She took the menu, pushed it down into the pocket of her apron, and scribbled her order on a tiny pad. When she left, Victoria leaned over to Myles. "It's my first time here. I hope you made a good choice."

He wiped his mouth with his napkin. "The food is amazing. Anything here is an excellent choice."

She squeezed in her shoulders and scanned the dining hall. "I didn't imagine this setting. I'm inclined to believe you."

He observed her curiously. "You're beaming. Does this mean your search is finally producing results?"

"Not really." She fought a smile tugging the corners of her mouth.

"Then you're dealing with it more formidably, for you're glowing." The glow seemed contagious, for his face turned red and his piercing hazel eyes widened in a deliberate attempt to force her to lock eyes with him.

She did, half-commanding her mind to stop unreeling her recent encounters with Slone and half-wishing each moment with him could have gone on forever. The gentleness in his arms when he helped her from his truck. The long talk late into the evening after he returned her car, and the many phone calls since, lasting into the wee hours of nights were at the forefront of her mind. She blushed from the emotions, and Myles watched, amused.

"Well?"

"Well, What?"

"Forgive me if I'm being forward, but the last time we talked you were frustrated with the way the search was going. Now, here you are radiating. Something changed. Do tell."

73

The waiter returned with the bowl of soup and placed it in front of her. Victoria circled the spoon around in it, tasted a half-spoonful, and patted the corners of her mouth.

"This is delicious."

Myles nodded an *I told you so* nod and scooped up the last of his. He dabbed the corners of his mouth again and pushed the empty bowl to the side. "I'm sorry you haven't found anything about your father, but, for what it's worth, seeing that twinkle in your eyes is a welcome change. What's the cause of it?"

She looked at him. "I owe it to the wonderful people I met. I didn't plan on that coming here."

"Oh?" Myles remarked.

"The people in this town are well-suited for the name. They're beautiful."

"How so?" he chuckled.

"I can't explain it, but I've found that an encounter can leave you somewhere between amazement and euphoric."

"Interesting. Tell me more."

"The people here are warm and kind. They offer help, and not the kind you pay for."

"Is there another kind?" Myles joshed.

"Oh, there is. But it comes from a place of mindlessness, I believe. People avail themselves without thought and expect nothing in return." She paused, understanding the sentiment she expressed was mostly due to Slone.

"Slone," Myles said, sliding his chair back from the table.

"How did you-" Her words were lost with the awareness of a distraction. Slone had walked into the restaurant and held off the greeter, making his way to their table on his own. Myles greeted him with a hearty handshake, and they pulled each other in for a quick hug.

"I was on my way to the church for our meeting when I spotted your car in the parking lot." He took full notice of Victoria and contained the pain piercing his heart in seeing her there with him. "I didn't mean to interrupt you."

"You're not interrupting us. We were just settling down for lunch." Myles pulled out the chair next to him. "Please join us."

"No," Slone said and looked with curiosity at Victoria. "I didn't see your

74

car out there. Are you having problems with it?"

She felt butterflies fluttered in her stomach, and she shifted in the chair, uncomfortably, before looking up at him. "No. I parked in the rear."

He didn't look away from her.

"Please join us," Myles said again, taking back his attention.

"I can't. You two enjoy your lunch. I have to get to the church to prepare for the meeting. I'll catch up with you there."

"I was planning to call you about that. I've decided to skip the meeting."

"Why? You've never skipped a meeting."

"There's always a first time, and this is it. I'm going home for a quiet evening when I leave here. I'm hoping you will carry on for me this time."

"I can. However, the deacons and ministers are expecting you, the pastor."

"Yes, I know. But even pastors need a break at times." He hiked his shoulders high and shoved his hands deep into his pockets.

The nonchalant response left Slone puzzled. "Are you feeling well?"

"Yes. Can I count on you this evening?"

"Of course. You know you can." He kept a steady eye on Myles that spewed concern.

"I appreciate you." Myles said, adding with jest, "And don't worry about me. I'll be rested and ready to win when we meet tomorrow night to play cards. You can make it. Right?"

"I've been waiting."

"Same time?"

"Same time," Slone confirmed and shook a finger at him. "Don't let anything get in the way this time."

"I won't."

Slone turned to Victoria with his heart shattered at the core. "It's good seeing you again, Mrs. Davenport."

She strained to face him and met the agony in his eyes when she did. "Yes, it is."

Slone left, and Myles sat down again. Victoria stirred her soup. "I wasn't aware that your relationship with Deacon Slone extends beyond the church."

"It does. I've known him all my life, and I can say, with confidence, he's one who is most suited for Beautiful as you described. Wouldn't you agree?"

She shrugged. "You've had a lifetime to determine that."

"It didn't take a lifetime, though. He's the best friend I could ever ask for, and I knew that in first grade when he took a punch from a bully for me."

Victoria was tickled.

Recognizing the effect, Myles continued laughingly. "The next day, after school, we double-teamed that boy, beating him senseless. I still remember him staggering like a drunk man and falling to the ground. We got into a lot of trouble with our parents and the principal over it, but it didn't matter to me because I knew then I had a friend I could count on. He's committed."

Victoria thought about the morning she awoke to the noise from Slone fixing her gutter. She had only been in town one night. "He does make an impression immediately."

Myles' giddiness from telling the story faded. "I imagine as a celebrity, it's challenging managing your privacy in public."

"It is, and that's another reason I love it here. Nobody knows who I am."

"Oh? When you said you parked in the back, I assumed it was for privacy. I thought, maybe, you didn't want to publicize your whereabout."

She reflected on his words. "I suppose that could be the case, instinctively."

"Instinctively? Did something alarm you?"

Her voice fell to a careful whisper. "That day I had the flat tire, a boy was watching me. Well, a young man." She narrowed her eyes, dredging up an image of him. "In his late teens or early twenties. Maybe. He's tall and thin. Short haircut. He walked away rather quickly when I took notice of him."

She continued with skepticism. "I saw him at the library a few days after that and then at the grocery store." Uncertainty crept into her voice. "At least, I think it was him. I thought it rather strange. He seemed to appear everywhere I was. I haven't been out much the past few days, but maybe instinctively, I was taking precaution."

"You should have told me."

"I didn't want to make a big deal about it. It probably isn't. After all, Beautiful is a small town with few options in places to go. There're only one library and one grocery store. I shouldn't be suspicious if I run into someone from time to time."

The words made sense in her ears and worked well to help diminish the deepening concern evidenced in the creases across Myles' forehead. He looked away, in relief, to the waiter approaching with their meals.

"The service is fast," Victoria commented after the food was spread out before them and the server left.

"That's how they distinguish themselves from the competition. Great food. Great service." Myles reached both hands across the table and took her hands. He closed his eyes and prayed a blessing over the food.

She didn't close hers. Remembering only her mother holding her hand in prayer, left her uncomfortable. She was a child then, and, as an adult, she hardly ever prays. Watching him do it, though, made her pledge to start doing so at least once a day.

When he was done praying, she opened her napkin, spread it across his lap, and dangled her fork back and forth over her plate until she picked up a piece of mushroom and nibbled on it.

Myles picked up his fork. "Does Slone alarm you, too?" There was a subtlety in the question.

She swallowed. "Why do you ask?"

"You were uneasy when he spoke to you."

"You're quite observant." Victoria picked at another piece of mushroom and put it into her mouth.

"It's the spirit of discernment. It's a powerful gift for decoding the obscure. It's how I know I should trust Slone." He looked at her firmly. "You can trust him, too."

She chewed and swallowed again. "You make a good case, needlessly. My intuition led me to believe I could the day we met at the bus stop."

"Then why the uneasiness in his presence?"

Victoria placed her fork on the plate. "It wasn't a distrust in him that made me uneasy. It's the extent to which I trusted you."

"I don't understand."

"You and Slone have a bond I was unaware of. In watching the two of you, I wondered why you never mentioned him."

Myles pressed back against the chair. "But I have. I sent him to meet you at the bus stop, to fix your car-"

She swept a wisp of loose hair from her forehead. "Each time he came, I was expecting you. You never told me to expect him." She sighed. "I wonder now if you told him about me before he met me?"

Myles thought about the many times he avoided the subject when Slone inquired about her. "I would never betray your confidence." He leaned over to her. "Do you think I have?"

"I don't know what to think. Apart, the two of you cast a different picture from what I saw of you together."

"How so?"

"You are his pastor. That's all I knew. I didn't know you were best friends, too."

"Why does that matter?"

"I want to know the nature of the relationships between the people around me. I don't like surprises."

"If his presence was disconcerting, you could have asked me about him. You could have asked me on day one."

"I wasn't uncomfortable then. I trusted you. When he told me you sent him, I trusted him. Until I saw the two of you together, I didn't know I was in the dark about your relationship with him."

"You're not in the dark. Everybody in Beautiful knows we're best friends." Hearing his rationale, he paused and reached for her hand. "I took for granted you knew, too. But how could you have known? You're not from Beautiful. You couldn't have. I wasn't mindful of that, and I'm sorry. Please forgive me."

Her guards came down with the sincerity in his voice. "I was a bit dumbfounded at seeing it, but I understand. No harm's done."

"Are you sure?"

She nodded and picked up her fork again. He followed, and they ate while the sound of soft jazz music soothed the air. When his favorite song played, he asked her to close her eyes and listen carefully to the saxophone. She did, and when she opened them and found him swaying slowly in rhythm, they laughed heartily. Her company and laughter was gratifying and made the quiet time he sought when he came there more satisfying than he imagined.

That night when he prepared for bed, he didn't seek refuge in his study. Instead, he climbed into his bed to the sound of his own selection of jazz music filling his bedroom. He had forgotten how much it, too, breathed life into him.

T he next evening, Myles was finally able to pass the time with Slone playing cards. He dealt a hand and asked about the meeting he missed. Slone gave him an update and then turned the conversation to Victoria.

"Rumor has it you have a personal interest in Mrs. Davenport. I wouldn't have believed it if I didn't see it for myself. Why didn't you tell me?"

"There's nothing to tell. Our lunch together was simply that. Lunch." He threw out a card and Slone followed.

"It appeared to be a lot more to it than that. The two of you were comfortable and seemed to be really enjoying each other's company." Slone fixed the rest of the cards in his hand.

"It might have appeared that way, but it was unplanned. Neither of us knew the other would be there." He threw down another card.

"I would believe it if you weren't so obvious in your attempts to avoid the topic every time that I inquired about her."

Myles glanced at him. "It's the truth. There's nothing to avoid or discuss." He looked back at the cards, studying them. I'll tell you this though. She likes being here. It's quite possible she might not leave Beautiful."

Slone placed another card on the table, and he followed. "If only she would visit the church; for if she decides to stay and join, her tithing would make a significant difference in the finances."

"You have information about her financial status?"

"It's obvious she's a woman of great means."

"Is that your interest in her?"

He looked steady at Slone. "You know me better than that, but I won't deny I recognize it as an opportunity to grow the church."

Slone placed all his cards on the table. Myles dropped his and gathered them up in a pile, laughing. "You used to be good at this. What's happening to you?"

"You tell me, Myles. What's happening to you?"

"What do you mean?"

"You secretly bring this strange woman, who you say you know nothing about, into town and flaunt her around in public. Now, you want her to be a member of the church, so she can fund it. What's happening to you?"

"Firstly, she came here on her own. I told you that. Secondly, I said, if she decides to join. There are other options in Beautiful."

"But you want her to choose yours."

"Don't judge me for that."

"My judgement of you is the least of your concerns. The whole town is already gossiping about the two of you. Members of the church board are asking questions not even I can answer."

"What questions?"

"The same ones they ask about you and Ronnie."

"Slone, you know me. It's not what it looks like."

"I do know you, and something is going on here. So, if it's not what it looks like, then you better tell me exactly what it is."

Myles reflected on Slone's emotional response the day he asked him to fix her tire, and the way he looked at her when he saw them having lunch at the restaurant. "I know you, too, Slone, and maybe it's you who need to tell me what is going on here."

Slone stood. "I'm not the pastor. I don't have to justify my actions in the manner you do. Despite that, I wouldn't be a friend if I didn't warn you. Neither the ongoing saga between you and Ronnie nor whatever it is you have with Mrs. Davenport looks good to the board. You're playing with fire, Myles, and somebody is going to get burned."

Myles pushed back from the table. "I think we should try this another time when you're up for the challenge."

Chapter Seven

Across the railroad track, where the sound of trains roaring through the town at odd hours of the night was loudest, Nena lay alone in her apartment staring at the ceiling. The vibration from yet another train rattled the window, but she was used to it. It only prompted her to look at the clock on the nightstand. It was nearing midnight. She hoped that was the last train. Possibly, though not likely, the last disturbance of the night.

She barely had time to enjoy the possibility of such tranquility when she heard sirens over the fainting sound of the caboose in the distance. She tossed aside her blanket and reached for the pink terry cloth robe at the foot of her bed. Slipping her arms into the sleeves, she searched the floor with her bare feet to find her bed slippers and then hurried to the window, making it just in time to see the flashing light from the ambulance disappear out of sight.

Nena rubbed her weary eyes and looked two stories down. Other occupants in the apartment building were also peering out their windows. If it were daylight, they would huddle in the street to tell each other their version of why the ambulance had come into town, what they think happened, how it happened, and to whom. But it was nighttime and only drunks, holding up their trousers with one hand and carrying a can of beer in the other, flocked the railroad track. No self-respecting woman would be caught out there with them. Nena shook her head and left from the window, tightening the sash around her body.

She sat on her bed and wrapped the ends of the robe between her thighs. A glance at the clock again showed only two minutes passed since she last looked at it, but it felt longer than that. Time passed slowly when she's up at nights waiting for him.

She patted the side of her head and took off the scarf, allowing her hair to fall loosely over her slender shoulders. Caressing her lips with the tip of her tongue, she wondered why she avails herself to him. It's not that she didn't know the answer. It's that she hadn't figured out a way to exist without him because of it.

It was then she heard it. The sound of keys jiggling in the door and laughter. Sweet laughter. The kind that came from lips laced with liquor. Relieved, nonetheless, Nena pushed herself up from the bed, switched on the light, and hurried to the front door.

"You're drunk, Aiden," she whispered in disgust when he stumbled through the door. She held him up and led him to the sofa. "You're lucky you made it up the stairs without falling."

"Tell me something I don't already know," he mocked heartily and fell backward from her arms into the sofa. Shifting in it, he tumbled to the floor but managed to pull himself back up with legs sliding loosely with each attempt.

Nena watched, feeling grateful she didn't marry him when he asked her to but foolish to be stuck with him anyway - at least with that part of him. The part he didn't mind her seeing but hid from the rest of the world.

"Do you- do you remember- when- when-I asked you - to marry me?"

She looked away. It was a topic she continually avoided, and was relieved he only brought it up, now, when he was least able to discuss it.

"You said- you said-" He stuttered but was still determined to engage her into a conversation. "Gimme a minute, Nena, I'll tell you exactly what you said." He wiped his mouth with the back of his hand, and shaking a finger at her, answered his own question.

"You told me," he kept on, partly angry and partly incoherent, "You told me to pour out the liquor in my bottle, 'cause a man can't think when he's drunk. That's what you told me, Nena." He wiped his mouth again, somewhat in triumph.

"You should have listened, Aiden."

She went to close the door and caught eyes with the neighbor across from her apartment hurriedly closing her blinds. She knew then what the rumors in Beautiful would be at sunrise. It was the least of her worries, she found when she locked the door, and felt Aiden behind her, trapping her against the closed door.

"Aiden, don't," she begged and faced him.

"You're right. I should have listened to you."

The motionless glare in his eyes would have frightened her if she hadn't grown used to seeing it. Now, not even her heart beat faster when he approached her that way. He tried to kiss her, but she pushed him away. Then, she felt it. The violent sting of the back of his hand ripping across her face. Nena fell to the floor and quickly drew up her hand to protect her face from another possible blow. It didn't come this time.

Aiden dropped down beside her and scooped her into his arms. "Babe, I'm sorry. Are you okay?"

She inhaled, and her body relaxed.

"Why do you make me do this to you, Nena?

She eased out of his arms and rested a shoulder against the door, pulling the loosened robe back around her body.

"You know I can't handle it when you refuse me. Why do you make me have to treat you this way?"

Nena held down her head and brushed the tip of a finger across her swollen lip, but he clutched her chin and forced her face back to him.

"Babe, I'm sorry," he whimpered. "I will never hurt you again. I promise."

Hearing the apology, evoked no emotions in her. She expected him to say it and everything else he said. "I'll stop drinking. I promise I will, Nena. I'll stop drinking."

She braced against the door and pulled up from the floor.

"I'm sorry," Aiden sobbed, as she walked back to her bedroom and closed the door.

Nena stood in front of the mirror, keeping her focus on her swollen lip. It was evidence of the way things changed between them, and how it remained the same.

The telephone rang and broke her focus. She wondered who would call at that hour of the night, but the curiosity was not enough to make her answer. She had to focus on her ordeal. Suppressing tears, she switched off the light, and crawled back into bed.

On the other end of the telephone, Dorothy prayed for Nena to answer, as she made her way through a somber crowd gathered in front of Victoria's house. With her heart drumming, she neared an ambulance that woke everyone when it came down the street with its sirens blaring and stopped in front of the house.

With no answer from Nena, Dorothy shoved the phone into her purse and forced her way up the steps unto the front porch. It was as far as she got before the paramedics yelled for her to move out of the way, wheeling Victoria out on a gurney. There were bruises on her face and blood penetrating the bandage on her head when they pushed passed her.

"Oh, God! Let her be okay." Dorothy bent at the waist and squealed.

An hour before the commotion, Victoria sank into her bathtub, weary from another search that produced a lack of information about her father. A glass of wine she purchased at a restaurant where she had lunch earlier, and the warm water protruding from the powerful jet spa massaging her body, lessened the stress from the search that day. Feeling relieved, she finally got out of the tub, dried, and slipped into her nightgown.

Daubing her face with night-cream, a noise from her bedroom drew her attention. She supposed something from her closet had fallen and decided to see about it. It was dark in the room when she opened the door, but she caught sight of a shadowy figure, visible only from the light escaping the bathroom, moved toward her. Another figure emerged from her closet. Her eyes focused enough to see there were two masked men in the room. Victoria screamed and dashed back into the bathroom. She snatched the wooden towel rod from the wall and hunkered behind the closed door. The next few seconds were all she had to accept the danger facing her was real.

The men were already beating down the door and soon kicked it open. Despite her desperate plea for them to not hurt her, she felt a hand grip her hair. She lodged the rod at the man's crotch, and he let go crumbling to his knees. Victoria staggered up to her feet in dire hopes of escaping but came face to face with the man's partner. In a split second, the back of his hand across her face sent her floundering back to the ground. The rod fell from her hand.

He locked his fingers into her hair and dragged her across the floor back into the bedroom.

"Where's the money?" The guttural voice was urgent.

"I don't have any," she said in a breath above a whisper.

He flung her up against the bedpost, and Victoria grabbed her rib cage and twisted in pain. She tried to scream but breath had abandoned her.

The man knelt by her and clutched her throat. Tightening the hold, he asked again, "Where's the cash?"

She gagged.

He loosened the hold and motioned to his accomplice, who had finally regained footing. Following the order, he knelt beside her and pressed an object against the side of her head.

She reached up to shift it away and, on contact, discovered it was a gun. He pushed it up against her head and bashed her with it without warning. Blood trickled down her face.

"Don't make this hard for you," he whispered. "Give us the cash, now."

Victoria wiped the blood from her face with her nightgown. "I have jewelry. They're very valuable."

He dragged her up from the floor. "We want cash."

"Then you're in the wrong house," she found strength to yell.

"Where's the jewelry?"

"In the middle room closet."

With the gun in her back, they forced her down the dark hallway and shoved her into the room. Victoria went to the closet and switched on the light.

"Turn it off and don't try anything else foolish."

She flipped the switch again and searched a shelf in the dark for the box of jewelry.

"Open it," he demanded when she brought it to him.

She did, and he raked around in it with his hand before ordering his accomplice to take it. When he did, he shoved her hard to the floor. With the gun pushed deep into her side, he snatched the diamond ring off her finger and warned her, "If you say anything about tonight, I'll come back and finish the job."

Victoria lay almost motionless and watched them climb out the open window, she was sure was locked when she went to her room that night. She waited to be certain they were gone, before she staggered back to her room, crouched at the foot of her bed, and dialed 9-1-1. It felt like a lifetime passed, waiting for help. By the time it arrived, she had collapsed on the floor.

The police scoured the house, while the paramedics performed rhythms of CPR to revive her. When she regained consciousness, they bandaged her head and wheeled her out of the house.

Dorothy followed the paramedics, begging in vain they tell her the status of Victoria's condition. It was her responsibility to take care of her and watching them put her into the ambulance and drive away rendered her helpless. She thought to call Nena again. It was the protocol in such situations, for she always knew the pastor's whereabout to inform him of any crisis. With the previous calls unanswered, however, Dorothy dialed Slone's number instead. The groggy voice on the other end was a relief.

"Deacon Slone, Mrs. Davenport has been hurt. The ambulance is taking her to the hospital," she blurted.

Slone jolted up in his bed. "What? What happened?"

"I don't know. There are cops all around the house. The paramedics bandaged her head, put an oxygen mask over her face, and rolled her out of there. She looks dreadful."

Slone ripped the sheet from across him. "Meet me at the hospital."

Dorothy made her way through the crowd, catching hints of the gossips already brewing questioning Victoria's true identity, why she came to Beautiful, and what might have happened inside that house. Many of them who wondered, had only heard about Victoria since she moved into the house and only a few had even gotten close enough to say hello. Dorothy wanted to stop and dispel every whisper of untruth but had only time to silence one.

"Don't spread lies about people you don't know. I'll tell you about her when I return from the hospital. Until then, get Rayne and take care of her for me." The woman lived in the house next to hers and their daughters were becoming best friends. She handed the woman the key to her house and left.

Dorothy arrived at the hospital minutes after Slone. He was standing at the front desk when she rushed inside and threw desperate arms around him.

He held her until she let go. Shaking, she scribbled her name below Slone's on the list of visitors and flashed the clerk her driver's license for ID.

"Is she going to make it?"

"We'll know when we see her." He showed her the room number on a card the clerk gave him, and she locked arms with him, hurrying them toward the elevator. It moved at a snail's pace up to the third floor and opened with a ding. They exited and made way down the corridor to Victoria's room.

The door was ajar. Slone peeked in, and they entered with caution. A warm dimmed glow of light hugged the tiny room. There was a table in a corner with a plastic water jug and white foam cups on it. In the bed, against the back wall, was Victoria, swaddled in white linens.

Myles was there too, sitting by her bedside holding her hand. He let go quickly and stood to greet them.

"Slone. Dorothy. You're here."

Slone passed him to Victoria.

"Thank God you're here, Pastor." Dorothy flung her arms around him and buried her head in his chest. "I called Nena, but she didn't answer." She looked up at him. "How'd you get the news so fast?"

"One of the paramedics knows me well. Mrs. Davenport mentioned my name, and he called me when they took her from the house," he said with eyes on Slone.

Slone looked at Victoria through moist eyelids. There were needles taped to her arm and a bandage around her head.

"Are you ok?"

In pain, she managed a groggy, "I think so."

"What happened?"

"Those thugs again," Myles answered. "They broke into the house with a gun, stole her jewelry, and left her with a fractured rib and concussion."

Slone was still fixed on Victoria. "Did you see who did it?"

"They wore masks," she whimpered.

A still silence blanketed the room. Myles broke it with a quiet voice. "I was about to pray with her when you came." He took Victoria's hand again and reached for Slone's. "Will you join me?"

He accepted and extended a hand for Dorothy's. They bowed heads and closed their eyes. Myles cleared his throat. "Deacon Slone, lead us please."

Their eyes met with controlled conflict. It was brief but long enough to expose the emotions were still unsettled between them. Slone closed his, and a heavy moment passed before he submitted to the appeal with a delicate, "In the name of Jesus."

Myles gripped Slone's hand, securing it in his, but the prayer became a struggle. Over and over, he called on the name of Jesus, and each time Myles strengthened the grip of his hand.

Finally, the Spirit warmed within him. He centered his focus on Victoria but found his heart deeply vexed as he imagined the chilling ordeal she endured. The fear she must have felt in the presence of masked gunmen sent his attention to God, and a frightening thought of *what kind of God would allow this to happen* grieved him.

"God! Why?" The question followed with a deep desperate moan that pierced the room. Myles clutched onto his hand with an urge that begged him to take control.

Victoria opened her eyes to the warmth she felt in his grief and watched his eyes tremble from holding back tears welling behind his closed eyelids. She couldn't remember anyone grieving for her in that way and quickly caught a rolling tear at her cheekbone.

A heavy silence filled the room and she closed her eyes. In the silence, Slone took heed to a spiritual shift and surrendered to God. When he spoke again, it was of thanksgiving.

"God, while we preferred this not to have been, thank you for not taking her so soon from me." He paused. "Um... from us."

Hearing the choice words, Dorothy peeked at Slone through a half-closed eyelid. He swallowed a lump in his throat, and she shifted her attention to Victoria. A calmness was on her face. She was almost motionless- too afraid to open her eyes.

Myles seemed equally unmoved by the prayer, agreeing with enthusiasm, "Thank you, Lord."

The words replayed in Dorothy's ears as a question. "So soon from me?" And she wondered if anyone else was even listening to the prayer. It was a struggle to quiet the voice in her head trying to make sense of what Slone said, but she managed and forced her ears to tune in to him again.

"Thank you, Lord, for being with her through the valley of the shadow of death, for her presence reminds us of your promise to never forsake us in our time of need. Be her comforter on her journey of healing. And Lord, I pray you'll restore unto her peace within her soul."

He looked at her, and a pair of unfamiliar eyes, full of gratitude, met him. He nodded in acceptance of it, and in the private endearing moment whispered a gentle, "Amen."

Nena awoke early to the sound of a dog growling. It was the sharp bark that brought her fully out of her sleep. She rubbed her eyes with her ears tuned to the subsequent growl. A separate bark came and then chattering. The walls in the apartments were thin. If they weren't careful, everyone in the building would know each other's business. She was most cautious of that.

A twitch in her bottom lip reminded her of the horrific night she had, and she crawled out of bed and knelt at her bedside. On her knees, however, she could not find the right words to say to God. She had prayed all the words she knew already and couldn't bring herself to pray them again. The memory of a message Myles preached months before, reminded her that sometimes it's enough to kneel in silence. The memory was timely, and she stilled. The dog barked again. A baby cried. And there were more chattering. She endured it until she felt spiritually strengthened.

Nena rose, determined to drown out the sounds from her neighbor with a strong humming of her favorite hymnal in the shower on full blast. When she dressed, she noticed her swollen lip, and dabbed powder over it, but make-up wasn't enough to hide it. Hopelessly, Nena sucked it in and left the apartment, carefully stepping over Aiden asleep on the living room floor.

The sun was rising and painting a golden glow above the horizon. Nena couldn't ignore it. She made her way down the stairs, took her camera from her bag, and aimed it toward the sky.

"Early mornings are the only time it makes sense why this old town is called Beautiful," she grumbled, snapping a picture and capturing the magnificent sky. A bird flew into her view and carried her attention to a tree. It perched on a branch but quickly spread its wings wide, ready to take flight again. Nena pointed her camera and captured the flight with one click. She held the camera at her side and watched, wondering what such freedom felt like.

Absorbed in the thought, it took a neighbor backing out of a driveway honking the horn to bring her out of it. With a quick wave and a mouthed apology, she tucked the camera back into her bag and hastened to her car. Shifting into reverse, she reflected on the day Aiden's life fell apart.

It was a week before their high school senior prom. He had come to her back porch and knocked on the screen door. When she opened it, he blurted, "Nobody asked you yet, right?"

"Asked me what?"

"You know." He stalled. "To the prom."

"Are you asking?" Nena remembered saying, dryly.

"Yeah."

"I don't hear you asking." She folded her arms and turned away from him.

"I just did," he said impatiently.

"You're asking about the wrong thing then," she snapped and turned to go back into the house.

"Nena," Aiden called after her. "Go with me."

"That's not how you ask."

"Stop playing. Go with me."

"You're supposed to ask and not demand that I go with you."

"Well, are you going?"

She shook her head, tiredly. "I'll think about it." He had to ask again before she finally said yes.

The day before the prom, Nena's father took her to Langston to buy her a new dress. They spent hours at the hair salon, leaving with her hair pinned up in a bun. Then, they drove to a spa for manicure and pedicure.

The evening of the prom came. She put on the long powder-blue spaghetti-strap dress and draped a sheer blue scarf across her shoulders. She chose a pair of silver high heel open-toed shoes to show off her white-tip painted toenails.

Sitting on the sofa in the family room, she waited for Aiden to escort her. Hours passed. When he finally showed, he left from his car holding a brown paper bag. He was not dressed, either, for the occasion, and, from his bloodshot eyes that met her at the door, she could tell something horrible happened.

"I've been at the hospital all day with my mom." He spoke without apologies and was filled with infuriation. "Someone broke into our house. In broad daylight," he groaned, punching into thin air. When he settled, he grabbed hold onto her and slid down at her feet. "I don't think she'll make it, Nena," he sobbed.

She dragged him up and wrapped her arms around him, but he was stiffened with anger in the embrace. She held him, hoping he would feel the love she had for him.

"She's all I have." He eased away from her and sipped from the bottle in the paper bag. "I will find who did this. I swear."

Nena looked at him with tears streaming down her cheeks. "She just might make it. You have to believe."

He wiped his eyes and took notice of the single white rose, amidst baby breaths, tucked in her hair. Soft pink lipstick colored her lips. The long silver earrings dangling from her ears matched the silver necklace around her neck and silver shoes. His eyes lingered on the well-fitted blue evening gown. He watched her brushed the loose strands of hair from her face. In the evening sun, the tears glistened in her eyes, and he knew she felt the pain he was feeling. It made her even more beautiful to him.

"You dolled up like this for me?" He was grazing his hand across the white rose as he asked, and he wiped tears settling in the corner of her eyes with his hand. When he touched her face, she held it there. Feeling the warmth of her hand against his, he leaned in and kissed her lips. The alcohol was distinct in the kiss, and she drew a dislike for it. She turned away, but Aiden drew her back to him and held her.

"Marry me, Nena."

The proposal came with no obvious thought. "We'll be graduating in a few weeks anyway, and if I lose my mother, you're all I have left." He continued as if he, too, was trying to make sense of what he was proposing. "My dad left before I was born. If I lose her, you're all I got."

Nena dared him to pour out the liquor in the bottle, and he asked her why.

"Because a man can't think when he's drunk," she told him.

Before the night ended, Aiden's mother transitioned. It was the worst night of their lives. She knelt beside him in the hospital room and faced him. With tears running down her cheeks, Nena promised she would never leave him. The moment, still vivid, made her body quiver as she entered the parking lot, choosing to park a few spaces down from the entrance to the grocery store. Releasing herself from the memories of that tragic evening, she walked briskly to unlock the chained door.

Inside, she began the day as usual- removing expired products from the almost empty shelves and restocking them with more of the same items, knowing soon she would be removing those as well. No one was buying them anymore, and she wondered why the owner hadn't accepted that the customers' taste and needs were changing. Until he did, however, working there was her major source of income, and her best prospect in Beautiful.

The thought was daunting. Fortunately, a loud knock on the door saved her from dwelling on it further. Nena checked her watch. It wasn't time to open to the public yet, and it was unusual for a customer to come so early. The knock came again, and with it, a voice from the other side of the door.

"Nena, it's Dorothy."

"What are you doing here already?" she asked opening it.

"I tried to reach you last night."

Nena went behind the counter. "I couldn't answer the call."

"You didn't hear what happened to Mrs. Davenport, I guess."

Her eyes were fastened onto the cash register, and her index finger moved across the number pad, keying in her code to open it. She didn't even look up when she answered. "What happened to her?"

"Thugs broke into her house and robbed her at gunpoint."

The drawer popped open. Nena pushed it back shut. "What?"

"They stole her jewelry and roughed her up pretty badly," Dorothy went on.

Nena stepped aside from the register. Her forehead crinkled from concern.

"Thank God, she will be okay," Dorothy said, lessening the worry. "She managed to call 9-1-1. The police officers and the ambulance showed up with lights flashing and sirens blaring, but those thugs ran off before they got there."

Nena sighed and shook her head.

"Everyone crowded the street to find out what was happening at her house. It was a commotion out there.

Nena nodded, aware the ambulance she saw crossing the railroad track was for Mrs. Davenport.

"I had to push my way through the crowd to try and see her," Dorothy continued. "But they wouldn't let me near her. I was devastated watching them wheel her away."

Her focus shifted to Nena's lip. The swelling was still visible. "Are you ok?" The question came after an awkward pause.

"Me? Yes." Nena sucked in the lip and repositioned herself.

"It must have been an ordeal for you. Did you call Pastor?"

"I called Deacon Slone when you didn't answer." Her voice dropped to a whisper when she said his name, and Nena's probing eyes begged her to continue.

"By the time we arrived at the hospital, she was checked into a room and Pastor was already there, holding her hand."

Dorothy leaned in closer to her. "I tell you, Nena, when Deacon Slone walked in, Pastor let go so fast you might believe he was engaged in wrong-doings. And Deacon Slone." She eased back with her hand on her hip. "From the look in his eyes, you would think he was the one who caught him."

"Mm," Nena grunted. "What do you think that was about?"

"I don't know." She paused, reflecting on Slone's prayer with unsettled curiosity. "I couldn't put my finger on it. But something is going on, and Pastor didn't want me to catch on to it. After we prayed for her, he hurried me out of there to see about Rayne. He called me early this morning with a list of things to buy for Mrs. Davenport."

Dorothy searched her bag for the sheet of paper on which she jotted down the items. "Here," she said finding it.

Looking over the items, Nena mumbled, "Well, whatever it is, it'll come to light. Nothing stays a secret long in Beautiful."

Centering on Nena's lip again, Dorothy agreed. "You're right about that."

She left the store that morning with less than half of the items on the list, and she was not the only one that day. Nearly all the other shoppers spent more time spinning their version of the incident than they did shopping.

Nena listened to the stories from one customer to another, all of them eventually pointing to it as evidence of the downward spiraling of Beautiful. It was another day of more gossips than sales.

She closed the store with the usual ritual of balancing the cash register and preparing the bank deposit slip. Then she locked all the funds she collected in a safe for the owner to retrieve at his convenience and chained all the doors. On her way home, she prayed, silently, for Mrs. Davenport and worried about managing her bills if the store went out of business.

When she pulled into her parking spot, Connie, her neighbor from downstairs, stuck her head out from the front door, hiking her youngest baby up onto her hip and ushering another child back into the apartment. Her short stocky frame stalled in the doorway until Nena was out of her car.

"Nena, did you hear about that woman who got robbed last night?" She spoke with a voice that was meant to be a whisper, but curiosity carried it higher.

"Yes."

"Do you know her?"

"I've met her."

Nena glanced away from her up to her front door. Aiden had come out of her apartment, dressed in a light-blue striped shirt tucked neatly into his well-pressed navy-blue pants. His black leather briefcase was strapped over his shoulders and he gripped his phone at his ear. A subtle gust of wind met him at the top of the stairs, rustling the long thin blue tie hanging loosely around his neck. He struggled between keeping the tie in place and the phone at his ear as he jogged down the steps.

"I told you I had too much to drink last night," he spoke firmly.

Nena cringed and looked away, but Connie didn't take her eyes off him. He was silent until he came to the foot of the steps.

"I'll see you tonight. I promise," he laughed, ending the call.

Aiden tucked the phone into his briefcase, and finally looking up, he saw Nena. He went to her, guardedly. She expected him to be gentle when he slipped a hand around her waist. He was. His body brushed against hers, and she smelled his cologne. It was her favorite. He searched her eyes with care, gliding the back of his hand lightly down the side of her face. He was tender. A contrast to the way he was the night before. The delicate touch sent her heart weaving between an array of tertiary emotions based in love and sadness.

As she stood before him emotionally exasperated, Aiden tilted her face up with a finger beneath her chin and lowered his lips onto hers. His lips were soft, and he was patient. Her hand went mid-way to touch his face as her heart sank. Unable to settle on what to feel, she brought her hand down and let his kiss linger without resistance, while her neighbor upstairs perched in the window, and Connie, still stuck in her doorway, watched.

"Babe, I'm sorry," he whispered desperately into the kiss. There was something penetrable in the way he said it that soothed her. Her emotions yielded, and feeling her calm, he let up and glided his thumb carefully across her lips. She closed her eyes, opening them to the ground.

"Nena." He was pleading. She looked up at him, and he mouthed, "I love you." She nodded, smiled, and walked away.

Entering her apartment, a dozen white roses on the tiny dinner table in the kitchen welcomed her. She stood with her back against the closed door and looked at them shimmering in the light breeze and dim sunlight flowing in through the half-opened window. She didn't want to touch or smell them. *They are white, and they are roses.* That was all her weary emotions allowed. Her heart couldn't feel anything more. She went into her bedroom and threw her body across her bed. And there it was. A white envelope tucked behind the clock. It wasn't hidden. Just secured. Nena opened it and found enough cash to pay her bills for the rest of the month. On a card in it, Aiden scribbled: *I'm sorry for hurting you. Please Forgive me.*

Chapter Eight

The news of the violent attack spread fast, and, within days made Mrs. Davenport a household name in Beautiful. The pastors from almost every church in, and near, the town brought their prayer warriors to the hospital every day to proclaim healing upon her. The continuous inflow of strange faces overwhelmed her. If it wasn't for Myles, Slone, and Dorothy at her bedside daily assuring her the visits were customary, she would have insisted it stopped.

She was relieved, nonetheless, when the day came that her doctor released her from the hospital. By then, Myles had gotten a security system installed in the house. When he brought her home, a representative of the company was there to show her the new features. She practiced setting the alarm, but Myles was still uneasy about her being there alone. He went to all the rooms and checked the windows to ensure they were locked and suggested that Dorothy stay with her for a few nights until she was used to being back in the house.

"I can't let her do that. She has her own home and a child to care for," Victoria said.

"It's only a precaution. You're still healing, and you'll need round the clock assistance at least for the next few days."

"I can manage."

"I know, but she has already agreed, and I insist she stays."

At nightfall, Victoria accepted Myles was right. She needed someone there. Ordinary sounds she had grown used to was now impossible to ignore. Dogs howling, car engines revving in the distance, and crickets chirping were amplified in her ears. She listened for hours, unable to fall asleep. When the sound of night quieted, the memory of the attack surfaced, and her heartbeat escalated.

Dorothy knocked on her door and whispered, softly, "Mrs. Davenport."

Victoria sat up in the bed. "Come in Dorothy." When the door opened, she asked, "Will you turn on the light?"

"You're awake. Good." Dorothy flipped the light switch. "It's time for your medication." She handed her a glass of water and took out a pill from the pill bottle on the bedside table. "How do you feel?"

Victoria swallowed the pill and handed the glass back to her. "I feel better, but I'm glad you're here."

Dorothy touched her arm lightly. "I wouldn't have it any other way. You rest, now. I'll remind you when it's time for your next dose."

The next morning, Victoria awoke early and sat in the rocking chair by the window. Looking out into the open yard, she accepted the attack as one that could have ended her life. Grasping the full meaning of it, she accepted, too, some of life's most precious moments are fleeting. The luxury of Crystal Falls and the fame from being a world-renowned ballerina, though precious, suddenly fell short of value. Living a more purposeful life became pressing, and the ability to breathe meant she has the opportunity to do so.

It starts with fulfilling her deepest desires, she decided and pondered accepting Myles' help or hiring a private detective to locate her father. Dauntingly, in either case, there were no leads to pursue. She had no names, no pictures, and no clue if he was even still alive. They were locked away in her mother's heart, and she couldn't reach them.

Locked away, too, in her heart was the image of a boy she longed for secretly. She often reached for memories of him to comfort herself at will- like the first time she mentioned him to her mother. It was at the height of her frustration in her marriage.

"It is wiser to think of what you have instead of what you're missing," her mother warned.

At the time, it made sense, but with her husband gone now, she couldn't stop thinking about what she was missing. Her heart bled from the likelihood of never knowing, considering no one has even mentioned his name since she arrived in Beautiful.

The doorbell rang, releasing her heart from sinking deeper in despair. Tightening the sash around her pastel pink satin robe, she hastened to answer it.

On the other side of the door was Slone. Her face bloomed with delight in seeing him. Expecting Dorothy when the door opened, Slone's eyes bulged in the shock of seeing her instead. She was supposed to be sick and in bed, but there she was wearing a glow he didn't expect either.

"Victoria."

She couldn't hold back the delicate laughter. "Slone." She eased back from the doorway.

He accepted the hint to come in through the half-opened door. Their bodies touched as he passed her, and when she closed it, he took her into his arms with the unbridled passion of his youth. She responded readily, wrapping her arms around him. Slone cradled the back of her neck with one hand, while the other roamed her body and drew her closer. Their lips met with hunger, satiating the urgency of a flaming desire sprung out of control. Burning from the heat at her core, she moaned, deeply.

"Careful," Slone cautioned himself, remembering she was still healing. He buried his head into her shoulder.

"I thought I heard the doorbell," Dorothy said coming into the living room.

"It's just Slone." Victoria gathered her robe over her shoulders, grateful she didn't catch them in the act.

"Dorothy, good morning," Slone greeted her.

"Good morning, Deacon Slone. I'll have breakfast shortly. Will you be staying awhile?"

"He can't, " Victoria said quickly and turned to him. Her eyes carried a desperate plea for him to not stay.

"I just wanted to see how she's doing." He looked at Victoria warmly. "I thought she would be in bed. It seems you'll have to work harder to keep her there."

They laughed.

"Don't worry. I will," Dorothy said, making her way to the kitchen.

Victoria opened the door, and he left with a warning. "You should be in bed. Full recovery takes time."

She agreed, and he palmed her face, raise it gently, and met her lips with another kiss. She closed the door and rested her back against it, calling out,

"Dorothy, bring a cold drink to my room. It's turning out to be an extremely hot day." Fanning with her hand, she went back to her bedroom and crawled back into bed.

Dorothy took a glass of fruit juice to her. "Deacon Slone is right, you know. You shouldn't be out of bed yet. I'll get the door the next time the doorbell rings."

Victoria sat up, sipped from the glass, and placed it on the table. She cleared her throat and tapped the edge of the bed for Dorothy to sit on it.

"Do you know why I came to Beautiful?"

"I've wondered," Dorothy admitted, positioning herself on the bed.

"I wanted to be free," Victoria explained.

"Free from what?"

"From people who think it's their job to take care of me. I wanted to be free to take care of myself."

"That's why you came?" Dorothy forced out a dry laugh. "I wish I had someone to take care of me, and here you are running from it?"

"Why don't you have someone to take care of you, Dorothy?" The question held more concern than curiosity.

Dorothy's eyes watered. "I must show you something." She hopped off the bed and left the room. She returned with a small picture frame and handed it to Victoria.

"I carry this everywhere I go. He was my husband and Rayne's father. He was a good man, and he took good care of us until he died a few years ago."

"I'm sorry. How did he die?" Victoria examined the face of the man in the picture.

"He was coming home from work late one evening. The rain was pouring. He lost control of the car and hit a tree." She looked away from Victoria.

"I lost my husband in a similar way, too," Victoria told her. "He was coming home from a business trip. It was a stormy night. He never made it home."

"I'm sorry. I didn't know." Dorothy put her hand to her mouth, wishing she could take back the story.

"Don't be. You couldn't have known." The softness in her voice was clearly forgiveness. "It's been over a year, anyway. I'm dealing with it better."

She handed the picture back to Dorothy. "Your husband has a striking resemblance to Pastor Avery."

Dorothy sat at the edge of the bed again. "They're brothers."

"Oh?" That the people in Beautiful were too unforthcoming with their relationships, came as a thought she might as well accept.

"It was quite a big deal marrying one of the Avery brothers," Dorothy smiled, shifting herself into a more comfortable position on the bed. "Those brothers could have any woman they want, but my husband chose me." She looked at Victoria and longingness replaced the twinkle in her eyes. "And he loved me deeply. I could feel it in my heart."

"That explains why Pastor Avery hasn't pursued you."

Dorothy rolled her eyes. "Besides that, Ronnie would never let another woman near him."

"Who's Ronnie?"

"Uh. She's trouble, to put it mildly. They were high school sweethearts-broke up years ago, but she can't get over him. She shows up at the church whenever she feels like it and lay all her problems on him to keep his mind occupied on her. The poor man has to work overtime just to handle his own affairs."

Victoria laughed. "What about Slone and the other eligible men in Beautiful? Why haven't they pursued you?"

"I've known these men all my life. They and my husband were friends. It wouldn't be right."

"Sounds like you've given up on marrying again."

Dorothy ran a finger over the picture of her husband in the frame. "Not really. I've struggled since I lost him. I had no income, and the money he left us didn't last long. It would be good to have someone to help share the burden, and I'm sure Rayne would like to have a father."

"I meant for love," Victoria said flatly as if to reject any reason for marriage other than for love.

"Are you looking for love, Mrs. Davenport?"

"Isn't everybody?"

The doorbell rang again, and Dorothy got off the bed. "You stay right here. I'll get it."

At the door, Dorothy greeted members of a church who brought groceries, and in the days that followed, more church members came. Some brought cooked meals, some offered to help with chores, and some just prayed. Victoria welcomed them to keep with the town's custom, but the attention drove her crazy. Everyone knew her by name now. The privacy she wanted coming there was slipping away.

"This is a small town," Myles explained one day, sitting next to her on the front porch listening to her dilemma. "We exist as one big family up here. When one person is hurt, we're all hurt, and we take care of each other. Besides," he said with compassion, "You didn't expect for a woman of your status to sashay into town, and it remains a secret forever. Did you?"

"Not forever, but I didn't wish for the intrusion," she frowned.

"Open your eyes, Victoria. You're the only one in Beautiful who can afford a helper. You drive around town in a Jaguar for God's sake! Heck! You get dolled up just to sit on your front porch," he laughed, bringing attention to her, sitting cross-legged in a red strapless ankle-length sundress and a white shawl draped over her bare shoulders. A wide-rimmed red hat and matching backless high-heeled slippers completed the ensemble. Her eyes were hidden behind dark sunglasses.

"If it wasn't for that unfortunate incident, nobody would feel comfortable enough to approach you."

Victoria squirmed and took off the sunglasses. "I've spent a lot of years in the public eye. You think I'd be used to the attention." She looked away adding, "The truth is, I don't enjoy it. I never did."

"So, you thought coming to a small town in the middle of nowhere would solve that," he mocked under his breath.

"I wasn't seeking total anonymity," Victoria asserted. She uncrossed her legs and walked to the edge of the porch where she braced against the wooden rail. Frustration crept upon her face. Myles followed after her and rested a hand on the back of her shoulder.

"I know you weren't, and I'm not blaming you for the intrusion. You must understand, though, apart from an annual play the school puts on for the community, our people are not exposed to theatre, high fashion, ballet, and things of that sort. The opportunity to intermingle with someone who has is rare." He giggled. "It's downright intriguing in fact. So, don't let the attention alarm you."

"Going from obscurity to become the talk of the town makes me believe I will never escape the public's attention." She let out a desperate sigh. "I only wanted to find my father. Quietly. Without anyone knowing who I am. I wish I was afforded more time to do so."

"Let me help you, Victoria."

"I've thought about it, but I don't have any information you could use yet. Without verifiable information, your only avenue is to approach every man in Beautiful and ask if he is my father."

"A beautiful woman like you would have a long list of old men lining up for that role."

"But for the wrong reasons. Never mind that my mother's reputation would be ruined in the process, and the tabloids would have a field day with it."

"I didn't think of that."

The tension on her face diminished and warmth found a place there instead. "I appreciate you wanting to help. I promise I'll let you know when I find some clues you can use."

Myles rubbed his hand across the back of her shoulders and patted her. "I'll be waiting right here until you're ready."

The wait was longer than he expected. When he visited her again, nothing had changed still, except for her desire to stay in Beautiful.

"Mother was intentional in erasing every trace leading to my father. I've wasted my time coming. I might as well go back to Crystal Falls."

"Then you'll never find him for sure."

"I know. But I've searched just about every box in the attic, searched the school archives, and read every newspaper ever published in and around this town, and I still have no clue."

"You might have overlooked something. He couldn't have vanished into the thin air. Not in this small town, anyway. You have to keep searching."

"There are a couple of small boxes in the attic I didn't open. I can't imagine anything important in them. Maybe I should see to be certain, but I'm prepared to accept it if they, too, lead to a dead-end."

"Let's hope they don't."

Recognizing her return to Crystal Fall meant closure to a significant part of her life, she waited for days before climbing up the ladder again. Hope was all she had when she brought down the boxes and searched through them. By the time she re-taped the last one, the rainy season had passed, the women in Beautiful were spending more time out in the yard, caring for their gardens, and the town had gotten around to filling the potholes. Life in Beautiful was returning to normal.

At least it was for everyone else but Slone. He couldn't get Victoria off his mind, and he couldn't risk seeing her again. They spoke almost every day on the phone but that too was torturing, he confessed to her one night.

"Wanting you in my arms makes having these conversations challenging," he rolled onto his back with the phone to his ears and told her. "But you're not ready for anything more, so I have to stay away, for the temptation is strong. I can't cross that line if we can't be more."

The typical church services were not so normal either. Myles was expecting more members to begin showing up for church again. But during one of the worship services, he looked out from the pulpit and wondered if it was still raining in Beautiful. It was disheartening to see the empty seats increasing, and he prayed an extra-long prayer before the worship service that morning.

It was wise that he did, for if it weren't for the few faithful members dancing in the Spirit and waving handkerchiefs to usher him on, he wouldn't have been able to deliver the message with the usual passion he was known for.

After the service, he disappeared into his office, burdened. The attendance had been dwindling for months, and the decline in tithes and offering had the church on the brink of a financial disaster. Myles sat at his desk. He pulled out the folder he kept in the drawer and combed over the pages in it. After much thought, he picked up the phone and called Victoria.

"Myles," she answered with delight.

He reclined his chair as far back as it allowed him and got to the point. "I know you've been preoccupied with other things, but you must be concern with the balance in your bank account. We should set a time to discuss it."

She was silent, and it prompted him to check if she was still on the line. "Victoria?"

An almost inaudible sigh told him she was still there.

"Well?" Myles pressed, urging a response.

When she spoke, it came with intense pauses between words.

"I'm- I'm embarrassed to admit- after giving you control of the account, I- I didn't think of it again."

"Really?"

"You see, Edward handled our finances. I- I just assumed- you'd know what to do with it."

"I see." He brought the sizable balance on the bank statement back into his view. "Well." He cleared his throat, buying time to figure out the best choice of words. "With the work that was done on the house, Dorothy's salary, and paying the hospital bill, there is still a huge balance in the account. I can come by tomorrow and explain the transactions line by line if you'd like."

"How about I meet you at the church? It's time I leave out of this house again."

Myles detected a touch of sparkle in her voice. It was the first time he heard it since the attack, and it was enough to convince him to agree.

"Sounds great. I'll see you tomorrow." He hung up the phone and placed the folder back into the drawer.

Victoria held her phone at her ears and closed her eyes. A mental picture of Edward sitting at a big red oak desk in his office at their home emerged. It was there he conducted business and took care of the household finance. She didn't dare enter in there when he was sitting at that desk. If she needed him, she stood in the doorway and spoke from there. On the occasions when he did lift his head to acknowledge her, the long impatient sigh signaled her presence was an unwelcomed interruption of something far more important than whatever she had to say.

"Uh," Victoria said in disgust of her passivity. Her mother colored it such an honor to have a husband who knew how to take charge of things. Neither of them ever considered how she might manage if she had to do it on her own.

A key turning in the doorknob took her attention. The door opened and Dorothy stumbled in, hugging together two brown paper bags full of groceries. She gently pushed the door shut with one foot and greeted Victoria with a winded, "How're you Mrs. Davenport?" as she scurried into the kitchen.

Moments later, Victoria heard pots touching. She heard water running from the faucet and faint sounds of cutlery clinking. At any other time, these sounds would go unnoticed but hearing them suddenly disturbed her. She went into the kitchen, unable to stand it.

"Can I get you something, Mrs. Davenport?" Dorothy asked.

Victoria shook her head. "No."

Dorothy busied herself again with unpacking the groceries, but Victoria's presence in the kitchen was distracting.

"Is something wrong?"

"You're here earlier than usual," Victoria said, ignoring her puzzled countenance.

"There wasn't much in the pantry at church, so I went shopping and came right over to get your dinner started." She wiped sweat from her forehead with the back of her hand.

"And Rayne? Where is she?"

"With her friends from church. I allow her time with them since there's no one at home to play with as you know."

Dorothy picked up a knife, but Victoria took it.

"Don't you have friends, too?"

"I do."

"Take the evening off and spend it with them."

"But what about your dinner?"

"I'll be fine." There was confidence in her voice. "I've been learning my way around this kitchen. I believe I can manage for one day."

Dorothy was not amused. "You've been cooking?"

She nodded.

"So, you don't need-"

"Of course, I still need you," Victoria interjected when she saw the troubled look on her face. "I also want you to have quality time for yourself. There'll be no more running out of church for the sake of taking care of me. This is your day off with pay from now on."

"You're paying me to not work?"

Victoria laughed.

"Should you be doing that?"

"Of course. Go ahead and take off the apron."

She unstrapped it, and Victoria took it from her. Patting her hair back into place and straightening her dress, Dorothy told her, "Some of the women from church are going to White Roses for dinner. They begged me to come."

Hanging the apron on a hook inside the pantry, Victoria encouraged, "You should. You deserve to enjoy some free time with them." She escorted Dorothy back to the door.

Alone again, Victoria went into the kitchen and took a half-eaten covered dish from the refrigerator. After warming it in the microwave, she sat at the table and said a grace her mother taught her as a kid. Dangling her fork, loosely, between the asparagus and squash, she landed it on the salmon, cut a tiny piece of it, and put it into her mouth. She chewed it slowly, not only because her mother taught her to, but remembering Dorothy saying it was an ordeal finding a grocery store with salmon, she wanted to savor it.

She did not like to eat alone, for she found her mind strayed and tended to linger on unpleasant things. Aware of it, she forced her thoughts past the horrific night of the attack to a place less frightening. Europe. It was there she spent her younger years with her mother dancing, and it was where she met Edward.

She was a teenager and training at his studio when they first met. A prominent respected owner of a dance company, also, he was a busy man. The only way to get his attention, Alana thought, was to stage a well-orchestrated encounter with him, and turn it into a meeting. She watched him scrupulously, taking notes of his habits. On a day she knew he would be at the studio, her mother walked right into him, accidentally, she held. Offering a long embarrassing apology and tossing of hair between small talks, she enticed him to stay and watch Victoria in rehearsal. Edward agreed and was quite impressed with her technique and artistry. He watched her dance for years after that. Then, one day, he chose her to perform with his dance company.

Soon, she became the principal dancer in many of his sold-out shows, amidst a brewing secret romance that developed, much too quickly she admitted. The fifteen years difference in age didn't phased him, and his high-profile status in the industry excited her. Despite his age and status, Alana thought they were perfect for each other. They were married in a private ceremony, much to her mother's delight, and it thrust them into a very lavish lifestyle.

Her appetite diminished, thinking of the years that followed. She hoped, after the marriage, to perform less and start a family. But Edward had other plans for her, demanding that she perform more. When she shared a desire to take time off, he moved out of their bedroom and refused to come back until she agreed to a grueling schedule. To please him, she did. And it was the only way, it seemed, she could please him, for when she was not on stage performing, nothing else about her mattered.

Victoria pushed away from the table, conscious of every bite she had. It was how she maintained her weight during that time. Staying thin was a major concern for Edward, and she wouldn't dare disappoint him or her mother by gaining a pound.

She rubbed her belly, remembering the joy she felt when she did gain a few pounds, despite her strict regimen. It was caused from being pregnant, and that was the only reason why Edward agreed she didn't have to dance anymore. Of course, by then, he was of age and secretly desiring fatherhood while he could. Her mother easily convinced him to leave Europe. After finding the perfect home in Crystal Falls, she carried out her pregnancy and gave birth to their son.

The thought of Noah filled her with pride and made her feel alive. She went back out onto the porch where a chilly breeze met her. Victoria sat in the chair and crossed her legs, thinking, a change in season was soon to come.

Chapter Nine

Victoria awoke with anticipation of the meeting with Myles. She toyed with many options of what to do with the money in the account. *I could replace my jewelry. I'll need them in Crystal Falls.* Another thought came to send Dorothy and Rayne on a vacation to somewhere they've never been. *That might be anywhere. They have never been far from Beautiful.* She went into the bathroom and contemplated expanding it. *A master bedroom should have a big bathroom.*

The possibilities continued to flood her mind when she raked through the tiny closet contemplating what to wear. *Every master bedroom should have a spacious closet,* she thought, forcing apart her clothes packed tightly in it.

A light blue floral-print chiffon dress fell from a hanger. She took it and held it up in front of her before the mirror. The flutter sleeve A-line dress was knee-length, with a demure V-neck she felt suitable for a meeting at a church. *This will do,* she decided, turning from side to side for a better view.

When she left the house, she saw it was the perfect choice for the beautiful blue sky that greeted her. She let down the windows to feel the breeze swaying leaves on trees along the side of the road. When it touched her face, it carried her back to the last time she was at that church. The day started much like that morning, she remembered, with a clear blue sky and the cool breeze against her face. But before it ended, it had turned into a day she would never forget.

The casket positioned in front of her and her mother. The solemn songs the choir sang. The sadness on the faces of the grievers. She, dashing out of the church, in tears. The young boy.

She centered on him. *Whatever became of that young boy?* Victoria wondered. Will I ever see him again? She mulled on it and the many other unanswered questions that brought her to Beautiful until she pulled into the parking lot.

At first sight of the church, her body grew weak. The long narrow brick-layered church, narrower than she remembered it as a child, stood near the edge of the mountainside and looked like a tunnel into an abyss. The two pieces of four-inch wide wood, forming a cross about two feet into the air, looked frail atop the wooden steeple- a contrast from the tower of strength it was supposed to represent. A flood of every emotion she wanted to escape unleashed inside her.

Victoria forced every step toward the building, but at the foot of the stairs, she couldn't go any further. The steps, with chipped and missing bricks, leading up to the church door suddenly became a journey too difficult to complete. The memory of her dashing out of the church and running down those steps and out into the churchyard left her shaken. After decades, facing those same steps, running away still felt like her only option.

You have to go in there, a voice in her head egged her. If not, what would Myles think of her not making their meeting? She took the first step. She took another and began a slow walk up the steps feeling her heart pounding.

Victoria went through the door and entered the foyer. She breathed, straightened her dress, and made her way toward a set of double doors with OFFICE etched above it. When she reached, the doors opened, and Slone came through them. Her heart fluttered, and she could tell he had unearthed emotions in her she wasn't ready to feel. It threw her off guard.

"Victoria!" His voice was rich with shock and jollity that made her name sound new even in her ears. Her heart begged to hear him say it again. He took her hands. "What are you doing here?"

"Slone!" Her voice cracked, and she swallowed before she spoke again. "I'm here to see Pastor Avery."

The pleasure in his voice dissipated into a disappointing, "Oh?"

He let her hands slipped from his, but his eyes asked, "Are you sure?"

"It's business," Victoria explained under the weight of it.

"It could only be you, I said when I saw that jaguar in the parking lot," Myles proclaimed, coming to the door. He stopped next to Slone and patted the back of his shoulder. "I was thinking, since it's such a beautiful morning, we should go out for breakfast instead. We can talk business after that," he said to Victoria.

It was just what she needed to hear- a reason to escape the memories of being there. "I would love that." There was eagerness in the response.

"You should come with us," Myles said to Slone. "After all, why waste a beautiful morning like this?"

"I'm answering the prayer line. Have you forgotten?" Slone asked him.

"There must be someone else who can answer the phone. You must come," Victoria insisted. "It'll be my treat."

The desperation in her voice did not escape him, but Slone insisted they go without him. "I'll have to take a raincheck."

"Then it'll be just the two of us," Victoria said to Myles, not wanting him to take back the offer.

"Anywhere special you desire?" Myles asked her.

"There's a cozy restaurant next to the movie theater. I've had breakfast there once and enjoyed it."

"Then it's settled. If you allow me a few minutes to make a phone call," Myles said checking his watch, "I will meet you there in about half an hour."

He patted Slone on the back of his shoulder again and went back to his office. Slone kept his eyes on Victoria, and she on him as Myles left.

"Good choice," he said with raised eyebrows. "It's probably the only decent place to eat in Beautiful, beside White Roses of course. The two of you should enjoy it."

He seemed unbothered with coupling them, and it infuriated her. It wasn't what she wanted him to say. *Why doesn't he just say what he really wants to say? Only a man's ego would make him not say what he's feeling and if that's the case, his is too inflated to endure any longer.* "I should go."

Victoria turned to leave with her heart crushed. Was she mistaken in interpreting his emotion as love, when he prayed for her in that hospital room? Was the love she felt when he held her and kissed her that morning meaningless? After all, she hasn't seen him since, and this interaction appears to want to keep her at bay.

Slone took hold of her hand before she left. "Just business." He was commanding it, and she was sure she detected jealousy in the command.

"Just business," she assured him.

When she did leave, Victoria cautioned herself to not think much about what happened in there, for doing so was robbing her of her energy. She needed to stay focus, and everything about him was making it difficult.

She arrived at the restaurant and requested a booth in a corner at the back of the room. Her server gave her a menu. She scanned it, settled on a cup of coffee, and gave it back. "My companion is joining me shortly. I'll order breakfast then."

Myles arrived only ten minutes later. He spotted her in the back staring out a window overlooking tall trees and shrubs and running her fingertips back and forth over the brim of a cup. She had on her dark glasses, and a scarf matching her dress draped from her head and tied under her chin. Deeply engrossed in the distress occupying her mind, he was already in the seat in front of her before she noticed.

"A penny for your thoughts," he joked.

Victoria took off the sunglasses, and pulling back the scarf, greeted him with a sigh of despair. "Thank you for suggesting we meet here."

"You're troubled."

"Puzzled, is more like it."

"Why?"

She tucked the glasses into her bag and took out a stack of letters. "There was a small locked box in the attic. I pried it open and found these." She placed them on the table in front of him.

"What are they?"

"They're letters from my mother to someone. I read some of them, but I don't know what to make of what she was saying."

Myles examined the fading words on the pages of one of the letters. "How old are these?"

Victoria picked up one of them and pointed to the date. "This one is a month after I was born, and it's filled with such sadness."

He read the letter silently, and then noted to her, "She takes great care in making the relationship appear platonic."

He read aloud to make his point. "I miss our time together, our conversations, and the way I could be myself without judgment, with you. I wish you were here to share in the experience of raising my daughter. I need your friendship very much now."

Myles looked at Victoria, perplexed. "Do you think this is to your father?"

"No. It's warm. She was never warm when I mentioned him."

He examined the letter more acutely. "She said, my daughter. Not our daughter. She mightn't have meant it for your father then. It could be a letter to a friend."

"Why didn't she mail them. They're all here. Like a journal." Victoria spread the letters out before him.

The server returned, again, with menus for the both of them. She decided on toast and eggs.

"I'll have the omelet with orange juice," Myles said without looking at his.

When the server left, he held up the letter to the light with squinted eyes. "It says, to Lola." He passed it across the table to her and pointed to the faded words.

"Lola? Mother never mentioned a Lola," Victoria voiced, examining the letter and searching her memory to be sure.

"I know of a Lola. Ronnie's mother. I don't think she would have any connections to your mother though. She was a prostitute I remember Ronnie saying." The words came out with little thought, and he wished he had spoken with more care.

Hope beamed from Victoria's eyes, nonetheless. "Ronnie? Dorothy mentioned her. She's your ex. Will you take me to her?"

She waited for him to agree, but he hesitated.

"Don't you see? She can tell me where to find Lola, and if this Lola is my mother's friend, she might know my father. You have to take me to her."

"Ronnie doesn't know where her mother is."

"I'm sure she has a way to find her if she had to."

"She doesn't want to find her."

"Why not?"

"Because theirs is a story of shame. A burden she's had to carry her whole life. She faces her reflection in that shame every time she sees her mother." He shook his head. "It's the ugly side of Beautiful. Whatever your family's reputation is, you inherit it. It becomes the lens through which folks in Beautiful view you. An unspoken rule it is, and it's buried deep in our culture. She didn't even try to escape it, but I know she doesn't want to face it." He quivered and shook his head. "I can't ask her to face it."

"Then tell me where to find her. I'll ask her."

Myles was silent.

Victoria touched his hand. "I've been carrying this burden my whole life. The fruitless search is unbearable. I finally have an avenue to pursue. It might be the only one there is."

Myles tried to avoid the desperation in her voice but found himself succumbing to it easily. "I did promise my help when you find information to go on." He cleared his throat. "Ronnie shows up at the church service now and again. I never know when she's coming, but she always let me know when she's there. You'll have to come to every service until she shows up again. When she does, I'll introduce you to her."

Victoria exhaled with triumph. Then she tilted her head toward him. "Was that an invitation to your church?"

"You can call it so." He braced back into his seat. "I'm aware of the many invitations you have from other churches, and I don't want to influence your decision regarding which one to visit. But if you want to meet Ronnie, you'll have to come."

"I see."

The server approached with their orders. Victoria gathered the letters and stuffed them back into her bag to make room on the table for the food. With their meals spread out before them, Myles took her hand. Brushing his thumb lightly, back and forth over her knuckles with every word, he offered thanks to God.

Victoria whispered, "Amen," when he was done, and he echoed it with emphasis in delight.

She picked up her fork, and he followed. "You said you were puzzled. I understand why, but in my spirit, I detected you were troubled. I guess it's because you appeared uncomfortable at the church earlier. Why were you?" He put a fork load of omelet into his mouth, steadied his eyes on her, and chewed.

"Nothing escapes you."

He swallowed. "Not if it matters."

She picked up the toast and broke a small piece at the corner. "I was unprepared for the rush of emotions that came over me. I haven't been inside a church in quite a while."

"I assure you you're welcome there." He dabbed his mouth with his napkin and reached for a folder in his briefcase. "Since it turned out we'd be alone, I figured we could talk business."

He opened the folder and placed it on the table. His fingers found its way to the bottom of the page of a bank statement. Victoria's eyes followed and widened.

"You barely spent the funds I transferred into that account. I thought repairing the house alone would cost at least half that much." She looked up. "How much do things cost around here?"

Myles giggled. "Apparently, not as much as in Crystal Falls. Around here, we bargain for the best price, and whoever offers it gets the job."

"You'll have to teach me how to do that. Bargain I mean." Victoria sipped from her cup, still studying the figures on the paper. When she put the cup down, she drummed her fingertips on the side of it freely.

"I've been thinking all morning what to do with the money in this account. I had no idea it was so much." Her fingers stopped and her eyes bulged as if a light came on in her head. "I have more ideas now, and even one to benefit you and the church."

"How so?"

"Well, I didn't see the entire facility, but from what I saw, it could use some beautification."

He wiped his mouth again and straightened. "We have our challenges in getting some things done."

"A sizable donation will help you overcome those challenges."

He bent towards her with deep dimples appearing on his flushed face. "That's quite generous, but I'd rather you accept my invitation to visit first. If we're lucky, Ronnie will be there, but if nothing more, you'll have a chance to hear my message. If you like what you hear, and you still want to have a financial impact, to further the ministry, then we can talk about it."

He sipped the orange juice and wiped his mouth with the back of his hand. "You must know, however; I will be more interested in talking about your soul than your bank account."

"I know, and I appreciate it. So, yes, I accept the invitation."

"Good. You have no idea how much I've prayed for the opportunity to introduce you as my special guest."

Chapter Ten

In the early morning, Ronnie sat in the rocking chair looking out from her father's bedroom window. The morning dew on the front lawn glistened in the rising sun, and birds chirping, flew from limb to limb on a tree in the center of the yard. In the otherwise quietness that usually blankets the town on Sunday mornings, the cry of a newborn baby in the house next door did little to break her trance.

She was reliving the memories of weeks of legal jargon amidst episodes of tussles to keep the attorney off her. Her reputation had preceded her, she sensed when she met him. And, while she was willing to go along with some flirting if it meant he would work more diligently to get her what she deserved, she was not willing to give her body fully to him as he expected. Her resistance to the blatant advances slowed him in moving the legal process forward. It might have even stopped it if she hadn't secretly recorded some of his advances and used it as leverage.

A butterfly flew passed the window and her eyes followed it to where it landed on a patch of cherry-red petunias. It sat there for a while. Ronnie kept her eyes on it, welcoming the opportunity in the distraction from her tired mind.

When it flew away, she turned to her father stirring in his bed. He rubbed his eyes and pushed the sheet down from his chest.

"Daddy."

He blinked slowly.

There was love in his eyes. She couldn't detect that emotion in all the years when she needed it most but seeing it made up for every time that she doubted it. There was acceptance too. She looked longingly at him, appreciating all of it.

"I was waiting for you to wake up. I'm going to church today. It's been a while since I've gone. Do you want to go with me?"

Julia walked into the room. She bent over her father, kissed his cheek, and pulled the sheet back up below his chin.

"Daddy needs his rest, and the last thing Pastor Avery needs is for you to start showing up at his church again." She faced the mirror, fiddling with a midnight blue bow attached to the back of the black pillbox hat on her head. "Besides, he has a new woman in his life. She's rich and sophisticated. You should think about moving on with your life."

Ronnie turned away from her sister and looked out the window again. Since their father signed a will the lawyer drew up, giving Julia the house, the fighting amongst them ceased. It was the DNA test results Ronnie insisted on, however that eventually quieted them. Despite taking her in as a child, her father never called her his daughter or intervened when the rest of the family made her feel she didn't belong in the house. His silence on the matter left her fighting the family alone and even caused her to question her legitimacy in being there. When he agreed to the test, he assured her knew he was her father and the result wouldn't matter. But, for Ronnie, having the indisputable evidence, which she waved in her sisters' faces, did. The fighting was pointless after that.

"Sis, I know it hurts to hear it, but I think you should know. It's not a secret. Everybody in Beautiful is talking about it."

She waited for Ronnie to react, and when she didn't, Julia went and stood next to her. With a hand resting on her shoulder, she stared out the window with her.

"I wouldn't feel right if I'd let you walk back into that church not knowing. It's time you move on with your life. Lord knows you've spent enough years waiting for that man to desire you again."

Ronnie acknowledged the truth in the statement and half nodded to the pity pouring from her eyes and lips.

"Do you have another church you might like to attend? I can take you there on my way."

Ronnie patted her sister's hand, shifted it from her shoulder, and got up. "No, but I'll be fine."

Julia opened her arms and took her into a long firm hug that had Ronnie forcing her way free to catch a breath.

"I'm praying for you, sis."

"I know you are," Ronnie said.

Julia straightened the blue jacket over her black dress and left the room. It was a while now since she attended church. The long hours at the hospital and the rehabilitation center with their father took up most of her time. Taking care of him, after they brought him home, proved to be more than she could handle, even with the help of all her sisters. It drained her.

The falling out with Myles for recommending the lawyer to Ronnie didn't help either. He was the family's pastor, and when he took sides, it left a toll on her. She didn't trust any other pastor after that. The ordeal left her spiritually hungry. In deciding to reconcile her broken relationship with Ronnie, she decided it was best to make amends with her church family as well.

Julia almost collapsed when she entered the foyer. Dorothy scurried to her, noticing the exhaustion on her face the moment she came through the door.

"You came back. Pastor Avery will be so happy to see you." She helped her to a chair and fanned her until she regained her strength, and then they waited at the church door with the others to be ushered into the sanctuary.

Among them was Victoria, the woman everyone in town was whispering about. Julia couldn't take her eyes off her. She stood poised in a pair of yellow strappy stilettos, a form-fitting yellow dress and a sheer knee-length jacket with beige polka dots. Clutching a yellow satin purse to her body with an elbow, she held a stone face hidden under a beige wide-brimmed floppy hat, pulled down to her forehead.

Myles came into the foyer to receive her, but when he saw Julia, he cut a path straight to her with open arms. "Julia, welcome back." He glanced around. "Are your sisters with you?"

"No. They're home helping daddy."

He fixed attention on her more earnestly. "How is he?"

"He's resting better."

"That's good news. We're praying for God's healing on him."

A long prayer, which delayed their entrance into the sanctuary, finally ended. The door opened and an usher came out to them.

"It's good to see you." Myles patted the back of her shoulder and hastened away to Victoria.

"Victoria."

She flipped up the edge of her hat, and he cocked his arm. She took it at the bicep, and he escorted her to a seat in the front row. After everyone was seated, he went to the podium as usual to welcome the congregation. This time though, he began with acknowledging Julia's return, which brought everyone to their knees with an arousing applause.

"We also have a very special guest visiting us this morning." He smiled widely and then weakened. "Some of you might have already heard of her from the report of the horrendous attack upon her life right here in Beautiful. You might have come to know, also, she's one of the world's most celebrated ballerinas, and you probably have since wondered why she's here in our small town. What you might not know is that her roots run deep in Beautiful, as she is the great grand-daughter of the man who planted this very church."

Gasps spread across the pews. Slone walked in amidst of it and sat across the aisle from her. At seeing her, he blinked to be sure his eyes weren't deceiving him. But well absorbed in Myles' introduction of her, she didn't notice him.

"Until recently, I would have opted for many flattering words to describe her," Myles continued. "But today, I find only one is most fitting. Courageous."

He asked Victoria to stand.

"Please help me welcome my very special guest this morning, Ms. Victoria Davenport."

He never addressed her that way. But hearing it as she stood, offering a cupped-hand wave to the congregation, she felt a shedding of a past to which she was no longer bound. In waving, she finally noticed Slone, and her face softened. He acknowledged her with a delicate nod and turned to Myles with eyes, fused with concern and displeasure. Myles pretended to not notice and went on to preach a bold sermon he entitled, Everything She Needs.

It was Women's Day, and he presented a fitting message with a twist, stringing together a set of unique characteristics of Jesus to construct the ideal mate for the women in the church.

He began with John 4, presenting Jesus' encounter with the Samaritan woman at the well, and highlighting His wisdom in recognizing the woman's needs. With each point, the congregants' interest piqued. He elaborated on Jesus' keen insight into knowing a spiritual filling would quench her needs. The members began to fan and sway in their seats.

From John 11:35, Myles spoke of Jesus' relationship with Mary and Martha, and His ability to connect with them emotionally, pointing to the tears He cried, too, as they mourn the death of their brother. It had the women looking left and right to each other, nodding in agreement.

By the time he built up to Jesus' ability to commit to His divine purpose and His strength to resist temptation, the women were on their feet. When he touched on the social challenges of everyday living and illustrated how each of the characteristics would work to enhance their lives, he brought tears to their eyes.

He was knowledgeable and engaging, citing scriptures that flowed from his lips like well-rehearsed nursery rhymes. He spoke with confidence in constructing an image of what a man should aim to be like to fully satisfy a woman but assuring the women that a relationship with Christ was the eventual answer to everything they need.

The delivery was not short on charisma either. His style of moving about the pulpit excited the congregants. He knew precisely how long to drag out a syllable to make the members moan and how long to hold back on completing a profound thought to keep them on the edge of their seats.

Victoria had never experienced anything like it. She listened and even stood with the congregation to affirm the message with applause.

After the service ended, Myles came down from the pulpit, intercepting a small group of women making their way toward Victoria.

"You were awesome," she said greeting him.

"No. Not me. It's God working through me."

She shrugged. "Whoever it was on that pulpit, I want to hear him again."

"I take it you approve."

"I do."

"Good. I'd love to see you come back again."

He looked about the sanctuary as if searching for someone. "Deacon Slone," he called out when he spotted him.

Slone came and whispered in his ears, "We need to talk."

Myles pretended he didn't hear. "Could you show Ms. Davenport the rest of our facility? The last time she was here, we didn't have a chance to show her around. You remember. Don't you?"

Slone moved closer to his side and whispered through clenched teeth, "This can't wait."

Myles walked away from him to drum up a conversation with someone else, and Slone shoved his hands into his pockets with frustration.

"You look upset?" Victoria noted, drawing his attention.

He faced her. "Not anymore. You're a perfect distraction."

She blushed.

"You look stunning," Slone added. "Had I known you would be here, I would have worn my Sunday's best."

"You look just fine." She reached out to straighten his lapel, and he gently cupped his hand over hers. They locked eyes at the touch, and he shoved his hand back into his pocket.

"Well, where should we start?"

"I would love to go out into the churchyard."

Slone looked down at her stilettos and pointed to the door. "Out there?"

"Yes."

"I don't believe that's what Pastor Avery had in mind."

"I want to see everything. Starting from out there."

"As you wish," he agreed, reluctantly, and led her out of the sanctuary, down the stairs, and out into the open churchyard.

"Did you enjoy the message?" Slone asked as they began to stroll.

"I think every woman in there enjoyed it."

"I'm sure, but I'm most interested in if you did."

"It was a beautiful message." She clutched her purse behind her back with both hands and kept her head steady before her. "He said the kind of things I imagine a father would tell his daughter."

"You imagine?"

She was silent.

"Your father. You never mentioned him," Slone noted.

"I never met him."

"It's his loss, you know."

"Mine, too."

He glanced at her, but she held her attention straight ahead.

They neared an oak tree, and Victoria lagged and then stopped. "There used to be a wooden bench under that tree. What happened to it?"

Slone thought, and his eyes widened. "Yes. That was a long time ago. How did you know?"

"What happened to it?" She asked again.

"It got old, and they knocked it down."

They strolled further. "How did you know about that bench?"

"I remember seeing it when I visited the church with Mother. It was a long time ago. I was still a child."

Slone dredged up a memory. "I remember, too, as children, we couldn't wait for the church service to end to run out here and play musical chairs on it."

She tried to stifle a giggle, but it graced her lips. He noticed it.

"You're amused."

"I just imagined you, as a boy, running around out here."

"And it made you want to laugh. I'm curious. What did you imagine about that boy?"

"I imagined you jovial. And sweaty. That's what made me laugh."

"Sweaty?" He smiled, and they continued until he reached the edge of the churchyard. "There's a beautiful garden in the back. It looks almost as beautiful as the one you're nurturing in your backyard. You should see it."

They walked to the back of the church, passed under a metal archway to the flower garden. Slone joked, "Do you see anything else that spurs another memory?"

She looked around and shook her head.

"This is it then. There's not much else to see out here."

They entered back into the church through a door that opened to the kitchen. She immediately noticed brown spots on the ceiling and remembered Edward replacing the entire roof of one of their homes when he noticed similar spots appearing. She listened as Slone explained their ministry of feeding the elderly and the homeless. He explained the challenges they face in keeping the pantry stocked to meet the growing need in the town. They went into the nursery, and Slone bragged about the plans to open a daycare one day.

"That's short term, though. Long term, we want to have a school for the children in the community."

He continued the tour, sharing the plans to integrate Christianity into every aspect of the operation of the school, and the benefits for the children learning to apply Christian principles early. Victoria listened with keen interest. When they finally made their way back to Myles' office, he pulled out two chairs for them.

"You finished the tour. Tell me, what do you think?" Myles asked.

Victoria sat, but Slone leaned against the wall. She looked around the small office. "Mother was closed mouth about so many things regarding her life here. It's hard to believe I have a stake in this. But I do, and I'm ready to help in any way I can."

Myles rolled his chair closer and planted an elbow on his desk. "How is your mother, by the way?"

Victoria crossed her legs. "She's well, but she's ready for me to come home."

Slone looked away from them.

A knock on the door drew their attention. It opened slightly, and Nena poked in her head. "Have you seen Deacon Slone?"

Myles pointed to him and Slone walked out of the office. When he was gone, he asked, "Are you ready to go back to Crystal Falls?"

"I thought I was ready, but I don't want to consider it since I could be close to finding what I came for, and I have to see that through."

Myles drifted back into his chair. "I'm sorry Ronnie didn't come today. She hasn't been here in a while."

"Isn't there somewhere else I could find her?"

"Nowhere you would want to be seen."

"I don't care where if it leads me to my father.

"You don't understand, Victoria. Ronnie lives a complicated life. Her whereabouts are unpredictable. She has to come to you."

"I don't want to wait on that to happen. I have to find her."

He bit his lip and shook his head. "It's not that simple. Not with Ronnie. Finding her could lead you into a compromising situation. A homeless shelter or an old broken-down house with men having only one thing on their minds."

"I'm willing to take the chance, and you promised to help."

Her voice fell, laced with disappointment, and it reached him like a wrench to his heart. He bore it in silence, waiting for the effect to subside. When he recovered, he had a sobering thought. "I know a private investigator who can help us. I'll set up a meeting for us to talk to him if you'll consider that approach."

Slone came back into the room. From the door, he saw tension on their faces and suspected he was interrupting something important. But what he had to say was important too. Holding the door open, he blurted, "We have to talk right now. Excuse us, Mrs. Davenport. Church business."

She rose, and he pointed her to a chair in Nena's office, avoiding eye contact as she passed him. He closed the door and went to the chair Myles pulled out earlier for him. "The church board is planning a meeting. They're gathering information, and I believe they're looking for answers you might not be ready to give."

"You believe?"

"Nena confirmed it. They haven't been exactly transparent with me these days. They say our friendship is clouding my judgment."

"Our friendship?" Myles laughed.

"Yes. The obvious tension hasn't changed that."

Myles looked away.

"I've been open and honest with how I feel about what I see going on, but that's between us, Myles. With them, I turn a blind eye to everything."

Myles turned back to him, puzzled. "I didn't know."

"You weren't supposed to know. You were supposed to trust that I have your best interest at heart. You're the most powerful preacher in this town, and you're beginning to get the recognition you deserve. I don't want to see you lose that, so I have to be honest with you even at the risk of our friendship, and my position on the board."

"They're after you?" The sincerity in the question was lost between the shock and the chuckle.

"Now they are," Slone repositioned himself more comfortable in the chair and chuckled. "But I've been pretending to be oblivious to it. I don't want any decisions about you being made without me at the table. You're not making it easy though," he laughed.

"How do I get us out of this?"

"Their main issue is your relationship with Ronnie. The charges for hotel rooms, clothes, dinners, and her frequent visits here- at her whim to see you. They think she's the kind of distraction that can ruin the reputation of this church." Slone leaned in closer from across the desk. "She hasn't been around lately. Tell them you severed ties."

"That wouldn't be true."

"Why wouldn't it be? Have you seen her?"

"No, but it's not because I haven't tried. I've called and left messages for her. She hasn't returned them."

"Well, it doesn't matter who severed ties. She's no longer a distraction for you. That's what matters."

Myles sighed. "According to the lawyer I asked to help her, she's his distraction now."

"You don't sound relieved."

"Why should I be? She's still a lost soul with no real sense of direction, and he's a married man with no good intentions." He sighed. "After all those months of free counseling I gave him and his wife to keep their marriage together, I didn't expect him to go down that road again. He was so grateful his wife didn't leave him, he begged me to find someone he could help, pro bono, as a way of thanking God. Some kind of thanks that was," Myles frowned.

"Focus, Myles. Their mess is not your problem anymore."

"I'm a pastor, Slone. Everybody's mess is my problem."

"You can't fix everybody's problem."

"The nature of my role as a pastor won't allow me to not try."

"You've done what you could for Ronnie, and God has given you a way out of that situation."

"That's where we go wrong. We assume if a thing benefits us, then it must be of God. That's not the case every time, and I assure you it isn't this time." He pounded a fist on the desk. "It's not in the character of the God I preached about in there to orchestrate such sinfulness. So, forgive me if I can't accept their mess as my way out."

Slone sat upright. "Then you have two problems to address before the board."

Myles braced in his chair, interlocked his fingers at his abdomen, and began to swivel the chair. "How so?"

"Mrs. Davenport." Slone felt his throat clogged, and he cleared it. "The rumor is you are in a relationship with her."

Myles smirked, and kept swiveling in the chair, rolling his thumb over one another.

"You must know it's not proper for a pastor to gallivant around town with an unmarried woman like you've been doing. Today, you introduced her to the church as Ms. Victoria Davenport. The board will never accept anything less than Mrs. Avery. Are you ready to call her that?"

Myles steadied the chair. "Is the answer to that question for the church board? Or, is it for you?"

Slone ran his thumb across the week's growth of beard under his chin. "You and the church board are my only concern right now."

"As it stands, then, I only have one problem to address before the board." He picked up the phone and dialed Nena's extension. "Send in Ms. Davenport, please?"

"Yes, sir," Nena said turning to Victoria. "Pastor is ready to see you again."

Victoria stood and straightened her dress. "Don't forget what I told you."

Nena nodded, hoping the rumors she was hearing were true. For based on the conversation they had, she believed Victoria would make a good First Lady for the church.

During their time together, Nena shared some of her challenges and fears with Victoria. It wasn't her intent to divulge her personal drama when Slone pointed her in, but Victoria asked about her job at the grocery store, to break the ice, and it felt easy to open up and share more.

They talked mostly about the business failing, the owner's lack of interest in doing something about it, and the resulting financial impact Nena was enduring. Victoria seemed genuinely concerned about the problems.

"Have you thought about relocating elsewhere and pursuing a professional career?" Victoria asked.

On that topic, Nena had nothing impressive to say. "Elsewhere? Me? No."

Living in Beautiful was simple living. It was all she knew. She never thought about leaving. She was grateful to have the job at the grocery store, and the only thing she enjoyed more was taking pictures. She never contemplated a professional career and wouldn't even know on what to decide.

"You've already figured out where you want to be at your tender age. That could be a good thing. You and that gentleman I met at the store should have the life you deserve, even if it's right here in Beautiful."

Nena decided a bit more transparency was warranted. "I don't know about him. I'm trying to live a Christian lifestyle, but he's wrapped up in worldly things."

"He'll come around. Either way, you have the opportunity to do what you want. Enjoy doing it."

"I'm afraid that won't be the case much longer if sales at the store keep decreasing."

"I'm already thinking of a way to change that."

Slone opened the door. "I hope we didn't keep you waiting."

"You didn't."

"Good. Will I see you here again next week?"

She took it as a good-bye. "You're leaving?"

"I'm only getting out of the way for now." He looked at Myles and closed the door.

Myles pointed to the seat, and Victoria sat in it again.

"Now, where were we?" He pressed back into the chair. "Yes. The P.I. Are you willing to try it?"

"I've thought about it as an option."

"You wouldn't need Ronnie, and you would only have to share what you know."

"A private investigator might be the way forward. I've gone as far as I can go on my own. It is time I try something new."

"I'll make the call then."

"Thank you." She sighed. "I'll be happy to have that mystery solved, for I believe there is a greater purpose for me being here in Beautiful."

"Oh?" He furrowed his brows in interest.

"I want to open a ballet school here. Young girls like Rayne should be exposed to art in all forms."

"How long have you been thinking about that?"

"Since I arrived and saw her." She leaned forward over the desk. "I believe I can do more than that."

"I'm listening."

Victoria shared a plan to revitalize Beautiful, starting with buying the grocery store. "There're acres of unused farmland north of here. I noticed it from the bus coming. It is perfect for growing fruits and vegetables to sell in the store. If people are willing to work the farm, having the job might reverse the rising trend of crime around here."

"How long have you been thinking about this?"

"About ten minutes," she laughed. "I also thought about the many products we have to travel to Langston to buy. The people there need reasons to come to Beautiful and spend their money, too, and we have way too many untapped skills for them not already doing so.

"It's a grand vision. It could keep you here for a lifetime," Myles warned.

She crossed a leg over the other. "I know."

Chapter Eleven

A crisp morning breeze met Nena at the top of the stairs outside her apartment. It was a welcome change from the summer heat and the rain she'd often hurry down the stairs to avoid. With the cloudless sky and cool breeze, she slowed, appreciating the thick flowery shrubs huddled between the rows of sugar maple and white spruce trees lining the edge of the busy Main Street to seclude the apartment building. Halfway down the stairs, a whistling red-winged blackbird steadying on a branch caught her attention. She thought to take its picture, but it flew away as she got her hand on the camera in her bag.

At the foot of the stairs, she noticed dirt on a pink rose pedal and stooped to brush it away. Once in her car, she tossed her bag into the seat on the passenger side and rolled down her window. The cool breeze upon her face made her more alert. A butterfly darted onto the pink rose pedal, and she shuffled through the bag, with haste this time, and retrieve her camera. One snap was all it allowed her before flying out of sight. But it was enough, she determined after a quick review of the shot. Nena put the camera back into her bag and backed out of her parking space for the drive to the grocery store.

On the way, she reflected on her conversation with Victoria, for in it was her last shred of hope for financial independence. Every night since they spoke, through prayer, she breathed life into the possibilities, and she hasn't wavered from the hope.

She arrived at the grocery store and took an empty spot at the entrance to the store. When she first got the job, straight out of high school, she picked parking spaces farther away. The business was booming and having available spots near the entrance was her strategy to attract shoppers to the store. Now, it didn't matter if she took the space closest or farthest away, no strategy was working to bring in more than a few shoppers per day.

Getting out of the car, she draped her handbag over her shoulder and checked the time on her watch. It was an expensive gift Aiden gave her a year before. Remembering him stumbling into the apartment, pinning her against the door, and forcing her to accept it caused a twinge in the pit of her stomach. She slid the watch off her wrist, stuffed it into a small pocket inside her bag, and dug deeper into the bag for the keys to unlock the chains on the door.

Nena looked around when she stuck the keys into the lock, and an image that had escaped her when she entered the parking lot, came into view. Parked across the street from the store, was a black Mercedes Benz SUV with lightly tinted windows. A man inside, wearing dark sunglasses, watched her. It brought an eerie feeling over her, for only someone in a high-paid profession or dealing in illegal activities could afford a vehicle like that, she reasoned within herself. And besides Mrs. Davenport, no one in Beautiful matched the profile of the former.

The possibility of the latter brought chilling memories, and she hoped Aiden wasn't involved in any illegal activities with such characters who would seek her out, again, in revenge against him. She hastened, with shaky hands, to unlock the chained door. When she finally opened it, Nena hurried inside and turned the deadbolt with her heart racing. She rushed to the counter and stood behind it with her hand on the gun Aiden gave her and waited. Seconds passed like hours, and after what felt like an eternity and nothing happened, she crept up to the window by the door and peeked out to see if the car was still there.

It was not. She took a long deep breath to calm herself and began her routine for opening the store. When she was satisfied with the display of goods and had put cash back into the register, she flipped the sign in the window from close to open, unlocked the door, and pushed it wide open.

There were more cars in the parking lot by then, with people getting in and out of them. Nena lingered at the door, taking note of everyone who passed her going in and out of the other stores. For the first time, she was deliberate in noting who they were as they greeted her, or she greeted them. They were people she knew by name or they had familiar faces, and she knew to whom they were related. All the while, she kept an eye on the spot where the mysterious vehicle was parked. It had not returned, and the stranger had disappeared with it.

Nena went back into the store, pondering why the car was there in the first place and why the man watched her so keenly. Wearied from finding no plausible reason, she adjusted her thinking to ridicule herself for overreacting. After all, it was just a vehicle parked on the side of the road. The driver could have been lost and was figuring out where he was. Why else would anyone in a luxury SUV just park there? Clearly, he was lost, she accepted, putting the matter to rest. She went into her office and refocused, again, on the hope she found in Victoria.

That hope and a fashion magazine helped her pass the time for another hour before the first customer came into the store. It was her neighbor, Connie, hiking a baby up onto her hip and dragging her young daughter struggling to keep up the pace. She walked up and down the aisles before picking up a box of diapers.

"No milk?" she asked Nena when she reached the counter.

"Nope."

"No bread?"

Nena pursed her lips and shook her head.

Connie placed the bag of diapers on the counter. "Your pastor and that woman, Mrs. Davenport, have been seen dining around town. I heard they're in a relationship. Did you know that?"

"Don't believe everything you hear," Nena cautioned her, keyed some numbers into the cash register, and gave her the total.

"I don't," Connie contested and paid her. "It's none of my business anyway," she mumbled under her breath, waiting for her change. "I've learned to mind my own business."

Nena counted out the change on the counter, and Connie gathered it up, adding, "Rumor has it, it's the reason for the breakdown of his long friendship with Slone."

On some occasions, Nena tried to quell the rumors, pointing out absurdities when she heard them. This time, she doubted her ability to have an impact one way or another. Luckily, the baby became cranky. He whined and slid down her hip. Connie hiked him up and changed the conversation to the struggles of being a single mother raising her children alone.

"I wouldn't have it any other way though. I love my-" The tearful baby twisted, let out a restless sob that progressively grew louder, forcing an end to the conversation in mid-sentence. She wiped and kissed his wet cheek, wrapped the handle of the bag around her wrist, and promised to share more of what she heard when they see each other again.

By the time another customer came in, hours later, it was clear the rumors were out of control. The different versions of the relationship between Myles and Victoria, laced with drama and trivia, both appalled and annoyed her. To her relief, though, none of the gossiping customers mentioned seeing the luxury SUV or the stranger in it. Nena supposed he must have long left town and resolved to put it out of her mind.

But the man hadn't left Beautiful. At least, he didn't for good. He had taken to explore the small towns from Beautiful to Langston. The sun was high in the sky, when, after a few wrong turns, he ended in Victoria's driveway.

Dorothy was preparing lunch when he rang the doorbell. He followed with a repetitive knock that made Dorothy hasten to open the door. Standing six feet tall, lean built with a slight muscular chest, he stepped back when the door opened. The sun glistened off his shiny bald head and his light brown eyes penetrated her.

"Good day, sir. May I help you?"

"I'm looking for Victoria Davenport. Her address lead me here. Is she home?" His voice was surprisingly pleasant.

In her peripheral view, Dorothy saw Victoria entering the living room with her arms wide open.

"Noah! What are you doing here?"

Dorothy shuffled out of the doorway, and he came into the house.

"Mother."

She flung her arms around him.

"Dorothy, this is my son, Noah." There was sheer joy in the introduction.

Dorothy greeted him with a handshake and excused herself, walking back to the kitchen with a listening ear.

Victoria took his hand and led him to the sofa. "Why didn't you tell me you were coming?"

"Why didn't you tell me someone tried to kill you?"

"How did you find out about that?" Victoria asked in shock.

"It's on every news channel in Crystal Falls with pictures of you in bandages."

She didn't think anyone would be so unethical to share those unflattering pictures, but she was sure it was for a price.

"The reporters say you were robbed at gunpoint and beaten almost to death. They've been following me around to get information since the story broke. And grandma? She has just about gone crazy over it. We want you to come home."

"That is my decision to make, and as you see, I'm fine, son."

"Are you really, Mother?"

"Look at me. I've never been better. I didn't tell you about it because I didn't want to worry you or mother, needlessly."

"The accountant and attorneys are worried too. They say you want to invest in a parcel of land and a building you saw."

"Why would that worry them?"

"In light of the attack, they believe it could be that you're being forced to make this investment in exchange for your safety."

Victoria threw her head back with a burst of uncontrollable laughter. When she gathered herself, she explained, "I understand the news reports and those awful pictures might have alarmed you, but no one is taking advantage of me. Besides, I'm a smart woman, and I can take care of myself."

Noah eased back into the sofa, eyeing her. She spoke again with warmth and content. "The incident was unfortunate, but, ironically, I feel most alive and very much at home here. I can't leave Beautiful. Not now, son."

"I saw the building, the land, and the surrounding towns. I didn't see any signs of economic development nowhere near here. Why make such an investment if no one is forcing you?"

"The investment is not in the building or the land. It's in the people, who I've come to know." She stood up. "You must be tired from the journey. Let's have lunch. Then Dorothy will show you to your room. He was tired indeed. After they ate, he slept until evening.

By then, the children were coming home from school. A school bus stopped near the grocery store, and a group of noisy students ran from it, making their way into the store to buy candy. Nena had a bag ready for one of them and handed it to a little girl who strolled in alone.

"Tell your momma I miss seeing her in church."

"Yes, ma'am."

The innocence in her voice when she reached for the bag brought Nena back to the day when she sat on the front porch of her father's house to braid the girl mother's hair and listen to her lament about being pregnant in an uncommitted relationship. To see the result of that pregnancy, a beautiful young girl she was, leaving the store running to her mother waiting in the parking lot was proof time passes quickly.

Knowing it was unlikely to serve any more customers that evening, Nena ran the day's report, took the cash from the register, and settled in her office to prepare the bank deposit slip.

Counting the cash, she heard a sound inside the store, and she peeked from the office. Surveying the aisles with curiosity, she came in further when she didn't see anyone.

It was then a man jumped across the counter and pointed a gun to her head. He handed her a bag and demanded she put all the cash she had into it.

It startled her. She didn't recognize the voice, and the ski mask over his head made it impossible to identify him. She stood in shock; unable to move. Then she felt the gun pushed up against her head harder.

"Do it."

Nena walked back into her office with the man following so close behind her, she could hear him breathe. She shoved the cash into the bag and handed it over to him. Within seconds, he darted back across the counter and disappeared out of sight.

Her body grew cold, and she trembled. Dazed, she managed to pick up the phone and call the police. But as she dialed, she heard sounds coming from the store again. Nena dropped the phone and ran quickly to retrieve the handgun she kept under the counter, getting to it just in time before the man approached her. Tears rolled down her face, as she pointed the gun to his head.

"You have five seconds to make it out alive."

"Nena?"

She sniffled, holding the gun steady.

"I'm Noah. My mother, Mrs. Davenport, sent me to talk with you about the store." He spoke calmly but pleadingly.

"She never mentioned having a son."

"I can show you my ID."

"Four seconds."

He didn't move.

"Three seconds," Nena said, tearfully.

He held up his hand. "Please put that gun away and let me show you my ID."

"Two seconds." She began to pray silently.

"Listen to me," he pleaded and reached across the counter to take the gun from her hand.

Nena closed her eyes and pulled the trigger. It clicked, and a deafening silence crippled them. She opened her eyes fearing the sight of his lifeless body sprawled before her, but the gun had jammed, and Noah's hand was still engulfing hers.

They were both shaking. She questioned what right she had to take a life if she had killed him and was relieved, she didn't. More tears rolled down her cheeks. He drew back his hands, leaving her with the gun. "I didn't come to hurt you," he told her, backing away with his hands up.

Two police officers barged into the store. As they shouted for Nena to drop the gun, Noah voluntarily lay face down onto the floor and placed his hands over the back of his head. One of the officers kept him down with a knee in his back and handcuffed him.

"Thank God you didn't hang up that phone," he said looking at Nena before motioning to his partner to go search the rest of the store.

"Are you okay?"

He knew her well. As children, they lived on the same street, and being three years older, he felt a responsibility to protect her.

"I am now," Nena said.

"What happened?"

"He robbed me at gunpoint and came back. He didn't expect I had a gun, too. He didn't even wear the mask this time."

The officer asked Noah, "Do you have your ID sir?"

"It's in the wallet in my back pocket."

The police officer retrieved the license and examined it. The address, Crystal Falls, caught his attention and then the name.

"Noah? Noah Davenport? Why are you robbing a store?"

"I didn't," Noah told him, as the officer helped him to his feet.

As one of the responders to the scene when Victoria was robbed, that officer had come to learn of her professional life and financial status through the ongoing investigation. He wouldn't accept her son, a man with access to such vast financial means, would commit such an act.

"Are you sure it was him, Nena?

She wiped tears from her eyes and scrutinized him further.

"Do you want to come down to the station and make a formal statement?"

She shook her head with her eyes still on him. "The man who robbed me had on a black sweatshirt with a hoodie attached." She turned to the officer. "I remember because when he jumped back across the counter, it fell off his head." Her attention went back to Noah in a dark grey sweatshirt, but no hoodie attached to it.

The officer took a pen and a small notepad from his shirt pocket and flipped through the pages to a clean sheet. "Do you remember anything else?"

"No. It happened quickly."

"I saw him leave the store," Noah spoke up. "He walked right past me. He's about my height and built and had a cross tattooed on his wrist. I saw it when he pulled the hoodie over his head."

The officer unlocked the handcuffs and Noah massaged his wrist. Victoria had suggested he rest and check out the store for himself the next day. She spoke at length about Nena and the financial impact the struggling store was having on her. The love she had for her work there and her desire to see it stay open and serve the town better. He listened to his mother's spiel about her dedication to the church and the hours she spends volunteering there. They compared her love for photography to the same his last girlfriend had and found more similarities between the two that almost discouraged him from coming.

It was the passion in Victoria's voice that compelled him to come. She spoke like a mother who has decided to expend all resources to capture the eluding dreams of her child to make her happy. The unwavering desire left him suspicious, so he wanted to see if she was the one taking advantage of his mother. That was the reason he didn't wait until the next day, as Victoria preferred. But standing across from her, watching her fight to hold back tears, he wanted to help her as much as his mother. If only he could remember something else about the man coming out of the store. Anything that could relieve the uncontrollable fear and frustration lodged in her eyes. But he couldn't.

"I'm sorry I didn't get a better look at him." He was staring at her the whole while.

The officer handed Noah his license, scribbled his number at the station on a clean page in the note pad, and gave it to him.

"If you think of anything else, you call me."

He took it and promised. When the officers left, she let out a tearful, "I'm sorry," and with a hand on her belly, bent at her waist from nausea crippling her. Everything went blurred. Her legs weakened, and a strong urge to lay down overcame her. She wobbled, reached for the edge of the counter to hold steady, but grabbed thin air instead. Strength left her, and she collapsed onto the floor.

"Nena," Noah shouted, sliding across the counter. He landed near her, stooped down, and raised her leg slightly from the floor.

"Nena. Can you hear me?"

She opened her eyes halfway.

"Are you okay?"

She heard his voice as if from a distance, and she saw him through blurry eyes. Nena blinked and blinked again before his face came into focus. She didn't recognize him. Still, she was grateful that he was there, for her strength had not returned.

"Are you ok?" he asked again.

She held a hand up to the side of her head.

"You need an ambulance," he said definitively.

"Who are you?"

"Noah."

"Noah?" She eased up from the floor.

"Don't move." He guided her head back to the floor.

"What happened?" she asked him.

"You were talking to me and then you passed out." That was all he divulged, evading the grittier detail on purpose.

But the events leading up to that moment were slowly coming back to her. She began to piece them together.

"Did I shoot you?

"No."

She found a minuscule relief in the answer and struggled to her feet. He placed his hand on her back securing her. Nena scanned the store and left from behind the counter to lock the entrance door. It was then she saw the black SUV she noticed that morning. More memories unfolded. She locked the door, leaned back against it, and slid slowly down to the floor. Noah followed all the while and sat on the floor beside her.

"This can't be just a regular day in this small town," he joshed.

She didn't respond to his attempt at humor. "Is that black Mercedes yours?"

"I rented it at the airport."

"Was it you in it parked across the street this morning?"

"Yes. Why?"

"Where'd you go when you left?"

"To see my mother."

Nena held her hand up to her head again.

"Are you sure you don't need an ambulance?"

"I should get home," she said.

"Allow me to drive you."

The image of her coming home with a strange man would undoubtedly anger Aiden and fuel more drama, which she could do without that day.

"It's nice of you to offer. Thank you, but no."

"Aiden," Noah laughed. "I forgot about him."

"You know him?"

"Mother told me about him when I agreed to meet with you." He continued laughing. "Actually, she told me about you and warned me of him. I suspect she wanted to put me on notice that you were taken."

Nena ignored the subtle flirting in the statement.

"It's no way I'm letting you drive home alone in your condition. Do you want me to call him for you?"

He was ruling out the option more than offering his assistance. When she didn't answer, he made another offer. "I'll drive you home then, to be sure you make it safely."

She was silent still. When the silence grew heavy, she asked, "How long do you plan to stay in Beautiful?"

"I'm not sure now. I came out of concern for my mother, and nothing so far has lessened it."

Nena stood up and brushed away a speck of dirt from the leg of her khaki pants. "There's a chance we'll meet again while you're in town. Hopefully, under a better circumstance."

She took a step but fell off balance. Noah stumbled up and caught her. One arm landed around her waist. He wrapped the other around her body. "You're not okay."

She steadied and parted from him. Avoiding the alarm in his eyes, she walked away, without incident. When she left to go home, Noah followed the whole way and parked in the space next to her when she reached. Nena rolled down her window. "Thank you. Please go now."

"You should see a doctor."

"And you should go home. Please."

"I'll leave when I see you go into your apartment safely."

"You don't understand. Nothing goes unnoticed in this small town."

"I understand. Which one is your apartment?"

She pointed up to it just in time to see her neighbor upstairs shift a vertical back in place.

"Let me help you up the stairs."

"No." Gratitude softened the rejection. "Everything people see around here becomes a story. I don't want you to become a story."

Connie opened her door and poked out her head. She looked around, drew back in, and closed it.

"I couldn't forgive myself if you fell," he protested.

"I won't fall."

"I want to be sure you don't."

"You leave me no choice. I'll show you that I won't." Nena stepped out of her car and went up the stairs. Reaching the top, she waved good-bye to him and went into her apartment.

At the small dinner table, pleading with Aiden to allow the police alone to find the man who robbed the store, her phone rang. Nena answered it with a gut feeling it was the owner of the grocery store who was calling. The store had been closed since the robbery, and she was waiting for his decision on when to open it.

"Hello." She said nothing more until she hung up the phone. "He's decided to not reopen the grocery store."

Aiden reached for her hand. "Don't worry about that. I can take care of you."

"I want to take care of myself. You know that."

"Come work for me at the club."

With a decisive, "That's not the environment I want to work in Aiden," she turned down the offer.

"Why not? I'm already giving you money I make there. What's the difference if you earned it?"

"I know what goes on at nights at your club."

"You can work the day shift. That's when the good old church folks come in there anyway."

She rolled her eyes. "Your girls work both day and night shifts. Giving me special treatment would be unfair to them."

"It's my club, and everybody knows you're my girl. If I say you work the day shift only, you work the day shift only. It's final. I make the decision on how to run that club."

"At the grocery store, I make important decisions, too." Her mouth twisted with disgust. "If the owner considered them, he wouldn't be out of business."

"But he did go out of business, and, up here, you don't have any better options than what I'm offering you."

"Mrs. Davenport has plans to buy the store. It might not be closed for too long."

"I know all about Mrs. Davenport's plans. The grocery store. The dance studio. Restaurant and photography studio. She wants to take over the whole damn town."

"Don't talk that way, Aiden."

"Why not? If she opens a restaurant, she could take away my lunch crowd and cut into my revenue."

"She's not trying to compete."

"She wouldn't have to. She has the financial resources to drive the whole damn town out of business."

"That's not her intent."

"It's business, Nena. What do you know about her intent?"

"I know God is using her to create more jobs in Beautiful."

"A job isn't what you want. I just offered you one, and you turned it down."

She looked away from him.

"What's she offering, Nena? That rich boy who came home with you the other day?"

She pushed back from the table, but Aiden grabbed her arm. "Is it?" His fingers sank into her flesh. "You're not that stupid to think I wouldn't find out about it, and I know you're too smart to take such a risk with nothing in return."

"It's time you leave," Nena said, yanking back her hand.

"That's the wisest thing you said, and I'll take your advice because I don't want to do to you what I'm thinking right now."

He opened the door and jogged hastily down the steps.

Chapter Twelve

Noah awoke to soft rays of sunlight beaming through the half-opened blinds in the window above his bed. A pleasing aroma seeping into the bedroom stirred him. He peeled away the cotton sheet coiled below his waist and slid a black t-shirt down over his bare chest as he sat up in the bed. Shuffling his feet into a pair of leather slippers at his bedside, he tightened the drawstring in his blue and black striped pajama pants and went into the bathroom across the hallway to freshen up.

He was prepared to ask Dorothy for his usual cup of coffee, but in the kitchen, he found his mother there instead, retrieving a tray of golden croissant from the oven. Victoria placed it atop the stove and took off her mittens.

"Noah, you're up early."

He giggled. "Where's Dorothy?"

"Home, I suppose. It's her day off."

She untied the apron from around her waist and hung it on a hook on the door inside the pantry. Taking napkins from a shelf, she spoke over her shoulder. "You two connected well. You talked through most of the night." She closed the pantry and placed the napkins on the table. I wasn't expecting you to be up so soon."

Noah took a croissant and tasted it. "This is quite delicious."

"Thank you."

He examined the piece in his hand and stuffed it into his mouth. "Did you make it?"

"You look astound." She made her way back to the stove snickering. "Did you wash up first for breakfast?" He reached for another one and she swatted away his hand. "There'll be none left when we sit down to eat."

Before they had that chance, the phone rang, and she hurried to her room to answer it.

"Hello."

"Good morning, Victoria."

"Slone." There was warmth in her voice.

"I woke up thinking of only you this morning. Will you be in church today?"

"Yes. My son, too."

"I heard he's in town. I'd love to meet him."

"I'd like that."

"Then I look forward to seeing both of you there."

They said goodbye, and Victoria pressed the off button and held the phone to her bosom. She didn't see Noah watching.

"Who was that?"

He caught her off guard. There was no way to hide the evidence of delight still warming her face.

"A deacon from the church." She placed the phone on the bedside table.

"Why'd he call you?"

"No reason," she shrugged and passed him at the door.

Noah followed her. "You were blushing."

Victoria went back to the kitchen and retrieved two plates from the cupboard. Resting them on the table, she admitted without looking at him, "He's taken an interest in me."

"And you in him." Noah leaned against the counter and folded his arms. "I can see it."

She placed the plates on the table.

"How much do you know about him?"

"Knowing about him is not my priority." Victoria answered. "I still have unfinished business here, and I don't want anything in the way of that."

She busied herself with shifting through the knives and forks in a drawer. She held up a fork and then a knife to the sunlight streaming in from the kitchen window and examined each before putting it back into the drawer. She examined another set and then another, and finally selecting two of the shiner ones, placed them on the table.

"How would his interest in you hinders you from finding your father?"

She planted a hand on her hip and glared at him.

"You're not talking about your father. Are you, Mother?"

She bit her lips.

"It's that guy, Darius. Isn't it?" Convinced he had uncovered a secret she didn't want him knowing, he pressed. "You're looking for him. Aren't you? I heard you talk about him with Aunt Olivia when Dad wasn't around."

"I might have wondered about him from time to time," she admitted, turning away to put the sweet flaky croissants and turkey patties on his plate. "But I couldn't have talked about him that much. I only knew him for a day." A slight giggle floating in her voice undermined the assertion.

Noah went to the table and she scooped scrambled eggs onto his plate. After putting less than half the amount on hers, she sat with him, took his hands, and blessed their food.

"Being here has changed you, Mother, and it's a beauty to watch," Noah told her when she said amen.

The change he saw that morning in the kitchen was not all he noticed that day. At church, she took notes in a notebook with pre-fill pages. He figured she must have been attending regularly to have that many pages filled. Noah tried to recall the last time they went to church in Crystal Falls but couldn't.

With all the changes Noah noticed, however, there was one thing that remained the same, and that was her ability to muster up the appropriate emotion despite what she was truly feeling. She proved it when the pastor introduced him to the church.

In the introduction, Myles offered Noah a public apology, on behalf of the town, for the unfortunate mix-up with the robbery at the grocery store that had him handcuffed on the ground. "We're a hospitable community marred by a few deviants attempting to weaken us at our core. But we are strongest at our core and it is where we cannot be broken."

It was then Victoria learned Noah was handcuffed. He told her about the robbery when he got home that evening, but he kept that part from her.

Victoria masked the shock with an agreeable nod as Myles impressed upon the church a need to reconstruct the minds of the younger generation. He talked about what Victoria was already doing to help, starting with a significant donation she made to the church. Identifying her only as a generous donor, he spoke of his plans to, not only expand the church facility to include a school with a Christ-centered curriculum for school-age children but incorporate leadership programs to educate the adults as well.

"My vision, if I'm allowed to bring it to life," he announced side-eyeing Slone, "Is to have a church with well-trained strategic leaders, equipped for leadership in the church and the community at large."

The grand vision lead him into his message with resounding applause, and it aroused a sudden suspicion in Noah that the church was the culprit taking advantage of his mother's financial means. He scanned the congregation with contemptuousness but saw Nena, half-way down the rows of pews, rising to her feet with an enthusiastic ovation. His mother's words that her investment was not in the building but the people instead, came back to him and he resolved to not accept so quickly his suspicion was factual.

He didn't take his eyes off her. Her hair was pinned up in a bun, the way it was that evening he saw her at the store. She wore no make-up, and her colorful long sleeve dress covered her from neck to ankles. He gathered she wasn't superficial or materialistic like the women he encountered in Crystal Falls. With flattery and an expensive gift, he had their attention. But Nena's simplicity left him lost in contemplation on how to get hers. As if his scrutiny of her was penetrating, she met his eyes from across the pews. He beamed in the instant, but she casually refocused on the pastor. He did, also, but with an impatience for the preaching to end.

The message was unusually short that day. An adjustment Myles decided to make to the church service.

"Scaling it back gives the members more time at home with their families and family time is worship time," he told Slone when he shared the idea with him in his office earlier that week.

Slone agreed, noting neither of them had a family at home.

"It's time we changed that. Don't you think?"

Slone shrugged. "Do you have a wife in mind?"

"It's just a thought right now."

"Why now?"

Myles pressed back in his chair. "Family is the lifeblood of the church. Besides, you must admit, we're way past our prime."

It was with the admission in mind Slone call Victoria that morning. He wanted to see her again. When the service ended, he greeted her with a lingering two-hand grip handshake. Standing less than a foot apart, she leaned in and straightened his tie. A casual exchange of compliments flowed between them, mostly on their attire - she, wearing a baby blue sheath midi length dress with sleeves flare at the elbows, matching six-inch ankle strapped heels, and a wide blue feathered hat. And he, a grey and white pinstriped suit, grey tie, and a white triangle-tip handkerchief peeking out of the breast pocket. Her usual delicate shoulder thrust, quiet laughter, and gentle head toss still fascinated him.

Noah watched from a distance.

Dorothy made her way over to him, taking his attention. "That was a good message. Did you enjoy it?"

"It was interesting."

"Thank God pastor mentioned the handcuff ordeal. I don't know if I could keep that secret from your mother much longer."

They laughed, and his attention shifted back to Slone and Victoria. "I heard nothing stays a secret long in Beautiful."

Dorothy moaned, "You heard right."

He turned to her again with much interest. "What's the secret about those two. He, in particular?" The subtle tilt of his head toward Slone drew a mischievous grin from Dorothy.

"Rumor has it, if he's vying for her attention, he'll have to compete with the pastor."

"The pastor?"

Her eyes widened with an inconspicuous nod.

Noah smoothed down his mustache near the corners of his mouth and deep lines crept between his brows.

"Don't look so troubled. Either one of them is a desirable catch for the women in Beautiful."

Her words failed to ease the apparent concern as intended. In fact, she managed to heighten it.

"The women in Beautiful?" He cast his eyes at Victoria, with the thought that he must take her back to Crystal Falls with him. She threw her head back in laughter and waved him over to them.

"She needs you. Go to her. We'll talk more tomorrow." He fought to not trust the assurance in her eyes so readily and went to his mother.

Being noticeably taller, he never passed on an opportunity to highlight the difference. He reached his long arm across her shoulders and squeezed Victoria in close to him with a cuddly hug. She, reaching just below his shoulders, slipped an arm around his waist. "This is my son, Noah." She was filled with the expected pride in introducing him. Her eyes danced, turning from Slone and fixing on him. Noah, this is Slone, the deacon who called this morning."

Noah extended a firm handshake that sent an indubitable message he was a subject of special scrutiny. Slone accepted the warning with a steady gentler hand. "Noah, it's good to meet you finally. Your mother speaks well of you." He gave Victoria a quick nod of approval and engaged Noah again. "Did you enjoy Pastor Avery's message?"

"He's a dynamic speaker, I will admit."

"I'm sorry you had that horrible experience. I hope the rest of your visit is more pleasurable."

"It has been already. I've met some kinder people since," he said, dismissing further talks of it.

"That's great to hear. We do want to reflect a better light."

"You have. That's why I'll have to insist Mother comes home with me. Otherwise, I might lose her to this town."

Victoria laughed, interjecting a report of Noah's academic accomplishments. "He's excelling at the university with a double major in business and theater. He can be dramatic at times."

"Business and theatre. That's an interesting combination. What is your plan?"

"I'm taking over the family business."

"He plans to expand into other areas of art, but he knows to do so successfully, sound business knowledge is important for understanding the interdependency of the different functions of the entire operation," Victoria chimed.

Slone took it in with hopes for spiritual guidance in the endeavor. "The Bible says you can achieve it if you put God first. You have only to believe His words."

Seeing the congregation dispersing, Dorothy and Nena among them, Noah said, "I'll try to remember that." He planted a kiss on his mother's cheek and excused himself, hurriedly, to catch up with them. Victoria and Slone moved to each other's side as he hastened down the aisle away from them.

"Nena." Wanting to not draw attention to himself, Noah's voice was barely above a whisper, and, as he discovered, not loud enough to attract her attention. He quickened his steps, but she and Dorothy vanished through the door before he caught up with them.

At the door, Myles, who dutifully greet everyone coming out through it, intercepted him with a hearty handshake and took him into a full hug with arms wrapped firmly around him.

"I hope that the unfortunate incident hasn't made you feel unwelcome in our town," he said when he released him.

Noah pulled his cuffed sleeves back to arm's length and straightened his jacket. "It hasn't."

"Good. You have a legacy here. You should know you belong."

"I didn't think of myself in that way."

"You should. Your history runs deep in Beautiful, and in this church especially."

Half listening, he nodded and glanced away. "I was trying to catch up with Nena. Did you see which way she went?"

Myles recognized Noah's disconnection from the sentiment of the church his forefathers built and from the town at large, but he quickly forgave it. After all, how could he embrace it if he hadn't experienced it?

"Nena? She went into her office."

An elderly woman came out of the sanctuary, and Myles took her hand in a handshake and held it. "Mother, could you show our special guest to the secretary's office?"

The woman's face brightened, and she locked arms with Noah, leading him away with peppy steps and eyes fastened upon his bald head. She took him two doors down and pointed to the office.

Nena was studying Myles' schedule when Noah walked in and approached her desk. He extended a hand to her. "I'm Noah."

She rose from her chair and accepted his hand. "We've met."

"We have, but you hoped we'd meet again under a different circumstance."

She drew back her hand slowly. "Better. I believe I said a better circumstance."

"I stand corrected." Noah looked around. "This is a church. You will agree there's no better circumstance under which we could meet. Is there?"

She blushed. "I can't imagine one."

"I have a thought. One that might stretch your imagination on that topic."

She eyed him with interest.

"I was driving into town and came upon a river, rippling at the edge of huge rocks along the highway. In a bend, where the highway finally veers away from it, begins a grassy trail that leads to a beautiful garden of wildflowers spread out wide, touching the bank of the river. If you focus only on the highway, you could miss the trail, easily. I almost did." He looked at his watch. "The day is far from over. Let's spend the afternoon there."

"It's tempting, but I can't today."

"You must. I have only a few more days in town. If not today, then when?"

She lowered her head to the desk, centering on nothing in particular. Noah pressed. "Tomorrow? You can tell me all about the grocery store. We haven't talked about that yet."

She raised her head again, but unsure of what to make of the expressionless young woman before him now, he added quickly, "Or, anything else that interests you."

"I'd like to talk about the store. I have ideas to make it better."

"Better," he echoed in relief of her acceptance. "There's that word again. I'll pick you up at noon."

"No. I'll meet you there."

"Okay. I'll see you there at noon." He didn't look away from her. "Do you have a favorite restaurant where I should pick up our lunch?"

She shrugged. "Not really."

"How about your favorite music?"

"I don't have a favorite.

Determined to draw emotion, he asked, "A favorite joke I should practice? I would love to see your smile."

The corners of her mouth curved up half-way.

"I'll take that."

Loud chatter drew their attention to the door. Dorothy pushed it open and came through it with Rayne. Seeing Nena and Noah facing her in stillness, she suspected she had interrupted them. She cleared her throat to signal her presence, needlessly, and Nena shifted her eyes from her to Noah.

"Oh." Dorothy giggled and covered her mouth. She tip-toed up to Nena and whispered into her ear. "Tell me everything later." Grasping Rayne's hand, she said to him, "I'll see you and your mom at the house tomorrow." She went back through the door in a hurry.

With most of the congregants gone, the foyer was scanty. She stopped at the church door and ushered Rayne to say goodbye to the pastor. He received her with a hug, searched his pocket, and slipped a ten-dollar bill into her hand.

"Thanks, Uncle Myles."

Dorothy thanked him, too, for his generosity, and waved goodbye over her shoulder.

Myles re-entered the sanctuary to find Victoria, who he noticed had not come out of there yet. At the end of the aisle, he saw her with Slone. They hadn't moved since Noah left them.

She had one arm crossed over to the other, clutching it at the elbow, and he had his tucked into his pockets as if there were the only place he trusted them. His keen attentiveness to her, the quiet laughter between them, and her subtle head toss hastened his steps to them.

"May I steal her away from you?" Myles asked, standing next to Slone and facing Victoria. "I have some good news, and I'm sure you want to hear it."

She hiked her shoulders unsuspectingly and loosened her hand from her elbow. Her eyes apologized to Slone for wanting to know what Myles had to tell her. Slone massaged the tension springing up at the back of his neck and stepped aside, giving her way to him. Warmth lit Myles' face. He placed his hand lightly at her back and escorted her into his office. Once inside, he pulled out a chair for her and sat at the edge of his desk with one foot planted firmly on the floor. The other dangled, intermittently, as he spoke.

"The private investigator found a Lola. We think she's the one your mother was writing to in those letters. She has agreed to meet with you." He picked up an index card from his desk and handed it to her. "Here's the address."

Victoria pushed up from the chair, took it, and flung her arms around his neck. "Thank you."

Myles sat motionless until she let go. He looked steadily at her. "Don't thank me yet. We don't know with certainty that she's the one we're looking for, or that she'll be willing to divulge what she knows if it turns out she is, indeed, the one. I don't want you to be disappointed."

"I know." Victoria checked the address on the card, locking it into her memory before dropping the card into her bag. She clasped her hands at her mouth, pensively.

Myles reached out and took her hands. "You're trembling."

"I didn't expect it to happen so fast or to be this nervous about it." She drew a hand back from him and held it to her chest. "My heart's pounding."

"You don't have to go through with it if you're not ready."

"I'm ready."

"We'll do it together."

Tears settled in the corners of her eyes. She dabbed them with a finger and laughed. "I'll need you with me. Thank you."

He let her other hand slip from his, and Victoria paced the floor. "When can I meet with her?"

"That's up to you. She's available when you are."

"Tomorrow," Victoria said. "Tell the private investigator I will meet with her tomorrow."

"I can't go tomorrow," Myles told her. "I'm leaving tonight for a speaking engagement at a conference. I'll only be gone for two days. Can't it wait until I return?"

"I couldn't bear the anxiety for two more days." Her misty eyes held an unyielding purpose. "I have to go without you."

The room fell quiet. In the quietness, a thought came to her. "Your friend-" Victoria hung on to the words, searching her memory for the name. "Ronnie."

Myles looked at her. He didn't blink.

"This Lola. Is she her mother?"

151

He went around his desk to his chair and faced her from there. "I didn't inquire that far," he replied.

"Oh? You seemed concerned when we first discussed her."

"She's less of an issue now."

He was quiet again. Victoria sensed his silence was not because he had nothing more to say. It was a thick silence that forbade her to inquire further. There was emotion in his eyes, too. Pain or anger. She wasn't sure which, but she was sure he hadn't broken through it. She pressed down the hat gently on her head and picked up her handbag. "I should find Noah and tell him the good news."

Sensing he was thorny, he stopped her. "Victoria, I'm sorry I came off short. It's not you." It was enough to make her hesitate. Pain crept onto his face, and he wet his lips readying to explain further but simultaneously deciding against doing so.

She felt the battle. "I came to Beautiful saddled with my own burden, and you took it on as if it was your own. Don't find it unbefitting if you need me to do the same for you."

His lips moved, and she waited for what he had to say, but laughter erupting in Nena's office stopped him. His attention went to the door between their offices and then back to her with a hint of curiosity. He had forgotten the sound of Nena's laughter. Hearing it again moved him from behind the desk, and he inched up to the door.

"Nena," he tapped lightly.

She opened it. "Pastor Avery." Her hand went up to her mouth. "We didn't know you were in there."

"We?"

She opened the door wider. "Noah and I were taking pictures."

"Silly pictures," Noah giggled, looking down at the camera, scrolling from picture to picture. When he finally looked up, he apologized. "We didn't mean to disturb you."

Victoria appeared next to Myles. "Noah. There you are. I was just about to come and find you."

He looked from Myles to her. "What are you doing in there?"

She entered into Nena's office. "Pastor Avery had a bit of good news for me. I can't wait to tell you about it. Are you ready to go home, son?"

Noah handed the camera to Nena. "I'll see you tomorrow?"

With pursed lips, she nodded and put the camera into her bag. Victoria went to her and whispered, "Be careful what you do with those pictures. In the wrong hands, you might find yourself with the kind of media attention you're not prepare to handle." She stepped back with eyes that seemed to search deep into Nena's soul and then turned to Myles, who was observing with a shoulder resting on the doorframe.

"Thank you again for everything. I'll let you know how things turn out." She offered him a quick wave. Myles bowed half-way to acknowledge it, and she left the office with Noah.

Outside, the sun beamed from the middle of the sky. A day never looked brighter to her. Victoria breathed in the air and went down the steps, poised, and with careful footing as if an audience was watching. Noah opened her door when they reached her car, and she got in with her focus fixed on the churchyard. Her mind, however, was thousands of miles away to Olivia's bedroom in London, where she first decided to find her father one day.

"What's the good news?" Noah asked, strapping the seatbelt across his shoulder.

"Pastor Avery hired a private investigator to locate a woman who might know my father. He found her, and she's agreed to meet with me."

"Mother, that's great. I want to be with you when you meet her."

"I sent a message to meet her tomorrow."

"Tomorrow?"

Her eyes bulged with excitement, and she bobbed her head up and down.

"I can't go tomorrow. I have a date with Nena."

The excitement dissipated into troubling impenetrable eyes. She touched his hand. "Son, you can't have a date with Nena. I told you she's-"

"Not available. I know," he interrupted. "It's a business lunch date to discuss the grocery store."

"Then you keep it as such. Do you understand me?"

"Don't worry yourself, Mother."

Victoria started the car and pulled out of the parking lot.

"Will you consider going on another day? I want to be there with you."

"I know you do, but I'll be fine, son. You go ahead and have the meeting with Nena. The information you gather about the store will help the lawyers proceed more speedily." She glanced at him. "And you can get back to the university and the life you have in Crystal Falls."

Chapter Thirteen

The night was especially long. Victoria tossed and turned, sleeping on and off mere minutes at a time. During one of those off minutes, when she switched from her side and stretched out on her back again, she became aware of her overactive heartbeat. Mindfully, she rested a hand on her abdomen, drew in a deep breath, and exhaled slowly with her eyes closed. The breathing was calming, but it was not enough to put her back to sleep.

Images of what the next morning might bring appeared, vanished, and reappeared repeatedly throughout the night. It was impossible to fall asleep again. So, at dawn, she left her bed before the alarm sounded, brewed a pot of chamomile tea and readied herself for the long drive.

Tension surfaced in her stomach as she left the driveway. She sipped the hot tea from a stainless-steel mug to ease the pressure. It was her go-to remedy when she felt overwhelmed. It never let her down before, and it seemed equally effective in serving its purpose that morning.

The fresh morning air blowing in from her window, let down halfway on the passenger side, cooled her moist face as she drove down the mountainside. She didn't notice the quietness of the small neighboring towns she drove through, nor the calm river along the long stretch of empty highway. The meeting, and the many possibilities that could come from it were all that mattered.

It was mid-morning when she came upon the sign, Hillside Manor, mounted unto a wooden pole about seven feet into the air. An arrangement of all-white and yellow daisies surrounded it at its base at the foot of a hill. She slowed and turned unto the narrow road up the hill. Reaching the top, it expanded into a spacious land with a one-story cedar log building amongst tall trees. Glare from the rising sun bounced off the glass door. She shifted into park and double-checked the address on the index card she pulled from her bag.

Victoria dropped the card back into the bag, dug in deeper for a pair of sunglasses she put on her face and got out of the car. It shaded the glare, but she wore it more to hide her puffy eyes she spent time trying to minimize with different beauty products before she left home that morning.

Entering onto the covered rectangular porch, with a swinging bench at both ends, an unwelcomed twitch in her stomach made her wish she had more tea. She bore it, nonetheless, and pushed the front door open. Inside the well-lit lobby was a gift shop, and a comfortable looking colorful sofa near a wooden table with magazines arranged neatly on it. She walked a brown carpet from the door to the front desk.

An overly charming young woman, considering it was still morning, stood up and greeted her with a sign-in sheet on a clipboard. Victoria removed the sunglasses and scribbled her name on the first line. Upon requesting to see Lola, the woman checked her ID and pointed toward a set of double doors.

"Press the red button on the wall and go straight ahead, Mrs. Davenport. She's in the room on the right at the end of the corridor," the woman instructed.

Victoria went down the corridor with her hand against her stomach calming the nerves going awry. When she reached the room, she noticed the door was opened. She tapped it nonetheless and peeked into it.

The bed was made up with white linen. A colorful quilt covered the bottom half of it. She noticed a small bottle of cocoa butter lotion and an open Bible on the dresser, and a plate of half-eaten breakfast on a table near a window. A woman wearing pink sweatpants and white t-shirt was in a chair there. Her hair, mostly gray, blended with black, was combed neatly into a long ponytail, and her eyes were fastened to a TV on the wall, tuned to a gospel station. She looked toward the door, hearing the tap.

"Come in."

Victoria walked into the room, a tad overdressed, the woman thought, in a pair of brown slacks and a beige blouse under a long brown cardigan sweater. The brown pumps and leather flap-over briefcase made her look professional, in fact. "You come to see me?"

With a nod and an extended hand, the words, "I'm Victoria," came out stronger than she expected. "Are you Lola?"

Lola wiped her hand on a paper napkin and shook Victoria's hand. "That would be me."

Her voice was innocent and sweet. It diminished the tension Victoria had inside her. "How are you?"

"Never been better." Lola pointed to a chair at the table and waited for Victoria to sit, studying her face. "They told me you'd be coming. Can't say I know you though."

"Thank you for seeing me in spite of that."

Lola scoffed. "Don't get no visitors up here. Didn't think I was in a position to deny one."

Victoria looked around the dull room. Even with the open blinds, and the morning sunlight beaming through the window, it could use better lighting. She imagined it must be depressing being in there alone.

"I understand. Still, I thank you."

"Why'd you want to see me?"

Victoria reached into her bag and pulled out a letter she chose from the stack she found in the attic. Her first thought was to bring all of them, but without her mother's knowledge and permission, she felt even one was straggling a line of privacy invasion.

"I wanted to know if this belonged to you." She passed the letter across the table but kept her hand on it. "Do you know Alana?"

Lola threw her head back with laughter. "Lana Grover? Think about her every day." The laughter faded. She touched her lips with a fingertip and dragged out a mortified, "She died?"

Amused, Victoria took her hand off the letter. "No. She's very much alive. She's my mother."

"Your mother?" Lola analyzed Victoria's face more keenly for a resemblance. She found it in her small pointed nose and narrow eyes. "I can see it. How is she?"

"She is well. That letter, she wrote it to you decades ago." She pointed to the name fading on it. "I don't believe she knew where to send it."

Lola picked up the letter. "She wouldn't have. Moved around a lot after leaving Beautiful. Thought she'd forgotten about me."

"You were friends?"

"Best friends. Went to the same school and church. Talked about everything, including those painfully embarrassing things we couldn't tell our parents. Got good memories of her." She turned the letter over, examining it back and front. "Her daddy put me in a play with her at the church, and I shared my candy with her at recess. Became best friends just like that," she snapped her fingers and laughed. "She didn't talk much to the other girls at school. Parents didn't allow it, you know. Quite different from mine. Mine let me talk to anybody."

Lola looked at the letter again and rambled off a story of when they played angels in a Christmas play. She talked about them studying for exams and the boys in their class who wanted to date them. With each story, she seemed to come more alive, and Victoria was content to listen to all of them.

"Try as they might, we wouldn't give those young boys the time o' day and vowed we wouldn't marry them either. Too playful," she shrugged with a bit of sophistication. "Not the older boys though. Now, they had our attention, but we didn't let them know," she laughed. "Fantasized about our wedding day and even picked out names for children we'd have with them. That's the kind o' friends we were." She sighed heartily and shook her head. "Silly. Just silly schoolgirls. Didn't know a thing about life back then."

She glanced out of the window. "Gave my daughter the name I picked out though. Veronica. Liked that name a lot. Turned out it was close to her father's, Victor. Didn't know it would be at the time I picked it out."

She drifted back to Victoria with quizzical eyes. "You said your name's Victoria? Victor your daddy?" Before Victoria spoke, Lola eased back in her chair. "No. He couldn't be. Lana was not that type of girl." She leaned into Victoria again with eyes narrowed to a peek. "But of course, that wouldn't matter to him. He's your daddy. Isn't he?" She sat up straight before Victoria answered. "Victoria! Hm. Why didn't I think of that name?"

Victoria had a name for her father. Finally. One part of her wanted to leap from the chair and hug the woman, and the other part wanted to go to her, bury her head into her bosom, and cry. Knowing she shouldn't do either, she held it together and sat in pretense that the information was not new.

"You know my father."

"He was a charmer," Lola laughed. "Wouldn't have guessed it, but don't fault Lana one bit. I fell for him first. Beat myself up for doing that for years after that." Seriousness briefed her. "No more though. He was a grown man. A married man at that. Our teacher. He should have known better, I say. We were just kids. Curious about stuff, but it don't mean we were bad. We had dreams you know. Big dreams of leaving Beautiful, becoming rich and famous, and living in mansions like we saw on television." She dipped her head toward Victoria and whispered, mockingly, "Nobody rich and famous ever come out of Beautiful, but what'd we know? Couldn't tell us nothing while we were dreaming."

Victoria reflected on hers and her mother's accomplishments. Could it be it was in those moments her mother shared with Lola that the drive to be rich and famous was birthed? She thought to ask more about the man Lola said was her father, to keep her on topic, but decided against it. It was clear, not having visitors made her hungry for conversations. If left to her own free will, she might divulge more than she would if asked. And Lola did.

She exposed contempt for the people in the town of Beautiful, alleging, "Misunderstanding of Biblical principles is what led churches to punish young girls who became pregnant too soon, by their standards, but not punish the grown men who took advantage of their innocence."

Her disappointment in families torn between protecting their daughters and the ultimate decision to sacrifice them to hide their shame was not lost either. "We ran away in the middle of the night to spare them and ourselves the shame. Lot to learn in ridding ourselves of that shame. About self and God. Self mostly, but God importantly."

Lola shook her head with disdain. "They used to say Beautiful is safe. Like everywhere else is the devil's playground." Squaring her shoulders with her head held high, she recited, "Beautiful is where our forefathers came to hide from the watchful eyes of the world." Dipping her head toward Victoria, she smiled. "Believe it, and you grow afraid to leave even when you have to. Truth is, it's no better. No safer. And there are more watchful eyes in Beautiful than anywhere else I've heard of."

Internally, Victoria flushed out multiple explanations for how her mother managed to stay ahead of that time. Being intentional and resilient were her most obvious qualities. She displayed them proudly and to such a fault that it made her appear inflexible and controlling. But seeing Beautiful through Lola's eyes revealed something more. Her mother had to be that way to control her own narrative.

"What stopped you from living out your dreams when you left Beautiful?" Victoria asked her.

Lola brushed up the back of her hair with a hand. "Reality. That's what. Life has a way of teaching you the difference."

She imagined her mother responding differently and in a way that suggests, life offers you the chance to create your own reality.

In coming there, she expected to learn about her father. She didn't expect to be enlightened on her mother instead.

"Would you like to go outside? It'll be a shame for this beautiful morning to slip by us, and we experience it only from the boundaries of this window."

Lola folded the letter. Stuffing it down into her capacious bosom, she bounced up from the chair. "Don't mind if we do." She shuffled her way around the table and stuck her feet into a pair of tennis shoes she had under her bed. On the way out, she checked her reflection in the mirror. "Do I look okay?"

She was taller than she appeared sitting behind the table and, except for her busty chest, slightly thinner, too. "You look great."

A warmth hugged her face and stayed as they walked down the corridor and out into the fresh morning air. Lola took the lead towards a garden bridge that crossed over a small shallow pond where koi and goldfish swam together. They sat near the edge of it on a swing bench and watched.

"Mind if I ask why Lana didn't come with you?"

"She's in Crystal Falls."

"Crystal Falls? Where those rich folks live?"

Victoria half giggled. "All kinds of people live there."

"The man who told me about you said you're from Beautiful."

"I'm only visiting."

"With your father?"

He lives there? She kept the question in her head, but her heart fluttered in her chest. Suppressing the shock from the revelation, she chose her next words carefully to keep her on the topic. "What was my father like? Besides charming, I mean?"

"Like a man," Lola moaned without hesitation.

"Mother never talked about him or any of the guys she dated in high school for that matter."

She rested a hand on Victoria's knee. "There were no other guys to talk about. And forgive her for not talking about your father. You're a lovely lady and all, but it could be her way of escaping the shame of being with that man."

The wind rustled the tree branches. Lola wrapped her arms around her body and looked out across the lush green hillside. Standing, she muttered, "Sure is a beautiful morning. Wouldn't be right to have you waste your day here with me. You must have better things to do with your time than deliver outdated letters."

"There's nothing more important I have to do. In fact, I'm enjoying your company. If it's the same for you, I rather we spend the rest of the day together."

Lola froze in appreciation of Victoria's desire to spend more time with her but questioned her worthiness. However, the warm smile affirming she was worth it, made her sat again, quietly.

"I saw a restaurant on a lake near here. We should have lunch there and then go shopping. My treat. Mother would be pleased to know we enjoyed the time together."

Victoria did not intend to tell her mother about her visit with Lola any time soon and had already decided to share what she learned about her father, only in part, with Noah when she returned home.

Rayne dipped her forehead to Dorothy for a good-night kiss. She kissed it and wiped the spot with her thumb. "Get in your bed and don't let me hear you playing around."

"Yes, ma'am."

Dorothy was home from her day's work at Victoria's house and was sitting by her window. On school nights, the children stayed in to do homework and prepare their clothes for the next day. The street was usually quiet. Any sound out there was enough to draw the neighbors to their windows with curiosity.

It was the sound of an engine that drew Dorothy. Noah's SUV, she discovered, after she shifted the curtain and peeked out into the street. When she left their house, he hadn't come home yet. Typical of young men always wanting to be anywhere but home at nights, she thought it not strange then, but from her window, something was causing her to think differently.

He parked in the driveway, hopped out, and open the door on the passenger side. Dorothy was sure it was Nena who he helped from the vehicle. She knew they were friendly, but there was something inappropriate, she thought, about the way he reached his arm around her shoulders and pulled her in close to him. She seemed unbothered when he nuzzled her neck, before his hand slid down her back and around her waist, as they went up the steps onto the front porch. Before opening the door, Noah scanned the surrounding. He escorted her inside and closed it.

Wondering what was going on over there, Dorothy waited in the window as long as she could for a clue. The hours passed. The light came on, and Noah drew the curtains close. An hour went by before the light went out. Neither of them came out of the house.

Tightening the scarf around her head, Dorothy left from the window and crawled into bed. On her back, her wondering spirit refused to surrender her body to sleep. She couldn't stop thinking about Nena. *Has she lost all sense of self? She's the church secretary for God's sake. The last thing the church needs is subjection to more rumors. Besides, she knows Aiden is not the kind to take infidelity lightly. The whole town knows he's domineering. He's been that way since high school. It's the only reason the church mothers haven't confronted her about his frequent sleepovers at her apartment since she gave her life to the Lord.*

Dorothy pondered, too, if Noah knew Aiden was spending time with Nena. Frightening imageries of altercations between the two men taunted her, and she hoped, for Nena's sake, what she saw from the window was not happening at all.

It wasn't just the inevitable altercations between Aiden and Noah that worried Dorothy. It was Nena's eventual heartbreak, as she expected, from being used by Noah that concerned her most. *He had only come to Beautiful to take his mother back to Crystal Falls. With Mrs. Davenport showing no signs of wanting to leave any time soon, spending time with Nena is simply a way to occupy his time before leaving town- for there is no way a young handsome rich kid like Noah would settle for a small-town girl in Beautiful.*

With that thought, Dorothy committed herself to be there for Nena if she should need a shoulder to cry on. She propped her pillow and closed her eyes, but a more troubling thought entered her mind. Since the brutal attack on Victoria's life, the people in Beautiful had come to embrace her as one of their own. With the negative publicity the town received on the international stage because of the attack, and the unfortunate incident that left Noah handcuffed at the grocery store, the pastors took aggressive strides to make Beautiful safe again. They continued to speak of the attack from their pulpits and made pleas for anyone who had information about the crimes to share it and help bring the culprits to justice.

Dorothy opened her eyes again. *It's not Nena alone who stands to lose if Aiden finds out about this torrid affair. Mrs. Davenport could suffer the consequence of it. If Noah's antics with Nena stir up trouble with Aiden, who everyone knows has a violent side, nobody is going to risk coming forward with information on her behalf. Besides, considering rumors are already brewing that Aiden sees Mrs. Davenport, a potential future business competitor, as a threat and wants to get rid of her, that sort of trouble will not be good for her at all.*

Dorothy speculations turned grave. *Could it be the affair between Nena and Noah is not what it appears? Could it be that Nena is being used as a pawn in a bigger scheme? It's no secret Aiden is calculating when it comes to his business affairs. But would he use Nena to get inside information on Victoria's plans? Or, is Noah using her to get the scoop on Aiden's plans?*

She sat up in the bed with a more devious thought. *Could Victoria be in on it, and Nena be oblivious to the scheme?*

She questioned if she knew Mrs. Davenport as well as she thought. Despite spending just about every day at her home and enjoying many friendly chats, there was still a lot she didn't know about her. The gut feeling she's hiding a secret of some sort didn't help either. She was sure Pastor Avery knew the secret, but he and Victoria were tight-lipped about it with everyone else.

Dorothy reflected back to when Victoria was searching through the boxes in the attic. *What was she looking for? Why did she stop? What were the trips to the library for? Why did those trips stop? Is she even able to go back home? And what did Pastor Avery have to gain from all of it?*

There were too many unanswered questions, and she decided she must talk with Nena before she gets herself in too deep. Somewhere in the agony, she managed a prayer. A long prayer that included a plea for the rescuing of Nena, "A naïve young woman. A holy woman who is committed to serving the Lord. A woman now under a spiritual attack," Dorothy prayed aloud with a heavy heart before drifting off to sleep.

Victoria arrived home well into the night and was startled when she saw them, Noah and Nena, cuddled together asleep on the sofa in the family room. It was late, and the house was dark when she entered it. She switched on the light and walked into the family room where she found them.

Noah stirred, rubbed his eyes, and tapped Nena's shoulder. She eased her head up from his chest, and they sat up together.

"Mother. You're home. How did it go?"

His voice was groggy. Victoria gathered they had been asleep for a while. She put down the bags full of assorted things she bought on the shopping spree and sat in the love seat across from them. "I didn't mean to disturb you, but I wasn't expecting-"

"This?" Noah pointed from himself to Nena.

She crossed her legs unamused. "Yes. What is this?"

Noah took a scarf from around Nena's neck and her hand went up to cover the bruises. He took down her hand gently, exposing them. Victoria's mouth fell open.

"What happened to you?"

"Aiden found out about our meeting," Noah told her.

"I wasn't expecting him to visit my apartment in the middle of the day," Nena explained. "It's usually busy at White Roses during the lunch hours. As I was leaving to meet with Noah, there he was at the front door. He asked where I was going. I didn't want to lie, but he insisted I answer. So, I told him."

Nena picked up the scarf. Wrapping it back around her neck, she added,

"I should have known better. I could see he was drunk."

Victoria glanced away from her to Noah with shock plastered on her face. He ignored it.

"I kept having this gnawing feeling in my gut urging me to go to her apartment and pick her up for our meeting, even though that wasn't the plan. When I arrived there and saw her on the floor, I lost it."

Victoria's eyes widened. "Noah, what did you do?"

"We scuffled, but he was too drunk and unbalanced to fight. I did more trying to settle him than I did scuffling. When he did settle, I talked with him like a man." Noah moved to the edge of the sofa. "He needs help, mother. We found a treatment facility in Langston for alcoholics and took him there."

Nena sighed. "He gave me power of attorney to handle his personal affairs and White Roses before he checked himself in."

"That's a big responsibility."

"He has no one else, Mrs. Davenport."

Noah put his arm around Nena's shoulder and coaxed her in close to him. "Hopefully, he'll deal well with the consequence when he gets out."

"The consequence?"

"Mother, Nena is an incredibly strong woman. Do you know after enduring that ordeal, she insisted we still have the meeting?"

Nena inched away from him and confessed, "I have a condition that makes me detach from traumatic experiences. It started as a coping mechanism when I was a young girl, but it's more than that now. Some ordeals don't even register. Most of that didn't."

"I detected the dissociative state today. We can get treatment in Crystal Falls," Noah assured her.

Victoria swallowed. "In Crystal Falls?"

"Don't pretend you don't see what's happening. I'm not leaving her with him. I want her with me in Crystal Falls."

"Is that what you want, Nena?" Victoria asked.

She spoke tiredly. "It's what I've prayed for. The opportunity Noah presented is more than I imagined. It's not only what I want. It's everything I need right now."

Noah reached his arm across her shoulders again and drew her back close to him. Their eyes met briefly, before he looked back at Victoria. "We talked all afternoon about your plans for the church and the town, and even developed some strategies to implement, beginning with the hiring process for the grocery store when you take ownership of it."

Victoria listened keenly and then spoke carefully. "What exactly did Noah offer you, Nena?"

"A job. A scholarship. A place to escape from here."

"What about White Roses? It's your responsibility now."

"We'll handle it with our other business dealings," Noah said. "After what I witnessed, I couldn't let her feel alone in that." She felt his gentle squeeze of her shoulder, and as if they could get any closer without her disappearing into his side, Nena snuggled into him. Noah's hand slid down her arm caressing it up and down, keeping her close. She drew confidence from it.

"We came up with a plan, and we met with the staff already to discuss it," Nena disclosed.

"An effective plan takes time to develop. Shouldn't you stay here and work on it some more?"

"There are plenty of reasons for me to stay, Mrs. Davenport. All of which could keep me here for the rest of my life."

"We decided it's either she comes back with me to Crystal Falls, or we spend the rest of our lives wondering what might have been," Noah said to his mother.

Detecting Noah was referring to her own personal dilemma and, to some degree, appealing for her support, Victoria uncrossed her legs and stood. "You seem to have everything figured out."

Nena went to her. "Not everything." She clasped her hands down before her. "I never thought I would leave Beautiful. Living here is all I ever imagined. Being with Noah, I'm able to imagine something more." Her face softened. "Something different." Her sparkling eyes fell onto Noah, briefly. "Something better," she told Victoria. With a pair of less than confident eyes, she canted her head to her left shoulder. "I'm unsure, though, if I will fit in with the socialites in Crystal Falls. Will you give me some pointers on how to cope?"

The humility filled the air, but it was the sum of compounded fear unveiling in Nena's eyes that resonated the most with Victoria. It was familiar. She wondered, too, if she would ever fit in with the people in

Beautiful the day she arrived, and all the experiences she had living in different countries and performing around the world didn't lessen that fear.

She reached for Nena's hands. "Who you are is enough, dear. Just be yourself when you get there." The motherly tone came with a bit of final advice. "Let them worry about fitting in with you when they come into your space." A gentle reassuring squeeze of her hands cemented the advice before Victoria let go and smiled. "It's been a long day. I must get some rest."

Noah gathered the bags Victoria brought in with her. "You didn't tell me about your meeting."

She took the bags and straightened her shoulders. "Tomorrow. I'll tell you all about it tomorrow."

He guided a hand up Nena's back to her neck, and his fingers moved in slow rhythm, massaging gently into her skin. Victoria watched Nena relaxed, and the fear disappearing from within her. She swept her eyes back and forth from each of them, and with a quiet unhurried sigh, walked away to her room.

From the window of the dark room, she stared out into the night. Feeling foolish for trying to rush Noah back to Crystal Falls to prevent the inevitable, she stepped out of her shoes and sat in the rocking chair. Her mind shifted to Darius. Not even time had erased him from her memory, she admitted. Why was she so naïve to then think putting distance between them would work for Noah? He was a lot like his father in many ways beyond his physical features, but he was more like her in her unwavering commitment to eventually have what she wants.

Her body grew weak, and Victoria closed her eyes at the thought of Darius again. The memories of him still made her warm inside. She relished in it for a while, carving an image behind her eyelids of the man he might have grown to become. His then lanky limbs suggested tall and strong. The compassion in his eyes, she could almost feel still. Piercing. She opened her eyes, but her mind was still reeling. Kind and caring. Passionate and attentive. Those things her spirit yearned for but fell short of having in an otherwise picture-perfect life. Victoria decided to make finding him a priority as soon as she found the man Lola said was her father.

With that settled, she fumbled through her briefcase for her phone and dialed Myles' number. The call went to his voicemail. After the brief lively jazz music played in the background of his greeting, she left a message.

"Myles, this is Victoria. My visit with Lola went well today. I'll tell you more when you return from your trip."

Chapter Fourteen

The alarm sounded, waking her. She rubbed her eyes and peeked over at the clock. It was morning again. Dorothy silenced the alarm and went to Rayne's room.

She was already dressed for school and standing in front of the mirror combing her hair. A quick brush to smooth out the curls at the back was all Dorothy had to do. And she didn't have to do that but doing it made her feel needed.

"I want to walk to the bus stop." Rayne said as she brushed.

"You can't."

"Why not?"

"Cause I said so." Dorothy put the brush on the dresser. "And don't question me like that again."

"Can I eat breakfast with my friends at school?"

"What's wrong with eating breakfast here like we always do? It'll only take me a minute to prepare."

Rayne was silent.

As if a lightbulb went off in Dorothy's head, she asked, "Are you planning to meet up with one of those boys at school?"

"No, ma'am."

Dorothy softened. "You can tell me if you are. I used to find ways to see your daddy when I was young and pretty like you."

"You were never young like me," Rayne giggled.

Dorothy laughed. "We met every morning in the cafeteria for breakfast. He always carried my tray to our table." She widened her eyes at Rayne. "You make sure that boy carries your tray to your table."

"I can carry my own tray."

"Make sure he knows that but let him carry it just the same."

"Yes, ma'am."

She stretched out her hands and Rayne took them. "Can I pray this time?"

"You have something to pray about?"

Rayne nodded.

"You don't have to ask for anybody's permission to pray. You can pray in your heart anytime you wish and about anything you want. Even if you're somewhere that forbids praying, God will still hear the silent prayers in your heart."

"But you always pray out loud."

"I pray in my heart, too."

"You do?"

"Of course."

"About what?"

"About anything. I was praying as I was walking to your room. I asked God to protect you while I was brushing your hair. Sometimes I pray while I'm driving alone in the car."

Rayne bowed and closed her eyes. She was silent for a while. When she said "Amen," Dorothy hugged her and then prayed openly for both of them. After she was done, she went back to her room to ready herself for the drive to the bus stop.

In the car, she asked Rayne, "Have you been rehearsing your lines for the play?"

"Yes, ma'am. I do every day. I know my lines and my castmates' lines."

"Don't forget to invite Uncle Myles to the play."

"I already did. I invited Mrs. Davenport, too."

Dorothy cast her eyes over at her. Her tiny body looked swallowed up in the big passenger seat. She tapered a sigh that would have drawn an inquiry from Rayne, who often asked if there was something wrong when she heard those long deep sighs. At the bus stop, Dorothy noticed many students, who were about Rayne's age, walking, and she told her, "Tomorrow, you can walk if you still want to."

She didn't wait for the bus to come before leaving that morning. Instead, when Rayne kissed her and ran off to join a group of students waving her over to them, Dorothy continued to the next town to do her grocery shopping.

It was late morning when she made it to Victoria's house. Hearing the keys jiggling in the door, Victoria opened it. Dorothy stumbled in with her arms hugging three grocery bags. She was taken aback at seeing Noah and Nena cozied next to each other on the sofa.

Noah hurriedly took one of the bags.

"Thank you. This used to be so easy."

Nena took one, also, inconspicuously nudging her with a shoulder and exchanging a girlish grin at the shock on her face. They went into the kitchen, and Noah left the bag on the counter, but Nena stayed, helping to unpack them.

"I didn't expect to see you here."

"I can tell you didn't."

Dorothy packed some of the groceries into the pantry and, speaking over her shoulders with a bit of concern, noted, "You looked quite comfy next to Noah."

"It's comfortable being around him."

"It could be easy to fall for him if you're not careful."

Her lips quiver from a suppressed giggle. "Why would I need to be careful?"

Dorothy closed the pantry door and stuck her hand to her hip. "He's young, tall, well-traveled, irresistibly handsome, and rich. You're a small-town girl. Aren't you suspicious of why he'd be interested in you?"

"I was, but I'm not anymore," Nena said thinking back to their meeting near the river when she did question his interest in her.

He was all about business when they sat at the table in the gazebo, and he questioned her about the changes and strategies she recommends for reviving the grocery store. Taking notes on every concept and idea, from tracking changes in consumer taste to building better relationships with suppliers, he probed her until they mapped out a plan to better serve the community.

Satisfied with all they accomplished, he spread out a red and white checkered covering over the table, and taking their lunch from a picnic basket he brought a long, inquired, "What trapped an intelligent young woman as you in an abusive relationship with Aiden? Tell me everything. From the moment you met him."

Considering he foolishly put himself in harm's way to protect her, she figured she owed him that much. Candidly, Nena shared her history with Aiden, as they ate, and he, in return, revealed the stories of his romantic encounters. He spoke ambitiously of a future she didn't dare dream and poured wine for them in disposable wine glasses. They drank, told jokes, and laughed. He enticed her into taking pictures of him near the river, of them together, and of each other. She snapped pictures of countless birds and wildflowers and of the sun painting the sky golden as it glistens in the peaceful river.

He easily won a bet guessing her favorite hobby, and she lost trying to determine his. He requested his reward for winning to be one dance with her, and reluctantly, she agreed. After a twirl and a playful dip, he brought her up into his arms and whispered, "You're discovering it."

"Oh. Allow me to guess again."

He didn't. Instead, he continued into a long slow passionate dance. Finding it easy to relax in his arms, she accepted a gentle kiss on her cheeks when it ended.

"Come back to Crystal Falls with me."

The idea seemed so far-fetched, she believed he could only have conceived it in jest. Easing out of his arms, she thanked him for the evening, and ran back to the gazebo to gather the leftovers and tablecloth.

He followed. "Tell me, what just happened?"

"I woke up." She brought two ends of the tablecloth together.

"You were not asleep. I asked you to come back with me."

"Why me?"

"I saw the look in Aiden's eyes. He knows he has lost you. If he had the opportunity to relive that moment you asked him to pour out the liquor in the bottle, he would do it without questions. If, by chance, you were to start over, every time he touched you, it would be with passion and not fear."

"What does that have to do with you or me?"

"It has everything to do with us. One can learn a lot about a woman from the regrets of the man who lost her. I don't want to relive this moment, years from now, with regrets of what I should have done." He took the tablecloth that kept her attention away from him and threw it on the basket. "We have a lot to offer each other, and to figure out together. So, tell me you're awake, Nena, and answer, are you ready to go the whole distance with me and see where this moment leads us?"

Victoria came into the kitchen. "Nena, aren't you coming back to join us?" She turned to Dorothy. "I was showing them pictures of my grandparents I found in the attic. Come and join us, too."

Dorothy and Nena followed her back into the living room. Victoria opened the photo album again. "My mother shared stories about them when I was a young girl. She didn't tell me everything, and until last night, I didn't think to tell Noah the little she did share with me."

"What happened last night to make you think to do it now?" Dorothy questioned.

"I met a woman who told me things I didn't know about my family. She filled the gaps my mother left. Last night, when I saw Noah packing his bags, it occurred to me, he was leaving behind a big part of him right here in Beautiful. If I didn't share these pictures and tell him the stories, he might one day realize he has gaps I didn't fill. I don't want strangers filling gaps for him."

She flipped to a page in the photo album and then to another, where she pointed to a picture of her mother and grandmother. They laughed at the hats they sported.

"Do you share stories with Rayne?" Noah asked.

"Come to think of it, I did this morning."

"Share everything you know with her," Victoria implored. "Don't leave her to confirm who she is through someone else."

Noah hugged Victoria's neck and kissed her shoulder. "I'm proud of you, Mother, for not giving up on knowing. Seeing the pictures of my great-grandparents and the generations before them seated right here in this house and in that church has helped me understand that I do have a stake in this town. I feel a deeper connection to the progress you envision for Beautiful. Nena and I will do all we can to support and further that vision with you."

Dorothy glanced at them in discreet, as Nena caressed him mid-way his back.

"I believe Pastor Avery was trying to help me make the connection when he cornered me after church and mentioned something of the sort about me feeling at home here," Noah reflected. "I didn't understand it then, but of course, my focus was on Nena," he laughed. "So, I wasn't trying to understand it then. I do now, however. Thank you, Mother."

"I'm glad you do, son. There are some things I understand a lot better, too, but there are more I have to unravel still. Which reminds me," Victoria said to Nena. "What time is Pastor Avery due back in town?"

"Late this evening." She checked her watch. "The time is going fast. Thank you for sharing your pictures and stories with me. I must get back to my apartment, for we have a lot to do today."

The light on the porch of every house lining the quiet street was on when Myles pulled into his driveway. He got out of the car and retrieved a handful of mail from his mailbox before dragging his bags into the house.

On a barstool in the kitchen, he sifted through the mail, piece by piece. One sent from the church made him halt. Tossing the rest onto a pile on the counter, he rose from the barstool and took it, along with his bags, into his bedroom.

Curious about the content of the letter, he leaned the bags against the wall, instead of unpacking them, and sat at the edge of his bed to read it. The polite greeting in the name of the Lord led straight into the church board's regrettable decision to dismiss him from his role, pending a scheduled mandatory meeting. That, he predicted, but he didn't foresee what he read later.

The timing of the meeting prompted a somber laughter. It was scheduled for the next day. That was hardly enough time for him to prepare a defense for the violations of the bylaws they outlined against him. He checked the date stamped on the envelope. It showed the date he left for the conference. Surely, they could have afforded him more than a day to prepare.

A knock at the back door further ensured time would not be on his side. He was not expecting anyone, but it was not unusual for Slone to show up at odd times, as it was, at the back door. It was what he did as a child, and in all the years they lived across from each other, Myles was hard-pressed to remember him knocking the front door. Despite their strained relationship, he was ready to welcome him. He dropped the letter on the bed and hurried to the door.

"Perfect timing," he said opening it, but it was Ronnie who stormed passed him into the house.

"Tell me it's not true." She was fighting back tears.

Her denim overall shorts stopped way above her mid-thigh to where the pocket edges peeked out from underneath. One of the straps was unbuttoned and hung down from her shoulder. Her white tube top, barely serving as a bra, exposed deep cleavage.

He closed the door with a deliberate concern that parted ways with his exploring eyes. *The season is changing. She'll need a long coat soon.* Securing the mental note, his eyes drifted between the birthmark on her thigh, and the tears running down her cheeks. "Tell you what is not true?" he asked.

"Everybody says you've taken up with that woman. Victoria Davenport."

He smirked. "So, you finally heard."

Her nostrils flared with a sniffle, and Myles went to her and cupped her face in his hands. The touch was gentle, and his hands were warm against her skin. She prayed for him to say it's just rumors and relieve the anguish in her heart.

Myles tilted her face up and lowered his just a breath from hers. Wiping away the tears with his thumbs, he whispered, "Let's forget you're here uninvited." He moist his lips and spoke softer. "Let's even forget that the neighbors who saw you come into my home tonight will be watching still to see what time you leave." His thumb grazed her lips. "Tell me, Ronnie, what's it to you if what you heard is true? You're not First Lady material. You could never walk in her shoes."

He glided the back of his hand gently down the side of her face, and his eyes turned cold. Every emotion in them told her he would enjoy watching her fall to her knees, begging him to say the rumor was untrue. But his words left her breathless. It took all her strength to not crumble to the floor.

Myles tapped a finger on her lips, shook his head, and went back to the door to open it.

She did not move. With a faint voice, she managed, "You're heartless. You have no soul. That alone makes you unfit for a pastor. Yet, there you are," she laughed, mockingly, and more tears rolled down her cheeks. "Does she know the pain you're capable of causing, Pastor Myles Avery?"

It was the first time she addressed him by his title, and it came with an undercurrent of anger in the tone. It got his attention, and he pushed the door closed, listening.

"Your rejection of me is stifling, but it's soothing compared to your sting."

"My sting?"

She sniffled and wiped her eyes with the back of her hand. "You're charming. I'll give you that. To not have that part of you is stifling. But there's another part of you, Myles, that experiences joy from the pain you cause. Seeing it, stings. Does she know it's your weakness? Or, does she think you're perfect, too?"

He realized he was mistaken. It wasn't anger. It was contempt. He folded his arms and leaned back against the door. "You think that's my weakness?"

"It's not your only weakness. You lack the ability to commit. You will draw her in and fill her with hope. Then, you'll break her heart and dispose of her. Is she prepared for that?"

"Why do you think of me in that way?"

"Because you did it to me."

He chuckled. "You did it to yourself. You," he pointed at her, "disposed of yourself."

"It was the only choice I had."

"I offered you a better choice than that."

"You offered me broken promises," she yelled.

"How was I to fulfill them with your legs wrapped around another man," he yelled back.

"You left me, and I stopped breathing. I didn't have much to give to another man."

"You gave plenty to other men."

"I was broken. They took what they could. I didn't give them my heart as you've done."

"Is that supposed to redeem you?"

"I didn't come for redemption."

"Why'd you come here then?"

She dried a tear and netted as much dignity the moment allowed. "To find out, where I stand."

He relaxed back against the door. "You're concerned I won't be there for you anymore."

"You're the only man I can depend on."

"Rest assured, Ronnie, nothing's changed. I'm still an honorable man of God."

"Do right by me then. Honor the promises you made to me."

"You made that impossible decades ago when you chose a different man."

"You chose differently first. Just like you're choosing again."

"My first choice was you, and I would have never hurt you."

More tears trickled down her face, and she opened her arms wide. "Take a second look, Myles. What you see is not a lie."

"You can't blame your pain on me."

Ronnie shook her head and laughed. "I might never be able to walk in her shoes, but unlike you, I can walk in my truth."

She went for the door, and he stiffened against it. Seeing her angry was the norm. The quiet pain was the hook. "Are you saying I hurt you?"

She sniffled. "Don't pretend you don't know you did."

"What I know is tomorrow, I have to stand before the church board, mainly because of you. Your very presence here, right now, is quite possibly the last straw in my downfall. So, while you're here, Ronnie, let's have this conversation, for it's long overdue. Help me understand. How did I hurt you?"

The question forced her to revive decades of unendurable memories that left her in anguish. "Where should I start?"

"From the moment you felt the sting."

"Your affair with Carlena. Are you sure it's where you want me to start?"

"I didn't have an affair with Carlena."

"I saw the letters you wrote to her."

"What letters?"

"I read every word in them," she contended. "They drove me crazy, and, I admit, I fell apart."

"I never wrote to her."

"You're a liar, Myles Avery," Ronnie spewed before a quick sniffle. She shook a finger at him. "God is not pleased with you."

He reached for her, and she pulled back. He reached again and forced her into the sofa in the corner of the room.

"Sit down, Veronica, and talk to me."

He hadn't called her that in more years than she dared to count, but she remembered he only did when his patience wore thin with her. She settled in the seat, and he knelt at her feet.

"I'm listening. What letters are you talking about?"

He was calm and void of the blatant disregard he often had when he looks at her. It freed her to relive before him the pain of reading the letters Carlena flaunted week after week. She recalled with ease the plans he made with her, and she stuttered over the details of the love he proclaimed for her.

Myles listened, wishing he had not let the heartbreak from seeing the picture of her in bed with another man prevent him from discussing it years ago. When she was done dredging up the memories, he asked if that was why she sent the picture to him.

She admitted it was. "You were making plans to come home to me. Then you stopped. With no explanation, you snatched that hope from me. I didn't understand it until Carlena showed me her letters, and I saw the same plans you made with me, you were making with her. I wanted to hurt you like you hurt me."

Myles' eyes fell to the floor. "So, you sent me a picture of you. Your naked body wrapped around another man in bed. Your birthmark in plain view assured no mistaken it was you."

"It was the only way I knew to hurt you."

"Carlena deceived you," Myles said and stood. "I never wrote to her and never saw her until the day we buried her."

Ronnie sprang from the sofa, contending, "I didn't imagine the words on those pages."

"They weren't from me, Ronnie."

"They were your words. You said them to me."

"Unless she stole your letters from your mailbox, those words did not come from me." He looked at her in anguish. "I wish I could prove it to you."

He was nothing short of pleading, and it brought her calm. She moved in closer to him and whispered. "You can prove it, Myles. Make love to me."

He recognized the kindled passion. He knew it well. It didn't come as blatant seduction or alluring innuendoes, but a breathy glimmer of surrender instead. A kind she mastered way too soon.

Myles looked away from her and she said, painfully, "In those letters, you pledged to love only her. If those words did not come from you, that was your chance to prove it to me."

"Sex is not absolute evidence of love."

"It is for you. It was for us."

"I'm sorry that with my young mind I distorted the meaning of love for you. I was immature, and you had no one to teach you better."

"What's better?" She scoffed.

"I know how to love better."

"We have a history of making love. Are you saying what we had wasn't good for you?"

"The whole town knows about our history," he mumbled and sat on the sofa. Taking her by the hand, he coaxed her to sit again with him, and he faced her. "Tomorrow, if the church board votes for me to step down as the pastor, it'll be, in part, because of that passion we shared. It has turned into a never-ending saga, which they plan to use against me. That, along with a list of mishandling of church resources as well as my personal finances I used to take care of you. They assume you must still be satisfying me. I've ignored the gossips and rumors, and I've lost members who saw you as a distraction I can neither resist nor control. Still, I never turn my back on you when you needed me. That, Ronnie, is evidence of the love I have for you."

"You said what you do for me you would do for anyone. It's a ministry you called it. How is that evidence of your love for me?"

"Doing it for you came with a cost, but I did it anyway because I love you."

"That's not the kind of love I need Myles, and nothing less will make the wrong you've done to me right between us."

He pressed her hand to his lips and held it there for a while, studying her. With much thought, he agreed, "Then I won't offer anything less, for I have mangled the image of your self-worth, and it's time I show you real love and try to restore it."

Embattled from the list of charges the church board outlined against him and knowing the longer she was there the harder it would be to dispel the rumors that were sure to come from it, he added still, "I only ask that you promise to never break my heart again."

Her eyes fell on him with a powerless desire. "I promise."

"You have to promise you will always trust me. And there is never a time I needed you to trust me more than I do right now."

"I trust you."

Fighting back tears, he whispered, "One last promise."

"Anything."

"Promise you'll never let another man touch your body again if he can't make you feel love the way I will tonight."

She swallowed hard. "I promise."

"Good. Come with me."

Myles led her down the hallway to his office, holding firmly onto her hand. Reaching the door, unsettledness crept into her, and she stopped.

"Wait."

"Please don't say you have a change of heart."

She faced him. "It's your change of heart that concerns me."

He let her hand slip from his.

"For years, I watched you grow as a pastor, and despite the rumors about us, gained the respect of everyone in Beautiful. During that time, as I watched you grow, you were watching me die inside. You knew I wanted your affection, but you withheld it. What's changed, Myles?"

He braced against the doorframe with his face up to the ceiling. "During those years which you speak of, I was learning to be a Godly man, but tonight, I realized after all that learning, I still didn't get it right. Not with you anyway."

Myles pulled her in close, taking her head to his chest. "For the record, you always had my affection. It is why I couldn't turn my back on you.

That came easy. It was forgiving you that came hard. That's what I withheld, Ronnie. But knowing you were deceived, that changed tonight."

He tilted her face up towards his, and a tear sneaked down his flushed cheeks. "I preach forgiveness, but I didn't live it. In all those years, I didn't forgive you, and it kept us enraged and stuck in a past neither of us intended. I'm sorry I took so long to free us, but I forgive you now. I hope you will forgive me."

She pulled away from him. "That's why you're giving in to me? You want my forgiveness, so you can be free? From me?"

The question ended in her throat, and he caught a glimpse of a desperate girl grasping for the right to exist without rejection. His heart, flooding with her pain, sank from the woman standing before him to that girl in his past. Both were drowning, and he pulled her in with arms wrapped around her like a lifeline.

"I'm not trying to be free from you. There was never anyone I desired more than you. When you were gone, all I had was God and the picture of you, the woman I love, in bed with another man. I was in anguish. That anger kept me bound, and I was not always kind to you. Tonight, I released it. I forgive you, and I'm asking you to forgive me, too."

She had forgiven her father and sisters, and they were trying to forge a new relationship to establish her as a legitimate member of the family, which may or may not work, she quietly admitted. Not knowing what a new relationship might be like with him and refusing to take the risk without trying to win back his love, she whispered, "I can't do that now."

"Then say, one day you will."

"If I can feel your love again, I promise I will."

He took her hand and led her to the chair at his desk with a heightened conflict between wanting to preserve his role as the pastor, and an unwavering desire to reconcile their past to the present which was steered out of their control.

She had been in the room before. It was his bedroom with pictures of them taped all over the walls. Those pictures were replaced with bold Bible verses and inspirational quotes. The light beige carpet replaced a brown one that covered the floor. She noticed the altar near where he stood. His bedside table was there, and a sofa took the place of the bed where they lay.

"You promised to trust me. Do you still?"

She was silent when he asked, but she nodded when he seated her and asked again.

"Good. Have a seat. I promise I won't be long."

He left, and she decided to examine the writings on the walls, wondering what became of their pictures. She centered on the inspirational quotes to assess their importance as a replacement. Reading one on morality by Mahatma Gandhi, she looked away. Boredom drew her back again. She read another on forgiveness by Martin Luther King, Jr, and on character building by Helen Keller. She browsed the many scriptures about love, faith, and peace, and suddenly, she couldn't look away from them. The minutes passed, and her eyes were glued to the wall. Finding wisdom in the words she read, she felt the room stripped of the passion she experienced in there.

Myles finally returned, carrying a basin of water and a towel over his shoulder. Kneeling on both knees, he said, "I know a greater love than what we shared in this room, and tonight, I want you to experience it."

At her feet, he bowed and prayed aloud, confessing his pride that caused her pain, and he asked God to forgive him. He prayed for spiritual healing in every aspect of their lives and that one day, she, too, will forgive him. As often as she heard him pray at his church, she couldn't remember him praying more desperately.

Ronnie sat still with a calmness warming within her, and tears running down her face. When he was done, he loosened the straps on her sandals and took them off. Her spirit weakened. Patiently, he washed her feet. Never looking up at her, he dried them with the towel and strapped the sandals on her feet again.

Their eyes met, and she uttered, "I never felt more-"

"Valued?"

More tears fell, and she swallowed. "Yes. Not ever- with anyone."

"That's what happens when you connect with God's love." He stood. "That love exists inside of you, Ronnie, and it reflects your worth as God sees you. It is more valuable than anything I can offer you, and it is everything you need to sustain you even without me." He took her hand. "It is the essence of that love I've been striving for in every interaction with you, but even I, a pastor, came up short."

He pulled her up from the chair. "I tried to shut you out of my life. I belittled you and was even dismissive of you. None of that evidenced the essence of God's love. Nevertheless, you desired to make your body available to me."

She looked away, but with a finger beneath her chin, he made her face him again. Through smiling watery eyes, he continued. "I was not worthy of you, Ronnie. No man is worthy of you if he can't bring forth God's love inside of you. Promise me again, you'll never give your body to another man if he can't make you feel the love you felt tonight."

"I promise."

T hey rode in silence under the starry sky, with the moon nearing high. Half-way, he fiddled with the radio until he heard the jazz music playing on his favorite station turned to low. The cool night's breeze from the open windows accompanied them.

It was decades now since they were alone for more than mere minutes. Between her blatant seduction and the church's growing suspicion, it was a chance he couldn't take. Over time, resisting her turned into rejecting her, but he hoped, through God's love, he had restored her.

They came to a stop in her driveway, and Myles noticed the light in Julia's bedroom window. She had not gone to sleep yet.

"Julia waited up for you."

"I expected she would."

Keeping a stone face steady on the window, he battled a desire to reach over and take her into his arms. Indulge in a final touch. Steal one final kiss.

"She loves you." He spoke from his head.

"She's trying, but I understand better now the love she's striving for."

The words drew his attention from the window unto her, but hers was still leveled on it.

"I better go inside, so she can finally go to bed." Ronnie unbuckled the seatbelt and got out of the car. She didn't look back when she went up the steps, and he didn't take his eyes off her until she disappeared into the house.

Gazing at Julia's window, again, he saw her enter the room, and by their silhouette, extended their arms to receive each other. Myles watched until they released, and the room went dark. Free-flowing tears trickled down his cheeks, and he waited for his heart's permission before he backed out of the driveway to leave.

He drove slowly, consumed now, with the challenges that were to come the next day. The list of violations and allegations, and a sudden doubt of his ability to explain them away. When he reached home, he went into his office where he found refuge. This time, though, he didn't find it there. It wasn't his spirit that was empty and adrift. It was his emotions, he realized that had come unanchored. So, he went to his bedroom and released the decades of suppressed emotions, for a woman he loved, going awry, and grieving the long blistering relationship, coming to an end.

On his bed, he listened to his voicemails, skipping over some of them. When he heard Victoria's voice, he held his breath. "Everything went well. I finally got a name." He repeated her words and stretched out across the bed. "Finally. Everything went well."

Chapter Fifteen

Myles sat at his desk in his office at the church, red-eyed and unrested from the few hours of sleep he managed just before daybreak. Facing the board wasn't the only thing that kept his mind busy- too busy in fact, to fall asleep that night. He was curious about Victoria's visit with Lola.

With anticipation of learning the information she received, and an unclear mind of the appropriate tactic to use in defending himself when he meets with the church board, he hurried to the office at sunrise. There he prayed as the sun mounted the sky.

Noises from Nena's office, a sign the members volunteering their time at the church were trickling in, disrupted his private moment with God. He ended the long desperate prayer and began to prepare to face the day. Scanning his calendar, he saw nothing, except the meeting, that took priority over speaking with Victoria, and it was still an hour before it was to convene. As he reached for the phone, it rang.

"Yes, Nena."

"A detective from the police department is on the phone. Do you want me to put through the call?"

"Yes. Yes, please do, but hold my other calls."

The detective was working the case in the robbery at Victoria's house, and Myles had been following up on the progress since she didn't want the exposure. After Nena was robbed, the public plea from the pulpit for information seemed inadequate and passive. So, he took a more aggressive approach, in contacting the police department and demanding swifter actions to solve the crimes.

"Hello, Detective."

"Pastor Avery, we have good news."

"I can use some."

"We recovered Mrs. Davenport's jewelry, including her ring, from a pawn shop in Langston."

"That is good news, indeed. Mrs. Davenport will be happy to have back that ring?"

"I'm sure she will. It's quite expensive."

"Did you catch the thugs who robbed her?" Myles asked.

"Not yet. Off the record, we believe it's a network that extends well beyond Beautiful, and the owner of the pawn shop is at the center of it. For now, I can't say anything more."

"I understand. What's the next step for Victoria?"

"We'll need her to come to the station and claim the jewelry."

"I can arrange it. Are there any new developments on the robbery at the grocery store?"

"We have that culprit in custody. Thanks to Noah for spotting the tattoo and another victim who picked him out in a lineup. He agreed to cooperate, so we're working to get more like him off the streets."

"What's next for him?"

"That's up to the judge," the detective said.

"Is he a suitable candidate for our mentoring program?"

"He fits the profile you presented."

"Be sure the judge knows."

"I'll do what I can."

"Thanks, detective. Keep me posted."

Myles hung up the phone and praised God in a moment of internal celebration of the update. It was all the more reason to call Victoria, so he dialed her number, cheerily.

"Myles." Victoria placed the cup of tea she was sipping on the bedside table. "Thank you for returning the call. How was your trip?"

"It was glorious. I'm sorry for not getting back to you before now."

"There is no need to apologize. I knew you would return the call when time permitted."

"Thanks for having the confidence. You said you got a name."

"Victor. Lola said his name is Victor. She said a lot more, but mainly that she and mother talked about naming their children after their fathers. I'm

Victoria. It makes sense. Do you know anyone by that name?"

"Victor?"

"She said he fathered her daughter too. Her daughter's name is Veronica."

"Wait. That's Ronnie," he uttered in disbelief. "That Lola is Ronnie's mother as I suspected?"

"Do you know her father?"

"Mr. Vic? Yes, but are you sure?"

"I'm not sure, but Lola seemed convinced of it. I have to meet him and find out if he is."

Myles leaned back in the chair, taking in what it would mean if Mr. Vic was indeed Victoria's father. Evidence of another infidelity would erode the foundation of the family structure at a time when they were trying to rebuild it. He closed his eyes. "The family has been through a lot lately. He's extremely ill. Are you sure you want to go through with this?"

"Yes, especially if he's ill. Time might not be on my side."

"You have a point. This is hitting home closer than expected."

"You sound distraught."

"For the family. Ronnie is a product of his infidelity. The sisters are only now able to accept it. I'm not sure they can withstand news of another infidelity so soon if it turns out to be the case."

"I hadn't considered the others involved, and the pain this could cause them." Victoria finally said. "But I have a right to know if he is my father. Can you tell me where to find him?"

"They'll never forgive me," he sighed, reflecting on Julia's disappointment when she discovered his role in getting the lawyer for Ronnie.

"Forgive you? Why would they have to forgive you?"

"Oh, Victoria, you don't understand."

"Myles, I believe I do." Her voice was restrained. "You said living up here is like being a part of one big family. It's clear. Your lives are very much intertwined, and your relationships run deep. Disrupting a family structure and causing them pain could make you appear disloyal." She breathed heavily. "This is as far as you can go with me. A step further might be perceived as a betrayal."

"You do understand."

"Clearly. Thank you for what you've done already. If Mr. Vic, as you called him, lives here, I will find him on my own. And don't worry, whatever the outcome, I take full responsibility."

"I'm still on your side."

"I know you are, and I appreciate you voicing it, considering your position."

"I have some good news to add to your breakthrough."

"Oh?"

"The police recovered your jewelry."

"They did?"

'They want you to come to the station to claim them."

"Of course. When?"

"As soon as possible." He added in the same breath, "I want to be with you when you do."

"Can we go today?"

"Um. Yes. I have a meeting this morning, however, and I promised my niece to attend her first play at her school later today. If you don't mind waiting, we can go this afternoon."

"Rayne invited me to the play, too. We can go there together after the play."

"Sounds good."

"I'll see you there."

Myles held the phone after they said goodbye, appreciating that the lives of the people around him were coming aligned, and accepting there was a major upheaval at the core where he stood. It was time he took control and steady the path of his course. He put the phone on the receiver and went to the conference room to await the board members.

With his future in limbo, the ten-minute wait felt like a life sentence. When Nena escorted the members in, he was relieved. They sat at the table, but he stood at the head of it behind his chair, gripping the top of it. There was never a time he needed his best friend more than when one of the board members called the meeting to order, briefly welcomed them, and asked Slone to pray. He did, intentionally keeping the prayer short.

Myles held his chin high when another board member read the violations against him. Membership declining under his leadership was the lesser of a list that progressively ripped into the core of his moral character.

"Misappropriation of the church funds, lack of ethical judgement, public fraternization, and after rumors of a rendezvous last night, we're hard-pressed to exclude fornication, all of which threatens the image and moral standing of the church." The deacon offered Myles the floor and sat.

"Thank you for the opportunity to make my case. Although, last night, when I read the allegations you outlined in your letter to me and listened, now, to them spoken aloud, I must ask, could it be that you have the wrong guy?" The sarcasm was deliberate. He nailed Slone with a long side-eye that made him clench a pen between his teeth.

Lodging eye-contact with each of the board members, he went on. "As a pastor, I pray you've examined the factors influencing your perception of the allegations and violation of the bylaws because those influencing factors say more about you than they say about me. Proverbs 23:7 states, "For as he thinketh in his heart, so is he.'"

He casually leaned over the back of the chair and said after a quick throaty chuckle, "I admit, I struggled with this scripture for years, taking it literally. In my simple interpretation, I thought, after all, if a man's action leads me to think he's a thief, does thinking it makes me a thief? That wasn't reasonable." He paused in deep thought and added, "Thankfully, I sought God for a deeper meaning, and He gave it to me." He straightened. "Bear with me while I share a story."

He began a slow pace around the table. "When I was a young boy, crime was rampant in Beautiful, like it's happening now. The businesses were being robbed and the business owners found it necessary to install alarms and put up steel bars over their doors and windows. Many of our businesses still have them."

He stopped. "I was in line at a store one day. A woman in front of me purchased an item, paid for it, and proceeded to leave. The alarm went off when she got to the door. She took a few steps backward, and the alarm stopped. She made another attempt to leave, and the alarm blared as she did. The cashier, who took cash payment for the item she bought, announced in a loud convincing voice, 'She stole something.'" All eyes were on the woman.

Myles paced the floor again. "The manager was summoned, but instead of being accusatory, she apologized to the woman quickly and thanked her for being a valuable customer, noting the alarm might have malfunctioned.

189

She asked to see her receipt, and seeing she paid for the item she had, probed further and asked, could she have made a purchase at another time and the product was still in her bag. The woman remembered making a purchase the day before. Cough drops, I believe. She showed the manager the unopened item, and the receipt, still in her bag. While the increase in crime may well have contributed to the cashier's perception, in her judgment, she exposed characteristics that reflected her thinking. The manager did as well. In thinking other factors might have been at play and wouldn't conclude so quickly, the woman had stolen, she revealed characters about herself. You can decide what those characters are according to your thinking."

Myles reached his chair. "It took years for the experience to make sense to me. I've since come to accept that much of what we perceive are influenced by factors, unrelated to the target of our observation. Those factors lend insight into who we are. So, I ask, have you examined the factors influencing your perception of the allegations you brought against me?"

A board member interrupted. "What happened at that store, then, is not the same as the situation you are facing, now. First Thessalonians 5:22 cautions us to abstain from the appearance of evil. That woman did not intend to set off the alarm nor could she control it. She had receipts for every item she bought which shows a deliberate action to even avoid it." He pointed to Myles. "You, however, you had control over the way you behaved and the poor financial decisions you made. You had no apparent intent to avoid this situation, which is why you're here today."

"Tell me, by whose standards have you judged my actions? Man's, or God's?" Myles asked.

"Both, and in both cases, you failed to meet the standard."

Myles straightened. "Clearly, you have not considered the standards Christ outlined in Matthew 25 when He said, For I was an hungered, and you gave me no meat. I was thirsty, and you gave me no drink. I was a stranger, and you took me not in. Naked, and you clothed me not. Christ said when you commit these acts against the least of your brethren, you do them unto Him. Yet, you said I misappropriated the church funds in paying for food and hotel rooms for an ex-lover." He grunted, bitterly. "I will ignore the implications in that, and ask, did it make her any less hungry or any less homeless because she is my ex?"

Another board member responded, "Romans 14 warns to not let your good be evil spoken of. This community has gossiped about you and her for years. The church has lost members because of your actions. So, if your defense is spending the church funds on her for food, clothes, and shelter is what Christ would have wanted, the witnesses who saw her coming out of your house in the middle of the night can cast shadow over that defense."

Myles smirked. "I am aware, as Luke 8:17 states, nothing is secret, that shall not be made manifest; neither any thing hid, that shall not be known and come abroad. The expenses I insisted on and approved to help Ronnie were not in secret. And, from the moment I opened my door last evening and she stormed into my home, until the late hour of the night I drove her home, I knew God's eyes were watching me. "So I ask you, by whose standards have *your* witnesses judged my actions? Man's, or God's?"

Romans 14:18 and 19 states for the kingdom of God is not a matter of eating and drinking, but of righteousness. Anyone who serves Christ in this way is pleasing to God and receives human approval," the member said.

"I believe I have served this church in a way that is pleasing to Christ, for helping those in need is a major function of the church. I know many of you have done the same for others who sought your help in private. Is she less deserving of such help because of who she is?"

The board member argued, "We cannot judge whether or not Christ is pleased with you. However, the fact that we are losing members is evidence you haven't received human approval. It is why the bylaws are in place. You must apply them, for they guide your actions in gaining that approval. Instead, you chose to ignore them and has put the reputation of the church at risk."

"I must say, in truthfulness, giving much consideration to all these scriptures, the standards set forth for how to love each other were the only ones I wrestled with, and they were the ones that guided me in carrying out the very actions you say now violated the bylaws. I am convinced; however, the standard of God, as I understand them, supersedes the standard set forth in the bylaws.

Another board member spoke up. "Pastor Avery, the bylaws are not suggestions. You don't have the option to decide when, or if, to consider them."

"I ask again, then," Myles said, "By whose standards do you prefer I assess the appropriateness of my actions? Man's, or God's?" When they didn't answer, he moved from his chair and strolled around the table. "Any of us can find a scripture to back our actions, especially if we are self-serving in applying it. So, I'll save you another excerpt as I address another charge you brought against me. In your letter, you say the final straw was reports of a relationship I have with Mrs. Davenport. That, I secretly brought her into town and spent time together, privately, at her home I renovated for her." He cleared his throat. "The more current rumor I believe, is we've been seen around town eating and enjoying each other's company. This, another questionable act, demonstrating my lack of judgment."

He positioned himself across from Slone and stopped. "I could not share the details of who she is or why she came because of pastoral confidentiality. She trusted me to honor it, and I did." He locked eyes with Slone and spoke as if no one else was in the room. "Earlier, I asked have you examined the factors influencing your thoughts about the allegations you brought against me? Just as it was with that woman in the grocery store, not everything is what it appears to be. If you ask the right questions like the store manager did, you'll find the answers you're looking for."

His voice fell to an intimate whisper. "Think, Slone. Think why I asked you to meet her at the bus stop when she came into town. Think about the house where you took her and the many occasions, I made you, not me, available to her. When you gave her a tour of the church grounds, could she have said something that jogged your memory of third grade?"

Slone threw the pen on the table and made a dash for the door.

The door opened as Slone raised his hand to knock. Not expecting to see him out there, Victoria gasped with a hand to her chest before she worked up a delightful, "Slone. What are you doing here?"

He stilled. The long burgundy and beige sleeveless sweater dress accentuated her curves under the unbuckled matching coat. The burgundy clutch purse under her arm paired well with the backless peep-toe boots and suggested she had some sort of formal engagement.

"Tell me the occasion isn't important," he managed.

"To Rayne it is." Her face glowed.

"Rayne?"

"She's making her stage debut in her school play. I promised her I'd come."

"It's that time of the year already?"

She nodded.

"At what time is the play?"

She checked her watch. "In a few hours."

"The school is only a fifteen-minute drive from here. Why are you leaving so early?"

"I want to get some flowers and a gift for her."

He looked over her shoulder into the house. "Dorothy. Where is she?"

"She went ahead of me. Rayne forgot her props. Anxiety I suppose."

"Noah? Is he here?"

Curiosity graced her face. "Is something wrong, Slone?"

He refocused. "No. Nothing's more right, in fact. Are you alone?"

"Yes."

"Good. We have to talk."

She opened the door wider and moved out of the doorway, allowing him to pass her into the house. When she pushed it shut, the nerves tightened in the pit of her stomach. It had been a while now since he showed up at her door. "What is it, Slone?"

He clasped his hands under his chin, with the tip of his fingers touching it. "You are so beautiful."

"Thank you." It was dry. "Forgive me. I detected a sense of urgency out there. I wasn't expecting flattery. What is it we need to talk about?"

He searched her face for something familiar but found nothing. "I keep meeting you for the first time."

Her brows knitted. "What do you mean?"

He moved closer to her. "I met a girl, and I met a woman. Now, I'm meeting the woman the girl became."

"You're not making sense."

"It didn't make sense to me either. I would have never guessed you are the woman that girl became. Tori?"

Victoria placed her purse on the sofa. "How do you know that name?"

"It was the first thing you said to me when we met."

She recalled when they met at the bus stop. Nothing presented a reason to say that name.

"It couldn't have been."

He didn't acknowledge the statement. "You were wearing a white dress, white shoes, and white socks. Your hair was long and thick. It flowed over your shoulders. A silver tiara held it back from your face. I remember because none of the girls I knew wore their hair like that. They wore big plaits and ribbons. And you," he shook a finger toward her, "You stood out among them. I knew you were not from around here."

"Slone, we never met before meeting at the bus stop."

"I was sitting on the steps outside the church door. You ran out of the sanctuary past me, went down the steps to the bench under the tree, and you sat there and cried."

Victoria's mouth opened, and her hand went up to cover it. Looking at him with relief and confusion, she said, "You can't be the boy I met that day. His name was Darius. You're Slone."

"Darius Slone," he corrected her. "My father's name was also Darius. By the time I became a teenager and girls were calling the house, it got confusing which Darius they were calling for. He loved the name, so I told him he could keep it. I made everyone call me Slone."

She studied his face, piercing eyes, straight white teeth, cool dark skin, bulky biceps outlined in the untucked blue plaid shirt, and his long muscular legs in the perfectly fitted blue jeans. She'd fantasized about what the young boy might look like as a grown man and wondered if she would even be attracted to him still, if they ever met again. She didn't have to wonder anymore. "You're the boy I met?"

He braced his shoulders. "I am Darius."

Victoria felt a twinge of panic grip her chest. She went to the sofa and sat, and he followed and knelt at her feet.

"Are you okay?"

She nodded.

"You're remembering."

"I never forgot," she whispered, touching his face. "How did I not know it was you?"

"It's been decades. I hadn't thought about that day for years. I wouldn't have guessed it was you either."

"It was my grandfather's funeral." She looked at him through blurry eyes. "I was just beginning to know him, and just like that, he was gone." She blinked, and a tear fell from her smiling eyes. "And there you were, comforting me."

Slone sat on the sofa next to her. "I wish I'd known it was you all along. When you spoke of your grandfather, I hadn't made the connection between you and that girl, and that girl and Mr. Grover, the man we buried that day." He eased back from her. "That's why you were crying. Everything is making sense. I remember that day only because it was special. As a kid, I don't know how I knew, but I knew something special was happening. Just about everyone in Beautiful was gathered in that church." He paused and added with a gentle squeeze of her hand. "And I remember the girl, but I didn't know she was you. And here you are still crying."

More tears dripped down her face. He wiped it away with his thumb. "Are you sure you're okay?"

She cupped her hand over his, on her face. "They're happy tears this time."

He looked longingly at her and then stood. "Victoria." An unwelcomed tension rose in his throat. He swallowed. "The first time you visited our church, Pastor Avery asked me to show you around the facility, but you wanted to start in the churchyard. When we got to a tree out there, you asked if there used to be a bench under it. Why did you remember that bench?"

She regained her emotions enough for a chuckle. "That bench was the only pleasant thing I remembered of that day."

Slone shoved his hands into his pockets. "We used to play around on that bench after church, you know. Then some days, I just sat there, and imagined the girl I met was sitting there with me. I wondered if I would ever see her again. The years past and the bench got old and worn. After the pastor knocked it down, somehow, I stopped thinking and wondering. In time, the girl faded from my memory. I forgot about her."

Victoria laughed. "Did you?"

"I didn't even think about her when you asked me about that bench."

"What I remember of that boy sitting on the step of the church is his name and the way he made me feel. I was embarrassed when I saw him watching me cry. He must have known it, too, because he left, but he returned, holding a small cone-shaped paper cup with water in it, and gave it to me. After I drank it, he took out his handkerchief and dapped my eyes."

"I sat next to you on the bench," Slone said, seating himself beside her again. "And I told you my name is Darius and asked your name."

"I said 'Tori.'"

"Tori," Slone echoed. "You no longer go by that name?"

She giggled. "Mother still calls me that."

"It's a cute name."

"For a little girl, but unlike my mother who hasn't noticed, you see I'm a woman now."

He took a full view of her. "That you are."

She blushed.

With the tension back in his throat, he asked again, "Tell me the whole truth, Victoria. Why did you remember that bench?"

"Something happened to me out there, and I've spent every day since, wanting it to happen again."

"Has it?"

She shook her head. "Not until the first morning I woke up here in Beautiful and heard you banging at the gutter on the side of the house."

"I don't understand. You wrote me a check and asked me to leave. Remember?"

"I wasn't always my best self, early in the morning." She suppressed the untimely chuckle in her throat and spoke in seriousness. "I noticed the gutter when we arrived the day prior. I knew it had to be fixed, and there you were that morning, fixing it. I was unready for you, perhaps. It was the first glimpse of the man I was searching for. The one who understood my needs and took care of it."

"You're implying no one took care of you."

"Not like that." She rolled her eyes and walked to the center of the room. "There was always something attached."

Slone went to her. "That boy only wanted to see you smile, and in his undeveloped mind, have a lifetime in return to take care of you."

"His presence was innocent and natural. He made me feel real." She hugged her arms around her body. "I never forgot that feeling."

"Was that the only thing you felt?"

"I was young. It was the only thing I could feel."

"That's the safest and most soulless answer you could give," Slone quipped.

"It's the truth."

"It's not the depth of your truth. You said you remember how he made you feel. Take me to the depth of what you felt."

She looked away, but he took her hands and held them to his lips. When he spoke again, he left his heart on the line. "I fell in love with the girl I met on that bench under that tree. She was beautiful. Delicate. Vulnerable. In all my life, no woman has excited me more. Not until I saw you get off that bus. You were poised with flare and class. I fell madly in love with you as I did with the girl I met. I knew I had to see you again, and nothing could stop me."

Her throbbing heart left her powerless to deny him her truth. "We were kids, but I know I fell in love with you, too." She touched his face. "You found a place in my heart that surrenders when it is touched. I've hungered for-"

"That touch again?" His mouth lowered over hers in mid-sentence, and at his best to finish her thought, he sent her mind in a spin with a kiss. It was slow and satisfying. Her lips parted to indulge him fully. He caressed her with gentle hands, reaching the nape of her neck with patience. She was warm and soft and tempting in his arms. It awoke him unto a spiritual consciousness that it wouldn't be good for him to continue life without her.

Drowning in the thought, he cuddled her face in his hands and pressed desperately upon her lips. Her hands found way under his shirt with a breathless moan, revealing she wanted him as much as he wanted her. He wished it were that simple- to take her. Right there- right then. But it wasn't. It maddened him that it wasn't. Slone pulled back, brushing his lips against hers. Settling her with simple kisses, he eased her out of his arms.

"I'm sorry."

"Don't be."

"I know you don't want to cross that line."

"I do. When it's right, I do." His thumb traced the contour of her lips. "Is that what you felt why you came back? Loved?"

"Yes. I wanted to feel that love again." She sighed and looked longingly at him. "I didn't want to leave Beautiful, but after my grandfather's death, Mother wanted nothing more to do with this town. When she took me away, it was only a part of me she took. We traveled the world, and I became a famous ballerina. But somewhere between the grand jete and pirouette," she laughed with a hand tossed about the air, "I lost the part of me she took. I spent years, living out her dreams. Then one day, I realized the last time I felt complete, I was sitting on that bench under that tree. I had to come back to rediscover me."

"Is that what you meant when you said you need space and time to figure out some things?"

"Yes."

"Have you?"

"It's a process."

"Are you where it's not a compromise to feel what I want you to feel?"

"It was never a compromise. I couldn't avoid feeling what you wanted me to feel no matter how much I tried."

"Are you sure?"

"I didn't want to compromise the off chance of reconnecting with Darius and experiencing me through him again. But since the first morning I woke up in Beautiful, I've been torn between you and the image of the man he might have become. That night you prayed for me in the hospital room, you touched my soul. I knew then it wasn't a compromise, for I've spent my whole life hoping to find Darius, but there I was, falling in love with you."

Slone reached into his pocket and took out a ring he bought and kept for years, for he had not found the woman he wanted to have it. When he left the meeting at the church, he had one thing in mind, and he drove to his house, first, for the ring. Kneeling before her, he took her hand, "I don't see a reason for us to spend another day apart. And if there is, we'll have to work through it because I am in love with you. Will you marry me, Victoria?"

Her face lit up, and her eyes glistened with tears. "Yes, I will."

Slone slipped the ring onto her finger and took her into his arms. With her tears wetting her cheeks, he kissed her.

"I have to go back to the church and tell Myles-"

"He'll be shocked to hear it," she wiped the tears and laughed.

"I was going back to tell him I'm sorry. Why would he be shocked? He already knows everything."

"Not everything. He doesn't know I was searching for you, too?"

"Me, too? Is there someone else?"

"My father. He only knows I was trying to find my father."

"You said you never met your father. You didn't say you were trying to find him."

"I have been since I arrived in Beautiful. It's the only reason I gave him for why I came. I didn't tell him about you."

"But he knows. He sent me to you."

"How could he have known? I kept that in my heart."

Slone's eyes widened. "I told him."

"You couldn't have. You didn't know who I was."

"I talked about you with him for months after we met the first time. He made the connection. He knew you were that girl all along. That's why he sent me to the bus stop to meet you. He found every opportunity to put us together, over and over, but I couldn't see what he was doing. I was so convinced he wanted you for himself."

"Why would you think that?"

"He was overly discreet about you. At the time, nothing else explained why."

"I asked him to be."

"But why would you want him to be if you're trying to find your father?"

"I didn't want anyone else to know I was looking for him. And, I still don't."

"Why not? It might help."

She shook her head. "Maybe. But think about all the men who might come forward, and they will, for their own personal gain. It could be leaked to the tabloids like the pictures of my injury. All those men claiming to be my father would embarrass my mother and call her reputation into question." She shook her head again. "I don't want to do that to her."

"I see. Are you close to finding him?"

"I'm closer. Myles was helping me connect the dots."

"Is that what those meetings and lunch dates with him were for?"

"Yes."

"Why didn't you tell me? Why didn't he?"

"I wasn't ready, and he's a man of honor."

"You said he was helping. Isn't he still?"

"Not anymore. I know enough to continue on my own."

He kissed her forehead. "I really must go now before the board makes a decision."

"A decision about what?"

He was already at the door. "Removing Myles from his role."

Chapter Sixteen

Nena knocked on the half-opened door to Myles' office and poked in her head. He looked up from the stack of papers he was perusing. "Come in Nena."

She crossed over the doorway and stood by the chair in front of his desk. "The board wants to inform you the vote is postponed until tomorrow."

"Why?"

"Everyone has to vote, but Deacon Slone isn't here to cast his."

He checked his watch. "Hm. Thank you." His attention went back to a document on the desk. He flipped it over and picked up a pen. But Nena didn't leave. Scribbling his signature at the bottom of the page, he asked, "Is there something else?"

"Yes, sir."

He looked up from the document.

"They didn't think one vote would matter anyway."

Myles braced in his chair. "They said that?"

"Only one board member, but I deciphered he was speaking for the rest."

"I see. Well, thank you." He slipped the signed document into a folder and moved it to a corner of the desk. Nena stood there still. "There's more?"

"No, sir." Her voice dropped, setting off a brief but weighty pause. "Not about that anyway."

He refocused on her. "What's it about?"

She sighed. "Now that you asked, I realize it's not the right time to talk about it, considering what you're facing." She turned to leave but threw up her hands and pivoted. "Then again, there will never be a right time for this."

Myles lay the pen aside. "A right time for what?"

She composed herself. "I'm sorry, Pastor. Never mind. I shouldn't have brought it up. It's nothing."

"You're stalling."

"I don't mean to."

"Then say what's on your mind."

"Is everything going to be alright around here, Pastor?"

"This, too, will pass. You know that."

"How can you be so sure?"

"Is that what has you troubled?"

She dabbed the tears forming in the corner of her eyes with a finger, and Myles pointed to the chair she was clutching. "Have a seat, Nena. What is it?" he asked when she sat. She unwrapped the colorful scarf from around her neck, and he leaned towards her with heightened concern. "You're bruised."

She rewrapped her neck with the scarf.

"I suspected it." Myles pounded the desk in anger. "Did Aiden do that to you?"

Knowing the widespread speculation of her abuse, she jumped ahead of the questioning. "Noah handled it."

"Noah?"

She nodded.

"Why didn't you come to me first?"

She shrugged, shaking off the question. "It's complicated."

"For whom? Me? In this role?"

"You're right. I guess I wanted to spare everybody the trouble of trying to protect me."

"You needed protection."

"That's why I was praying my way through it, Pastor."

"God works through people also. You should have come to me. The church. We would have helped you."

"I know, but he needed help as well as I did. And, as foolish as this sounds, I desired that he be helped more than be harmed. He is all I have. We're all we have."

"You have us, your church family. We can help you. The both of you."

She looked away from him.

"I can arrange a safe place for you."

Nena shook her head. "Thank you, but you won't have to. We took him to a facility in Langston. He checked himself in to a program for alcoholics." She paused and bit her lips. "Noah, Noah"

"Go on. What about Noah?"

"He asked me to go back with him to Crystal Falls."

"He asked you to do what?"

"He offered me a job."

"Did you accept it?"

"Yes."

"Are you sure about that decision?"

"No, but I'm sure I'm ready to take the chance. He offered me a scholarship through their company for college. I can't pass up the opportunity."

"He's offered a lot. I must ask, what's he expecting of you in return?"

"He wants to collaborate on Mrs. Davenport's business ideas for Beautiful. She plans to buy the grocery store, and we spent some time discussing the failure of it. He was impressed with my business insight."

"Mrs. Davenport is on board with the decision?"

"Cautiously. Noah and I are, too."

"I detected chemistry between the two of you."

"There is, but we're not rushing into an intimate relationship. He believes we can work more effectively if we're together in Crystal Falls."

"Where will you live? Crystal Falls is quite costly."

"He offered me their guest house. It'll be a start."

"He has an apartment off-campus. Right?"

"Yes, sir."

"Promise me you'll call, if you're in need while you're there."

"Thank you, Pastor."

"What about a church? Did he suggest one?"

Her voice fell again. "He doesn't have a church home, but we plan to find one when I get there."

"Will he attend with you?"

"Yes, sir. You sparked his curiosity," she laughed.

"Good. I will make a few phone calls and create a list of some to visit if you wish. When do you plan to leave?"

"Tomorrow."

"Tomorrow?" How will you be ready by tomorrow?"

"Noah is helping me prepare. Since I agreed to go, he's been at my apartment packing a few things I want to take with me, and he hired a moving company to take care of the rest."

"I see."

She interrupted a calm silence in which Myles was absorbing the obvious. "I'm sorry it's such a short notice, but Noah has to get back to Crystal Falls. I've been thinking. Dorothy will make a great secretary for the church. She knows what the duty entails."

"Mrs. Davenport wants to keep Dorothy on her payroll." He interjected a somber laugh and picked up the folder he placed in the corner of his desk. "Today, I was prepared to offer you the position, full-time, with pay. I was finally able to work it into the budget." He dropped it back on the desk.

"Really?" Her eyes brightened.

"Yes, but, you prayed, and God prepared another way out for you. Now, unless you have reservations about Noah's offer, I have to believe God was preparing this position for someone else." He pushed back from the desk and went around it to her with open arms. "Will you allow me to pray with you?"

She rose from the chair, and he took her into his arms, going into a long, powerful, and fatherly prayer. When he ended and opened his moist eyes, Slone was waiting in the doorway. He released her, and Nena closed her eyelids tightly to squeeze out the tears. She opened them with gratitude. "Thank you, Pastor. I'll leave you two alone."

Myles nodded and acknowledged Slone. "Deacon Slone."

"I didn't mean to disturb you."

"You didn't. Come in," Myles beckoned with a hand, went back to his chair, and sat.

Nena, in passing Slone, accepted a long embrace he offered.

"Are you okay?" Slone asked, letting go.

"Yes, I am." She took his hands, untying her knotted emotions to decide which to display. Appreciation surfaced on her face and in her voice. "I was always okay because I knew you were there if I needed you." Turning back and forth between them, she added, "Both of you. Thank you for letting me know you were there," she said and went back to her office.

Myles pointed to the empty chair.

"That was a powerful prayer. Even I felt the chains breaking," Slone said, settling comfortably into it.

"Hers or yours?"

Caught off guard by the question, Slone massaged his bearded chin with deep thought. "Mine's, equally," he affirmed. "I should have trusted you, and I'm sorry."

Myles bobbed his head, slowly. "How did it go with you and Mrs. Davenport."

"Victoria, you mean. We both know, neither you nor I is that formal with her except in our presence."

"I never thought you were," he smirked. "So, how did it go with Victoria."

"I asked her to marry me, and she said yes."

"Congratulations. I expected you would ask."

"You knew who she was all along. Why didn't you tell me?"

"I already explained."

"I don't buy your pastor confidentiality excuse. I've been loyal to you. You trust me."

"Fine. And it wasn't about trust. The truth is I knew when you saw her, you would have done, then, what you did today if I told you who she was."

"You're implying it was foolish of me to propose?"

"No. Today it wasn't, but months ago, when she first came to town would have been insane."

They laughed.

"People change, Slone," Myles continued. "When I realized neither of you recognized the other, I thought it was best you rediscover each other on your own. I wanted you, especially, to learn the woman she became without sentiments of who she was."

"I wish I'd known you had my best interest at heart. I believed you wanted her for-"

"I know what you and the rest of Beautiful believed," Myles sighed and cut him off. "But it didn't matter to me. For, as long as I kept her close, no other man stood a chance of getting close to her, except you."

"You risked your reputation for me."

"You did the same when you turned a blind eye to the church board concerns, even though you felt strongly enough to confront me, privately, about them. I appreciate that you looked out for me, and, at a time, you didn't know I was doing the same for you."

"What made you decide to give me the hint of who she is?"

He responded, pensively, "When we spoke this morning, she assured me she understood the bond we have with each other in Beautiful and released me of any obligations that might weaken it. We weren't discussing this issue, of course, but I trust it applied if she knew, fully, the tension between us."

"Thank you. I might not have figured it out without your help. She shuts down on topics that offered insight into why she came."

Myles shrunk into the chair with his face turning red and his dimples deepening. "There's another reason. I observed the two of you gravitate to each other after every service. If I don't step in to break you apart, you wouldn't know how to pull away from each other." They laughed. "Watching you fall, helplessly, in love with her, and she with you, I decided it was time."

"Was it that obvious?"

"To me it was. You, restraining yourself with your hands in your pocket but can't take your eyes off her. The grown man you are, in her presence, looked like a third grader again. It was time you knew the grown woman fixing your tie and straightening your lapel, even when they didn't need to be, is the girl you fell in love with way back then."

Slone rubbed his head. "Why did you choose the meeting to let me in on it?"

Myles pulled his chair closer to the desk, leaned in, and whispered, "I knew the bylaws requires every board member to have a vote if the issue at hand is concerning the conduct of the pastor. A thought occurred to me to delay the process. Wanting you to know who she is and needing to get you out of the room, the meeting was like a divine plan coming together."

They laughed, heartily.

"I was in no hurry to come back either. It was not until she explained everything, and I saw how wrong we were in judging your actions to be anything but of good intent that I hurried away from her to come back."

"She told you everything?"

"She told me about her father and that it was the reason the two of you were meeting. How you managed to keep that secret in Beautiful is beyond me."

"It is the best kept secret in Beautiful, but it wasn't easy, as you saw." He checked his watch. "We're meeting again this afternoon."

"She didn't mention you were meeting."

"The detective informed me they recovered the jewelry those thugs stole from her house, and we're going to the police station together after Rayne's play."

"I'd like to get my hands around the throats of those thugs."

"You'll have to wait for that. The robbery is connected to a bigger network, where they target the rich. They're still working the case."

"Does she know?"

"I didn't see a need to alarm her, so I didn't tell her that much."

His countenance fell, and he excused himself and went to the window. Sensing he was distraught, Slone joined him. "Is there something else I should know, Myles?"

He shook his head. "No. Not about that." They locked eyes and he said softly. "Rayne is playing Lady Marian in the school play this year. I just remembered Robin Hood was my brother's favorite story. He would be so proud of his little girl in that role."

Slone patted his shoulder. "He is proud, and he'll be there in spirit, watching and enjoying every moment of it with you."

"Will you be there?" he sniffled and pressed down his moist eyelids with his fingers.

"I can't. I'm working the prayer line."

"Of course. You should catch up with us at the police station when your shift ends."

The phone rang, and he went back to his desk to answer it. "Yes, Nena. Send her in please."

Victoria marched in, and seeing Slone, strutted to him. He slipped an arm around her waist. "I thought you were shopping."

"It turns out, I didn't have to go far to find a suitable gift." She spun around in his arms to face Myles. "So, I decide to drop by and find out why the church board wants to get rid of you."

"They think they have grounds."

"Does Mother know about this?"

"Your mother isn't involved in how things operate here. She wants only to know when we change pastors."

"Have they done so?"

"They haven't voted on it yet."

She threw her purse in the chair. "Well, you tell them my money goes wherever you go. They can vote on that too."

Slone wrapped his arms around her tighter and kissed the top of her head. "I'll be sure to do so when we reconvene tomorrow."

Sitting at the edge of his bed, Myles' mind reeled with outtakes of events from the day. Victoria and Slone's engagement stood out among them. The meeting with the board members. Nena confirming his suspicion she was abused. Her unexpected resignation, and the challenge it left him to find a replacement as dedicated as she. He clasped his hands on his head to quiet his mind, but it kept reeling.

The excitement in Rayne's eyes when the cast held hands, raised them in unison, and bowed deeply to the town's roaring applause at the end of the play brought both delight and despair. Myles closed his eyes to block the grievous reality of his brother not being there. The hours at the police station crept into his mind, and he opened his eyes, escaping to the blissful, "Slone," bursting from Victoria in finding him waiting at the station when they arrived. He chuckled at the image of Dorothy, wide eyed and a hand over her mouth, as Slone welcomed Victoria into his arms with a passionate kiss on her lips.

These were the highs and lows packed in one day, and, feeling deserving of a chance to break from all of it, he crawled into bed with jazz music playing in the background. The next day held its own course of order and upheavals, and as the pastor, for now, he must be ready to face them.

It came too soon. His playlist reached the last song, but he didn't hear it. A gentle rain against the window came and went. There was a siren. He stirred, pulled the sheet over his head, and was asleep again.

The hours passed, and an image of Nena floated into his consciousness. He opened his eyes. They were still heavy with sleep, but the sun beaming in the morning sky deterred him from staying under the sheet. He rubbed his eyes and got out of bed with a nagging thought that something significant was to happen to him that day. Drip by drip, his mind collected the spillover of the day before. "Morning came too soon," he grumbled, going into the shower, processing it.

When he came back into the bedroom, he slipped into a black jogging suit. Zipping up the hooded jacket, Nena entered his mind again. This was her last day before moving to Crystal Falls, and there was no time for the church to plan a proper send-off. He would have liked it. Although, after gathering some documents from his bedside table, he accepted that she wouldn't have. She didn't care for people making a fuss over her. He stuffed the documents into an old brown leather briefcase, pulled the hoodie over his head, and went to his car.

It was a slow drive to the church. Paying attention to nothing, in particular, he drove as if it was his last trip, and he needed to savor the memory of every inch of the journey. A thought popped into his head as he came upon their flower shop, and he made a detour into the parking lot, deciding on having an arrangement of yellow and white tulips delivered to Nena.

The exchange of pleasantries with the shop owner turned into a long request for prayers- the owner rambling off a list of her family members and friends with diverse ailments. It faded into a quiet disgust for what the church was doing to him. "It's not like anything about you and Ronnie is ever," she gestured with air quotations, "breaking news."

Myles laughed and signed the card for delivery with the flowers while she relayed the apparent consensus point of view on the current situation he was facing. "Don't get me wrong, everybody thinks that woman, Mrs. Davenport, is good for you, but nobody is disappointed she chose Slone. Ronnie wouldn't have it any other way. Besides, nobody believes a rich celebrity will stick around in this old town. It's better she idles her time with the deacon than with the pastor. The church board needs to give it time to blow over. You're a good pastor, and Beautiful needs you in that role."

Myles thanked her, and before he left, extended an invitation to the next church service if she had time.

Reaching the church, he pulled into his designated parking space and sat in his car, staring at the sign before him with his name in large lettering on it. When he finally decided to go into the building, each step up the stairs to the front door came with a heavy heart.

He opened the door to the foyer just as Slone was entering the sanctuary. Seeing him, too, Slone pivoted back, smiling wide-eyed and offering a riveting handshake. It was enough to suggest his role was safe. Myles stilled, trying to drum up gratefulness but was too disheartened for an easy transition on demand. Failing, he pulled Slone closer to him and buried his head into his shoulder, releasing within him the burden he bore. They hugged tightly, and Slone patted him on his back.

"What happened in there?" Myles gathered himself and asked.

"Let's just say the speed at which gossip spreads in Beautiful is not always a bad thing after all."

"What do you mean?"

"Ronnie heard about the meeting, and she popped in to clear up some things."

"Ronnie? What did she say?"

"That she didn't want to be the reason for your downfall. Then, a whole lot about distinguishing between romantic love, which she admits she still has for you, and God's love, which she chastised us for failing to recognize when you displayed it so boldly toward her."

"Ronnie? She did that?" He pulled the hoodie from his head.

"Yes. She even cited scriptures. I'm willing to bet everyone in there will judge her differently from this day forward." Slone paused to savor the possibility for her sake. "And, as it turns out my engagement to Victoria didn't stay private long either. After I confirmed it, and her intention to transfer her financial support to whichever church you pastor next, they didn't have a leg to stand on." Slone glanced at his watch. "We have a meeting scheduled in twenty minutes to inform you formally." He slapped his shoulder. "Get yourself together. You're late, and you look a mess."

Hurrying to his office, Myles reassessed his attire, complete with a pair of old white sneakers which held his attention for about a second. An impromptu personal reflection on his level of spiritual endurance set in, and he equated his sneakers to the frailty of his spiritual self. Taking pride he did not waver in his belief God's will would prevail in the whole ordeal, he conceded, too, his faith was weakened in the process. It was why he came ready to accept whatever the board decided but was even more prepared for a result much different from the one they made.

He brewed coffee in a small coffee pot in his office and sat at his desk, staring up at the clock on the wall. The twenty minutes past slowly with him clenching the cup of coffee as he sipped and tapping his fingers on the desk.

Then an hour came, and the meeting started and ended. It took only ten minutes for Slone to call it to order, pray, and formally announce the decision, noting one opposition to him continuing in the role as the pastor.

In the fifty minutes that followed, Myles sat at the head of the table in the conference room and listened as the board members justify their reasons for wanting to remove him from his role, and, awash with regrets, credited themselves for adjusting their point of view when credible information came to light. With slow nods here and there, signaling his appreciation, and an exchange of quick glances with Slone, when either one found a viewpoint peculiar, he passed the time with them.

The meeting adjourned, and the men stood, extending congratulatory sentiments for the good fight in overcoming the deceitful plot of the devil to persecute him and ultimately the church. They gave each other hugs- big bear hugs- with hearty slaps on the back of each other's shoulders. Some stole brief moments for private chats with Myles to reiterate no ill-will was intended in the process. Their triumphant laughter transformed inklings of discord into unity against a greater adversary. They laughed, and he laughed, shaking hands as they cleared the room.

From the far end of the table, Slone dawdled to him. It was the two of them left standing, now, side by side.

"It's over."

Myles shoved his hands into his pockets with a quiet, "What?"

"The ordeal."

"Oh." It was a distant *oh*.

"I'm relieved. I know you must be also."

Myles' attention was fixed at the door in front of them, reflecting on each member going through it, leaving him with their approval. Or, was it their reproach? He wasn't sure which was having a greater impact from the experience.

"Aren't you?" Slone landed a slight elbow to his side, urging a response.

"Aren't I what?"

"Relieved that it's over."

"Oh. Yeah."

"You're okay. Right?"

"Me? Yeah," Myles said.

"You don't seem okay."

"What makes you say that?"

Slone shook his head. "Nothing." Silence fell between them. "I have to ask," Slone spoke again.

"Ask what?"

"Did you no longer want to be the pastor?"

"Why do you ask that?"

"You seemed detached, and, with all the camaraderie that went on in here, you barely uttered a word."

Myles turned to him, still assessing his emotions. He found something he accepted as his truth. "Worn is what I am, Slone." I was trying to figure out what I'm feeling, and it's only now, I can say with certainty that I am worn."

"That's understandable. You faced a lot. Rumors. Suspicions. Innuendoes. Some of it lagged for years. But you're vindicated."

"It's deeper than that. I haven't knelt at the altar in my home in days."

"Why haven't you?"

"I feel an emptiness inside me that has nothing to do with my soul. It grew deeper as I faced the possibility of losing this church. I tried to fill it with jazz music when I'm alone at nights, but even that it's temporary. I wake up every morning swallowed up in this big empty space."

"You never mentioned feeling that way."

"I couldn't." He elbowed him back with a chuckle. "You were distracted."

"But not absent. You could have come to me."

"It's a peculiar position to be in as a pastor and your friend."

"It's not peculiar anymore, and I'm here, still. Talk to me."

"Ok. How about over cards tonight?"

"Same time?"

Myles nodded. "Same time."

"Sounds good," Slone said and then he retracted. "No, I can't tonight."

They faced each other like there was a sudden awakening.

"Victoria and I have agreed on a wedding date. She's coming over tonight to begin planning out the details."

"You set the date?" Myles' eyes glistened. "When?"

"Last night."

"No. The wedding date. When is it?"

"Oh. This time next year." He rubbed his forehead. "And if I'm to afford the elaborate version she presented to me, I better get to my shop right now."

The door creaked. Nena pushed it open and peeked into the room. "I thought I might find the two of you in here."

"Nena! I didn't expect you to be here. Aren't you leaving today?" Myles asked her.

"Tonight, to be exact." She crossed the threshold into the room and stopped. "But I wanted to say thanks, personally, for the beautiful flowers, and serve one last time when I heard you were still the pastor."

He hurried to her, and Slone followed, promising to tell him more about the wedding as plans develop. At the door, Slone begged Nena to agree she'll visit soon. She did, and he hugged her tightly before leaving the room.

Myles took her hand. "Thank you, too, Nena. I wish time had allowed me something grander than flowers."

"They were enough. Anything more would have been too much."

"I knew you'd think so." He looked longingly at her. "I'm glad you came."

"I am, too. Which reminds me," she added guardedly. "There's a woman in my office. Olivia Sinclair. She wants to speak with the pastor. I believe that's you."

"Olivia Sinclair? She's not on my calendar."

"She flew in from London this morning. Someone told her she could find you here."

"London? That's a long way. What could she want of me?"

Nena shrugged. "I asked. She said only to speak privately."

"Send her to my office."

Chapter Seventeen

S he stood about five and a half feet tall. Her light brown hair combed back from her face held lively shiny curls that rested on her broad shoulders. Her lashes, thickened at the outer corners, accentuated her piercing almond-shaped eyes. The long red and black plaid cashmere shawl draped around her, matched the touch of red lipstick softening her delicate full lips. Nena escorted her into his office, introduced them, and left, closing the door.

Myles extended a hand from across the desk. "Mrs. Sinclair."

She accepted the handshake. "It's Miss. And Olivia, please. If you don't mind." Her voice was gentle but urgent all in the same.

"Olivia it is. Please, have a seat. You must be tired after such a long flight." She sat and crossed her legs, and he sat too. "How may I help you?"

"I'm looking for Victoria Davenport. One of her neighbors said you'd know where to find her."

"One of her neighbors?"

"Yes."

"You were at her home?"

"I went there from the airport, but she wasn't at home."

"You could have awaited her there."

"I did for nearly an hour. The neighbor noticed and sent me to you."

"I see." Myles drummed the desk with his fingers. "She's not here either."

"Do you know where she is?"

He hiked his shoulders. "Shopping? Maybe."

"If she's gone shopping, I would have had a really long wait," she quipped, getting up from the chair. She removed her shawl, exposing the form-fitting red dress, and placed it over the back of the chair. Whipping back her hair, she sighed and put her hands on her hips. "And it was a long flight. Can you reach her for me?"

He smiled at the bold flirty act and contemplated the request, nonetheless. From the long flight, he expected she'd be exhausted. But she looked refreshed. Her make-up was intact, and the light foundation made her natural skin appear flawless. Her arched eyebrows and pair of silver teardrop earrings accentuated her radiance. There were no clear signs of fatigue.

"Is Mrs. Davenport expecting you?" Myles asked her.

"No. I wanted to surprise her."

"Ms. Sinclair, you came a long way to surprise her."

"I did, and I was sure she would be in bed when I arrived there this morning."

"The women in Beautiful are early risers."

"I wouldn't say that of Victoria."

"You presume to know her well."

She laughed. "We go way back."

Myles cleared his throat. "I'm curious about one thing then."

"What is it?"

"For you to know her so well, why she hasn't mentioned you?"

"If you find her for me, I'll ask her that myself."

He smirked. "I'd like to help you with that Ms. Sinclair, but I'm aware Mrs. Davenport is well known worldwide. I imagine since she left the spotlight, plenty of reporters are curious about her whereabouts. For all I know, you could be one of them."

"I see." She reached into her purse for out a postcard depicting the clock tower in the neighboring town and handed it to him. "Victoria sent this to me when she arrived here months ago. She sent more, but I traveled with this one." Smiling, she explained, "She warned me there are many small towns between here and Langston, and it's easy to miss the signs indicating which town you're in. I found the landmark on this one simple but distinct. It was my way of knowing when I neared Beautiful."

He was tickled at the profound reply, but, she, hoping to draw a more auspicious response, pointed to a spot in the picture. "She raved about this bakery. I had to stop and sample the bread for myself on my way."

He tapped the postcard against his thumb and checked his watch. Sensing ensuing impatience, she repositioned herself into the chair. "Pastor Avery, when Victoria told me she was coming here, I was sure it was only to put some old demons to rest. Then she told me about Slone. Deacon Slone," she said dreamily. "A man who could easily make her forget Darius ever existed." She shook her head. "She never forgot about Darius, so I was worried, and I became even more so when I heard of the violent attack in her home. I wanted to come right away, but I was performing in a play in Europe, and I couldn't leave at my choosing."

Myles rested his elbow on the desk and cotched his chin in his palm.

"I telephoned her after she left the hospital. She assured me she was fine, and nothing would distract her from finding Darius or her father. I believe you were helping her with that."

He widened his eyes, impressed she knew as much but not convinced the information couldn't have been obtained by a seasoned reporter.

"Anyway, I promised as soon as we wrapped, I was coming to see about her." She centered batting eyes on him. "Now, Pastor Avery, do you still think I'm a tabloid reporter, or that I am who I say I am?"

"Ms. Sinclair-"

"Olivia. Please," she interrupted.

"Olivia," he appeased, "Besides your name, you didn't say who you are."

She dropped her shoulders. "We're best friends. Like you and Slone." A hand went up to her mouth. "You must forgive me. We tend to assume everybody knows it. You can relate. Can't you?"

Myles recalled saying those words to Victoria, and becoming more inclined to believe her, declared, "Either you did a thorough research on your subject, or Victoria has been talking a lot."

"I did research my subject thoroughly, Pastor Myles Avery, and, although when I imagined meeting you, I had a completely different scenario playing out in my head, I can't say I'm in any way disappointed."

"I'm the subject." He smiled broadly.

"Victoria told me a lot about you. I was intrigued."

He pulled his chair closer to the desk. "I'm at a disadvantage then. How long will you be in town?"

"A few days."

"Have you had lunch yet?"

Satisfied she made an impression, Olivia taunted, coyly, "I thought I'd see my friend first and take a nap."

"Dinner then?"

"Perhaps."

Myles picked up the telephone, dialed, and held it at his ears. "Thank God you answered," he straightened and said.

"Are you alright?" Slone asked.

"I've never been better in fact. There's a-" He looked up at Olivia. "An angel sitting in my office. Her name is Olivia Sinclair."

Slone laughed. "You're joking."

"No."

"She's to be Victoria's matron of honor."

"She's a year early."

"Is she really there?"

"She is."

"Victoria thinks the two of you make a perfect match," Slone teased.

The breathy, "God, I hope she's right," caught Slone off guard.

"You're interested?"

His eyes glistened. "I believe we just established that."

"Does Victoria know?" The jubilant voice was stuck between relief and optimism.

"We're trying to reach her. Do you know where she is?"

"She's visiting Lola again."

"Lola? Why?" Myles whispered into the phone.

"Victoria wasn't forthcoming during their first visit and believes if she had been, Lola would have answered all her questions, especially those about Mr. Vic." Slone sighed. "I can't believe he's her father."

"She told you?"

"Yes."

"Why didn't you take her to him?"

"She thinks it's better if I'm not involved."

Myles pressed back into the chair. "She's right, you know. She alone has to fit that last missing piece of the puzzle."

Olivia reached across the desk and touched his hand. "Is it her father she's gone after?"

There was peace in her voice and a calmness in her touch that went through him. He nodded, and she cupped her hands over his and closed her eyes.

The connection they had with Victoria was obvious, but when she opened her eyes and met his, another connection, one much stronger, was evident, too. He took her hand into his and held it. In his spirit, familiarity with her inner-being unfolded, and he discerned he wasn't at a disadvantage after all.

"I should let Victoria know Olivia is in town."

"No, not yet. She wants to surprise her." He kept his eyes on her as he spoke. "Some things work better when they unfold as planned." He hung up and circled around his desk to her.

With Olivia's hand sandwiched between his, Myles looked up, hearing a tap on the door. She drew back her hand.

"Come in."

Nena walked in gingerly and closed the door. "Ronnie is here. She wants to see you."

"Now?" He was enjoying the lighthearted moment learning about Olivia- her spiritual beliefs, her dreams, values, pet peeves, birthday, food-

"Her father and sisters are here with her."

He pressed the heel of his palm to his forehead, questioning within himself why she came at such an inopportune time. "Take them to the conference room," he said with a groan and stood.

"I'm sorry, Olivia. This might take a while."

"I don't mind waiting."

"You've been waiting all day already."

"My father was a pastor. I understand the demands."

His heart skipped in awe of finally connecting with a woman who was aware of the demands of his role. "I need that in you."

"You have it." Olivia shooed him. "So go."

The door opened, and Noah, seeing Myles coming toward it whispered, "The people out there said Nena is in here."

Myles pointed to Nena.

"There you are," Noah said, coming further into the office, but noticing Olivia, he hastened to her instead. "What are you doing here?"

She met him with a hug. "I came to see your mother, but no one answered the door at the address you gave me."

"Mother left early to visit an old friend of grandma, and I left right after her to meet with the moving company."

"Is she moving back to Crystal Falls?" She was immediately thinking of a new reason to come back to Beautiful and see Myles.

"No." He went to Nena and took her hand. "We are going back to Crystal Falls. This is Nena. I told you about her."

"Yes, but I didn't know it was her."

Nena flashed probing eyes at Noah.

"This is Aunt Olivia. Mother's best friend."

"Olivia Sinclair." She inched towards her with a hand extended. "He said such wonderful things about you. It's a pleasure to formally meet you."

"The pleasure is mine," Nena glowed and met her with a hug.

"I was planning to steal Nena away for lunch. You and Pastor Avery should join us." He looked at Myles. "If you're available."

Myles reached into his pocket for his wallet. He handed Noah his credit card. "I have a meeting with those people out there, but please take this beautiful woman to lunch with you and bring her back to me as quickly as you can."

He walked ahead, leading Ronnie and her family to the conference room. Julia kept up, pushing her father in a wheelchair. When they were seated, he greeted Mr. Vic. "It's good to see you out and about again. How are you feeling?"

"I've felt better." His voice was weak and shaky.

Myles spoke gently. "You're well enough to get out of bed and come here today. I count that a blessing."

"He came to rededicate his life to the Lord," Julia announced. "With the health issues, the secrets, and only God knows what else, we want to be sure all is well with his soul."

"Is this your decision Mr. Vic?" Myles asked.

He nodded.

"Have you confessed everything unto the Lord?"

He coughed and, with a weak voice, spoke slowly. "I did some wrongs."

Myles touched his shoulder. "There was a time when grown men in this town did as they wished with young girls. Many men are guilty of this wrong." He looked away from him to the sisters and explained further. "The social norms, at that time, permitted it. No one held the men accountable. Their wives suffered in silence to keep their families together, and the young girls, who barely knew how to survive, were ostracized and made to leave town and live out their lives in shame. No one spoke of them again or gave thought to the children they bore. Those young girls and their children have voices that were silenced, too. Unfortunately, in my experience speaking with people in different congregations, I discovered this wrong was not limited to Beautiful alone. And it goes on still."

Mr. Vic pointed a shaky finger from Julia to Myles. From her purse, she handed Myles a check made out to the church. The generous sum was unexpected. "What is this for?"

Coughing between sentences, he declared. "I don't have long left on earth. I want to leave it a safer place."

"Our home is finally a safe place for our sister," Julia smiled, taking Ronnie's hand. "It took years for it to be so, and a lot of damage was done. We don't wish that for anyone else. Use it to create a safe place for other young girls in trouble."

She reached back into her purse for a white handkerchief. Dabbing the corners of her father's watery eyes, she added, "He knows a check won't undo the wrongs this town has done to its own. He only prays, now, for God to have mercy on his soul."

"Praying and confessing puts it in the hands of God to render His judgment. But as a society, to pray and confess is not enough. We must do our part to protect our young girls. Thank you for this generous contribution to accomplish this, Mr. Vic."

Myles looked up and saw Slone and Victoria at the doorway. As they came further into the room, he asked, "Are there more- children- other than Ronnie?"

Slone held unto Victoria's hand. They were moist and shaking. Mr. Vic nodded.

"Daddy. There are more?" Julia burst into tears.

"Is that your full confession, Mr. Vic?"

He answered with a slower nod and coughed. Victoria knelt before him and took his hand. "I'm Victoria Davenport. My mother is Alana Grover. I believe you are my father."

He squeezed her hand, and tears followed a wrinkly line down his face. "I prayed for a chance to see you again."

"You knew about me?"

"You were a little girl when I saw you."

A fit of anger surged in Victoria. She wasn't prepared for it. Her body trembled and, thankfully, her throat went dry, for she couldn't find the appropriate words to say. With all the planning for the moment when she would see him, she didn't plan what to say, other than, Daddy. Now, she had questions. Too many all at once. Questions the young girl in her wanted answers for, but the adult might reject, since he knew about her all along.

"Why didn't you look for me?"

"I did," he mustered. "When I saw you at your grandfather's funeral. Your mother hurried you into a car and drove away."

She felt the anger diminished, remembering when her mother did. She thought she was pulling her away from Darius. "I didn't know it was you she was hurrying me away from," she choked.

"I never got to tell you I'm your father."

"And I never got to say, Daddy."

Ronnie tugged Myles' hand. "You knew about this?"

"No, he didn't," Victoria answered quickly, rising to her feet. "Lola did. She told me everything."

"My mother? How do you know her?"

"She is my mother's best friend."

"You're a celebrity. Mommy doesn't know any celebrities."

"My mother was born in Beautiful and was schooled here just like Lola. They both dreamed of becoming celebrities, and faced with the same situation as your mother, my mother pursued it as her way out- out of this town."

"Mommy told you that?"

"Yes."

"How did you find her anyway?"

"I have my sources."

"Where is she?"

"Right now, she's on a flight to Crystal Falls."

Ronnie chuckled. "My mother? Crystal Falls?"

"Yes. I thought it was time the two friends reconnect, and they couldn't have been more excited about seeing each other."

"How long she'll be there?"

"That's up to them, but you should visit her at Hillside Manor when she returns."

Ronnie folded her arms and stared at her. "And you? Now that you're here, what are we supposed to do with you?"

"I've given no thought to that, dear," she said and rejoined Slone. She had questions she wanted answered, but not those Ronnie posed. They were questions that her mother avoided, and her father seemed too frail to confront. She looked up at Slone. "I've come full circle being in this church, with you, with my father, and a pastor. I'm afraid we might not have this opportunity a year from now."

"What are you saying, Victoria?"

"Everything I wanted for an extravagant wedding is suddenly frivolous to me. Gold-plated wedding invitations, long-stemmed crystal candle holders, ivory beaded chandeliers, and cakes on eight-tier cascading fountain stands matters little to what I have right here. This feels right."

"You want the wedding date to be sooner?"

"Yes, and there's no sooner day than today."

"Today?" Slone gasped. "What about your mother?"

"She doesn't want to come back to Beautiful."

"Noah?"

Victoria checked her watch. "There's still a few hours before there flight."

"You said your best friend, Olivia, had to be a part of it."

Victoria's hand went up to her chest. "Oh my. She'll never forgive me."

Slone winked at Myles. "I'm sure she will. If she understands your reasoning, I'm sure she will."

"Then I don't see why we should wait."

"There's just one more thing," Slone said.

"Sure. What is it?"

He led her back to Mr. Vic. "May I have your daughter's hand in marriage?"

When he nodded, Slone scooped up Victoria in his arms and twirled around, planting a long passionate kiss on her lips.

"Today is my lucky day. We're getting married," he turned to Myles in a burst of laughter.

"There's much to do," Victoria said elated when he put her down. "I have to find a dress. Please find Noah," she told Slone. "Will someone call Dorothy? Tell her to start preparing for the reception." She held her hand up to her chest. "Oh, I have to find a dress for Rayne. She'll make a beautiful flower girl." She soon entered full-blown panic mode. "Flowers. We need flowers. Lots of flowers to decorate the church."

Slone brought her back into his arms to calm her. "It's gearing up to be a beautiful afternoon. We have chairs we can put in the churchyard and have the wedding out there."

"The afternoons are slow at White Roses," Myles added. "It's decorated to your liking, and you love the food and atmosphere. We can rent the hall for a few hours and have the reception there."

She twisted in Slone's arms to face Myles. "Will they do that?"

"They've done it before for some local gatherings. I'm sure they wouldn't pass on the opportunity to do it for someone of your international status."

Victoria thought. "Nena is making the decisions there now. We should call her."

"Nena?" Myles asked astonished. "How will she do that if she's moving out of town?"

Victoria shook her head, flushing out the thought. "Aiden gave her power of attorney while he's in treatment. She and Noah has figured out a way to make it work."

"It's perfect then. I'll have Nena inform the staff to prepare for the reception."

"Tell her I want everything on the menu, and, to be sure it goes as planned, make her an offer she can't refuse."

Julia rose. "We want to help. After all, we're sisters now."

"Sisters." Victoria's mouth fell open with a breath of laughter escaping. "I have sisters. I didn't even think of you in that way."

"Getting used to having a celebrity for a sister, will take time for us, too," Julia laughed. "What can we do to help?"

"Take daddy home and get him dressed. The wedding is in three hours, and you're all invited."

Myles summoned the deacons and their wives back to the church to help him move the lectern and the white plastic chairs stacked in a room used for storage, out into the churchyard. They stabled the lectern under the tree where Slone and Victoria met and arrange the chairs in tidy rows on both sides of a make-shift aisle Myles created with a long strip of white poly-linen aisle runner, carpeting a path to the tree.

While the women tied colorful balloons to the back of the chairs, the men dragged the metal arch from the flower garden in the back of the church. A little frail, they propped it up at the end of the aisle runner in front of the lectern. Their wives gathered pieces of white tulle they used to decorate the pews on special occasions and wrapped them around the top of the arch. They swirled the material around the middle section and secured them there with white ribbons, allowing the flowing ends to graze the tip of the green grass. After a quick assessment of their work, and deciding it needed a fancy accessory to complete the decor, they rummaged through the storage room and found a big silver honeycomb wedding bell to hang at the top center of the arch. Satisfied, they completed the decoration with just enough time to hurry back home and dress for the occasion.

Myles was quick in readying himself, putting on his favorite black pinstriped suit and wool fedora hat. Before heading to the church, he made a quick call to Slone from the kitchen and asked him to open his backdoor.

Watching from the window, when he saw the door cracked, he grabbed his briefcase and ran across the backyard.

"Lucky for us, we had this moment planned way back in high school," he said entering the house, awestruck at the fashionable black tuxedo, white shirt, and patent leather shoes Slone sported.

"We didn't plan for this moment. If I recall, the plan was for you to wed Ronnie in the churchyard. I was to be your best man." Slone wrestled with the black bow tie. "We didn't plan for *you* to be both the best man and simultaneously officiate *my* wedding."

"I've officiated enough of them. I can handle both roles. Tell me, where's the ring?"

"In the same top drawer where it's been all these years."

Myles disappeared to retrieve it. When he returned, he put down his briefcase. "Let me help you fix this tie before we're both late for your wedding."

Victoria stood in the middle of her bedroom, wearing only a white strapless longline bustier and mermaid slip. On her bed was nearly every dress in her closet. Dorothy held up an off-white lace V-neck dress. "What about this one?"

"It's not long enough," she bemoaned.

Dorothy threw it on the bed with the others she rejected, searched her closet, and held up another one. "What about this one?"

"It's green. I can't get married in green. There must be another one I can wear."

"What about this one?"

The voice came from the door. She blinked, seeing Olivia holding a long white mermaid wedding gown in full display. The boat neckline, long lace sleeves, and the feathered train got her instant approval, and she met her with her arms outstretched. "What are you doing here?"

"I intended to surprise you," Olivia said, holding the gown away from them with one hand and accepting the embrace with the other. "Congratulations."

"When did you get here?"

"This morning."

"I didn't decide to marry until today. How did you know?"

"I didn't."

"But the dress-?"

Olivia came further into the room. "You can say the surprise was on me when Slone cut my lunch short with the last-minute wedding announcement."

"Slone? Does he know you're here? You met him?"

"Yes. Yes. And yes. We met at a bridal boutique near here. He asked me to choose the dress." Olivia looked at the bed. "He must have known nothing in your closet would suit you for this occasion." She handed the wedding dress to Victoria. "Go put this on. We'll catch up on the details later."

Victoria kissed Olivia and grabbed the dress. "The wedding will be perfect, now that you're here."

"And you're going to be a perfect bride in that dress. So, hurry. Your driver awaits."

Victoria looked back over her shoulder. "My driver?"

"Noah. He's awaiting you in your car. There wasn't time to find that horse-driven carriage Slone said you desired, but your convertible jaguar will do just fine." She fanned her away. "Now, you hurry and get dressed."

When Victoria disappeared into her bathroom, Olivia held out a hand. "You're Dorothy, I assume. I'm Olivia Sinclair. We're best friends. If you haven't heard about me, you'll have plenty of time after the wedding to learn all you need to know."

"It's a pleasure to meet you, Ms. Sinclair. Pastor Avery alerted me of your visit and asked that I remain quiet about it. I prepared your room at the end of the hall. Should I bring in your bags?"

"No, I'll manage. But thank you for offering and for keeping my visit a secret," she winked. "Slone bought a dress for Rayne, and the owner at the flower shop filled a small basket with rose petals for her to carry down the aisle. Noah has them in the car. You and Rayne must hurry and get dressed as well. We have only an hour left before the wedding."

She threw her shawl on the pile of clothes on the bed and pushed them back far enough to clear a generous space to lay. Removing her shoes from her tired feet, she moaned, "Lord, grant me, if only but a minute of rest."

The sun drifted across the western sky, layering the red, orange, and yellow leaves on the trees in the churchyard with a glow. There was an early autumn chill in the air. A soft breeze tousled the bright colorful balloons the deacons and their wives tied to the back of the chairs. They and a small list of carefully selected church members were trickling in and taking their seats.

Slone and Victoria selected those specific members to invite the next year, but with nothing more glamorous happening in Beautiful, when Dorothy called, they gladly accepted the short notice to come. Nena, with her hair combed down and spread across her shoulders, stunned in a long-sleeved lavender maxi dress took pictures of them as they arrived.

From the top of the church steps, Myles saw Ronnie arriving. The unexpected knee-length blue dress with a cape overlay shielding her curvy figure, made him gaze more intensely to be sure his eyes had not deceived him. With his Bible in one hand and a big brown shopping bag in the other, he made his way down the steps, calling her.

Hearing his voice, Ronnie stopped, but she didn't go to him. He knew it meant he had to come to her, and so he did. She barely held eye contact as he approached.

"You look lovely."

She turned aside, deciding against returning the compliment. What was she to say of him standing there in the long black clergy robe and white collar?

"The season is changing. I thought you might like this." He gave her the bag, and she pulled out a midnight blue wool coat.

"Thank you. I needed it."

"I thought you might."

She examined its full length, and images of the many sensual ways she could thank him rushed to her mind. Bidding still, the pleasure from it seeping through her veins, she stuffed it back into the bag. "Is that all?"

"Yes."

"I should go catch up with my sisters then."

In a change of heart, he stepped in closer. "No. Don't go yet. Allow me to thank you for speaking to the church board on my behalf. You saved my job."

"It was the least I could do. I was the main reason it was on the line in the first place."

"Yes, you were, but you didn't have to go the extra mile to save it. I heard you preached a sermon in there." They laughed. "Thank you for that."

"You don't have to thank me, Myles."

They stood silently, listening to their hearts as their eyes spoke. Hers, still longing and desperate. His, still restrained.

"Ronnie, I want to know you're okay. Are you?"

"Why wouldn't I be?"

"Well, since you looked upset earlier when you found out Victoria met your mother and that your father is her father-"

"And that she covered for you when I asked if you knew about it," Ronnie interrupted.

"She didn't cover for me, Ronnie. She has been in Beautiful long enough to know how much our lives intertwine. She was trying not to unravel it."

"So, you did know?"

"Not until Mr. Vic admitted his truth that I can say with certainty I knew."

She shook her head and twisted her lips. "The truth is such a burden. I guess daddy had to speak his truth to free himself of it. I can't say I fault him for that."

Sensing an underlying agony, he noted, "You didn't answer if you're okay. Are you?"

"Do you want my truth?"

"Yes, I suppose I do."

She positioned herself squarely before him. "It's simple. I don't know if I'm okay. This Christian journey isn't easy. I'm learning about God's love, but my body still hungers for yours."

He looked away from her and hung his head.

"I'm still angry with my mother for leaving me on a doorstep and with daddy for not protecting me," Ronnie continued, and he refocused on her again. "I'm trying to fit into a family that is welcoming me, but a part of me still strongly resents them for treating me like an outcast in the first place. I'm still angry with this whole town for that. And, as if that's not enough, this high-class socialite with more money you and I will ever know what to do with in a lifetime, has penetrated my life. I was afraid I'd lost you for good when rumor had it you gave her your heart. Now, I'm scared she'll replace me in daddy's and even my mother's heart. I can't afford to fly anybody to Crystal Falls on a whim. How am I to compete with that?"

She chuckled. "I'm trying to hold it together. You know? Pretend that I'm over you when yours is the only love I know. Pretend I feel like I belong in this big happy family, and that the thought of this woman, Victoria Davenport, isn't getting under my skin," she said through clenched teeth. "But pretending is not my truth. My truth is, I want to lash out at everybody who expects me to go along with *their* truth. Including you." She dropped her shoulders. "I'm trying. I am really trying. I pray every day, but I don't think I have the skillset for this Christian journey, Myles. So, I don't know if I'm ever going to be okay. That is my truth."

Myles sensed a lack of closure, among many other factors, was at play in the tangling of the re-emerging emotions she carried for him so openly. He dealt with it from a spiritual position just days before but accept it wasn't enough. Not even for him. For, looking at her embattled in the emotions, he still wanted to take her in his arms, and, if Godly principles permitted, love every ounce of her pain away. But it didn't, and it was time she faced it as he had.

"You say that's your truth, but it's not your absolute truth."

"How would you know if it is?"

"You spoke from your heart, and your words revealed your truth, but you're not listening."

"You have a way with words, Myles. But it's my heart, and it is my truth."

He tittered. "You say your body hungers for my love, but you don't have the skills for this Christian journey. Could it be it is not hunger you feel, but a disappointment in that I chose this path?"

"Is that a divine interpretation?"

"Maybe. But, if I thought it was your absolute truth, your body would never hunger for me again. You wouldn't have to pretend to be over me, for I would give myself to you freely, as a husband, right now. But I also know doing so would bring you agony. If I gave myself to you, you would only have the pleasure of familiarity. You, knowing what you have is not what you need, but being content in that at least, you know what you have."

She laughed. "I know what we had. It was everything I need."

"I'm a pastor, Ronnie. That *we* you speak of experienced the essence of my spiritual calling at its core. We didn't understand it, but it was why I was available to you. I was there every time you needed me. I came every time you called. I loved you in your distress, and it was satisfying to my soul. Being a pastor requires that I prioritize the needs of others in much the same way, and a pastor's wife must be willing to relinquish him to serve others in that same way too. I know for you to be with me, in that capacity, always having to release me to serve others at that level, would be agonizing to you, and in your heart, you know it as well as I do."

She felt an uncanny relief in the deeper truth he tapped as an unwillingness to entertain the image of him in that role surfaced in her subconsciousness. She looked away from him, but he took her hand and held it until he was sure he had her attention again. "If you had me in any form other than my divine calling, I would not be the man wanting always to be there rescuing you. And, in that form, I can't imagine you satisfied with me."

More guests passed, lodging the usual suspicious stares, but Myles paid little attention to them. Still holding her hand, he told her, "We have grown into our roles as different people. It's time we transition completely into who we have become. For who *we* were then, need *us* in our present self to process the emotions and challenges we're experiencing."

"You make it sound easy."

He kissed the back of her hand and let go. "It's not. Not even for me, a pastor. But I know doing it will make room for you to receive the love of a family that awaits you, the love of a sister you have yet to know, and the love of a pastor who will always be there for you."

A young boy ran past them, shouting, "The bride is coming! The bride is coming!"

"I should find my sisters," Ronnie said.

"And I should take my place at my best friend's side."

They walked together into the churchyard where the guests were gathered and found Mr. Vic, Julia, and the two sisters sitting center in the front row. Seeing Ronnie approaching, Julia picked up her handbag from the chair next to her and pointed her to it.

Slone watched from under the arch as Myles waited until she took the seat. He bowed gently and then faced Slone. Concern and questions were colliding on his face. To relieve him, he mouthed as he neared, "It's over."

Simultaneously, they sighed and faced the guests, who were clearly anxious for the wedding to start. At the far end of the aisle runner, Olivia appeared. Myles signaled to the lone musician at the keyboard, and he constructed a slow and delicate version of India Arie's Beautiful, filling the air.

With no planning, no rehearsals, no instructions on what to do, Olivia came down the path he carpeted to the tree, holding a lavender and white floral arrangement. Her curls were tucked above her shoulders with a lavender hairpiece, dripped with crystal rhinestone. The sheer lavender dress, knee-length in the front, with a maxi overlay in the back, flowed softly in the evening breeze.

Myles discreetly elbowed Slone, and with a shift of his eyes, drew his attention to her. He caught a breath and loosened his hands from behind him, cautioning himself, to enjoy the wedding, he can't occupy his mind with only thoughts of Victoria coming down the aisle to him.

As if Myles read Olivia's mind of what to do next when she neared them, he met her and cocked his arm. She gripped it in the bend, and he escorted her to one side of the lectern and kissed her lightly on her cheek.

"She deserves an award for pulling this off," Myles whispered to Slone when he returned to his side. "That little boy, too, who announced your bride's arrival." He would learn later from Olivia that she saw the boy in the parking lot and instructed him to run into the churchyard and announced it as loud as he could. She directed Rayne, also, to begin her slow march after she was about halfway down the aisle.

They watched Rayne following, sprinkling the rose petals, and Myles observed how much she grew since his brother's passing. Her thick hair, like his brother had, was combed into a ponytail and tied with a lavender bow matching her dress. Blushing, she waved to the boy as she came down the aisle but stopped when she saw Dorothy narrowing eyes at her.

It thrust Myles into a greater role to protect her, and he felt an obligation for her to know with certainty, he will protect her. Everyone must know, he accepted, she's his baby girl and that he will protect her from every ill-conceived thought manifesting to beguile her. When she neared him, he met her, took her hand, and guided her to a spot near Olivia. Stooping, he kissed her cheek and took his place behind the lectern.

Victoria and Noah took their position at the end of the aisle. The guests rose from their seats, and the musician switched selection to the bridal chorus.

Slone's mind went back to only a few nights before, sitting on his couch with her head resting on his lap, listing to the details of her plans for an elaborate wedding. A woman of considerable financial means, able to afford whatever she wanted, the man he was, was ready to put in the work it would take, to give her the wedding of her fantasy. The late summer wedding she desired. The white gown with a long train. The walk through an archway covered with green leafy wisteria vines, and to enter a church with dozens of lush ivory roses lining the aisle to the altar. She confessed although she was more unsure than certain she'd ever see him again, just dreaming of becoming his wife kept her spirit alive.

She spoke grandly, then, of walking down the aisle to the orchestral version of *Here Comes the Bride* played by a live chamber orchestra. But even in that majestic vision, he couldn't imagine her more breathtaking than she was, instead, moving effortlessly to the sound of the solo musician at the keyboard, to join him. Poised, her head high with a smile sweeping her face and illuminating the barrier of the veil that was supposed to conceal it. The sun, painting the evening sky golden, a backdrop that made every step that neared her to him more glorious.

When Victoria and Noah were under the arch, Myles led with a short prayer, after which, he shared stories in dramatic form, of Slone falling for Victoria when he met her the second time. He joked, although it almost cost him their friendship, it was amusing to watch, for he knew if he kept their paths crossing, they would remember the first time they met. He shared stories of how Slone pined in devastation that he might never see her again.

"It was his first major heartbreak, and we had only reached third grade," Myles laughed. "I don't believe he got over it until yesterday."

When he asked, "Who gives this woman to be wed to this man?"

Instinctively, Noah said, "I", placed Victoria's hand into Slone's and took the empty seat in the front row near Ronnie.

Epilogue

Victoria placed her light jacket on the back of her chair and went to the edge of the balcony overlooking their garden. She rested a hand on her stomach, breathed in the fresh morning air, and executed a slow relève to demi-pointe and a plie`.

"Adding the second floor was a brilliant idea. I'll never grow tired of watching the sun rise from up here," she marveled, as the sun spread its glow across the mountainside.

Slone watched from the table where they had breakfast before she began her morning routine. Sipping the last of his coffee, he pushed back his chair and went to her. "Redesigning the house more to your liking was the least I could do, considering the joy you brought into my life and the lives of others in this community. It's been an amazing year." He took a box from his pocket. "Happy anniversary, my love."

"I can't believe it's a year already. I've never been happier."

"Open the box, and we'll see if that sentiment still holds true."

Victoria opened it and saw a key taped to the bottom of it. "It's a key."

"To your dance studio."

She flung her arms around his neck and kissed him. "Thank you. It'll be great to start teaching Rayne and the other children in Beautiful. Where is it?"

"A few doors down from the grocery store. The space has been unused for years. It's perfect for you."

Her eyes grew misty. "I didn't imagine having it so soon."

"You deserve it," Dorothy said coming onto the balcony to clear the table.

As much as she liked the thought of owning a restaurant, she frowned on the responsibility for making one a success. That part of overseeing the operation, dealing with customers, suppliers, and keeping up with regulations was tiring, even in concept. She rather the private space that working for Victoria offered. There, she can be creative in doing what she loved most. Cooking.

"Oh, Dorothy. You knew about this and kept it from me?"

She groaned, "Deacon Slone made me."

In his defense, Slone chimed, "You contributed so generously to programs at our church and worked tirelessly to reopen the grocery store with products our people can use. It was time we gave to you in return."

"We?"

"Pastor Avery helped Deacon Slone hire the workers and they oversaw the renovation. First Lady Olivia made sure the interior was completed to your liking. I think it's the third best-kept secret in Beautiful," Dorothy laughed.

Myles and Olivia wedded six months after Slone and Victoria. The wedding was dubbed the second best-kept secret in the town. Myles notified key members of the church only the night before the ceremony, which Olivia's pastor flew from Crystal Falls to officiate. Slone was his best man and Victoria served as the matron of honor.

In helping to plan the wedding, she ordered dozens of ivory roses, months in advance, for delivery the morning of the wedding. When they arrived, she worked alongside the Deacons' wives, decorating the church in the fashion she desired for her own wedding. A live chamber orchestra played when Olivia came down the aisle. It was a vision they shared as young girls, developed more elaborately in their adulthood. In having little control over her wedding to Edward and racing against time when she married Slone, seeing the vision come alive for Olivia, with Myles as her husband, was gratifying.

"I knew they were perfect for each other the day I met Myles, and it took only one visit for her to fall in love with both the man and this town." Victoria gazed off to their adjoining backyard. "Her parents were like yours, you know. She was their only child. With both of them gone now, there is nowhere else I'd rather her be than here in Beautiful living across from me."

"You're blessed to have her as I am to have Myles. The unbreakable bond of authentic friendship is rare, and it is most precious."

A chill wind blew, and she shivered. Wrapping her arms around herself, Victoria agreed. "It is. Especially when losing a parent is such an expected reality."

Slone cuddled her. "You're thinking of your father again."

"One month was all I had with him, and then he was gone. Just like my grandfather. I wanted more time to know them better."

"You've learned a lot about your grandfather already, through his legacy here in Beautiful, and your father lives on in the four sisters. You have a lot of years to learn about him through them."

"Maybe. The relationship with them feels strained."

"Give it time. People in small towns cross paths daily. The experiences is what ultimately weaves us together, developing our relationships, naturally."

She frowned. "We've crossed paths enough. I don't know how to be sisterly."

Slone lifted her chin up to him. Looking into her eyes, he reassured her warmly, "Giving Ronnie your home, and the job at the grocery store evidenced otherwise. You believed in her. That's sisterly."

She stepped away from him, took his hand, and led them back to the chairs at the table. "Mother suggested Lola have the house when we decided to make this our home. She loathed the idea of her best-friend living alone in that facility. It made sense that Ronnie lived there with her. And the job was Nena's idea. I can't take credit for any of it."

"Your mother and Nena were instrumental. Somehow, Nena knew Ronnie's natural flirtatious ways could be put to good use in sales. She was right, and yes, they deserve credit. However, it was you who looked passed Ronnie's fury toward you and gave her the keys to your home and your business. You deserve credit for that."

She crossed her legs and mumbled with sarcasm, "Nena has a knack for detecting the social benefits of the very habit that makes one overbearing."

Slone laughed. "She does. Myles didn't peg Julia for a church secretary. She argued despite her tendency to be melodramatic, her readiness to ask Ronnie for forgiveness and her devotion to repairing the broken relationship within their family demonstrated an ability to take responsibility and resolve conflicts. She insisted those traits are important for the role of church secretary."

"She is wise beyond her tender years."

Victoria centered, again, on the sun rising and reflected on Myles and Olivia's reception at White Roses. The event brought the establishment instant global recognition and was already making it a sought-after location for formal events. But Aiden agreeing to host the reception didn't come easy. When he completed the program at the facility for alcoholics, he was drenched with anger over Nena running off with Noah, and he held Victoria personally responsible for it. She would not have been able to get close to him, much less persuade him to host the event, without Nena's advice to negotiate like a shrewd businesswoman, prioritizing the benefits to him for agreeing.

In a telephone message, Victoria guaranteed Aiden access to the international market if he agreed, and it stirred his interest. A promise to leak pictures of the reception at his restaurant to tabloids with a global audience brought him to the table. Outlining the benefits of having her as a cooperative partner was her leverage for calling a truce.

"I am most fortunate to have her as an addition to our family business, and I know she'll make a great wife for my son when they complete their studies."

Feeling another chill in the air, she took her jacket from the back of the chair, and Slone draped it across her shoulders. She retrieved an envelope from one of the pockets and gave it to him. "Happy anniversary, too, my love. I can't wait to see my new dance studio, but we must hurry. Our flight to Dakar leaves this afternoon."

About the Author:

Laura P. Jones, a Jamaican native, currently resided in the United States. She is a graduate of Florida A&M University and Barry University. She holds a Ph.D. in Global Leadership from Lynn University and is a Business Professor and entrepreneur.

Growing up in a Christian family, the church was more than a spiritual environment. It was her social space. Her experience in that space is the source from which she develops many of her characters and lends meaning to her stories.

She is married and has two sons.